YEARS In The MAKING

TABLE OF CONTENT

August

Chapter 1

Emillie Kate Van der Berg

Maybe if I jumped out of the window, everything would stop going so fast? I haven't moved from the spot where I'm standing since we came inside. I'm starting to wonder if I'm becoming rooted here. Maybe I'm turning into Groot. The room is relatively large for a dorm. Two twin-sized beds, stripped of everything but mattresses, are pushed against either wall. Both are high enough that I'd need a stool to climb on. But I can tell Jay will be able to get on rather easily.

"Emi, move. The movers need to bring Jay's stuff in," My mom tells me, her voice stern and smooth. I slide over a few steps.

Jay's room has a large window overlooking part of the New York City skyline. It smells like fresh paint. All his stuff is being brought in, and I can't bring myself to help unpack. If I help unpack, then this whole thing is real.

He's really going to college, and I'm not.

I don't want to admit that, not yet.

Jay comes over to me, his steps measured and slow, a smug smile on his face. I narrow my eyes, not liking that smile one bit. His smile spreads as he watches me. I take a step back. With each step he takes toward me, I take another back until I hit his roommate's desk.

"I thought the point of inviting you to come was so you could help unpack, not attempt to grow roots in my floor permanently."

"I didn't know I was invited for manual labor; I figured it was because you wanted to tell me goodbye." I raise my chin and look him in the eyes. His eyes seem lighter today.

His smile stretches. *"Why would I say goodbye? You're an hour's drive away, thirty without traffic."*

"It's New York; there's always traffic," I counter.

"Smart ass," he mutters, his arm brushing against mine. *"You, okay?"* he asks a moment later. I force a nod.

This day is not about me. He's moving into the college of his dreams. I will not cry and make this about me. I've been fighting tears for a few weeks. Whenever I think about him at college, a wave of sadness washes over me.

"You sure?" He presses, taking his phone out of his pocket and checking the time.

"I'm sure. Are you okay? I mean, are you happy?"

He nods, standing up straighter. "*Yeah, I think so. I mean, it's just school. I've been doing it my whole life. Now I just get to leave my dad's house.*"

I roll my eyes, biting back a smile. A few minutes later, Jay distracts me into helping him set up his bedsheets.

"*Do the sheets the way you do yours,*" he whispers. I purse my lips and roll my eyes, but I do them the way I do mine, unpacking the pillows Mom bought him.

As I tuck the sheets in, I glance at Jay. He leans against his desk, his arms crossed. His tight black T-shirt shows off his muscles. His brown hair pushed back; I could feel his eyes on me, so I looked away. A staring match with James Averell is very intense. I've been avoiding them for a while. He moves closer, his arm pressing against mine, 'helping' me with the sheets. When his hand grabs mine, I look at him.

"*What are you doing?*" I ask him, looking around for my mom. She's on her phone by the window. She's probably texting Jay's dad updates about what's happening. He doesn't answer. Instead, he pushes his hand higher on my arm, leaving a path of heat. I snatch my arm away, moving down the bed to tuck the sheets in.

"*Em,*" he starts, the sound of a knock on the door interrupting him.

An average-height guy with ginger hair, freckles, and shiny green eyes stands in the doorway. A blue duffel is thrown over one shoulder, a backpack hanging off another, and a red duffel in his hand. My guess is Jay's roommate has just arrived.

Jay doesn't move from standing behind me, so I elbow him and tilt my head in the guy's direction. He grabs my hand and drags me over with him. I try to put up a fight, but Jay is undeterred.

The guy unpacks two large monitors. I don't know how he was able to fit those into his duffle bag along with a mouse, keyboard, a laptop, and thick headphones like I've seen Jay wear. The guy sets everything up on the desk and throws the rest of his bags on his bed.

Looking at us, he smiles, his teeth slightly crooked and his cheeks soft and round. "*Hey, nice to meet you guys. I'm Caden Davies.*" He has an accent. Where is he from?

Jay nods. "*I'm Jay, and this is Emi.*" Caden's eyes flash to me, and he waves. Jay wraps his arm around my shoulder.

"*Nice to meet you,*" I say, shaking Caden's hand.

"*You go here too?*" he asks.

I shake my head. "*I'm still in high school,*" I say *sadly.* "*I go to school in Greenwich. Our hometown,*" I explain. Looking over my shoulder, I see Mom on her phone leaning against the window, her pressed capri pants and white blouse fitting her body. Her hair is styled in a low bun. Not a single errant hair was out of place.

Aurore Van der Berg is the perfect socialite, and everyone who's met her knows it. She's worked for that title. She's done everything to be perfect, even though she wasn't originally thought of that way. She is always ready to have her picture taken. Always wearing the newest fashion designs and jewelry Rick and Thena get for her. Always saying, without saying, that she belongs in this elevated social strata. Always believing that she has earned it. She shifts on her feet, her large wedding ring sparkling from the sunlight.

Jay and his roommate make small talk, neither one of them enjoying it. Caden's computer chimes, and he turns and sits down, opening it. Jay leans down and looks at the screen, his eyes widening. Before I knew it, he and Caden started discussing software and the apps Caden opens.

After a few moments, I concluded that both Caden and Jay love video games and coding. Therefore, they're the perfect roommates.

My mom walks over, her heels clicking against the floor, "*Emi, we have to go meet your sisters for lunch,*" she checks her watch. "*The car will be here in five minutes. I'll be waiting downstairs.*" I nod and take a step away from Jay.

I avoid his eyes, looking around the room. Some of his posters are on the wall, and most of his clothes and a few of his favorite sneakers are unpacked. Finally, it all starts to set in—he's really going to college. We'll never go to the same school again; we won't live less than ten minutes from each other.

I glance at him, and his hazel irises are locked on mine.

"*I'll miss you,*" I whisper, my whole body feeling slightly colder. I wrap an arm around myself, rubbing my arm.

"*I'll miss you too, but I'll text and call you so much it won't be that bad. I'm only an hour's drive away.*" He pulls me into him, his body pressed flush against mine. He's warm.

I squeeze him, resting my head against his chest. After a few seconds, I feel myself away from him, forcing a smile. I tell him and Caden goodbye and leave the room. The hallway to the exit is filled with people chattering and bustling this way and that. But the car ride is completely silent as Mom and I drive away. It makes me miss Jay even more.

How am I supposed to get through this year without my best friend?

Chapter 2

Emillie Kate Van der Berg

Our shopping bags have been left in the car. Mom and I wait inside a large Thai restaurant on the Upper West Side. Neither of my sisters has arrived yet, but Mom's already ordered appetizers for the table, and I'm on my second Coke.

Mom had *insisted* on taking me shopping for clothes and accessories for the new school year. She knows I wear a uniform, but that never stops her. Within the first thirty minutes, she had already bought me five dresses I'd never wear—unless forced—some blouses, undergarments, socks, and two new pairs of Chuck Taylors I had to beg her for. The whole experience was awkward and stiff, but neither of us commented. We never did. We never talked or acknowledged the awkwardness of our dynamic, and this time was no exception. She squeezed my hand when we pulled away from Jay's dorm; that was an affectionate pep talk in her world.

The sound of approaching heels clicking on the floor draws my attention. My eldest sister, Elénore Thena Van der Berg, slides into our booth. Her jet-black hair hangs down her back, every strand glossy and straight. I feel my fingers subconsciously flit to my own hair—much curlier and resistant to taming. Thena wears a black skirt, a matching silk blouse, and her usual four-inch heels. Her cold eyes narrow on the appetizers that had just been placed, and she holds in a comment. Mom knows Thena hates being ordered for, but she does it anyway.

"I said to be here at two-thirty, not two-forty-five, Elénore," Mom says, breaking the tense silence.

Thena's shoulders stiffen as she opens the menu. *"I had to speak with my assistant. Something came up."*

Mom responds with an annoyed sigh and opens her menu.

Ten minutes later, my other older sister arrives, her sunshine blonde hair pushed back with sunglasses and a yellow sundress with a bold floral print. Like me, she has curls, but her blond tresses grant her far easier acceptance into the crowds our family frequents than my dark textured curls. *Isabell Brigette Van der Berg*—Bell for short—radiates beauty and warmth in an arresting way. Thena gives off her own aura of beauty and power, but there isn't ever much warmth involved. The two exist on opposite ends of the gorgeous people spectrum.

"Sorry I'm late," Bell chirps. But, of course, Bell was always late; she was only on time when Tristan—her boyfriend—came with her. He liked being on time, probably so he could impress Rick, our stepdad.

"It's fine. We haven't even ordered yet," Mom responds, closing her menu and looking at Bell warmly.

I can practically see the waves of irritation coming from Thena, but I don't say anything, nor does she as she eyes the appetizers again.

"*How was dropping Jay off?*" Thena asks. I grab one of the spring rolls that Mom ordered and put it on my plate.

"*It was okay. I think he likes his roommate, so that's good.*"

Thena nods. We all order food while Mom examines her social calendar for the rest of the month. She's saying something about needing to catch up from our vacation. We had landed from our annual summer trip a week ago. I'd spent the week with Jay, sleeping, eating, watching movies, driving around, and going to the bookstore. It was a good week for me, but my mom told me it was a waste of time. In her opinion, there were important people at the Cape I should have been getting to know.

She just didn't get some things, and my summer weeks with Jay was one of them. I focus on Thena. Her eyes are on her phone, probably reading an email. Her skin is a honeyed bronze from summer; her full lips are pursed as she reads whatever is on her phone, her manicured nails hovering over the screen. She must feel my eyes on her because her attention snaps up, and she stares at me, her cheekbones intimidatingly defined as the light catches their angles.

She narrows her eyes—that always seem a little less blue in the summer—at me. "What?"

I shake my head. "*Nothing.*"

Our food comes out: my plate of fried rice, Mom and Bell's salad, and Thena's grilled chicken with fried rice.

"*Are you excited for school?*" Bell asks, smiling widely. I return the smile. It feels stiff on my face, an effort. Maybe she can tell, but she doesn't comment on it.

"Kind of."

"You should be. This is your senior year—a year of change. You get to apply to colleges, go to prom, graduate," Mom kept going, but all I could focus on was a year of change.

I didn't want a year of change. I didn't want to go through each month wondering what was in store for me. I was becoming drained just thinking about the rollercoaster I'd be on.

I start my senior year on Monday, a new therapist on Tuesday, and no Jay.

Summer was gone, and now I had to return to the real world. It was a little colder and less optimistic than I remembered.

September

Chapter 3

Emillie Kate Van der Berg

I remember I'd never get excited over the first day of school when I was little. Thena would lay everything out, pack lunch for all of us, and ensure everything was perfect. She loved school and always has. But I always dreaded it. When I met Jay, it got a little bit better. He was there, right beside me every step of the way. We'd always have lunch and at least one blow-off class together. I wouldn't panic or freak out; I'd just clutch his arm and keep going.

Now I'm all alone. Standing in front of my mirror, wearing my white blouse, navy blue plaid skirt, a blue blazer, and my navy-blue Converse—that Bell and Thena got for me—untied. My name and graduation year are embroidered in green writing above my left breast pocket.

Emi Van der Berg 21'

I "accidentally" missed my hair appointment yesterday, so now it's damp in its natural state. The curls and coils are down and thick with a leave-in conditioner, moisturizer, and a little gel. Mom complained about it for thirty minutes last night, but Thena waved her away, telling her how I present myself is my choice.

Rick, Mom, and Thena are downstairs. Rick and Thena discuss something while Mom arranges the kitchen flowers our cook—Lucinda— picked out. I sit down in my chair and bite the toast, my stomach heavy. I can only swallow one piece.

I look at the newspaper on the table. There's a picture of Mom and Rik standing and smiling on a red carpet. The header reads *Every Event Aurore and Rick Van der Berg Will Attend This Fall.* I'm used to pictures like this, but this picture feels more magnified for some reason. It feels like more attention is on me. More eyes are watching, waiting for me to screw up.

The front door opens, and Bell's cherry blossom perfume infiltrates the air. She walks in wearing a short blue dress and flip-flops, holding a bouquet of flowers in one hand and a box of donuts in the other. She plops the donuts on the table and runs upstairs with the flowers.

I pull out a glazed donut. It's warm and light. I inhale it in one bite and quickly grab another one. The heaviness of my stomach disappears with each bite.

I can hear Bell's footsteps coming down the stairs. *"Ready?"* Bell calls from the front door. I nod and get up. Thena follows me, her heels clicking behind me. We walk outside and find Bell waiting inside her yellow Jeep Wrangler, the doors off. I climb into the backseat—right in the middle—and Thena climbs in the front.

"Would you rather have Tuesday dinners to start next week or this week?" Thena asks, looking over her shoulder at me.

"Whichever is easier for you. It's your house."

"Bell, which one is good for you? Are you going to be in town?" Thena asks. Bell taps her finger against the wheel, stopping at the gate and letting us out of our neighborhood.

"Next week. I have to fly to L.A. tomorrow morning but return Wednesday afternoon."

"Next Tuesday, dinner at my house. I'll buy food." Thena always does.

When the gate opens, Bell presses the gas, and we shoot forward, going fifty-five miles per hour down the long streets, not slowing down until we're in the school zone. I don't bother to complain. Bell has a but-did-you-die approach to critiques of her driving. Cars lined up, all trying to enter the parking lot or drop their kids off. Bell swerves around everyone and stops closer to the front. I grab my backpack (the one I've used for the last four years) and slide out of the car. Before my second foot can hit the pavement, Thena grabs my wrist.

"You will get through this year without James. I know you will. You don't need him. Trust me," I nod, squeezing Thena's hand, hoping some of her confidence transfers into me.

My homeroom teacher handed me my schedule:

- Computer Science
- Calculus
- AP Comparative Government
- AP Art
- Lunch
- AP Biology
- Creative Writing

Who signed me up for *three* AP classes? I close my eyes, counting to five, then open them. I look at my schedule again. There are still three AP classes. I told my counselor I wanted AP Art, creative writing, and a free period. Instead of a free period, I got AP Biology when I barely passed Biology last year. The class went too fast, and we did a lab every day when I thought it was just notes and a slideshow. Apparently, Grier Academy likes to do integrated sciences to really "push" the students. It just pushed me toward a mental spiral.

I text Jay a picture of my schedule, and he responds a minute later.

Jay: Looks like your mom got a hold of your counselor. No free period?

Me: Nope! I asked for one, but she probably forgot to write it down.

Jay responds less than a minute later, saying, *"No, she didn't. You know it, and I know it."*

Maybe she did. I don't respond to him; the bell rings, and I listen to my homeroom teacher, Mr. Ginny, go on about the importance of our senior year and how this is the last year of our childhood. By the end of the thirty minutes, I'm on the verge of tears. *Why do I have to be reminded that I'm growing up?*

Sometimes, I understand Peter Pan. Not the dark, kidnapping innocent children part, but the idea of never wanting to grow up. *Sometimes.*

Computer science isn't so bad. My teacher is energetic and seems to enjoy the whole teaching thing.

As I walk to Calculus, I give myself a mental pep talk. I can handle these classes. I will make Grier Academy my b*tch. I will do well in my senior year. I will *not* cry. I will not cry *to Jay*. I will pass all my classes.

Despite my pep talk, I'm contemplating dropping out by the time I leave Calculus and head to AP Art. I don't understand anything in Calculus, and it's obvious everyone else there does, and AP Comparative Government makes little sense. I write what is on the board and look through the textbook. I don't remember the teacher's names; they rushed through intros and began teaching.

People file into the classroom. The tables are arranged like a typical art class, and I sit at one in the back. The room has light, wooden tables with paint stains and stools, two on each side of the rectangular-shaped ones. The teacher hasn't arrived yet; the passing period has three minutes left.

"Cool if I sit here?"

I snap my head toward the sound, and I nod. A girl I don't recognize sits on one of the stools next to me. I try to look at her out of the corner of my eye, but I can only glimpse her in small snatches without seeming like a creep.

She has light curly brown hair touching her chest, light brown skin, and a nose with a smooth bridge. Her cheekbones are sharp yet still soft, and her jaw is the same way. From what I could tell, she doesn't wear a skirt, just a blazer and pants, and the buttons on her blouse were crooked.

"I'm Liv." She introduces herself with an easy smile on her face.

Relieved that she has broken the ice, I respond quickly, *"I'm Emi."*

The bell rings, and an average-height, thin woman walks in with a large iced coffee. She smiles at all of us and waves, her glasses sliding down her nose and her chopped dark brown hair framing her face.

"Hi, artists! Welcome to AP Art. I'm Ms. Han." She pauses and moves toward her desk, depositing her coffee and purse. *"This year will be relatively chill, besides the AP exam in May. You all will be competing against each other for our annual art competition. All you have to do is make an art piece of your choice, write a one-paragraph description, and turn it in. To remove all bias,"* I can feel eyes on me as she says that, and I shrink a little, *"names will be removed from each project."* She lets her words sink in, then claps her hands.

"Okay, now that's out of the way, I won't have you all stand up and say your name." Thank God. *"I'll just come by and ask you all individually. There's a syllabus with all your projects for the semester. Any questions you have, feel free to ask, but this is all about you."*

Ms. Han makes her way around the room, writing our names on paper. I read over the syllabus. Every quarter, we have a project due and check-in dates along the way.

"Oh, this will be good," Liv says. I look up, and a tall blonde girl sits down directly across from Liv.

I recognize her. I've seen those eyes before, that same cold stare.

"I didn't know you were taking AP Art," Liv remarks, her voice lazy and smooth.

"That's all that was left" the girl fires back, *"If I knew you would be here, I would've chosen AP Psychology."* The blonde girl dramatically rolls her eyes and then glares at me.

"This is Clara," Liv says, gesturing towards the blonde, not much enthusiasm in her voice.

"I'm Emi-"

"Emi Van der Berg, I know. You're Jay's friend, right?"

The pieces click. I've seen her and Jay kiss before, my sophomore year. I nod stiffly.

"*I didn't know you were a Van der Berg,*" Liv says. I shrug my shoulders.

"*It's not that big of a deal,*" I respond, moving my eyes back to my paper.

"*You had an older sister, right? Allison?*" Clara asks, still glaring at me. "*She died a couple of years ago, right?*"

I nod.

"*Way to kill the mood, Clara, bringing up dead sisters. You just met this girl,*" Liv defends, sitting up straighter in her seat. I can't stop the smile from spreading across my face. Liv turns to me and says, "*I'm sorry about her. She's used to hanging out with people with zero personality and a lack of empathy.*"

I cringe inwardly. This is uncomfortable.

"*At least the people I hang out with can remember what they did last night. Don't all your friends compete to see who can get the most blacked out?*" Clara snaps back.

"*Oh, Ms. Han, it's so nice to meet you!*" I cry, directing everyone's attention to the teacher approaching our table—anything to stop Liv and Clara's conversations.

Ms. Han cheerily smiles at the three of us. Every other table is filled with four people, and then it's just us three. "*It's nice to meet you all, names please.*"

We each say our names, and she checks them off her roster. "*Just to warn you, these are your permanent seats for the rest of your year.*" Then, before any of us can react, she moves on to the table in front of us.

Oh no! Hopefully, Liv and Clara can get along better. But by the glare on Clara's face, that seems doubtful. Each project has a rubric attached, which is uploaded on her website. I pull my sketchbook from my backpack and begin drawing. Liv does the same. And Clara scrolls through her phone.

"So, what college did Jay end up going to?" Liv asks, breaking the quiet of our table.

"Columbia. It was his dream school. He only applied there."

"Why would he do that? Is he an idiot?" Clara exclaims.

"No, he did it because he believed he'd get in. Jay is not an idiot; he's confident, and he knew if he didn't go there, he didn't want to go anywhere else," I snapped at her. Her eyebrows raise, and the table goes quiet.

Liv does a slow cap, and I turn to look at her; her smile is wide and contagious. She reclines in her chair. *"Well, well. Van der Berg has claws!"* Liv squeezes my shoulder in encouragement, and I smile without thinking at the friendly remark.

Even though I feel Clara seething across from me, I still feel a little victorious. Jay would have joined in on Liv's clapping and would probably kiss me on the forehead. Liv and Clara don't say anything for the rest of the class. I have no idea what I'm sketching, but I know there would be sharp angles, light shading, and no focal points.

Once the bell rings, we all begin packing up. Clara hadn't taken anything out. She just sat tapping into her phone and looking between Liv and me. I tried to ignore her eyes.

"You know what? I think you and I will be good friends, Van der Berg," Liv says.

I bite back a smile.

"I don't know. Van der Berg is kind of a mouthful. Don't you think Emi or Em is easier?" I ask.

Liv shrugs

"Mm, maybe." Liv stands up and stretches, her shirt rising.

Clara watches with rapt attention. Then, when she catches me looking, she shoots me with a withering glare.

"I'll see you, Van der Berg."

Liv's attention turns to Clara.

"Try not to bring up dead family members next time. Can you handle that?"

"You'll remember this conversation? That'd be a first," Clara snipes back. Liv smirks and leaves, leaving Clara glaring at me.

"Uh, w-well, I have to go to lunch. See you!" I scurry out of the room.

I eat lunch alone in the cafeteria. Grier Academy may cost a fortune to attend each year, but the food doesn't usually taste like it. I look around at all my classmates. They talk and laugh with each other, all fitting in. And then there's me. I don't look like them—they're white and lean. My skin is a deep brown with curves that draw attention. And I don't talk or act like them. I'm an outsider in every way except one: money. But not even money can obscure the obvious differences, and with each minute that passes, I feel it even more.

By the end of the day, I have 30 calculus problems, two chapters of Comparative Government notes, a biology section of notes with a corresponding lab that I have to complete in order to pick a lab partner, and a syllabus to sign for creative writing. One of Rick's drivers picks me up from school, and I sulk most of the way home.

I   tried to talk to my counselor at the end of the day, and it...went in a way I didn't want it to go.

I knocked on the counselor's door, and she looked up from her computer, a terse smile painted on her pale face and her blank brown, almost black eyes. *"Emillie, what can I help you with?"* I sat in the chair across from her desk and pulled my schedule from my backpack. I handed it to her, and she looked over it. "What seems to be the problem?"

I didn't know if she was joking or not. It wasn't until the silence had stretched that I realized she was being serious.

"I didn't sign up for any of those classes besides AP Art and Computer Science. I also requested a free period since I'm a senior," I explained in a rush.

"Well, your sisters both took classes more advanced and rigorous than this. I'm pretty sure your eldest sister, Elénore, participated in multiple clubs, even went to Welton Prep for a semester, and did their online summer programs."

Yes, Thena did all of that and started creating her own company, and Bell has been naturally good at everything she's done since she was a child.

"With all due respect, Ms. Pace, I'm not my sisters," I blurted out.

She smiled. It was stiff and cold. *"No, but you can try to be more like them."*

###

No one is home when I arrive, thankfully. I head straight to my room. If I sit down and do all my homework, I'll be fine. I try to convince myself. I stop when I see what's waiting on my desk. Bell left me a bouquet of flowers. The flowers she brought over this morning were for me. I just thought they were for the bathroom or some common area.

She wrote a small note:

I hope your Senior year is filled with brightness.

If you need anything, I'm a phone call away.

Love u,

Bell.

I smile and pin the note on my bulletin board that Jay and Thena hung up one year ago, and now it's filled with papers. I look around my room. It's mostly clean—no clothes littering the ground; my bed's unmade, but my desk is clear, and all my new clothes and shoes are put up. I change into pajamas, sit at my desk, pull everything out, and begin working. I fell asleep some time between chapter two of Comparative Government and the fourth AP Bio question about hydrogen bonding.

When I wake up, it's midnight. I finish the rest of my homework and climb into bed. I get two hours of sleep before I have to get up.

I know the school year will only get more challenging, and that small truth makes me want to stay in bed for the rest of the day.

Chapter 4

Emillie Kate Van der Berg

My new therapist's office is twenty-five minutes away in a small shop outside of Manhattan. The building is a three-story brownstone with a fire hydrant-red door that has a shiny gold handle. My old therapist's office was on the first floor, yet, for some reason, my new therapist chose the third floor. The stairs are steep, and they creak as I climb them.

My old therapist moved to Oregon, so I had to find a new one. I'll miss the other one. Neither one of us talked. I usually brought a book and lay down, and she called her boyfriend. She wrote a report to my mom each week telling her I was fine, and I continued to come so she could continue to get paid. It was a good transaction; one I intend to negotiate with my new therapist.

Jay always said that therapy was some people's safe haven, but, for me, it was just another check my parents wrote because I wouldn't lean into it. I wanted to laugh and cry when he said that because he was right. And I felt a little shitty about that, but not enough to open up. There wasn't much to say, and there's more important shit to worry about than the errors my counselor made with my class schedule.

My appointment starts at 5:00 p.m., and it's been that way since I started going. Every other Tuesday at 5:00 p.m., therapy.

I wait outside until it's 5:00 p.m., and then I head inside. A young woman stands on the other side of the room, her back facing me. She's still unpacking. Boxes are stacked up by the window, and her desk is covered with files and packs of unopened folders and pens, both colorful. There's a small olive-green sofa with decorative throw pillows and a navy-blue captain's chair across from it. I look around, dazed for a second. Everything's so bright it almost reminds me of Bell's room, just more books and papers.

The lady turns around, a bright wide smile on her face and her eyes crinkling at the edges. She's wearing a flowy, ruffled skirt, ballet flats, and a graphic T-shirt with a corny saying - Kind is the new Black.

"*Come on in, sit, and we can get started.*" She ushers me in with excitement. I sit on the sofa and look at the windows covered in ruffled white curtains.

A minute later, she sits on the oversized captain's chair, her feet not reaching the ground. She sits with one leg under her and the other hanging forward. Between the sofa and her chair is a bare coffee table.

"*I'm Lily Young.*"

"*Emille, but everyone just calls me Emi.*"

"*Nice to meet you, Emi. Why don't you tell me a little about yourself.*"

Okay, I can do that. And then I'll bring up the negotiation I plotted quickly in my mind.

"*Uh, I have two older sisters, Thena and Bell, and an older brother, and my mom married my stepdad, Rick, when I was ten turning eleven, and I met my best friend, Jay, when I was eleven.*"

That was good enough—vague but still enough that she should be temporarily satisfied.

I open my mouth to start the negotiation, but she beats me. "*How old are your sisters?*"

"*Thena is twenty, and Bell is eighteen. They both live in New York. Bell just moved there over the summer since she graduated. Thena goes to Yale but only has classes a few days a week, so she just commutes New York. She works a lot, and her office is in New York. It's a lot of driving, but she doesn't care because she graduates next winter,*" I ramble. This isn't going the way I planned.

"*And what does Bell do?*" She asks, her voice soft and inviting. It's hard to resist answering.

"*She's a model. She's landed a few covers on stores online, but my mom's trying to get her onto 'Harper's Bazaar,' 'Elle,' or something like that.*"

"*Do you want that?*"

I don't like that question so I side-step it.

"*Do you have any siblings?*" I redirect.

She smiles and shakes her head.

"*I'm an only child, sadly. It seems like fun having sisters.*"

I stiffen, and by the slight tilt of her head, she notices.

"*Not always.*" I clear my throat and shift in my seat. "*So, I have a proposition for us.*"

She raises her eyebrows, her teeth digging into her bottom lip.

"*I'm listening.*"

"So, my last therapist, Dr. Hemphill, and I had an agreement where I'd keep coming here, we wouldn't speak, and she'd write a report saying I was doing okay, and she'd send it to my mom."

"And you want that to happen with us?"

"Yes, I think it'd be nice. Don't you?"

She smiles and stands up, going to her desk. She goes through the files, strands of dark brown hair falling in her face.

"Dr. Hemphill was your therapist for three years, correct?"

"Yes."

"Why does your mom keep sending you to therapy if your notes have been doing good for the past three years?"

"She thinks I need it."

"Why?"

I've asked myself that same question, but never long enough to think about it. I shut it down before it opens something more, something a little deeper, a little darker, and a little more real. But this lady doesn't need to know that.

I shrug my shoulders.

"Okay. Well, we can try and find out together if you want. Tell me about your best friend—James?"

His name must be written in the file. She sets the file back down and walks back to her chair.

"I call him Jay, and pretty much everyone else does too. He graduated with Bell a few months ago and now goes to Columbia in the city. He's really smart, and I think he might want to go into designing his own app or something, but I don't know. I just know he wants to take over his dad's company then let the board of directors do most of the work."

"How did you and Jay meet?"

"My stepdad, Rick, and his dad are close friends. They grew up together. Jay and I met at my birthday party one year ago. Then he came over again the next day, and it was just that from then on. Us." I smile at the memory of our meeting.

It was awkward but familiar at the same time. I think about our other memories, the summer weeks, the movie dates, the sneaking out of my bedroom window, the sleepovers we weren't supposed to be having, the drunken nights, and the other ones we act like don't happen.

"Is there anything romantic between you and Jay?" Lily Young presses. I haven't decided whether I want to call her Lily or Dr. Young, and I can tell she won't mind either way. Neither one seems right yet.

I thank my lucky stars that my skin does not show my flush; one of the lovely and rare scenarios when my skin tone is working for me, not against me with strangers. I can feel my whole body warm up, though.

"No, we're just friends."

"Do you want to be more?"

"Are you dating anyone?" I ask her. Back to my deflect and pivot strategy.

Her face brightens, and she holds up her left hand, a small oval-shaped diamond ring, and a matching band on her ring finger.

"I've been married for three weeks. We just came back from our honeymoon in New Orleans. We spent the week eating seafood and sweets, drinking, and sightseeing. Have you ever been?"

I nod.

"I'm from Louisiana."

"And you moved here when?"

"When I was ten, my parents divorced, and then my mom married Rick, and we moved to Greenwich, Connecticut, full time. Now I live there."

"How is your mom and Rick's relationship?"

"Good." I look at the clock. We have twenty-five minutes left.

"Are any of your sisters in a relationship?"

"Uh, Bell, she's been dating this guy, Tristan, for a couple of years."

"Is your brother in a relationship?"

"Maybe, I don't know. I don't even know where he's at right now. He likes to travel and be on his own."

I can't blame him; I think to myself. The Van der Bergs are a hard bunch to surround yourself with. Expectations that—for everyone but me—must be reached. Alexander comes home when he pleases, usually after both mom and Rick have badgered him about it.

I last saw Alexander at Bell's and Jay's graduation party. He stayed for the night, smoking a cigar with Rick, Eric—Jay's dad—and Mr. Yates. All of them sat outside around a table wearing suits with glasses of brown liquor in their hands. Jay went over and made conversation with them briefly, but then he joined me inside.

I don't mind the questions Dr. Young asks as long as they're in the safe zone, things people could find out if they went on Thena or Bell's Instagram or, maybe, if they took the time to Google.

But I can tell she's going to push. She's too interested and too good of a listener not to. I'm not good at outsmarting people with my words. I've been practicing for years, but still, some questions stump me, making me second guess my next answer and whether I want to tell the truth, evade it, or tell parts of it.

"And what about your dad?" She asks, her eyes focusing entirely on mine, a small warm smile still on her face. It works but not enough.

"He died when I was ten. Heart attack." The words are easy to say. I've been saying the same sentence for almost eight years.

"I'm sorry for your loss."

I shrug.

"It's been a long time; I hardly think about it," I lied. It doesn't sound like a lie. It sounds believable, and I don't know if that's good or bad.

"It's okay if you do."

I want this session to end. I don't think Dr. Young is going to accept my proposition, and I know my mom's not going to let me stop coming to these sessions. I have until my eighteenth birthday to see her. I check the clock again; only ten minutes have passed, and I have fifteen minutes left.

"Are either one of your parents dead?" I ask. I'm back to my one rusty trick.

"No, my parents have been married for twenty-seven years."

Oh, that makes sense. I examined Dr. Young more closely—long brown hair, eyes the color of toffee, an oval-shaped face with smooth lines, and a nose close to symmetrical. She's pretty and bright. Her smiles meet her eyes, and her cheeks have a flush that comes from happiness, or maybe she's hot from her office. It feels like the right temperature to me, but it might be hot for her.

"Is your office hot to you?" I blurt. She blinks and chuckles at the questions.

"No, is it hot to you? I can turn the AC on if it makes you feel better?" She moves as if she's going to get up.

"No, no, it's fine," I assure her.

She stands up and grabs a file from the box. I know it's mine because she brings it with her and sits back down. I don't know what's written inside, but she's reading it closely, taking her time with each page. It's not thick. Maybe an inch. Dr. Hemphill didn't take many (any) notes. This comforted me for some reason. As though I knew more about her than she did about me.

She was fifty-seven, originally from New Hampshire, married an electrical engineer who was allergic to grapefruit, apricot, and rosemary, had no children, and lived in a small townhouse thirty minutes outside the city. She lived closer to New Jersey than she did to New York City. Oh, and she also hated going to warm places for vacation. She got sunburnt too easily, and her husband slept too much. I may not have a folder, but I do my homework too.

"Why do you think you're in therapy, Emi?"

I don't answer. The only answer that comes to mind is because of my mom.

"Okay. Do you think you need therapy?"

"Everyone needs therapy," I joke. I heard Jay say that one time. I think he didn't want me to be sad that I had to go while he and Bell went to a party.

"Why do you think you need it?"

I get up. She follows me with her eyes. I look at the clock, and we have ten minutes left.

"You're not going to agree to my proposition, are you?"

She closes the file and shoots me a small smile while shaking her head.

I nod, forcing myself to accept this. *"I think I'm done for the day."*

"Okay."

I leave the bright, cheerful office, racing down the steep stairs, my hand gripping the railing. I think I did well. I told her about my sisters, brother, Rick, Mom, and Jay. It was more than I planned to tell her, but it was all good.

I repeat that in my head until I get home.

Chapter 5

Emillie Kate Van der Berg

Every month it comes, and every month I dread it to the same degree. On the first Sunday of every month, the Van der Bergs, the Averells, and the Yates all host a Sunday brunch at the local country club. The club shuts down for brunch, no one besides us is there, and no one comes until we leave. It's mandatory for everyone to attend.

The only good thing about these Sunday brunches is that no one outside our three families attends. Every family—aside from mine—in the club is two things: wealthy and white. But what we are missing in white, we make up for with wealth. Or at least that is how my mom tries to play it. It's still safe to say that the club is a little uncomfortable unless we are with Rick, then everyone is welcoming. He's one of them.

I stand in front of the mirror, in the Jack and Jill-style bathroom I used to share with Bell detangling my hair for brunch. Now it's just me, Mom, and Rick in this huge house. Being an only child is not working for me. Their attention is constantly on me, and it's harder to blow off school, therapy, or anything else. Hopefully, they will be distracted soon.

My natural hair, parts of it still wet from my shower and the products I combed through, hangs down to almost mid-back. As it dries it will shrink slowly towards my shoulder blades. I wear a simple brown dress and black Converse on my feet. It wasn't what Mom picked out, but I hadn't worn what she wanted me to wear in a while and I think she was finally tired of struggling with me on it.

As I reach the top of the stairs, I see Rick waiting at the bottom, typing on his phone, his short blonde hair styled and in a fitted gray suit with a crisp white button-up shirt underneath. His dress shoes make a little sound as he walks back and forth. Mom is probably either finishing getting ready or already fluttering around chirping orders at the chefs in the kitchen who have baked and packed one of "her" famous desserts to bring with us.

He must hear me come down because he looks up and smiles, pocketing his phone.

"You look nice, Emi. Is that dress new?"

I nod.

"I think Bell got it for me." I'm not sure.

"It's pretty."

"Thank you."

Rick and I have a quiet relationship. We don't talk much, but it's always pleasant when we do. He's also been there for most things. He taught my siblings and me how to drive and open a bank account, and he has been at most, if not all, of our events. He's present; both he and Mom are.

Mom comes downstairs, filling the quiet air with the sounds of her heels clicking. Both Rick and I look at her. Then, out of the corner of my eyes, I see Rick smiling at her as she comes down. Her hair is pulled back in a tight neat updo, and she's wearing a soft green dress and matching green high heels, her purse in one hand and her oversized sunglasses in the other.

She sighs.

"Emilie, I left a dress out for you last night." Usually, Jay and I would've snuck out by now and met them there after stopping for coffee or donuts. Now I have to ride with them. Life with no Jay.

"Sorry.," I mumbled to my mother.

I don't know what else to say. The dress she'd chosen was designer, conservative, and far from my style. Plus, the heels were at least three inches.

"Well, it's too late to change," she mutters. Rick squeezes my arm, and we all make our way to the car.

###

Both my sisters, Jay's dad, and the Yates are already here. Everyone but Jay has arrived, I sit in my usual seat, and Thena sits where Jay usually sits. I know she does it so I'm not alone, and I appreciate that. The staff takes our drink order. I order a coffee and a cup of orange juice on the side.

I look at my plate, praying everyone decides to eat fast. I draw shapes on the empty plate in front of me. Thena and Bell talk to each other about an upcoming fashion event in New York. I already shook my head, saying I didn't want to go. Photographers will be there, and my chances of being photographed are high. They always try to take pictures of the family.

"Which classes are you taking?" Thena asks me, I look up, and she puts her coffee to her lips. I tell her my class schedule.

"I didn't know you liked biology, seeing as you barely passed last year."

I smile. *"I don't, but I have a good partner."*

The first week of my senior year is done, and I'd already failed a quiz. But on the bright side, I have Liv in all my classes. Unfortunately, after that initial art class, she ditched the next two days of school, so I didn't know our schedules synced up until the third day when she sat down next to me in AP Bio.

"That's good. Thena states stoically. If you need any help, please tell me. If you need anything, I have all my old notes, worksheets, PowerPoints, papers, and projects."

I nod. *Do we have to write papers for that class?*

I look at Bell, who is sipping a cup of apple juice, her hair down in loose waves and a beige floral sundress on. She smiles at me and raises her glass in a cheers motion. I smile back and raise my orange juice. Bell and I don't usually talk much about these things. I typically talk to Jay while Thena and Bell are immersed in their conversation.

Now that he's not here, the whole dynamic feels off, but I doubt either Thena or Bell would admit that.

"Sorry I'm late." My head snaps up at that voice, the voice that's filled with so much sarcasm it hangs in the air.

Jay walks in wearing a crisp navy-blue shirt, black slacks, and a pair of sneakers as he sits in Thena's usual seat, the one directly across from me, on the left side of Bell and to the right of the chair that's been empty for close to three years. The chair we don't talk about.

"You took my seat Elénore," Jay says drily, leaning back in Thena's chair.

"Maybe if you were on time, I wouldn't have to take your seat. Or would you rather I leave my sister to sit by herself?"

"There are two other people on that side." He smiles at me. *"Miss me already?"*

"Hardly noticed you were gone."

We both know it's a lie, but that's okay.

He and Thena end up switching five minutes later, the smell of his soap and cologne hitting me as he sits down, his chair touching mine. Our food comes out, and we sit even closer. He eats the eggs off my plate, and I take the potatoes and onions off his.

"How's school been? Made any friends?"

"Yes, I have."

He arches an eyebrow, not believing me, and I smack his arm.

"I have!" I insist. *"Well, I don't know if she considers us friends, but she sits by me, and we talk. We have three classes together, not including art."*

"Are you having fun?" I can hear the concern and worry in his voice, and it's deep in his eyes.

"Yeah, yeah, it's been great," I lied. I keep my eyes locked on my plate.

He doesn't need to worry about me, not right now, not over whether I'm having a good time at school. I'll be fine. There are more important things than me eating lunch alone. The simple truth is school was better when he was there; now he's not, and I have to deal with that—all on my own.

"How's college going?" I ask, redirecting the subject back to him. We've been texting and calling each other most of the week, but I've kept the calls short, not wanting to keep him from anything.

"It's been pretty good." His smile stretches slightly before he adds, *"hell, it's been great, Em. The freedom, the amount of time I have for coding and shit, and my professors are actually competent, not just elitist blowhards who kissed ass and greased palms to get their jobs."*

He takes a bite of his French toast.

"I've met some cool people too, and the parties are parties, not much different from high school, but they last longer and the people are more interesting."

Wow. I don't know what I'm feeling. I'm so happy for him on the one hand, and then on the other—the selfish hand—I can't help but worry whether I fit into his new life in the city. I don't know if I fit into this world, he's creating for himself. I recognize the sinking feeling that my best friend is outgrowing me. I can't hold him back, but I don't want to let him go, so I force a smile and tell him I'm happy he's having fun because I am.

When breakfast is over, and while our parents are still talking, Jay grabs my hand and leads me out of the room. Thena and Bell are talking about something, but I catch both of their eyes before I leave. Thena rolls her eyes, and Bell smiles and wiggles her eyebrows, sending me an obvious wink.

If anyone's encouraged my crush on Jay, it's been those two; more Bell than Thena. One day, they confronted me about it, and I admitted I liked him, but said I wouldn't risk our friendship to explore it. I kept the intimate stuff to myself. They both hugged me and told me if he didn't see the person I am, then it was best we were just friends.

Jay and I take the stairs to the first floor and go to the golf course. He grabs a pair of keys off the hook and pulls me into a golf cart. This is not the first time he's done this. The first time was when I was thirteen and he was fourteen. We got it stuck in a pond, and when we told Rick, he just laughed and paid the owner of the country club so we wouldn't get in trouble. The next day he taught Jay how to drive a golf cart properly.

"Where are we going?" I ask him. He drives it as fast as it can go, a little under 20 mph.

"I don't know. I figured we'd drive around. I might as well spend as much time as possible with my favorite person." He shrugs his shoulders and smirks at me. I roll my eyes.

"Oh, I'm sure you'll find a new favorite person in a few weeks." I try to tease, but my voice is too vulnerable for it to be a joke.

He puts his arm around my shoulder, and I lean into it, the smell of his cologne stronger. He has one hand on the steering wheel. The sun is shining, and the smell of fresh-cut grass is growing stronger as we proceed.

"You'll always be my favorite person Em; no distance can change that. I promise you."

I wonder if he knows that he just eased some of my worries. They all seem minuscule under the crook of his arm, the brunch getting farther away from us.

Chapter 6

Emillie Kate Van der Berg

I spend Monday in a haze of exhaustion and boredom. Liv doesn't come the whole day, so I sleep in most of my classes besides art, where I actually draw. Clara also skips, so it's just me and my drawing. I use my sketches to distract me from my loneliness and the homework to distract me from dinner with my parents. I just have to figure out what I'll do when the motivation for schoolwork stops. What will I do to occupy my time?

In creative writing, we start a journal of thoughts. My teacher, Mr. Fields, says keeping track of our thoughts, especially the repeated ones is important. I like him. He wears cardigans with jeans and promotes reading and free thinking. He literally has a poster that says, *"I wholeheartedly promote reading and free thinking!"*

Tuesday was infinitely better than Monday. For starters Liv was in school on Tuesday. She must have sensed my relief because she said she'd start coming to school more often. She and Clara didn't talk in art class at all. The awkwardness at our table was physically uncomfortable so I talked to Liv about the brunch I went to, and she told me about the party she went to. Liv and Clara have a weird friendship. Sometimes they're mean to each other, and other times they're polite; almost too polite. It doesn't pay to try to intervene in either mode.

As Liv filled me in on the party she'd attended, she mentioned that she also got a new piercing. I looked her quickly over and asked where the piercing was. She didn't answer me. Instead, she stared at Clara leaving me hanging waiting for a response. Clara's cheeks flushed a deep pink then excused herself from the table. The whole exchange was standard Liv weird. I wasn't up for digging into their absurd dynamic so I changed the subject. Even that exchange couldn't quell my excitement for sister's dinner.

On Tuesdays, we have a sister's dinner at Thena's house in the city. Rick agreed he could drive me to Thena's but got stuck at work, so his driver was arranged to take me there. Sister dinners start at 6 pm every other Tuesday, always at Thena's. I always bring something sweet, Bell brings drinks, and Thena provides everything else. They started this when Thena moved out, and now it's a tradition. I try to never miss them.

Thena lives in a white brownstone on the Upper East Side. Every time I come, I always pretend I'm in *Gossip Girl.* That is because of the extravagance of the houses and all the expensive cars parked on the street. It's one of the few times my parents' wealth doesn't bother me. Rick and

Thena chose the brownstone a year ago; now it's hers. She told me it was one of his investment properties, and she pays rent to him every month, but she plans on buying it for herself before she graduates.

The outside is a soft cream with a large navy-blue door and red brick steps with a black railing leading to the front door. She always has a floral wreath on the door. Today there is a soft pastel motif. I ring the doorbell, and a second later, Bell opens it.

She beams at me while pulling me inside, barefoot in a short flowery dress, her hair half pulled back in its most natural state, some waves tighter than others, and some more loose from the coloring and constant heat she puts on it. When we were little, her hair used to be light brown, while Thena and I had dark brown, but now I'm the only one who still has her natural hair color. Their hair colors fit them, though. I couldn't imagine Bell without sunshine blonde hair and Thena without jet black.

I look for Thena, and Bell says, *"She's on the phone."* I follow Bell into the living room, sliding my shoes off at the door and stuffing my socks inside. The feel of Thena's smooth hardwood floor calms me.

Her house is large, organized, and clean. Nothing is ever out of place, and the decorations are something out of a magazine. She has an oversized gray couch in her living room with a black coffee table. The usual magazines, and candles have been removed and replaced with packs of soda, coasters, and paper towels. The food hasn't arrived.

I can see Thena in the kitchen, wearing a black dress, her high heels off, and her hair in a tight bun on top of her head. The kitchen has black marble countertops, cream cabinets, and state-of-the-art appliances. There's a large bouquet of flowers in the center of the island. I plop down on the couch, sprawling out. Bell lays on the floor right below me.

"Do you like your apartment?" I asked. She had moved in with her boyfriend over the summer in an apartment in Brooklyn. I haven't been over yet; I just know it's near a train, and she hates hearing it sometimes.

"It's growing on me."

Bell is the type of person to love things at full speed, with everything she has in her, which is why I know she hates her boyfriend Tristan's apartment but won't tell him.

"The only living arrangements that should ever grow on you are dorm rooms," Thena coolly says, walking past us and going to the front door. She opens the door, pays for the food, and returns to the living room. Her rug is covered in towels to prevent stains, and we all sit on the floor, *not the couch.*

I sit in between them, always in the middle. Thena takes the food out of the bag. Boxes of sushi, white rice, dumplings, and egg rolls are placed on the table. Bell's eyes brighten as she takes in everything. The only meat she eats is fish, and even then, only in small increments. I'm pretty sure she's been a pescatarian for five or six years now, and the only reason she even consumes fish is because Mom and her manager told her to.

Thena passes out three plates, and we serve ourselves our food.

"How do you like your new therapist?" Thena asks. I grab chopsticks and break them apart.

"She's nice. She talks a lot and is kind of pushy, but she's fine."

"You've only had one session with her, right?" Bell questions. I nod. *"Anything exciting at school?"*

"There's this art competition that's been announced. It sounds cool. My chances of winning are low, but I'm excited about it."

"Why do you think you won't win?" Thena's voice is cold and stern, and I know I've said something wrong.

"There are a lot of talented people in AP Art with more experience than me. Most of them go to summer camps and spend their time at big art schools or are applying to huge ones, and I don't do any of that." I keep looking at my sushi. I grab one of the California rolls and take a bite.

"Do you want to do those things?" Bell asks. I look at her, and she has an encouraging smile. Her encouragement doesn't catch me off guard, but her smile does.

"I-I don't know."

Everyone in my art class has an idea of where they want to go or what they want to do. Ms. Han had us go around and say our plans for the future, and when it came to my table, Clara was the only one who said something. She wants to go to Brown to play lacrosse.

Ms. Han said she'd ask us again when college acceptance letters come out and see what we have planned. I have time, but by now, Thena already had a business plan, and Bell had already started getting ready to move out.

"Well, just because those people study and consider themselves art experts, or whatever, doesn't mean you don't have an opportunity to win. If you want to win that competition, then you can. You just have to work ten times harder than them, and that's something you can do."

I nod, forcing myself to believe Thena's words. Maybe I can. Do I want to? Am I serious about art? Or is it just something I've always done?

"How's Elénore Co.?" I love her company name; it sounds so expensive, and I think she knows that.

Her top lip lifts.

"I've been meeting with potential investors, but I need to come up with an event or show to show off what I have to offer. I refuse to go into a meeting with nothing but my name, or more importantly, the Van der Berg name."

I nod in understanding; people would invest simply because of who our stepfather or mother is, and that's not what she wants. She wants her own name and to accomplish things on her own merit. Very admirable if you ask me.

She opens her phone and pulls up the Elénore Co. Instagram. She has one thousand followers and a few pictures, none of which have people's faces, just two necklaces showcased on different necks and a few bracelets. Thena admitted to us she was struggling with getting more business. I think she's playing it a little too safe, but I'm not a business expert.

"Maybe have a gallery walk, like you do in museums or art exhibits. Rent out a small room and show what you got," I suggest.

"Or a fashion show with neutral colors so people only focus on the jewelry."

"I could do both," she says.

Thena goes silent, obviously thinking about the idea, then opens her phone and begins typing, probably to her assistant. Her assistant is a housewife who Thena met at a boutique in Soho a year ago.

I haven't met her, but I'm pretty sure Bell has, and Bell says she's a sweet person, so I take her word for it. I finish two dumplings and go for another one.

"How's school without Jay?" Bell asks, her mouth filled with rice and a spicy tuna roll.

"Swallow before speaking," Thena says, a hint of disgust on her face.

Bell makes a big show of swallowing, then mouths, *"Sorry." "It's alright. I made a new friend. She's cool. I'll be okay."* The last thing I want is Thena and Bell worrying about me. They both have busy schedules, and I don't want them to have to add me to it. Thena needs to focus on her company and finishing college, and Bell is trying to grow as a model.

She's been modeling since she was fifteen when she hit a growth spurt, landing her at 5 '9 ½. Mom capitalized on that, and a few weeks later, she had a contract at one of the biggest modeling agencies in the country.

When I found out she got the contract, I got her favorite cupcakes and snuck them to her, so Mom didn't say anything. Bell is probably the only model on earth who eats carbs.

I look between them, my two older sisters, neither living with me anymore. They're in their own worlds in a different state and city than me. It's a short drive, but it's not the same. The people closest to me have all left me for New York City.

"I miss living with you guys," I admit in a whisper. Both their eyes soften, and Bell pulls me into a hug.

"I miss living with you too." Bell kisses the top of my head, and I soak up the smell and warmth of her body. She always smells like cherry blossoms; both her soap and perfume have the same fragrance.

"Though we may not be living with you, we are still with you these next few months. You'll get through this," Thena assures me. I wipe the lone tear from my eye and force a shaky smile. *"It's a lot of Mom for one person to manage."*

If anyone gets the pressure of living with Mom, it's them, Thena more so than Bell. I've avoided Mom and Rick so far, but it's only been two weeks. I spent most of my summer with my sisters and Jay, and now I have to do this by myself.

I don't want to leave Thena's brownstone. It feels warm and inviting. It kind of feels like home, but soon Rick will be outside waiting for me, asking me how it went. I'll say good and look out the window so he doesn't see my tears.

Chapter 7

Emille Kate Van der Berg

"You know, if you actually go out, the whole loneliness thing might fade," Liv says, sipping a Monster energy drink. It's been a week since my sister's dinner and Liv has been at school every day. We're sitting outside in the courtyard, sharing a bench. She had someone bring us sandwiches and drinks since neither of us has our driver's license.

"I'm not lonely," I retort, taking a bite of my warm sandwich. The bread is toasted, and the cheese is slightly melted. *Heaven.*

"Then why do you always look like you're sporting a broken heart?"

"That's my face, you jerk," I playfully snapped.

Liv laughs, and I join her. Liv wears an oversized hoodie that looks a couple of years old, navy-blue pants, and high-top Vans that have definitely seen better days. She's never worn the school uniform skirt like all the girls are supposed to, and no one says anything to her about it.

Today in art, Clara asked what we were doing for lunch, and Liv said anything without her. Clara's face turned three shades redder, and I was afraid to make eye contact with her for the rest of class. Now Clara is glaring daggers at us from her table of friends across the courtyard.

"There's a party tonight," Liv informs me.

"On a Tuesday night?" I ask, my eyes wide in disbelief. Liv chuckles and nods.

"It's at this boy's house in Greenwich if you want to come."

I sigh inwardly. *What is everyone's obsession with stupid New York?* *"Uh, I can't. I have therapy."*

"Oh shit! Cool. What's your therapist like?"

"Bubbly, nice, really interested in getting to know me." I focus on my sandwich, inspecting the tomato and watching some of the juices seep into the thick pieces of meat.

"Sounds cool. How often do you go?"

"Every other Tuesday."

Liv nods, chugging some more of her energy drink.

"I used to go to this bakery every Thursday. It shut down. I think the owner died. Her husband had died a few years before."

I look at her. Her tree-trunk brown eyes are fixed on the space between us.

"They had some good-ass brownies." A chuckle escapes my lips, but I stop before it turns into laughter. *"They were warm and gooey but not just straight batter."*

I softly laugh, and before I can stop myself, my laughter causes me to choke on a piece of my sandwich. When I recover, I find Liv's eyes looking off into space. I try to see where she's looking and find her eyes on a pair of green eyes filled with fire. Clara stands up and walks towards us, each step more forceful than the next. By the time she reaches us, I'm filled with dreadful anticipation but remain stoic.

"What's so funny?" she asks, staring down at us, her eyes flickering between us. I don't know what to say, so I let Liv take the lead. This feels like one of their games.

"Nothing that concerns you," Liv answers coolly, sipping her drink.

I refuse to get lost in this match of theirs, so I pull out my phone. I contemplate texting Jay but decide against it. He's probably in class or having lunch with his roommate or someone he's met.

Bell told me that most people's social circle doubles, triples, or even more during their first couple of months at college, but by the end of their first semester—sometimes even quicker—they have their *'real'* social circle. She said it was what happened when Tristan went to college. I wonder how big Jay's social circle is now?

"Don't you have anything to say?" Clara's voice snaps me out of my thoughts. I look up, and she's standing above me.

"M-me?" My voice is meek, and I can feel my whole body warm up, thankful no one can tell I'm blushing.

"Yes, you. Why are you sitting there with that dumbass look on your face?"

"Leave her alone. You're being a bitch to someone who doesn't deserve it. Leave!" Liv barks at Clara. They continue their glare off for a few more seconds before Clara turns around and leaves, her blonde hair whipping with each stomp.

I released a breath I didn't know I was holding.

"God, she's really terrifying. And I have Thena as an older sister!"

"Clara's more intimidating than your older sister?" Liv quirks a brow, obviously knowing Thena's reputation.

I think about it.

"Yes, without a doubt. I'm pretty sure Thena's never been cold to me."

I've seen her make people shrink from a glare, but I'm pretty sure the hardest she's been on me is still considered one of her softer levels.

The bell rings, and just like that, lunch is over. We get up and slowly make our way to our next class. AP Bio is on the third floor, and that usually takes us five minutes to walk to. We stroll more than we walk. Our teacher is reading the agenda by the time we make it to class.

I sit by my partner, Bryce, and follow his lead. He takes out his notebook and starts taking notes, and I attempt to do the same. A few minutes later, we have a new project to begin. Our teacher turns on the lights, turns the projector off, and sits at his desk to let us work.

Bryce turns to me, his large framed glasses pushed to the top of his nose, his collared shirt and blazer perfectly fitted. Bryce's skin complexion is notably pale, and his eyes resemble Liv's, just darker.

He smiles at me, and I smile back. I like Bryce. He's nice to me and doesn't treat me differently or try to isolate me. I feel like a regular, seventeen-year-old girl.

"This project is worth thirty percent of our grade and will be due the day before our midterm." I nod in understanding, writing down the date. *"I don't want to make you feel bad. I really don't."* His cheeks start to pink, and I can't stop my smile from spreading. *"But I can handle this project. I know I can, and I know that if I asked you to help, you would. But I can handle this."*

Oh, I expected something a lot worse. I'm not upset or hurt that he wants to do it himself.

"Bryce, it's really sweet that you'd think that'd hurt my feelings, but it doesn't. Honestly, I'm not good at this class, I wasn't good at regular Bio, and I was just put in here based on my last name. If you told the teacher you didn't want to be my partner anymore, I would totally understand. I'm not a good partner at all. I'll help with organizing stuff and whatever. But I promise it's okay, Bryce," I ramble, my hands twiddling with themselves.

Bryce nods and smiles, a flash of relief passing his face. The whole class, I organize our spreadsheet and make things as easy as possible. We pack up our stuff when the bell rings, and Bryce grabs my arm.

"You're a great partner, Emi, and a nice person." His face is red when he finishes, but I smile and nod, leaving behind him. *I'm a great partner.*

As a nightmarish surprise, Mom arrives to pick me up after school. She rolls down the window and waves, her big black sunglasses covering her face. I sigh and walk towards the car, getting in the front seat. She takes in my attire and then turns back to the road.

"Have you been in contact with James recently?" she asks as we pull out of the carpool line.

"Kind of."

"Well, make sure you give him the right amount of space so he can enjoy himself and have fun. Don't become a burden while he tries to enjoy himself," she scolds.

"His father told me James and his roommate have already received five noise complaints. I mean, boys will be boys. I'm surprised he's even going to his classes." She laughs, her pitch high and resonant like a church bell. "Remember when he started going to all of those parties a year or two ago? God, Eric wanted to ship him off."

"I remember," I mutter. I look out the window. I can feel Mom's eyes on me, but I don't know what else to say and I don't want her to see the concern on my face. *Is that what his life is back to?*

Dr. Young waits for me in her chair. I ignore her for the first several minutes until the silence stretches for an uncomfortable amount of time, and I've shifted in my seat more times than I can count. She is good at the waiting game. Better than me. So, I speak.

"*This year I got put into two extra AP classes that I didn't choose to be in because of my last name, and when I'm in those classes, I feel like everyone there knows I don't belong. I'm not smart enough. All I bring to the table is my stepdad's money and last name.*" I sit further up on the couch, and I feel my eyes burning. "*Thena has done everything independently, even if people have accused her of trading on her name. She always has facts and the scores to back up her efforts, and I…I don't have that. I don't bring a substantial amount of good qualities to the table,*" I admit with a weak chuckle. I wipe a tear from falling.

Dr. Young smiles and sits forward.

"This is stupid. I shouldn't be complaining about this. Some people would kill for the opportunities I'm given, and I'm complaining about them." I force a weak laugh and look away.

"How do you feel when you're in those classes?"

"I feel like if I make a mistake, everyone will see it and begin to judge me and hate me a little more, and each mistake is just another thing I can't do right."

"And how do you cope with that?"

"I don't know...I usually just let someone else lead and try to stay out of the way. I try to make myself as invisible as I can. When you're invisible, no one can see the mistakes you make."

"They also can't see you," she adds. She's right. I can tell by her voice that that's not a good thing, but it works for me.

Sometimes I'd rather be invisible than face everything.

"How often do you find yourself comparing yourself to your sisters?"

"Doesn't everyone compare themselves to other people? Isn't that part of being a teenager?"

"To some degree, yes."

"I don't hate or want anything bad to happen to my sisters. I love them. They're my best friends and are always willing to be there for me. I just wish that when people saw me, they didn't see the little sister of Thena, the successful serial entrepreneur, or Bell, the model. I will always be their talentless little sister, and... I'm trying to be okay with that."

I don't want to talk anymore; I'm starting to feel too much. I don't want to cry and throw myself a pity party. I also don't want Dr. Young to think Thena or Bell have done something wrong to me. They're not the bad guys.

"I know you love your sisters, Emi; I think you love them and Jay more than most things. But I also know that when you pour all your love into them, you only leave drops for yourself."

Two sessions, and she's figured that out. I don't know what to say or how to respond, so I just nod and pull one of my legs under me. Maybe I should've gone to that party with Liv.

###

Mom and Rick were waiting for me in the kitchen when I got home, and a plate of food for me was left out. I sit with them and listen to them talk to each other about their week and upcoming events. They asked me how school and therapy were, and I told them it was good. I leave before dessert and go to my room, forcing myself to work on some of my homework. I draw in my sketchbook for a little bit, then shower. When I come out, I crawl into bed, get on my phone, and go on Instagram. Using Bell's account, I found Jay's account. He has almost thirty thousand followers, yet he's never posted.

He's been tagged in a post. He's standing by a tall, beautiful girl, and both have red solo cups in their hands, smiling as they talk to each other. She has dark brown hair that falls to her shoulders in thick waves, her smile wide, and her eyes an olive green, kind of like Bell's, just not as bright. She's really pretty. Their arms are touching, and he looks like he's having fun.

My heart collides with my chest. I decided at that moment that I now know what's best for both of us. I cannot remain in this purgatory, and he has clearly found a new, full life without me.

October

Chapter 8

Emillie Kate Van der Berg

"Please just answer your phone," Liv says with a groan. I force an innocent expression and furrow my eyebrows.

"What's wrong with my phone?" I know what's wrong with it. It's been buzzing in my back pocket on and off for the past ten minutes. Liv freezes, her hand a few inches away from a bag of chips.

Currently, we're walking through the grocery store, finding snacks for the football game. Liv convinced me to attend it, so I'm honoring her wish. Our small handheld basket is overfilled with junk food. My phone buzzes again.

"Check your phone, or I'll leave you here."

I gasp. *"You wouldn't."*

She turns to me with a look that says, *"Try me. I dare you."*

57

Two missed calls from Jay. Two text messages from him as well, and a text message from Thena. I leave the texts from Jay unopened.

Thena: Would you like to go on any last-minute college tours?

I think about it.

Me: Not necessarily. Do you want to see any?

Thena: Seeing as I already go to college, no. Let me know if you want to see any, and I can arrange the details.

Me: Kk.

"It was just my sister."

"Mmh, I'm sure." Sarcasm drips from Liv's voice, and I narrow my eyes at her.

Feeling particularly chatty, I'd filled Liv in on my plan to put distance between Jay and I. She said it wasn't my most brilliant idea, but she supports me. I also may have shown Bell and Thena the Instagram picture of Jay at our most recent Tuesday night sister's dinner.

Thena investigated the girl, and we found out that she was a sophomore at Columbia, and her major was computer engineering. I'm sure there were juicer details, but that was what Thena told us. Her name's Miley something, and she's from London. Meaning she has an accent—a cute posh accent. Neither of them said anything about why I was asking them to stalk her.

"Quick question: how did you find the picture if you don't even have an Instagram?" Thena asked me. I pocketed my phone.

"I sometimes use Bell's or Jay's account."

I helped create Jay's account, so I like to think of it as ours.

I refuse to re-join social media officially. The copious amounts of judgment that live there gives me immediate anxiety. I can't bring myself to do it. I thought my FOMO would kick in by now, but it hasn't. When I get the urge, I just lurk from Jay or Bell accounts. Plus, in the short period I did have an Instagram, life wasn't going too well for me. Things happened that shouldn't have happened, and now everyone, including me, is cautious about letting me fully rejoin.

###

The football game is chilly and loud. The stadium is packed with parents, students, and people from the town. Mostly everyone's changed from their uniform. The fall air is crisp and still, not much of a breeze. Liv and I sit on the edge of a bleacher, our snacks in our hands and our eyes locked on the game. The other team has the ball.

"Emi, what do you like doing?" she asks, turning to me. I look at her, a Twizzler hangs out of her mouth, and a cigarette sits behind her ear, half hidden by her hair. "I've never asked you that."

I shrug. *"I like movies, books, and junk food. And amusement parks are cool too. What do you like?"* I ask her. *Are you supposed to ask your new friends these questions?*

"Partying."

"Is it that fun?"

"It's a good distraction."

"From what?"

"Life, things you don't want to think about, anger, pain. Anything really."

Is that why Jay used to party so much? Was he feeling things he didn't want to feel? I want to pull out my phone and call and ask him, but I can't drag him back to the past. These past two weeks, I feel like I've been constantly battling between letting Jay go and wanting to hold onto him. I hope this goes away with time, and eventually, he'll stop calling, and I'll get better.

I have a session with Dr. Young on Tuesday, and I'm thinking about telling her about it. She is growing on me. I haven't had any bad days in a while, so I might as well soak up her eagerness to help while I can.

Chapter 9

Emillie Kate Van der Berg

"How have you been, Emi?" Dr. Young asks, crossing her legs, her long flowy skirt reaching her ankles. Her hair is curlier today. I like it.

"I've been okay. How have you been?"

"I've been good. My husband and I are thinking about getting a dog. It's just a question of who will get up and walk it early in the morning in winter. We're from Florida, so the cold isn't our specialty."

"Do you like the cold at all?"

"It's beautiful," Dr. Young muses. Her smile has a sparkle to it. *"Do you like the cold?"*

"Sometimes. I like it when it's Christmas, and it's still that bright white before the dogs pee in it, before it starts mixing with all the dirt and becomes slush by the road. I don't mind the cold. I can stay inside."

"Do you like being inside? You're not an outdoorsy person?"

I chuckle lightly.

"No, that's more of Bell's thing. I like watching Marvel movie marathons in bed. The only light in the room came from the television. I'm not so much the snowboarding or hiking type, but I should try to go for Bell's sake." I rub my hands down my thighs. *"Do you like outdoorsy stuff?"*

She nods.

"I like surfing, and I've been on a few good camping trips, but I also like movies, pizza, and museum dates. I could go for either, honestly."

Dr. Young gets up and walks to her desk. It's more organized now. All the boxes are gone, and more pictures and knickknacks litter the room. The coffee table separating the sofa from her chair has a candle, a stack of magazines, coasters, and a chart of colors, each color representing a mood. If I could paint her room, everything would need to be mixed with white, no dark colors.

"How have you and Jay been?" She asks, bringing a cup to her mouth. I don't know if it's coffee or tea, but Dr. Young looks like she drinks only iced coffee or tea, no in-between.

"I've been avoiding him. I haven't been answering his calls or texts."

She sets her cup down and walks back to her chair, sitting down before she asks me, *"Why?"*

"I'm not doing good, and he is. I can't drag my best friend down. I won't."

Tears burn my eyes, but I blink them away. I believe in this wholeheartedly. This seems like the only way for him to succeed and prove his dad and everyone else who doubted him in high school wrong.

"How aren't you doing good, Emi?" She presses, her hands crossed.

"I don't know…I'm not meeting a bunch of new people or having the time of my life. I'm static, and he's growing. I don't think that goes together."

A familiar, cold, feminine voice in my head whispers, *you never belonged with him to begin with.*

I look at the clock. We have five minutes left.

"Bye, Dr. Young."

"Emi, wait," she walks to her desk and writes down her phone number. "I don't know why I haven't given this to you sooner. Probably because you always rush out of here." She laughs. I'm happy it doesn't upset her or hurt her feelings that I do that. She hands me a sticky note with big lettering, her phone number and full name sprawled out.

"Call me if you ever need anything or want someone to talk to."

I nod and leave.

Rick's driver, Dave, picks me up, and I'm grateful it's not Rick or my mom. When I get home, Rick and my mom are dressed up, and Rick is staring at her affectionately. I sneak past them and go upstairs, locking myself in my room. I climb into the shower and take a long shower. My phone is playing a playlist I'm pretty sure Jay made last Spring when I was having a bad day. I get out and wipe the fog off the mirror. I look at myself.

I think I've gained ten pounds since the end of the school year. I didn't work out the whole summer and ate anything I wanted. No one would be able to tell unless I wore a bikini, and I haven't worn one in a long time. If I go swimming, I usually just wear a one-piece and keep an oversized T-shirt on the whole time. I don't want people comparing my body to everyone else's.

I don't fall asleep for a while and contemplate calling Dr. Young. Instead, I call no one. I turn the volume on my cartoons a little higher and wait for sleep to pull me in.

Chapter 10

James Averell

The thing about Emi Van der Berg is that she's not a good liar. She cares too much to learn the skill correctly. She's also not good at subtlety. So, it became apparent rather quickly that she was avoiding me. No texts back. No calls. No FaceTime's. She went utterly ghost; I'd be worried if I didn't have her location and both her sister's contact information.

I do the only reasonable thing I can think of: drive from Columbia to her house. I park just outside her long winding driveway and punch the code into the walk-up gate. Her room is towards the backyard; an old ladder leads up to the roof, and it's just a window knock from there. I climb the ladder, the whole process from memory. Her parents like me, but not enough for me to be in her room at night. I've snuck into her room hundreds of times. I pulled the window up; she had left it unlocked. She always forgets to lock it unless I tell her to.

I climb inside and find her lying on her bed, in pajamas, and a book she's read hundreds of times in her hands. She doesn't notice me, so I climb down from her window seat and onto the floor.

She jumps up, her book flying out of her hands. I smile at the reaction. I walk towards her large bed with its flower-designed sheets, matching white silk pillowcase, and decorative pillows Thena gave her. Her shirt rides up as she moves, and I catch a peek at her *short* gray sleep shorts.

"Jay!" she yelps in surprise. I kick my shoes off and climb onto her bed as she shifts back further. I grab her arm, stopping her from moving. She's two spaces from falling off. She realizes and whispers a thanks.

"What a-are you doing here?" she asks, pushing her wet curls behind her ear.

"Came to see you," I murmur, sitting beside her, the smell of her soap and shampoo filling my nostrils. I like her scent and the way it's always the same and never changes, not as we've gotten older and not after everything we've been through. *"I missed you, Em."*

Her eyes soften like they always do, and a smile stretches her soft face.

"I missed you too, but you should be at college with your new friends."

"I want to be with you, my best friend," I tell her, my voice stronger and more serious than I intended it to be.

"I don't want to keep you from…" She trails off, looking for her remote. Her show has gone off, and she hates the show that's about to come on. She finds the remote and changes the channel.

"Keep me from what?"

She shakes her head.

"Are you spending the night?"

"Do you want me to?"

"Do you have any morning classes?"

"Answer the question, Em," I whisper. She shifts nervously, her knees touching my hip. I grab them, and she stops moving, her eyes locking on mine.

"I want you to."

"Then I will."

She blows out a candle she had lit and climbs under the sheets.

"You haven't come by in a while," she whispers after a few minutes.

"I know. I've been busy with classes and these random lunch meetings with my dad. I'm sorry, Em."

She doesn't stiffen or soften; she just stays still.

"It's okay."

My dad better not have lied to me again. If his advice screws me, I might have to take drastic measures like crashing one of his cars (again)... the possibilities are endless, and my partner in crime lies right next to me.

"We're not in a fight, are we?" I ask. Her curls are falling in front of her face. I lean up and push her hair back. Emi and I have gotten into maybe two fights in our six, almost seven, years of friendship. Each fight lasted maybe less than a day, but we've been in some off periods. Some months we don't talk about it.

I lean closer to her. Her big brownish-greenish eyes widen, tracking all over my face like she's memorizing every angle and planning to put me in one of her sketchbooks, the books she keeps hidden all over. Her brown skin feels warm under my hand.

"No. Why would you think that?" she gently asks, scooting closer. left. I bite back a smile. *"Uh, because you've been ignoring me,"* I say with amusement.

She shrugs, her eyes flickering toward the television.

"I just want to make sure you're not mad at me."

"I'm not," She exhales, her minty breath hitting my nostrils. She won't offer to explain her behavior over the last several days, and I won't push her to. Emi and I stayed like this—her leg touching mine, her small hand on top of mine, her rings cold, and my hand grasping her knee. She sleeps with most of her jewelry on, occasionally removing a necklace or a bracelet if it digs into her skin too hard.

At moments like this, I can forget about my dad, college, all our troubles, and the turmoil she keeps hidden in her head. It's just Emi and me, locked away in her childhood bedroom, a room with traces of me and our memories. I hope the distance doesn't put any more walls up. We live less than an hour away from one another, but she's too intimidated to visit me, and I've been advised not to visit her. It makes each minute hurt.

She climbs off the bed and grabs me a pair of shorts from her drawer. They're either a pair she's stolen or a pair I left over. She turns around and lets me change out of my jeans. When I finish, she's under her sheets. She smiles and encourages me to do the same. I do. When I lay down, she moves closer, laying her head on my chest like she's done a million times.

"I missed you," I say again. I can feel her smile.

"I missed you too."

A feeling of pride and happiness takes over me, one I haven't felt since I left for college. I miss Emi more than she knows. I don't think she knows how much she means to me, and maybe that's my fault, but either way, I'm tired of this. I want us back at the same school. I want to see her every day with no more walls between us.

But I can tell that when morning comes, and I have to go, the walls between us will be back up. So, I just wrap my arm around her shoulders and pull her to me. She holds onto my shirt with one hand, and the other stays on the remote. I wait for her to fall asleep, her breathing becoming shallower and her body a little heavier as she pushes further into me.

I'm lulled to sleep by her breathing, and I hope that whatever has happened with her, she tells me and lets me back in.

Chapter 11

Emillie Kate Van der Berg

"I saw Jay's truck parked outside when your mom and I came home last night," Rick says over breakfast. Mom is still upstairs, which means she's either hung over or in a bad mood.

I freeze, my donut inches away from my mouth. What am I supposed to say in this situation? If I were as bold and irreverent as Jay I would say *"fuck off,"* I think that was what he'd say to his dad. But I'm not Jay. I remain frozen as my mind whirs awake, searching for a lie.

"He left something here, and I told him to come by and pick it up," I lied. That's a good lie.

Rick's lip twitched.

"At three o'clock in the morning?"

"You guys came home late," I muse, taking a bite of the glazed donut that is still warm. *"Fun night?"*

"Very," Rick answers, amusement dancing in his ocean-blue eyes. I like his eyes. *"Thankfully, your mom was too drunk to notice it. Is anything going on between you two?"*

My whole body warms. I shake my head. *"No, no. Just friends."*

"I'm not going to tell your mom or threaten you with punishment, just be safe and remember you can talk to me." I nod. We eat in silence.

Mom's footsteps are heavy as she comes down the stairs, her hair in its natural wavy state piled on top of her head, and her silk pajamas hidden behind a thick robe she only wears in the winter. She sits beside Rick, sipping a coffee that I'm guessing he brewed for her.

"Morning, crotee," Mom says to me, her French creole accent thicker with her morning voice. She doesn't speak French often, but when we were little, she and *Meme* only talked to us in French. It wasn't until I was nine or so that it stopped altogether. She still speaks it on the phone, and I know Thena does too, but I think Bell and I lost it somewhere along the way. I can still understand it, but my pronunciation is awkwardly American.

"How'd you sleep?" she asks, putting some yogurt in her mouth.

I glance at Rick, and he hides his smile with his coffee cup.

"Good. How'd you sleep?"

She wrinkles her nose. Without all the makeup, the perfect hair, and designer clothes, she looks like my childhood - before life happened.

"I slept okay; your sisters should be coming over shortly. I think they want to make plans for Halloween." I open my mouth to remind her I usually just find something to do with Jay. But she beats me to it. *"I know you usually do God-knows-what with James, but his father says he has plans, so*

your sisters are coming over to ramp up the festivities. You should go out with them. Mingle with some of Bell's friends."

Bell's friends are all models and in their mid to late twenties, and as Jay says, 'too vapid to hang out with us.'

"I might just stay home or go out with my friend, Liv," I mumble around my mouthful of donut.

"You made a friend?" Mom's eyes widen in disbelief, and I can't really be mad or hurt over her reaction.

"Yes, we have a few classes together. I went to the football game with her."

She nods.

"Excuse my surprise. It's just that you've never been social or good at mingling like your sisters. Seems like it was a good thing James went off to college. You've come out of your shell! Oh, this is wonderful! I can set you up with Arthur. You know the Ransier's? Well, their son broke up with his girlfriend a few months ago, and his mother told me he was looking to get back out there."

I start shaking my head. I do not want to be set up. I've told her this before, and her exasperated response is usually, *"Your sisters were not this difficult at your age."*

I'm the difficult one.

The front door opens while Mom goes on about another one of her *"friends"* sons to set me up with. I'm trying to shrink further into myself. Between her ramblings she glances disapprovingly at my donut, I dropped it on my plate after her third side eye and haven't picked it up since.

Thena and Bell walk into the breakfast room. Bell is wearing black shorts and a tank top, and Thena is in a modest black dress, her heels clicking with each step. Thena's hair is in a sleek high bun, the pieces tightly twisted, and her usually dark blue eyes glint cooly at our mother. *"She does not want to be set up with one of your friends. Leave her alone,"* Thena says tersely, sitting next to me. Bell stands and shifts on the balls of her feet. Mom changes the subject.

"Isabel, how are you and Tristan?"

"Oh, we're fine. He might be getting a promotion pretty soon."

"That's good," Mom chimes, a small smile on her face.

"Actually, he was wondering if there was any way he could come to the Turkey trot?"

Rick stiffens, his coffee still in his hand.

"And he wants to know if he can come to Thanksgiving."

"If that's okay…" Bell hesitates.

"No, he cannot come to Thanksgiving. Now as for the Turkey Trot, it's a public event. If he pays the $55 registration fee, I can't stop him from joining." The usual smile is gone from Rick's face. *"But our hotel rooms are full; no space. So, he'll have to stay in your apartment,"* Rick adds.

"Our apartment," Bell corrects softly, grabbing a strawberry off Rick's plate.

Rick grumbles. *"I'm sure he thinks it is but I haven't seen him cough up a dollar for the rent yet."*

I bite back a laugh. I'm pretty sure Tristan and Bell split the cost for everything. At least that's what she told us. Rick's funny when he's being sassy.

"You're doing that thing again," Mom reminds him with a small smile.

"What thing?" he asks, his eyes focusing on her.

"That sassy, snarky thing."

He rolls his eyes. *"You try being the only guy around four women. You would get sassy too."*

I laugh, and his lips lift, a small laugh escaping him too. Mom tries to bite back a smile, but it peeks through. *"I'm surprised I haven't started eating ice cream out of the carton and crying at hallmark movies,"* he snorts.

"We do not do that!" Mom defends. I think we all have at least once or twice.

"Emi does it the best," Rick continues. *"She does it in her room and has tacos or pizza with her."* My eyes widen, and Rick just laughs. Mom's eyes narrow on me, but all the laughter distracts her. I'm sure she is calculating the carbs in his comment.

Thena squeezes my hand. I look at her, and she leans closer.

"Do you want to come to dinner with me tonight? I have reservations at this Italian restaurant in Little Italy. Bell said she can't come because she has a shoot in the morning, then something with Tristan." Thena rolls her eyes and waves her hand as if the very idea of Tristan is completely absurd. I have to hold in a smile.

"I'd like to go," I whisper to her. The idea of a dinner in the city with Thena seems exciting.

After breakfast, I sneak back up to my room and straighten it up. Liv texted me a picture of her sitting in Taco Bell late last night. It was almost two a.m. in the morning when she sent the photo.

Me: Did you go alone?

Liv: Yea. Had the munchies.

Me: Are you okay now?

Liv: Yea, just hungover.

I'll call her later in the day and make sure she's okay.

Thena knocks on my room door a little before seven. She opens it without waiting for me to say come in and looks around. I know it's not her typical standard of cleanliness, but my room is passable. She just has a way of looking at things, like our mother, that makes people immediately second guess themselves.

"Ready?" she asks. I nod and walk out with her. Mom and Rick sat in the sitting room, looking at a stack of papers together. We wave, and they both look up. Rick smiles and waves while Mom narrows her eyes.

"Emi, don't you want to put on one of the dresses I got you? You never know who you'll run into." In other words, *Who Thena might run into it.*

"She looks beautiful. we'll see you all later," Thena answers for me.

Dinner is amazing. We sit at a table in a more secluded part of the busy restaurant. Laughter, talking, and the faint sound of jazz music fill the air. I can't stop the smile that overtakes my face. I love restaurants filled with so much life you can't help but sit there and hope it soaks into you.

"Who's singing?" I ask Thena when we make it to our table.

"Ella Fitzgerald," she says briskly, opening her menu. The waiter comes over, and Thena orders us both Shirley Temples and herself a glass of white wine for when the food comes out.

"You remembered," I whisper, a smile stretching my face.

Whenever we go to a more upscale restaurant, we always order Shirley Temples. Bell, Thena, and I have done it since we were little. Our dad made them for us for my sixth birthday, and we all got sugar drunk. Mom freaked and tried to chase Bell and Alexander around while Thena and I stayed by Dad in the backyard. Looking back now, it's a bittersweet memory.

Thena rolls her eyes. *"Of course, I remember, little sister."*

The waiter comes back and sets our drinks down. I take a sip; not enough syrup, too much Sprite. It's a balance not all places have mastered.

"I'm going to be transparent with you." Thena starts right in. I nod, bracing myself. *"Mom has already scheduled a college tour at Brown. I made it clear to her that you didn't want to go to one, but she didn't listen."*

Why can't she just listen to me?

I don't know if I want to go to college, and it seems like everyone expects that of me. I haven't sat down and gotten excited over the prospect of college. A million emotions float through me, but the one that seems to stick is anxiety.

"Talk to me," Thena urges me. I can feel the waiter hovering near us, trying to decide if he should come and take our order.

"I-I don't know. Should I go? I don't know if I want to go to college, Thena."

The waiter approaches. Thena orders penne alla vodka, and I order chicken parmesan with a side of spaghetti.

Thena crosses her hands. *"If you don't want to attend college, that's fine. You don't need to go just because Mom wants you to or because I went. You know that, right?"*

"Yeah," I lied. We don't talk about college or Mom for the rest of dinner.

I soak up the time I have with her and try not to think about Jay or anything else.

Chapter 12

Emillie Kate Van der Berg

I think Clara and Liv have found the perfect balance of hostility and tolerance. All three of us are working on our 'projects.' I decided to make a paper Mache lion. I hope to give it to Thena for Christmas, but it's not close to being finished. I'm on layer one of the paper Mache, and I can tell it might need another layer, and I have to carve out the head.

Liv is making a large face mask with paper Mache, and Clara is trying to paper Mache a house someone else made for her. It's a beautiful house, but she obviously didn't make it herself. She's not very good at art.

"Liv, I have a question," Clara begins. I can already tell this won't be good. *"When you waste your life away at those parties, what do you do to occupy yourself?"*

"What do I do or who do I do?" Liv smirks at Clara. Clara's cheeks flame and I can't help but crack a smile. Clara brings up Liv's partying habits at least once a week, and each time, Liv has a different comeback.

"What's so funny?" Clara snaps at me. I almost dropped the piece of newspaper that was in my hand.

"God, leave her alone," Liv groans, her irritation apparent.

"Why? Clara snaps back. Are you sleeping with her too?!"

Liv rolls her eyes.

"You are far too invested in my sex life. I'm not your boyfriend, Clarette."

Clara's blush spreads to the tips of her ears. Her boyfriend is popular and notorious for being a playboy. I see him and Clara at school events together, both of them looking at different things, his arm always lying stiff on her shoulder.

"Emi, how many people?" Clara asks, her glare set on me.

Oh no. *"How many people, what?"*

"How many have you slept with? If you don't want to say you don't have to. Clara cannot put you on trial," Liv assures me, her eyes focused on her mask. She's applying the paper Mache on the nose; everything else is mostly covered.

"One," I tell Liv more than I tell Clara, but I can tell Clara's listening.

"Jay?" They both guess. I nod.

"Woah," Liv whispers. She looks at me with a slight smile on her face. She angles her body more toward me and lowers her voice. *"When did that happen?"*

"Summer going into junior year. We were both a little tipsy, and its kind of just happened. We never talked about it again," I whisper to her. I'm not ashamed of it; it's just not something I bring up. Jay and I have never talked about it after, so telling a bunch of people seems weird.

I was a virgin, and he wasn't, but it didn't bother me. It never had. I was—maybe still am—a little jealous of the girls he spent time with, but I never said anything. The night it happened, we had both been drinking at Rick's Hampton house, and it was late. There was a party a few houses over that everyone had gone to. We left to go back home, drinking the bottle of vodka Jay had stolen and eating whatever food we could find. One minute we were sitting in my bedroom, laughing about the people at the party, and the next, his lips were on mine.

He kissed me, and it was soft and warm, but I could tell her was holding back for my sake - like he knew he wanted more, but he didn't want to scare me off. I looked into his hazel eyes, and they had darkened. I nodded, leaned forward, and kissed him again. I kept my bikini top on and mostly hid under the covers. I remembered it clearly—every kiss, the way our bodies fit together, his ragged whispers, and moans... I remembered it all, but the next morning, I acted as if nothing happened, and he did the same. Like I had just dreamed it.

"Was it good?" Liv asks me, a devilish smile on her face.

"I can only imagine. He's a hell of a kisser," Clara adds. I freeze and look at her. She was one of the many girls Jay had attached to his hip my sophomore year when our fledgling friendship was tense. Back then it felt like we were constantly standing on the edge of something we couldn't voice. I hated seeing him with those girls. I never thought I'd speak to one of them, though. I'm not part of their crowd and most of them have already graduated. Clara was the only girl he was with that was in my grade. Maybe that's what hurt the most about him kissing her. Or maybe it's the fact she looks *nothing* like me, with her blonde hair, pale skin, and pale green eyes. I don't look like any of the girls he was with, and they all

looked like girls he would be with, girls that made sense. I now remember that was the part that hurt most.

"Damn, Clara! Your boyfriend's so bad in bed you're bringing up a kiss from two years ago. Sad case." Liv feigns disappointment and shakes her head, and I can't stop the grateful laugh that escapes me. Liv really is a solid friend. Clara looks annoyed, but I can't stop giggling at Liv's well-timed outburst.

Clara doesn't talk much for the remainder of class. Liv and I both focus on our projects, cleaning up everything when Ms. Han announces we have ten minutes left in class. As I clean off one of the paintbrushes I was using, I notice Liv and Clara standing close to each other, speaking in hushed voices. Clara's cheeks are a soft pink, and Liv's smirk is more relaxed. Later in biology I consider asking Liv what that was about, but think better of it. Instead, I listen to her tell me about her plans for tonight.

She's going to a movie with one of her friends, and I'm going to therapy.

Dr. Young waits for me in her chair, sitting up straighter and more serious than she has before. *Uh oh.* I sit down across from her, and she doesn't speak; neither one of us does. She usually starts with pleasantries and then waits for me to start talking. Today she seems more stern. Unwilling to play my game of burning the first 15 minutes with awkward silence.

"Remember how you tried to propose an idea of you not speaking and me telling your mom you're doing okay?" I nod. It was a failure, one that I've been hoping she reconsiders. I don't think she will, though.

"Well, I have a proposition for you." I don't know whether to be excited or welcome the feeling of dread that's begging me to let it enter. *"Every session, you stay the full hour and are honest with me. When I ask you a question, you answer honestly. You tell me everything you're comfortable with, and if you don't want to talk about something, you tell me. But you don't leave. And I won't tell your mom a thing we talk about. Everything stays between us. I'll even send you a copy of what I told her."* She stands up and walks closer to the table until her legs brush against it.

She lets her words sink in, letting me think about my decision.

"Do we have a deal?"

I would have to open up to her, but maybe I could better understand myself. Perhaps it wouldn't be so bad? I could keep Allison and Dad in a separate box, away from Dr. Young and everyone else. I can do it. I'll keep the necessary walls up and, from there, move forward.

I stand up and stand across from her. We're almost the same height. She extends her hand, and I reach for it, shaking on it.

"Deal." I give her a small smile, and a wider one spreads on her face. I can feel the relief.

Fifteen minutes into the session and Dr. Young has just been reading over my files and asking probing questions about the notes - basically trying to see what 'happened' to me. Nothing too bad has come up. My dad died, my older sister died, and I'm the youngest child. Worse things have happened to people, I remind her.

"Emi, what did your dad do?"

Great, she has already jumped into the topics I wanted to remain cordoned off.

"He owned a shipping company. It was really successful, I think. It's still in the family but it's run by a board. He was a great dad. I don't remember him ever being gone on long work trips— he liked to be home…with us."

"And your stepdad, Rick?"

I smile.

"Rick owns a record company called 'Roar' records, which he created when he was nineteen, I think. It's in L. A, but he works out of a satellite office here in the city. And he also owns half of Berg Theatres; his uncle owns the rest. His dad made a fortune on Wall Street, but Rick doesn't focus much on the finance sector. He's all in on music and entertainment."

"He's done really well for himself, hasn't he?" Dr. Young asks, a bewildered expression on her face.

"Billionaire boys club well," I say wishing she wasn't so impressed. Aren't therapists supposed to be too well- grounded to be impressed by money?

"And Jay's parents?" she presses.

"Averell Sports. Sports equipment and a few retail stores in big cities."

She nods.

"I'll admit that I knew you were wealthy, but hearing the extent of it - that must affect you in some ways. Does it ever feel like too much?" She asks. I like that she immediately gets it. That money is as confining as it is liberating.

"The money thing can start to feel like a lot," I say. "But Rick's money is his, and Mom's money is hers. And of course, Jay's family money is their concern. In the end, I don't have money - even though Rick likes to remind all of us that we are his heirs and will carry the money mantle forward when he goes."

"Speaking of Jay," she says, scribbling into her notes. *"Have you seen or talked to Jay recently?"*

"He snuck into my room a few nights ago and spent the night. It was nice, and he left before I woke up, though." I have no idea why I blurted that truth out to her. She had to be a witch.

"Did you guys talk about the distance you've been putting between you two?"

I shake my head.

"Not in depth. We just watched cartoons and talked. He's slept over a lot, so it felt natural." She smiles. She likes hearing about Jay. Or maybe she just likes hearing about my life. I'm ready to change subjects and regain control of this session though, so I move on.

"When I went to dinner with Thena the other night, she told me my mom had already scheduled a college tour with me at Brown. I never asked or really wanted her to do that."

"Do you feel like she makes decisions for you often? Your mother."

I nod. *"My mom listens, but she never changes her course of action. She's attentive towards Bell and her modeling career and helps and supports Thena's business, but when it comes to me, it's like she's pushing me to be more like them. Bell didn't go to college, but her career was picking up. Thena and Alexander both did. And I'm not a model, so I kind of have to."*

"You don't want to go, not even a little bit?"

I've lied to Thena about wanting to go because I know how much she loves learning and pushing herself, but I don't. I shake my head.

"School's never been for me. I struggle to get C's sometimes, and I always feel like I'm not good enough. I don't want to feel that for another four years, probably five or six knowing me."

"Well what do you like? What makes you feel good? You're not less of a person because college isn't for you. It's better to know yourself than to struggle pretending to be someone else."

"I don't know," I admit. Dr. Young nods and sends me an encouraging smile.

"You'll figure it out. You're only seventeen, Emi. It's okay that you don't know."

November

Chapter 13

Emillie Kate Van der Berg

I have spent the last two weeks rewatching *Gilmore Girls*, attempting to force myself into the fall spirit. It hasn't been much of a success, but I managed to get a C on my AP Bio quiz, no cheating necessary. Bryce smiled when I told him, and he said I just needed to get a B on the next one, and I might be able to get a B in the class. I didn't want to pop his bubble, so I nodded and agreed.

The Turkey Trot is in two weeks, the weekend before Thanksgiving. Mom has been *"subtly"* encouraging me to start working out so I'm in better shape. I agree and then go to my room with the junk food Liv has brought me hidden in my backpack.

Liv came over yesterday and fell asleep on the second episode of *Gilmore Girls*. When someone called her phone for the third time, she got up and slid on her shoes, waving at me and leaving like she'd been here a million times.

My phone starts ringing, the sound muffled by my pillows. I flip all of them over until I see it. I don't bother to look at it before I answer it.

"Hello?"

I'm too focused on Jess right now. I only watch the show for him, and maybe a little bit for Logan, but not so much for Rory. I *love* Chilton Rory but not so much Yale Rory. Another reason, college just isn't for me. I'm sure if I tell Dr. Young that reason, she'd laugh.

"Hello?" I repeat.

"You know there's a new Marvel movie coming out." Jay's voice comes through the other side, and I freeze. *"I know you've seen the previews already; hell, you've sent me three trailers of it."* I'd seen the previews a couple of weeks ago for *Eternals.* I'm craving to see it, and it comes out on Friday.

"Yeah, Friday, right?"

"Yup! There's a midnight showing that day too." It takes me a day to prepare for midnight showings, but something about starting your day off with a movie always makes me a little happier.

"Bell likes midnight showings."

He chuckles. *"So do you, or am I mistaken with a different Emilie Van der Berg."* I can't stop smiling. *"Well?"*

"Well, what?"

"Do you want to go see it? I thought I was making that obvious by bringing it up."

"Uh, I can't. I have to help my mom with something."

He sighs. *"You know, it kind of hurts you're ignoring me. Don't tell me everyone at that school stopped being shitheads as soon as I left. Was I the problem, Em?"* His voice drips with sarcasm and false concern.

"I didn't know Gryffindors could be such smart-asses," he retorts. My smile stretches, and I can hear it in my voice.

"I try to defeat all the odds laid out for me." I already know he has a dry smile on his face. I can practically hear it. We really are book nerds at heart.

"So, do you want to come to a party this weekend?" he pressed again.

"You know parties aren't really my thing." I say.

He's silent for a while. *"Don't tell me you found a new best friend,"* He jokes but without a smile in his tone.

I can't lie or ignore the question, not when it's apparent how much it hurts him. I can't hurt him; I don't want to hurt him.

"No, of course not. I just don't want to hold you back. You should be enjoying yourself, not worrying about me."

"Em-"

"I gotta go. I'll talk to you later." I hang up before more tears fill my throat.

Why am I like this? Why do I desperately want him all to myself and to go back in time to all our good memories and not face the future? Maybe I know that, inevitably, he'll find out too much. He'll really know me and not love me anymore. Jay and I have crossed the line between friendship and a relationship one too many times, and each time I lose a little more of myself to him.

Chapter 14

James Averell
February 17th, 2015
Six years ago

Blue dress. Blue dress. I keep reminding myself what color dress Rick said she'd be wearing. Blue dress, tight curly hair, and light brown skin. He came over last week and told Dad and me about how his girls were finally coming home. His new wife, Aurore, had finally tied up everything she had in Louisiana, and she and her five kids were coming to live with Rick in Connecticut.

He kept telling Dad and me, *"My girls are finally coming home."* He turned and looked at me, his smile not wavering. "You'll love Emi. She's shy and sweet, but if you give her some chocolate, she'll start opening up. She loves chocolate. She sneaks and eats it before breakfast."

His smile was soft. He really loved them. He always told Dad about the things happening in their lives.

That same night when Dad went to help Rachel with boxes in the garage, Rick pulled me to the side to talk to me.

"I want you to try to find Emi and be nice to her. I'm not saying you have to be her friend, but she could use a good friend. Be yourself. You're a good and sweet kid. I know you'll treat her well."

Rick thought I was a sweet kid? One of the coolest and nicest guys my dad was friends with thought I was sweet. Most of the time, people *told* me to be sweet and to think of others, but he already thought it. It made my chest swell with pride. I nodded and promised him I would. I cared so much what people thought of me back then.

Where was she? I was walking through the ballroom and hadn't found her yet. Everyone was dressed up, and there was a table with stacks of presents piling high in the back, a lot of envelopes, and some large over-the-top boxes. She was turning eleven, right?

I finally found her standing against a wall. She fiddled with her hands as she looked around with wide eyes. Her two older sisters stood near her. I brushed a hand through my hair and adjusted my tie the way Rachel always did before we left and walked over.

I took in Emi, her eyes too big for her soft face and her nose kind of like a button. She was short, and her dress went past her knees, the bottom of it puffy and ruffled. She wore black dress shoes with white socks. Her curls were tight and barely hit her shoulder.

I walked up and stood across from her, eyes widening as she looked up at me. I was maybe five feet then but still four inches taller than her.

"Happy birthday Emi," I told her, standing up straighter. She didn't say anything for a while. She just stared at me. *"I'm James."* She nodded and whispered a small thank you.

Her sisters introduced themselves. *"Thena,"* the blue-eyed one said, her eyes cold as she looked at me. Everything about her was intimidating even as a teenager.

"Isabel." I nodded at both of them. Thena was pulled away, her short heels clicking against the hardwood floor and Bell eventually drifting off.

Emi looked more panicked than she did before and started scratching her arm. I pulled the chocolate from my pocket and held it out. Five kisses in the palm of my hand.

She looked at them and then back up at me.

"For me?" she asked, her voice quiet and timid. I nodded, and she took two of them. She handed me the wrapper, and I put it in my pants pocket.

"Are you having fun?" I asked her. She shook her head and opened the second chocolate.

"Thena made a friend, and so did Bell."

"Have you made any friends?"

She shook her head, and her curls bounced and swayed with the movement. When she finished her second kiss, she looked at my hand expectantly, so I pulled more chocolate out.

After taking a bite, she started to look around the ballroom, stopping and pointing at someone. I followed her small finger.

"Who's that?" she asked me in a whisper as if someone could hear us.

A tall, slender guy stood by Thena. His wavy brown hair was slicked back, and his tuxedo fit him like a second skin. We could see his smile; I only knew one person with that much confidence at fourteen.

"Nick. His parents are close friends with Rick and my dad."

"Are you friends with him?"

"Yeah, kind of."

It was hard to be close to Nick. He was too smart for most people and was self-assured with everything he did. We never had much to talk about, but he was nice to me and listened to me if I did say something. But he hung out with a snobby crowd and I couldn't take them in large doses.

"I-"

"Emi." Both of our attention turned to a tall woman. Her hair was brownish, and she had a full face of makeup on with glossy lips and was wearing a short dress and perfume that I could smell from a mile away. Hiding her chocolate in her hand, Emi shrank more into herself as if that were possible. I knew that the lady wasn't her mom. Aurore was sweet, and she never tried to scare anyone. Whoever the lady in front of us was, she wasn't nice. I stood up straighter and tried to shield Emi, but it didn't work.

"Emi, introduce me to your friend," the lady commanded.

"T-this is James. James, that's Allison. She's my oldest sister."

Allison's eyes flashed

"Half-sister; we share the same dad," Allison explained, her lips pursed as she took in me, then her eyes shifted to Emi. *"Happy birthday Emilie."* She stood straight and left the party, Rick and Aurore following her.

"God, she's scary!"

Emi laughed.

"She is. She's even scarier when she's tired."

"How old is she?"

"Twenty," Emi answered, shoving a piece of chocolate in her mouth. She finished the rest of the chocolates, telling me about her old house in Louisiana and the trip Rick had taken her and her sisters on last summer. They went to Disney World and then to the beach. Emi fell asleep in the sand and had to wash her hair while everyone else got ice cream, but Rick and Thena brought her some back.

Emi and I talked until it was time for her to cut her cake. After that, Rachel took me home.

The day after the party, I convinced Rachel to take me to Rick's house. She did but also insisted on bringing some brownies. I thanked her and raced out of the car; their housekeeper led me to the backyard. Nick, Thena, Bell, and Emi were all in the backyard. Snow was still on the ground, and Bell was running around, occasionally jumping into different piles, while Emi watched her with a broad smile.

When she saw me approaching, she stood up and walked over. Dressed in an oversized winter coat and snow boots, she kind of looked like a marshmallow.

"Rachel made these for you guys." I handed her the case, and she sat them on one of the snow-covered lawn chairs and opened them. Her eyes widened, and a smile spread across her face. She ate a brownie and looked over her shoulder. Thena and Nick stood together watching Bell.

She didn't say anything. I could tell she was waiting for her sisters to rescue her at any moment. Rescued away from me. She closed the box of brownies, though I could see she still wanted to keep eating. Her eyes stared longingly at the box in her hand, but she stopped eating them.

"Are they not good?" I asked her.

She shook her head.

"No, they are. I just don't want to eat them all right now." She traced a finger along the top of the box.

"Why not?"

"Because then they'll be gone, and I'll never get them back." She sounded so sad.

"I'll bring you more, Emi. I'll always bring you more if you want," I promised. I understood her hesitance to eat them all. Things left, people left, and they never came back.

She smiled up at me, and a tear fell down her face. She quickly wiped it.

"I cry too much. I'm sorry."

"Don't be. I don't think I cry enough."

She softly laughed.

"I can cry enough for both of us."

I smiled.

"You cry for us, and I'll bring you brownies every time Rachel makes them."

She sighed.

"Dream team."

Emi opened the lid of the container and handed me a brownie. *"If you eat it, you have to come back,"* she warned me. It sounded like she was trying to scare me off, but if anything, I was more intrigued. I grabbed the brownie from her hand and shoved it in my mouth. I finished it in two bites. Her mouth dropped open in shock.

I smiled at her, pieces of brownie on my lips and chin. *"What? You thought I wouldn't eat it?"* I teased. I didn't blame her for thinking that. I would've thought the same thing.

We stayed outside until our hands went numb, then we snuck inside and sat on the floor in her living room, eating some snacks her housekeeper, Lucille, brought us. Rick walked past us on the phone, and when he saw us, he winked at me and smiled. He looked happy, but I felt ten times better. I had my *own* friend, one that didn't care about who my dad was.

Chapter 15

Emillie Kate Van der Berg
November 20th, 2021

Present Day

I don't want to move from the bed. I can hear Thena moving around in the bathroom, and Bell snuck out a little while ago to talk to Tristan. He was not at the hotel with us, so he kept calling her phone until she answered. It woke all of us up, but I was the only one still in bed.

We got to the hotel last night. Thena and Bell picked me up from school, drove to Mom and Rick's place, and helped me pack for the weekend. The run isn't until Sunday, but we all check in Friday night and spend Saturday together as a family. It's a tradition, one I continue to try and get out of.

I won't have to see Jay until the pre-race dinner tonight. Mom has constructed an itinerary for us to follow, but I already have a plan to sneak away so I can mentally "prepare."

The bathroom door opens, and the sound of high heels clicking draws close. I can hear Thena sigh, and I know she's already seen me still in bed. She opens my suitcase and picks out an outfit. It hasn't snowed yet, and I hope it stays that way until we return home. Running three miles in the snow sounds like slow, excruciating torture. I'm cringing while imagining the feel of ice-cold socks.

"You were supposed to be up thirty minutes ago," Thena tells me, flinging the covers off me. She's already dressed in a black dress with black tights underneath and red high heeled boots, and her hair slicked into a high ponytail. She must've gotten her hair straightened recently.

"I'm sorry," I murmur, sitting up. I yawn and stretch, looking around the room: one Louis Vuitton suitcase neatly stacked on the dresser with heels adjacent to it, a bright yellow suitcase in the corner by the window with half-open clothes spilling out of it, and my black duffel by the bed with no sign of mess.

Thena sighs. She goes into the bathroom and turns on the shower.

"Shower, get dressed, and I'll wait for you out here. I need to make sure my term paper was submitted anyway."

I do as she says, grabbing the black jeans, black sweater, and UGG boots she picked out for me and taking them to the bathroom. When I'm done showering and fully dressed, Bell and Thena are both in the room. Thena's computer is open in her lap with her phone to her ear, and Bell is eating a bowl of strawberries.

I grab my phone from the nightstand and check the messages. Liv has created a group chat with her, Clara, and me. Great. Now I can referee their sniping outside of school too. I open the chat to see how bad the thread is.

Clara: Olivia, what makes you think I want to be included in this group chat?

Liv: You can leave.

And that was the end of that. I didn't know why Liv had made the group chat, but I plan to ask her about it later. She and Clara were starting to get along better. Liv even laughs at some of Clara's snarky comments, and Clara hasn't cursed either of us out in a while. Good progress.

"Come on! I called us a car," Thena says. We followed her out of the room.

###

Halfway through breakfast, my phone starts ringing. I flip it over and check. Jay has called me three times already. I click the power button and stuff my phone under my thigh. He goes to school in this city. He could show up at any time, and there wouldn't be much I could do about it. But ignoring his calls is a power that I do still have, and I plan to leverage it. He hasn't snuck into my room again and hasn't invited me to another party. Maybe his efforts are dwindling. Maybe he's done trying. If that's what I want, I should feel happy. But the happiness hasn't manifested.

"Mom says we should be back at the hotel for lunch. I think she wants to be included for the rest of the day." Thena rolls her eyes and grabs her credit card from her limited-edition Louis Vuitton wallet she bought for herself last Christmas. I clock its value and realize that her business must be taking off more than she lets on.

"Maybe Rick's working, and she feels lonely," Bell suggests. She leans forward and grabs a strawberry from my half-eaten French toast. She dips it in the whipped cream and practically moans. *"That's the most sweets I've*

had in about two weeks. " My eyes widened. I had an entire bag of Snickers minis last night for a snack!

"Why can't you have any sweets?" I ask her. Disbelief and guilt creeping into my voice.

"I have a shoot on Tuesday. It's for a catalog spread for a boutique in Malibu. They want crop tops and high-waisted jeans, so I just need to make sure I don't gain anything I shouldn't," Bell explains, eyeing my plate of fruit and whipped cream. The French toast was more than sweet, maybe even too sweet.

"Oh." Thena stands up and heads to the door, so I follow suit. I hold the door for Bell as the wind whips at us, welcoming us to the cusp of an east coast winter. *"Do you still like modeling?"* I ask as I trail her down the walk.

"Sometimes." Is "sometimes" worth no sweets? *"I think most people like most things, most of the time. I don't think anyone ever likes something 100%."*

"No, but they love it enough that the bad times don't seem as bad. Not just because someone's forcing them to do it," Thena answers, her eyes staring right at Bell. Thena's eyes soften, and I feel like I'm missing something.

I can tell they've had this conversation before; I just wasn't there for it. Sometimes I feel like I miss so much of their lives, and they try to be there so much for mine. I wish I knew a little more about theirs, and they knew a little less of mine.

"Let's hurry before my hands freeze off," I tell them, making a show of shivering. Bell laughs, and Thena rolls her eyes, her lips twitching. We walk the four blocks to the hotel, and Rick's assistant is waiting for us when we enter.

She waves us forward, and we follow her up to Mom and Rick's suite. The ride is silent. His assistant taps her heel on the floor the whole way, and as she leads us to the door, she looks nervous. I know his usual assistant, Christina, is doing something else for him.

Rick and Mom sit in the lounge area with a breakfast tray in front of them.

Mom's eyes narrow on us. All three of us sit on the couch near them, and I take in their whole hotel room—a large California King size bed; floor to ceiling windows, nothing amiss, rumpled or disorganized.

"You three could've waited for me," Mom scolds, holding her cup of coffee. *"First, you three insist on driving down here yourself instead of having Emilie ride with us, and now you sneak off for breakfast before asking either Rick or me if we'd like to join. How do you think that makes us feel?"*

Rick looks completely fine. He's eating his breakfast with a satisfied look, his plate of eggs, toast, and sausage links almost gone. He pours another glass of orange juice and smiles at me. I smile back and take the freshly poured cup from him and sip.

I look at the newspaper in front of him. On the front page, in bold writing, it reads:

Following the success of Averell Sports & Berg Theatres, film & music moguls Rick Van Der Berg and Eric Averell solidify their status as two of the wealthiest businessmen in New York City.

"Congratulations!" I told him.

He shrugs his shoulders, a small smile on his face. *"I've had better accomplishments."*

"Emilie," Mom snaps as I look at her. *"Why were you so mopey at the last brunch?"*

Ah, the last country club brunch. I didn't say anything and stared at the menu and then the food the whole time. Jay came halfway through. His dad said he was busy at a meeting with one of his professors. I didn't talk to Jay the whole time. He made a few attempts at pretending everything was the same -playing with the escape artist ringlets of hair that broke loose from my high bun and drawing random shapes on my napkin. But I remained as stoic and distant as I could with my heart galloping against my own ribs. When it was time for me to leave, he kissed my forehead and said goodbye.

"I-I was tired, had a lot of homework, and was up late the night before." I muttered a poorly crafted lie to satisfy my mother.

Mom nods. *"I hope your grades are where they need to be. We have that Brown tour in a few weeks. I think Eric might want Jay to come along so he can have some more options also."*

I want to ask her why Jay would need more options, but I don't. I just nod and try not to think too hard about the C I have in AP Bio and the C I'm struggling to keep in AP Comparative Government. The best part about that class is that we watch documentaries sometimes.

"Now, who wants to go shopping?" Mom asks with a slight smile, Rick rolls his eyes, and I can say with one hundred percent certainty that I agree with him on that sentiment.

###

"Please pass the butter," Bell sing-songs from next to me. I pass her the butter, and we both reach for a piece of warm bread. When we both take a bite of the bread, we both moan, and I can't help but laugh. She laughs with me and wrinkles her nose. We dip our bread into the butter and sip our Shirley Temples.

"What are you going to get?" After a long day of shopping and doing things for the charity that the race is raising money for, we're all now at an Italian steakhouse in Lenox Hill. Eric and the Yateses have joined.

Mrs. Yates's blonde hair is blown out, and half is pulled up. Her turtleneck reminds me of the cream-colored one Mom wore a few weeks ago. I'm not surprised. I'm pretty sure they're best friends. Mrs. Yates has one of those *"I used to be an 'it' girl back in my day, and I'm still the shit, but I'm probably the humblest person ever and do completely normal things like snort when I laugh and wear pajamas until noon"* type.

I scan the menu again and find one of the usual dishes I get. *"I'll get Spaghetti with French fries."*

Bell gasps and looks at me with stunned, bright, olive-green eyes. *"That might be the best combination I've heard of. I think I'll treat myself to some mac and cheese and just run extra hard in the morning."*

I nod in agreement. *"That might be the best plan I've ever heard of, but who am I to talk?"* I shrug my shoulders and shove another piece of bread into my mouth.

"Where's Tristan?" I ask her, the chatter of the restaurant getting louder.

She stares at the basket of bread that we're hogging. *"He had to work. He'll see us all tomorrow."*

I nod. I don't know for sure, but I'm pretty sure Tristan works at a company that does investments and mergers. I'm also pretty sure his status and salary is low in that company. The fastest way to draw my mother's ire, is to be both broke and unambitious. *"He works on Saturdays?"*

Bell looks away, nodding. *"Are you excited to see Jay tomorrow?"*

"Uh, I guess. He probably won't come. You know how much he hates these things."

"He does," she nods in agreement. *"But he loves spending time with you."* I can feel my whole body warm at her comment.

"Emi," Mrs. Yates says, drawing my attention from Bell. I look at her, and she's grinning at me. *"Your mom tells me you'll visit Brown in a few weeks. When I went with Nick, he took one look at the campus and shook his head. I wanted to see their stadium, but we barely crossed the grate."* She laughs. This is what happens when Mrs. Yates gets to her second glass of wine before the food comes out—she brings up Nick and everyone's mood shifts.

Thena freezes. It doesn't matter what she's doing; she always freezes as if she's been struck at the mention of Nick. Bell and I watch her out of the side of our eye.

"You know he loved these races, thought it was good to see rich people sweat." She chuckles, and Mr. Yates reaches over and wraps his arm around her shoulder. He loudly clears his throat and forces a stiff smile. When Mrs. Yates looks into Mr. Yates's eyes, a wave of sadness comes over her, and she leans further into him.

"You know, when Thena took Bell, Jay, and me to Yale, I knew that I wouldn't be able to get in. I think it was the Latin on the school sign that really threw me off." Everyone laughs. Maybe some of them are forced, but I don't mind.

"I'm surprised Yale was even on your list," Mom adds. I force a sheepish laugh, and everyone else chuckles along. The jab was at my expense. But I don't mind them laughing at me as long as Nick isn't brought up again and Thena releases some of the tension from her shoulders. I know the counselor would have something to say about me offering myself as a sacrifice to change the subject, but this is how it is. How it has always been.

Chapter 16

Emillie Kate Van der Berg

Forty-seven degrees feels like forty; there's no wind. *Feels like freezing.* I want to start running; I need to start moving. We decided to walk the three blocks to the starting point of the race hoping to warm us up. I can say with confidence that it didn't work.

"Pull your ear warmers down now," Thena tells me. I do, and my ears start to warm. Apparently, you're supposed to let your ears get cold so the warmer can fully warm them up beyond just your normal ear temperature.

I look down at my outfit: thick leggings, two socks (one regular length, another hitting my calves), a long sleeve undershirt, a T-shirt, a zip-up running jacket on top, and all my hair pulled into a ponytail—a ponytail that took fifteen minutes and three breaks to soothe my aching triceps to finish.

Today may be one of the few times my sisters aren't in their usual outfits. Thena stripped herself of her heels and wore the same thing as me, just shorter socks, and Bell exchanged her dresses for shorts with the same top layers on.

Mom and Rick are somewhere huddled together, staying warm and out of the spotlight. Mom likes to choose when to be photographed because chances are the picture will end up online. Thousands of people are here. Photographers stopped along the way to take people's photos as they ran. The finishers will get a medal, hot chocolate, s'mores, and a few snacks.

"Did the Yateses show up yet?" I ask Thena, staring at the time, counting down how many minutes we have until we can start. Twelve minutes.

Thena nods. *"I saw them walking towards Rick."*

We have eleven minutes.

"Where's Jay?" Thena asks, reading my mind.

I shrug my shoulders; I haven't seen him at all today. He usually meets us outside of our hotel before the race. He didn't come to dinner last night either. Maybe he stayed in his hotel room with his dad. Eric never runs. He always meets us at brunch afterward and smirks at us like we're all idiots for running in forty-degree weather. *Maybe we are.*

"Let's go get some water before we start. You don't want to get a cramp, do you?" Thena's voice snaps me out of my thoughts.

I shake my head; I'd rather not cramp up on mile two. We speed walk inside a small store, the heat warming me. I rub my hands and flex them, hoping my gloves work a little better.

We stay inside the shop for a while, not leaving until two minutes are left. Until the starter pistol. The crowd has tripled, and I have to grip Thena's arm to stay beside her. Bell always says these are the moments she's happy the paparazzi don't follow her around.

When all the Van der Bergs are together, we're photographed. Most of the time, Bell can go places without recognition, but Mom told me she's doing a big project in December that'll add more "fame" to her name. There's been a few articles about Thena also. Eric has had his fair share of interviews in magazines and articles published about him; same with Mr. Yates. Rick says it's the reason he only has two friends: Eric and Mr. Yates. Because they're the only people who understand the money and attention we generate.

The announcer counts down, and when it's time, a blank gunshot goes off, and we all take off in waves. I hesitate for a few seconds, then start running. Everyone pushes past me, and I finally begin jogging, following the path. Thena looks over her shoulder for me and waves me forward. I catch up, and we jog together. I can tell this isn't her usual pace, and when it takes us ten minutes to do our first mile, my breath has quickened, but hers is steady. I'm holding her back, and it's clear as day.

"You can go. I'll be fine," I tell her between labored breaths. Two more miles. *"P-please g-go,"* I beg. Thena must sense my seriousness because she nods and picks up her pace. It takes a few seconds then she's out of sight. I am immediately relieved to be gasping for air without an audience.

I don't stop running though. I keep going, even when my lungs start to burn. The sign for mile two is taking forever to appear. I feel someone's hand slide across my back, and before I can properly freak out, I smell who it is. I look up, and a cocky, smug smirk is aimed at me.

"Jay," I breathe. He's wearing a long sleeve T-shirt and joggers.

"Em," he responds, his smirk spreading. He doesn't look a bit out of breath. A fact that both irritates and impresses me.

"What are you doing here?" I manage to ask between breaths.

He looks around and furrows his brows. *"Is this not the line for Starbucks?"* I roll my eyes. *"Running, Em. We do it every year."*

I nod. We do. We always run the 5k together, sometimes stopping halfway to walk or to eat whatever snacks we brought, but we always finish—usually the last ones.

We don't talk for a while; we pass the mile two checkpoint, and I can feel myself smile. Jay starts to pick up the pace, and I do the same. This is different from past years. I don't know why but I'm taking the run seriously - like I have something to prove. The worst part about mile three is a hill—a steep heel. We have to push ourselves to get to the finish line. My legs usually start burning, and the ground seems to become a temptation - a lovely place to lay down and take a break.

"You'll make it. We both will. Even if I have to carry you up there."

I laugh. *"You can't carry me up a hill."*

He gives me a slow once-over, pausing on my chest for a second, then landing on my face. Think friendly thoughts. *"You know I can."*

His confidence makes me believe he can carry me up that hill with ease. But I don't want to try it.

The hill approaches. I take a deep breath, and Jay looks at me. He nods; I nod back, and we push, leaning forward a little to counter gravity and incline. We keep going even when the burning in my thigh's spreads to my calves, even when I see people pushing past us and others stop running altogether and lean forward on their knees. I keep going, and so does Jay. We keep going together, he won't leave me behind.

When the finish line comes into focus, I run harder, Jay staying with me. When we cross the finish line, I stop and try to catch my breath. Jay smiles down at me, and I don't think before I throw myself in his arms. He catches me with one arm and squeezes me into him. Maybe it's the dopamine but I feel exhilarated.

"We did it!" I cheer. He laughs and nods, kissing my forehead.

"Emi!" Thena approaches, and I pull away from Jay. Her pale skin is flushed, and pieces of her baby hairs have slightly curled, but she has them pushed back with a headband I didn't know she had. *"Are you okay?"* She asks, looking over me. I nod, and she stops her inspection when she notices my smile. *"Come on. Everyone's waiting."*

"How long did I take?" I ask her, holding onto her arm.

"Thirty-two minutes."

I nod. Last year it took me 46 minutes, mostly due to screwing off with Jay. I feel a sense of pride swell at my improved time.

"What was your time?" I can see everyone come into view. Mom and Rick are speaking to each other. There's a sheen of sweat on Rick's forehead, and Mom is patting a paper towel around her neck, her eyes narrowed as she looks around.

"Twenty-two," she huffs. That must be a bad time for her. Thena's always going on runs to burn off steam and stress, usually for miles at a time. I know the only thing that slowed her down today was worrying about me running alone.

"You know, if you had just left me from the beginning like I told you to, you would've been faster," I remind her. She glares at me and keeps walking forward.

When Jay and I join the circle, the Yates join as well. Mrs. Yates' skin is flushed, and her baby blue eyes are bright as she smiles. Another theory I keep to myself is that Mrs. Yates and Thena go on runs together. That's their idea of hanging out.

I wonder if Thena has a large group of people she hangs out with that I don't know about. I know Bell does—all her model friends and maybe even some of Tristan's friends. I don't know any of their friends. Cost of being the youngest, I guess. I also never tried to find out, because I'd always had Jay. I looked around for Jay then. He was gone.

Sunnyside Up is a quaint brunch place a little outside of Manhattan. It reminds me of the place Dr. Young told me about during our last session. It always smells of burnt coffee, bacon, and sunshine, in that order. In that session I told her about the spots I used to eat at with my parents in Louisiana, and then I stopped because those times felt too far away to matter anymore. She asked about other parts of my life and told me more about hers. I like those sessions when we can just talk about random little things, and I don't feel like a patient.

"Emi," Thena says, snapping me out of my therapy musings. I look at her, and the waiter waits patiently behind her. *"Drink?"*

"Coffee, please, vanilla creamer on the side." I smile, but I can tell it looks shaky. He nods and scribbles it down. Brunch after the run is another hallowed tradition.

Jay's arm is on the back of my chair. He managed to reappear like a ghost just when we arrived at the brunch spot. I didn't bother to ask where he'd been. *"Latte and a glass of apple juice."* Jay taps on the table, and I look at him out of the side of my eye. There's a stiffness to him like he's waiting for something.

"*Where's Tristan?*" Mom asks Bell after everyone's drink order is taken. He's supposed to be here.

"*He got called away for a family emergency.*"

"*Thank God,*" Jay mumbles loud enough for most people to hear. I elbow him in the ribs.

"*I think your speech went over really well, Ror,*" Mrs. Yates tells Mom, quickly changing the subject.

Mom gave a speech after the race, thanking everyone for donating and coming out to show their support for the cause. Bell went up and waved, not really saying anything. The race raised close to a million dollars, plus the donations Rick, Eric, and Mr. Yates made.

Mom shrugs. "*I think so too. I just don't need you-know-who to bother me on Monday with something I could've done better.*" Rick chuckles. "*You know she will, that woman-*"

I stop listening to them.

"*Since when do you drink lattes?*" I ask Jay as the waiter sets our drinks down.

Jay smirks.

"*Since I've been forced to attend parties and make my eight A.M. lectures. Lattes are my new best friend.*"

"*I've been replaced with lattes?*" I pour cream into my coffee.

"*Lattes don't ignore me or cancel out on traditions for shit reasons.*" Ouch. "*What'd you replace me with?*" He doesn't give me a chance to say anything before he adds. "*Don't tell me you're dating again. I thought you ended that after those pricks' sophomore year.*" His eyes darken, and his frustration and anger are seething from him. His voice is cold and hits me right in the chest.

"I-I'm not dating again," I whisper. I feel like people are listening to our conversation. Or maybe I'm being paranoid. "I haven't replaced you. I told you we both just need to focus on our own stuff."

"I'm going to need a real reason, Em. I have mine, but what the hell are yours?" He stares at me. His vehemence takes me by surprise and I can't open my mouth and lie to him. What am I supposed to say? I feel like I'm constantly holding you and maybe everyone else in my life back, so I'm distancing myself from you. I can't say that. So I say nothing.

"Christmas." His tone softens just a little. "You got one month, kid. Then I want a real reason. No more lies." His voice is gruff and low, almost like a warning. He gets up and leaves, brushing his dad off along the way.

I can feel Thena's eyes on me, but I avoid them as best as I can.

One month to come clean.

Chapter 17

Emilie Kate Van der Berg

Thanksgiving is in two days. It's 2 p.m. on a Tuesday, and I'm sitting in Dr. Young's office watching her put away a file she had out. Our session today is only forty minutes.

"Tell me, how have your sister dinners been? You haven't talked about them in a while."

"They've been good. We have dinner together every other week. I usually do homework and listen to Thena's business plan. I'm not much of a planner, but I try to give my opinion. Sometimes we all just watch Netflix until it's time for me to go home. They're just normal for me. I don't really talk about them unless something crazy happens."

"Still ignoring Jay?"

I nod.

"He confronted me about it at brunch after the race. He's mad at me, and I can't really blame him. I'm being a shitty friend, but I'd rather give him space than hold him back."

"Do you know for sure that you're holding him back?" She looks at me with understanding eyes. We've had this conversation almost every time I've come to therapy, and she knows it.

"I feel like it…and I don't like the way that feels."

She walks over to her chair and sits down.

"How's school going?"

I grimace.

"My grades aren't too good right now. I'm not failing any classes, though. Liv came over two weeks ago, and we ate Taco Bell in my bedroom. I like that she treats me like a regular friend, not a charity case. I think Liv might be becoming one of my close friends, and I don't know… It feels good having someone you can count on, someone that doesn't know all the shitty things about you. I think some people just want to have someone who still sees them as a good person and not the whole picture." I pause, realizing that I said all of that out loud what was only supposed to be in my head. Dr. Young doesn't respond though. She just softly scratches some notes onto her notepad and then looks up.

"Are you excited for Thanksgiving?" I ask her. Distract and deflect are still my favorite habits. Her smile spreads, and she nods.

"This is the longest I've gone without seeing my family, so I'm excited. My parents aren't the best cooks, but what they lack in skill they make up for in enthusiasm," she chirps. "Most of the time, we just watch movies, eat Chinese food, and just all spend time together on the dock." She says. "What does your family do for Thanksgiving?"

"My mom and sisters all cook, and then we invite Jay's family and the Yates' for dinner. It's private, and you can't invite anyone outside of the core group. Everyone dresses casually, and we all eat before the adults go somewhere and talk, and the rest of us usually eat dessert in the kitchen."

Thena and Bell were coming home today and would leave next Sunday to return to their apartments. I know Bell is excited to be home, but I don't know about Thena. She likes living by herself, but I think she likes visiting in small spurts.

"Does your brother come home for Thanksgiving?"

I shake my head. Alexander rarely comes home for the holidays, and we've all slowly started to accept that. Mom still struggles with it, but she's kind of had to. I know he calls her regularly; she mentions what he's up to over dinner, or I overhear her and Rick talking about him.

"I think he's in Moscow." He texted Bell a picture of the Kremlin and a picture of him at a Russian restaurant with two cigars and two cups of coffee on the table. He and Bell both send pictures of the stuff they're doing.

"Do you think you'd ever want to travel like your brother one day?"

"I don't know if I'd want to be alone that much. I feel things could get bad, and I would just be lost. But it'd also be nice not having to worry about people babysitting me."

She tilts her head to the side. It's what she does when thinking about something. I never know how deep she will go, but she usually lets me talk about things I want to. *"You don't think your family trusts you to make your own decisions?"* she asks. I am thinking of responding with a resounding NO, when she adds another question. *"Do you trust yourself to make good decisions?"*

This freezes me in my tracks. I look at the clock and immediately stand up. *"It's time. I hope you have a good Thanksgiving. I'll see you later, Dr. Young."*

She smiles and waves, still scrawling notes in her file. *"Bye, Emi. Text me if you need anything."*

I nod. We both know I won't, but it's always sweet when she says it.

Bell waits for me outside in her bright yellow Jeep Wrangler, the doors and top both on. She rolls down the window, waves, and makes a loud gobble noise. I hurriedly walked to the car, climbing into the front. She pushes the gas, and we pull out of the parking lot. We lock eyes when we reach our neighborhood gate, and she smiles at me. Her olive-green eyes sparkle with happiness when she looks at me. Her cheeks are soft, but her face is still undoubtedly modelesque. The sculpted cheekbones were a gift from my mother's genetics.

"I miss living with you."

"I miss living with you too, but I'm happy you're happy with your boyfriend."

Bell nods but averts her gaze. *"Yeah, happy,"* she whispers.

Chapter 18

Emillie Kate Van der Berg

"Emillie, wake up!" Mom yells, pounding on my bedroom door. I don't move. If I stay still, she might give up and go away.

"Why are you pounding on her bedroom door and screaming before six in the morning?" Thena questions her, the agitation evident in her voice. *Before six!!*

"If she were up with everyone else, I wouldn't have to."

"It's not that hard of a task to knock and peek into her room and wake her up. But, Mother, if it's too much for you to do that, then I will."

If they are going at it in the hallway, the whole house can probably hear them. I sit up. The last thing anyone needs is Thena and Mom fighting before the cooking starts.

I open my room door, and Mom and Thena stand across from each other. Mom is dressed in silk pajamas and Thena in workout clothes, her running shoes off and replaced with thick slippers I know she only wears when she's here. She has her own slippers for her own house. Meticulous Thena would never walk barefoot or wear her running shoes inside.

"What's up?" I ask groggily. Mom's dark green eyes meet mine.

"You need to get up and start helping with the prep work, and we need canned cranberries and pineapple."

"I'll go to the store."

"You can't drive Emilie," Mom reminds me, her tone somewhere between frustration and anger.

"Bell and I can take her," Thena suggests before turning around and walking to her old bedroom down the hall.

"All three of you don't need to go to the store Elénore!!"

Mom huffs and walks away, and I close my room door and start getting ready. I can still feel the sleep in my body. My eyes feel heavy. I lean against the bathroom sink and close my eyes. I jolt awake the moment I lose my balance. *I need a caramel macchiato.*

Bell and Thena wait for me downstairs. I force a smile and follow them out to Bell's car. I sit in the backseat and resist the urge to lean all the way over and lay down. The grocery store is less than fifteen minutes away.

The store's parking lot is less than a quarter of the way full and people are walking inside just as it opens. The fall-turning-winter air is cool and nips at my cheeks and lips. I hug my fleece jacket tighter and walk a little faster. Bell walks with her eyes locked on the store and an added quickness to her stride.

I grab a shopping cart and begin pushing. We pick up the items Mom told us to and then get extra things I need for the desserts. I'm not much of a cook, but I can make a mean pound cake and, if I'm lucky, a good red velvet cake. Bell is good with sweet potato pie, and Thena can make anything if there's a recipe.

"*I need coffee,*" I mumble, grabbing more red food coloring.

"*We'll get some after we finish,*" Thena says, putting a fruit tray in the cart. "*We're not waiting until eight o'clock tonight to eat.*"

"*How long were y'all up before I got up?*" I ask them, putting the food on the conveyor belt as we check out. Our cashier still looks half asleep.

"*I had just returned from my run, so maybe forty-five minutes.*"

"*Fifteen minutes, maybe,*" Bell says, her eyes flitting to the side. *Is she lying to make me feel better?*

Before I can question her, we're already done checking out. We're pushing our cart outside. The parking lot is a little fuller now. There are at least ten cars in front of us in the drive-through line for Starbucks, but we still wait, the sound of the Spice Girls coming through Bell's speakers.

"*What does Tristan do for Thanksgiving?*" I ask her. Her smile drops a little, and I instantly regret bringing it up.

"*He usually stays home since he and his parents aren't on good terms with his father's side of the family.*"

I nod in understanding. Tristan's dad's business went under a few years ago, and ever since then, his dad's side of the family has pretty much cut them off. I know Bell has been there for him every step of the way, especially now as he works up the corporate ladder. I'm happy for him because Bell is happy for him.

"Maybe Rick would let him come over if he knew," I suggest. Ever since Rick met Tristan as Bell's boyfriend, he's disliked him. When he and Bell were just friends, Rick was okay with their friendship, but when they started dating, everything quickly turned south.

"Unlikely," Thena snorts.

She's probably right, and I think Bell and I both know that. It's why neither of us says anything until it's time to order our drinks. Bell orders an iced latte with three pumps of espresso, Thena an Americano with a splash of cream. I got a caramel macchiato with extra whipped cream and caramel.

We sit outside the house drinking our coffees, music playing in the background, and the cold slightly seeping into the car. None of us are eager to go in. Cooking for Thanksgiving is sometimes more stressful than it is fun. Dinner isn't usually served until late, and it's one of the few events we have that people don't get dressed up for. Although I am the youngest, and aware that my older sister's keep certain things from me, moments like these - when we are all telepathically on the same mental wavelength, are the moments I feel like I belong. The shared understanding that we are sitting in what may be the last peaceful moment of the day feels like a cozy blanket on a winter day.

"When should we go in?" I ask. Bell has already chugged all her coffee.

The front door opens, and Ricks peeks outside; he looks at us and waves us inside with pleading eyes. Mom tries to force him to cook, but Rick has never had to make a meal in his life. He usually preheats the oven, carries the ham into the oven, gets the ham out of the oven, and makes sure everyone has something to drink.

He jogs to the car and opens the trunk. He carries the bags inside, and the three of us get out and follow Rick inside.

"Oh, come on, girls! It won't be that bad. At least your grandma's not coming."

True, because everything is a little worse when *Meme* Louise comes.

Chapter 19

Emillie Kate Van der Berg

Things are not going well. Thena and Mom have fought over almost every dish. Bell and I are keeping busy with the desserts, but there are only so many ovens to use, and right now, they're arguing over what needs to be put in each oven based on temperature and cook time.

"The ham does not need to go in until noon. It takes three hours, not eight."

"Which is why we should get started on it now," Mom insists, her shoulders tightening as her anger rises.

"No, what needs to be baked is the pound cake because that will taste just as good cold."

Thena grabs the pound cake in its bundt pan from my hand and puts it in the oven, the oven slamming shut. Thena stares at Mom with a glare so strong Mom pauses momentarily.

"Why must you always be this difficult?!" Mom stresses, throwing her hands in the air.

"I don't know. Maybe the same reason you treat me like a child when I'm twenty years old."

Mom rolls her eyes. I can tell she wants to say something else, but she doesn't. Instead, she walks away, her huffs and mutters of annoyance following her.

Thena stares at the spot she was standing in, then turns to Bell and me.

"Let's hope she doesn't come back."

I help Thena with the sides as best as I can. Mom returns two hours later to ensure everything is up to her standards. She then checks the ham that Rick put in at her prodding. Rick leans against the island with a beer in his hand. He tries to console Mom, but after a while, he just stands there and focuses on his drink.

Thena moves around the kitchen with quick, efficient steps. She doesn't ask anyone for help and pretty much ignores Mom. She's made most of the food, and I've kind of just been deadweight, but she hasn't kicked me out like Mom usually does. She just gives me something else to do while my cakes bake. I've cut up the sweet potatoes and started making the second batch of basting juice for the ham.

She moves closer and tastes it.

"More mustard, then you're good. When you finish, put it by the stove." I do what she says.

Bell and I keep busy avoiding the anger simmering from Mom.

Guests start arriving at eight, and when the first guest arrives, the ham comes out of the oven. *Perfect timing.*

###

As always, Jay and Eric are the first to arrive. Jay has a look of annoyance and boredom on his face, and Eric wears his usual charming, slightly twisted smirk. They never bring anything. Sometimes Jay sneaks a small bottle of Vodka and gives it to me. The last time he did, I hid it in my room, and when our parents went to talk, we made drinks. Thena didn't even say anything about it when she discovered us. She just held out her hand, and we passed her a cup.

Jay enters the kitchen wearing jeans, a collared Polo shirt, and a suit jacket his dad probably made him wear. His brown wavy hair is messy, like he just woke up. He scans all the food and then nods.

"No turkey. Tsk tsk."

Thena rolls her eyes. *"You know Mary brings the turkey. Besides, what did you bring? Obviously not your charm,"* she snaps at him; her eyes are narrowed, and her hand is gripping the countertop so tight her knuckles are turning white. Jay nods and smirks.

"No, but I did bring refreshments and other things." He opens his jacket and pulls out two smaller-sized bottles of Tito's Vodka and a joint.

"I'll take the refreshments, and the other thing can go." She waves the joint away like it's spoiled, but grabs the vodka. Jay laughs and tucks the joint into his breast pocket. She goes to the cabinet and takes out cups for all of us.

"Where's Bell?" Jay asks, grabbing Sprite from the fridge.

"Talking to Tristan," I answered. Jay and Thena both roll their eyes and start pouring drinks.

Why does everyone hate Tristan? Jay hands me a drink. I can barely taste the Vodka. *Is there any in here?* Thena takes a sip of hers and closes her eyes. She can taste hers. Bell comes downstairs a few minutes later, her hair down, mixes of tight and loose waves falling down her shoulders.

"Hey, Jay! How have you been?" She asks him, grabbing her cup and taking a sip before even asking what's in it. She swallows it and smiles, looking into the cup. She wiggles her eyebrows. *"You brought us a gift? That's very sweet of you."*

Jay smiles. *"I try."*

He winks at her and chugs the rest of his cup. *"I've been good. How have you been, Bell?"* His voice is softer, and he leans more on the counter like he's really trying to listen to her. *Is he flirting with my sister?*

"I've been good, working, sleeping, eating... all that fun stuff."

"You sleep now? No shit," Jay drawls. He grabs the rest of the vodka and empties it into his cup, adding two splashes of soda.

The doorbell rings, and I hear Mrs. Yates's voice coming through the foyer.

"About time. I've been starving over here," Eric calls, walking into the dining room. Jay rolls his eyes and gets up, walking past me.

I tune out during dinner. I can't stop trying to figure out if Jay was flirting with Bell or if he was just being nice. Is it bad I can't tell if he's being friendly or flirting? Am I supposed to be worrying about this? I'm the one who said I wanted distance, so I can't be mad at him for being distant. But Bell has a boyfriend, and she's, my sister! He can't flirt with her! I'm his best friend, or at least I was. I look between him and Bell. They would look good together—both tall, both model materials, and they both live in New York City, so they could hang out.

She knows I have a crush on him, right? She has to know. Maybe he was flirting with her, and perhaps he's been flirting with other girls at his college. Because that's what people do when they're young and single, they flirt, have one-night stands, and experience things.

Yet I'm not doing any of those things, and I don't want him to either. But what I want doesn't matter. I can feel myself spiraling but I don't know how to make it stop.

"Emi." Someone says my name with enough force that I can tell they've been saying it for a while. I look up, and Mom's staring at me with a stern look in her eye. *"Pass the yams."*

I mutter a weak sorry and pass the yams. Everyone keeps talking, and I focus on putting food on my plate.

I hate myself for going down that rabbit hole, but I hate myself more for doing it in front of others.

I focus on dinner and everyone there. I participate in the conversations and try to forget everything I was just thinking. I keep trying even though I can feel it nagging me in the back of my mind.

Chapter 20

James Averell

Emi's daydreaming isn't a rare occurrence. Most of the time we hang out, she daydreams at least once. Sometimes she gets so lost in her thoughts, and all I can do is hug or talk to her until she snaps out of it. But Emi daydreaming while wringing her hands isn't something that happens a lot.

After dinner, all our parents go into Rick's office to talk, and the rest of us move to the kitchen, the desserts on the island. I grab Emi's hand before she reaches the kitchen, pulling her away. She yelps and falls into my chest, tripping over her own feet. Her frizzy hair is pulled back, and her curls fall down the back and a few down her face.

"Are you okay? What happened at dinner?" She knows what I'm talking about. I know she knows.

"I'm fine, and it was nothing. I was just thinking." Her eyes flit away from mine. I squeeze her hand.

"About what?"

She stares at me, biting her lip. I can see her turning over the truth in her mind, deciding whether she'll tell me or not. She sighs and closes her eyes.

"Were you flirting with Bell? Do you like her? Or girls like her?"

I can't stop the laugh from escaping me. Emi's eyes widen, and I see embarrassment seeping into her body. She starts to move back, and her blinks last slightly longer than they should. I grab her before she can take another step, pulling her back into me.

"I wasn't flirting with her. I don't have a crush on your sister. Why would you think that?"

"Do you find girls like her attractive?"

I shrug. *"Not really. I know what I like, and Bell isn't it, no offense."* I look at her, and she's not relaxed. I can see the anxiety in her eyes. *Is she jealous?* I move closer, my chest an inch away from hers. I grab her hand and squeeze it. Her hand is warm as she squeezes mine back.

"Emi, I'm not dating anyone."

Dating has always felt forced to me. There's no point. It seems forced and artificial. And up until now, I've had Emi. A real, no pomp, no fake friendship that didn't require *"dates."* I feel like she is slipping away though.

"You're my best friend—just you. I'll remind you every day if you want me to." I squeeze her hand, pulling it into me. She smiles and nods, her breathing a little heavier. She doesn't know what to say.

I laugh and kiss her forehead, her shampoo hitting my nose. Her hair smells like eucalyptus, and I can still smell it even when she pulls away.

I pull her into the kitchen away from our families. Her sisters are acting like they aren't eavesdropping, but they have gone unnaturally quiet. I grab my drink and sit beside Emi, pulling her chair next to mine, her thigh touching mine. If I could, I would always be this close to her. She shifts away just enough to break the contact and my chest tightens. I want to shake her. To demand that everything go back to how it was. But I know her, and I know she is battling a million worries that crowd her brain. I can't push her.

"*Christmas*," I remind Emi, whispering in her ear. She nods. I chug the rest of my drink.

Emillie Kate Van der Berg:

I'm on my second drink, and everyone else is on their third or fourth, but no one has begun acting drunk. I'm pretty sure Jay's been giving himself most of the Vodka and everyone else barely a splash, but no one says anything. The conversation has been shockingly calm for a while. Even mom is laughing her genuine ringing laugh from her perch next to Rick on the sofa across the room.

"*So how often do couples go on dates?*" Bell asks, her eyes looking between the three of us. I try to think. Liv doesn't go on any dates; she usually just comes back with stories about her weekends, some of those stories involving sex.

"*My friend Liv goes to parties every week, and I think that's kind of like a date.*" Jay laughs and shakes his head. Bell joins him. "*Isn't it?*"

Jay shakes his head.

"*Emi and I used to go out almost every day, but they were just hanging out.*" Jay sneaks a look at me over his glass. "*I know my roommate and his girl go on dates like once a month when they're both home.*" Why did Jay throw us in this conversation? He was definitely looking for a reaction.

"*It just depends on the couple; some couples are happy with going on dates once a month, and others are happy going once or twice a week,*" Thena adds. I nod in agreement.

"*Why?*" I ask. Maybe Bell and Tristan haven't been going out a lot. "Do you and Tristan not go on dates anymore?"

"*We do. It's just harder because I'm working more now.*"

That makes sense. Bell does seem a little busier. Every sister dinner, she has another shoot scheduled, most of them after the holidays and a few before Christmas. I think she has one coming up in a few weeks. It's in Toronto. She invited me to go, but the idea of photographers, models, and being a third wheel didn't sound appealing. I passed.

"*Makes sense. Thena, how often did you and Nick go on dates?*" Jay asks, his eyes locked on Thena's.

Silence.

I think this is worse than when Mrs. Yates brings up Nick because he's her son, so it's understandable, but Jay's never brought him up in front of Thena before, not since Nick left.

Thena stares at Jay, her eyes losing all softness and happiness that was there before. They're so blue now—clearer, and they contrast her pale tawny skin. I swear the room chilled a few degrees. I shiver. "*Maybe-*" Bell tries to speak.

"How often?" Jay talks over her. *"I know you guys did the same clubs, but when he graduated, what did you guys do?"* Jay stares at her, taking another sip of his drink and putting it back down. He's not sober. He can't be.

I grab his arm.

"Stop," I hissed. Thena hasn't moved, and I don't know how many more times someone can ask her about Nick before she loses it. Even the always composed Thena has limits.

"You know he's not dead, right? He's going to come back one day."

I shake his arm. *"Stop! It's Thanksgiving, and you're being mean."*

Why is he doing this? Why is he talking about him knowing how she gets? Jay looks at me and freezes for a second, scanning my face.

"Just stop," I whisper.

I look at Thena. She won't look anywhere but at Jay. I can see emotions that I don't understand swimming through her eyes. I can see her shoulders tense, her knuckles turning white, and her collar bone protruding through her Oxford blue dress, one of her favorite dress colors.

"Leave." That's all she says, and he does. Jay grabs his jacket and leaves, the door slamming after him. I don't follow him. My sister is squeezing the marble bar top as if she can break off a piece.

I do the only thing I can do: I distract her.

"You know Jay is drunk, right? Hey, remember when I was eight, and Rick took us to Disneyland?" Distract and deflect.

December

Chapter 21

Emillie Kate Van der Berg

Every December 1st since we moved to Connecticut, I come downstairs to a house filled with anything and everything Christmas. The tree is trimmed with a specific color scheme of ornaments and tinsel, with neatly wrapped presents stacked underneath. As the month goes on, the number of gifts grows, and so does the smell of pastries that Lucille makes. It wasn't always like that, though. Before, there was Dad. Dad used to decorate with us, lifting me to put a star on the tree and letting Bell run around and throw tinsel at anything she wanted. He loved Christmas, and in turn, so did I.

I stare at the decorations, wondering, as always how I didn't hear them setting any of this up. The tree is at least ten feet tall, and the stockings are all neatly hung above the fireplace; everyone has one. All our initials are on them: *RVB, AVB, ETVB, IBVB, EKVB.* Rick always says Van der Berg deserves to have the V and the B represented, so that's what we do for everything.

It's beautiful, but it's not our work. It's someone else's, someone else's goal and aesthetic. It's nothing like the way Dad used to do it. The decorations Thena, Bell, and I would make out of paper, and the ornaments that were older than us are gone. The longer I look at it, the angrier I get. The anger turns into sadness before I can even process it.

I force myself to look away from the tree and the neatly wrapped presents under it. I need to go to school. I have to finish my art project since finals are coming up.

Liv waits outside, in a beat-up old-school car. The paint is chipping off, and the back windows don't roll all the way up, so we will sit in the car with the heat blasting and our winter coats and hats pulled snugly against us. I don't mind it, though. Liv's fun to ride with, and she always brings me a breakfast taco.

I climb in, and she hands me the taco while digging through her pants pocket for a lighter, a joint in her lips. I look at the clock, and it's 7:47am. Our school starts at eight, and I live maybe ten minutes away. We're going to be late. And who smokes a joint before breakfast?

I eat the breakfast taco, moaning as the first bite hits me. Liv rolls down her window as she pulls out of my driveway. Mom's car is gone, but Rick's is in its usual spot.

"How are you?" I ask her, the pungent smell of weed hitting my nose. I wrinkle my nose and roll down my window. Showing up second-hand high isn't something I have planned for today.

Liv shrugs.

"Living. You?"

I shrug, mimicking her response.

"Living."

She turns up the music, and the sound of Amy Winehouse fills the car. I nod along to the words; I like her songs. I love painting to her music, especially "Back to Black." During the bridge, I always feel something changing in my strokes. My path and view shifted, and my mood shifted along with it.

Liv parks in the lot further back, the courtyard and front entrance deserted. She stubs her joint out and puts it inside a glasses case that she slips inside her door. I follow her inside.

We part ways after each receiving a tardy pass and a disappointed glare from the front desk lady.

Ms. Han comes by our table. It's five minutes into class, and she's been checking on everyone's work, coming by with feedback from our midterm projects we turned in six weeks ago. We're closer to finals than midterms, but no one says anything.

She hands Clara her paper, and Clara looks it over with the same satisfied nod I've seen Thena do when something goes her way. Then, she smiles at Liv and me and sets our papers before us.

I read her note: *I love it! Very creative, and I can see the focus you put into it. 100/100! Amazing Job, Emi!*

I smile and tell her thank you, and Liv does the same. Before tucking it into my folder, I take a picture and send it to Thena and Bell.

Bell responds first.

"Woo!!! Good job!! My favorite artist!!"

I smile at the message and *"heart"* it. My revelry is interrupted by Clara's grating voice.

"Why do you smell like weed?" Clara asks.

"Probably cause I smoked some," Liv causally answers as she types on her phone. I peek at Clara, and as usual, she's glaring at Liv, her cheeks a soft pink.

"Before school?"

Liv nods. She pockets her phone and picks up a paintbrush, putting a finishing touch on her mask. She pushes her small drawing to the side and looks over the large mask covered with intricate designs.

Clara scoffs. *"Is coming to school sober that hard of a concept?"*

"Not really. I just didn't feel like doing it."

Liv walks away, turning in her large mask for her final project. Of course, Liv finished hers a week earlier than she needed to. She was barely trying and still running circles around me. Our finals are the week of the thirteenth, and we leave for break on the seventeenth, a day before the Gala.

"Liv, are you going to any parties this weekend?" I ask her as she sits back down. She stares at me for a second.

"Are you and Jay still not talking?" she asked me. I furrow my eyebrows, not knowing what that has to do with anything.

"We're not."

Especially since after Thanksgiving, I didn't call him, and he didn't call me. I heard from Mom that Jay went to a formal for this class he's taking and that his date was an heiress. I almost threw up everything in my stomach. My appetite didn't return until close to midnight that night, even though she told me before I went to school. So much for Mr. I'm- not-dating-anyone.

Liv nods.

Sanchez is throwing a party."

She's told me about him before. Sanchez goes to our school and is the quarterback for our football team. From what I've heard, he's sweet and is dating this girl who's in college. He throws parties once a semester, always before finals. Liv likes Sanchez, but she likes the people who go to his parties more.

"*You want to go?*" Clara asks.

I shrug.

"*I might. I don't know yet; it depends on how therapy goes,*" I joke. I'm slightly kidding. But so far, all my therapy sessions have been good. Dr. Young isn't too pushy, and she's sweet and warm. I like being around her.

Liv laughs.

"*I'm sure you will hit a life-changing revelation today. If not, we can get tacos before we go to Sanchez's. It's good to have something on your stomach.*" She winks and leaves the table, grabbing her backpack and her phone.

There are ten minutes left in class. Two minutes later, Clara follows her, grabbing her stuff and not bothering to say goodbye. For two people that can't get along they can't seem to remain apart either.

###

Liv's not in creative writing, so it's just me and another girl, Annabell, at our table. Mr. Fields gives us an idea of what our final will be: a five-page paper about one of the books we've read this semester.

Everyone in class except me and maybe a few others groan and shake their heads with a look of frustration and anger. Mr. Fields just smiles, his store-bought pearly whites showing.

"Second semester is when creative writing comes into play, folks. You just have to push through the literature analysis aspect of it." Mr. Fields says in a calm and reassuring tone. I take out my notebook and narrow down which book to write about.

It can be any book of our choice. I spend the rest of the period writing down ideas and narrowing down my favorite books. When it's time to go, I don't feel any dread or panic about going to therapy. Hmmm. I'm not sure when that shift happened.

I'm actually thinking that I might tell Dr. Young about the way Dad used to decorate the house. If it starts to feel too heavy, we can just go back to talking about her Thanksgiving break.

Chapter 22

Emillie Kate Van der Berg

Something feels off about Dr. Young when I walk into her office. She's sitting in her chair, waiting for me, and there's a file on the table. I think it's from her earlier patient. I close the door and sit across from her; she smiles at me, and I smile back.

"How was Florida?"

"It was good. How was your Thanksgiving?"

"It was okay. The food was good. I made the desserts, and Jay was there."

She nods but doesn't comment. There's definitely something off about her.

"Emi, Dr. Hemphill sent over the last of her files on you last week. One of those files was from two years ago." She is maintaining eye contact now in a way that sets my skin to crawling.

Oh. I don't know what to say.

"You want to talk about it?" she asks softly.

I shake my head, my body beginning to fill with dread.

"I just want you to tell me what happened, and if you want, we can talk about how retelling it makes you feel."

I nod. That's fair. I want to tell her but I don't want our sessions to turn into this subject forever and ever on repeat. I can't stop squeezing my hands, my rings pressing into my fingers.

"Take a deep breath," Dr. Yung says, noticing my hand wringing. I take the breath. Then I begin talking.

"Allison. She was my older sister. She died at the beginning
of my sophomore year. It was a car accident. She was
with friends. They... the car collided with another vehicle.
The other people lived, but no one in Allison's car did.

It wasn't a good year... Nick had left, and Thena was so
devastated that she went into some kind of bubble that we
couldn't reach her in. Bell had started dating Tristan,
so she had him and I was just... lonely. I became inconsolable.
Nothing could make me feel better, and I couldn't get better.
But I don't know if I even wanted to... I just wanted the sadness
to stop. I didn't care how.

It's not like I held a gun to my head or anything. I'm not crazy.
I was swimming, one of the only things that felt like a release and
while I was underwater, in the perfect quiet I just thought...
what if I stay here. What if I don't surface? All of the hurt was above
the surface - or that's how it felt. I was just numb. The idea of coming

up and taking a breath was terrifying. I don't know what happened.

I guess I just got stuck in that thought and before I knew it I was

being resuscitated. I mean I would have come up on my own…

I think. Eventually. They say I lost consciousness. I know it was scary

for my family so soon after Allisonl. But I'm fine now. No one

believes me, but I am."

I shrug still wringing my hands. I look at Dr. Young, and she smiles - so much understanding in her eyes. But how could she possibly understand?

"What happened after that?" She prompts me to continue.

"I started going to therapy twice a month instead of once a month, and I started dating…er seeing Jay." My body starts to heat in embarrassment as I think about it. *"Jay had started partying a lot before all of that, and we were sort of distant. But after the pool incident, we got closer. I felt better, and Jay was a big part of that. We hung out more, and I was happy. So yeah, I was fine then, and I'm fine now."*

"Are you? Are you okay now?"

"Yeah. I am."

I don't know if that's true, but I'm not in a dark place, so that's good. I think this general feeling of being a little lost is normal right. Am I supposed to wake up every day smiling, feeling like I'm on top of the world? Should I feel so excited and happy to be here and go to school, then go home, avoid my parents? Am I supposed to be happy that I only spend two hours with my sisters every two weeks when they can make the time? I see Dr. Young more than I see them. And they're only getting busier.

How am I supposed to feel like I'm on top of the world when everyone is basically leaving me behind?

"I'm okay. I'm fine," I tell Dr. Young. I don't care if she believes me. I'm not even sure if I believe me.

I appreciate that Dr. Young keeps it light for the rest of the session and when I leave, I text Liv.

Me: I want to go to Sanchez's party this weekend.

Liv: Be ready at nine.

Chapter 23

Emillie Kate Van der Berg

"Why are you even going to this event again?" I stifle a laugh. Only Thena would call a high school house party an "event."

I walked out of my closet, and clothes were strewn across my floor and most of my furniture. Thena's practically sitting on her hands, so she doesn't pick up any of them and do my laundry. I stand in an oversized sweater, which I have repurposed as a dress. She came over to help me pick out an outfit, a gesture that almost brought me to tears. My hair is pulled half back, a hair clip hiding the hair tie I used. Thena brought over some new products to help contain the curls and frizz. For someone who always has bone straight hair, she sure knows a lot about frizz fighting

She stands up, stepping over as many clothes as she can. I followed her into my closet, which needed to be cleaned out three years ago. Most of the pants don't fit me because Mom purposely bought some of them a size or two smaller to 'give me something to work towards'. I cried to Jay (and a little bit to Thena) when she did that.

Thena scans the closet, opening the stuffed drawers. When she opens my second drawer and clothes get stuck, she glares at me.

"What will you do when you have to move out?"

I bite my lip. *"Call you?"*

She sighs and rolls her eyes but doesn't say anything. She pulls out a white bralette, a large black shirt, black ripped jeans, and a pair of Converse.

"This is a really basic outfit," I note, sliding the jeans on.

"And? It's cute, and it fits you. You don't like tight dresses and corset tops, so just put it on. Don't change your style just because you think everyone there will be wearing something else," Thena says. She leaves my closet, and I change. If I had Thena's confidence, my life would be much easier.

I leave my closet and slide on three necklaces. Thena sits cross-legged on the edge of my bed, her black heels hitting the floor.

"Are you sure you want to go to this thing?"

I nod. I need to. Especially after therapy on Tuesday. *"Do you need a ride? I can take you before I go to dinner."* She has dinner with Rick and a lawyer she's thinking about hiring.

"Nah, Liv's taking me. We're getting food before."

I look at myself in the mirror. The shirt hides my hips and stomach falling past my butt, my jeans are tight, and if I pull my shirt up, I think my insecurities would try to fly out and wrestle me back into bed, and I wouldn't be able to leave the house. Insecurity is a powerful thing. But standing next to perfect, svelte Thena, there are very few things I could be other than insecure.

Thena walks me outside where Liv is waiting. I climb into Liv's car, and without looking back at Thena, we pull off.

First, we go to Pepe's. The small, older restaurant has only a few booths and even fewer tables. Liv walks us to one, and I sit across from her. She wears a black cropped tank top, high-waisted black boyfriend jeans, and old faded Converse, her hair pulled into a bun with flyaway pieces. I can tell she didn't even pull them out. She has just mastered effortless shabby chic. She is appraising my clothing choices as well.

"I like your outfit. Very 'Pinterest' of you," she says - a joke in her voice. I narrow my eyes at her, and she just laughs.

"Thena picked it out."

A waitress sets down a bowl of chips and guacamole. I dip a chip in the guacamole.

After we order, Liv says, *"Don't eat too much."*

"Why?"

She smirks. *"More to throw up."*

Oh.

I don't know what I had imagined for Sanchez's party, but I can already tell I'm behind. I eat one of my tacos, and Liv does the same. Sanchez lives ten minutes away. Liv parks a block away, and as we walk by the endless cars between our parking spot and the party, it starts to hit me just how big this party is. Even though it's winter, no one among the other partygoers headed the same direction as us wears a jacket, their breath puffing visibly into the cold air as they laugh.

Sanchez lives in a smaller mansion, the outside brick with gray trimming. The garage is
open with couches and a table, and people are packed inside.

Liv pushes us through the small line outside the door, and the sound of music and shouting amplifies. Inside I completely forget the weather. The house is tropically warm, and most of the furniture has been cleared out. Liv grabs my hand and pulls me with her as we go into the kitchen, where she hands me a drink.

I sip it and immediately start coughing. Liv smiles and throws her drink back, not even wincing. A tall guy wearing a muscle T-shirt and a backward baseball cap enters the kitchen. Liv turns around and waves at him.

He walks over with a broad, lopsided smile as he hugs her.

"I knew you would come! Rex is out by the pool." Liv nods.

"Sanchez, this is my friend Emi."

Sanchez smiles at me. *"Tyler Sanchez, nice to meet you. You Jay's girl?"*

I shake my head. *"Uh, we're just friends."*

"She's Jay's girl," Liv says, refilling her drink and mine.

I shake my head, and Sanchez laughs, moving toward a bucket with more beers. I follow Liv outside to the pool, the smell of marijuana, cigarettes, and alcohol floating in the air. We walk towards a guy sitting on a lone chair next to a cheap, yellow, faded couch that doesn't look like it belongs in Sanchez's house. I sit on the couch and make myself comfortable.

Liv leans down and hugs Rex, kissing his forehead. He smiles. It's a really nice smile. It'd be nice to paint because his teeth are straight and the perfect size, not an over- or underbite. He wears a flannel shirt like me and jeans with white Vans, his pale skin resembling the moon, and his ginger hair is cut low. Rex is an attractive guy, very attractive. From what I can tell, his eyes are dark green.

"Who's that?" he points a finger at me, and I smile. The drink has definitely started to hit me. I like this feeling. I feel light and warm. If it dropped ten degrees, I wouldn't feel it.

"Emi. She's, my friend. She's cool."

I smile and squeeze her hand. She laughs and rolls her eyes.

"I need something," Liv tells him. Rex sighs but pulls something from his pocket and hands it to her, a lighter flickering in front of Liv's face. She lights a joint up, inhales deeply, and then passes it to me. I shake my head, and she doesn't hesitate before passing it to Rex.

"What else do you need? I know that's not it."

She leans closer and whispers something. *What is she asking for?* I don't ask; I just finished my drink. I've gotten drunk before, and I've felt like this before, but now I kind of want to stay like this. Rex hands her something, and she turns to me, grabs my hand, and I look at her.

"I'm going over there." She points to an area by the back door. *"You'll be able to see me. Yell if you need anything,"*

I nervously flit my eyes toward Rex.

"Rex will look out for you," she quietly assures. I nod and smile. I watch her walk towards the back door, standing by it. She refills her drink and then answers her phone.

"You want some punch?" Rex asks me. I nod and hand him my cup. He pours me some, and I sip it. It tastes like pink lemonade with a kick of something. I like it. The punch came from a large Gatorade jug, the kind they have at sports games. People walk up to it and refill their cups, then walk away.

"This is really good! Who made it?" I probably should've asked that before I took a sip, but I trust Liv and, by default, trust Rex.

"Sanchez," Rex answers.

I nod and continue to drink, finishing half before Liv returns. She sits next to me, and she and Rex talk about the party that happened during Thanksgiving. Then Rex brings up his plans for Christmas. I finish my drink and lean forward.

"Refilllllll, please?"

Rex smirks but does as I say.

Liv doesn't notice; she's watching the house, and I'm sitting on the edge in the closest seat to Rex. I take a sip and smile. I look up, and it looks like Clara's here, dressed in a short black skirt, black platform heels, and a black lace top, her blonde hair a stark contrast to her gothic black ensemble. She doesn't look phased by the cold.

"Is that Clara, or am I drunk?" I ask Rex, staring at her as she walks towards us.

"It's Clara. Her boyfriend's standing by the door, checking somebody else out." Rex lights up a cigarette.

Liv stares at Clara, her eyes a little brighter, and Clara stares at her, eyes narrowed as she takes Liv in.

"Well, well, well. If this isn't a first, I don't know what is. Oliva Brunes sobers at a party!" Clara smirks, crossing her arms over her chest.

"It's cuz I gotta watch Emi."

I frown.

"Oh, so you'll stay sober for Emi?" Clara takes a step forward, and I try to take one back but remember I'm sitting down.

Liv shrugs.

"What are you doing here?"

Good question, Liv! Clara talks shit about these parties in almost every art class.

"Chet wanted to come." She gestures towards her boyfriend, who's smoking a cigarette, his legs crossed as he speaks to one of the guys on the football team. Chet smiles and nods.

"Mmh, I'm sure." Liv stands up and leans down to whisper in my ear. *"I'll be right back. "*

I shake my head. Nothing bad could happen to me out here. Right now, I feel incredible. I want to stay like this. It isn't until both Liv and Clara walk away that I wonder where they went. I turn and ask Rex, who's taking the whole party. *"Hey! Where'd they go?"*

"My guess is to fuck." he says casually.

My eyes widen, but I don't say anything. The alcohol is slowing my thought process down but my brain is whirring life - walking back through all of the interactions I've witnessed between Liv and Clara.

"Probably in the bathroom or a pantry. "

"B-but Clara has a boyfriend," I stammer. Embarrassed by how childish I know I sound.

Rex shrugs. *"And? Those two are like rabbits. Last week they did it in my car. "* He scoffs at the memory, seemingly annoyed.

"Oh shit!" I exclaim, some of my drink sloshing on my hand. It splashes Rex, and he doesn't even blink. *"I'm so sorry. "* I rush out, wiping at his hand. I keep wiping even after the liquid is gone. It's an oncoming spiral and I know it. The revelation about Liv and my embarrassment is messing with me.

Rex grabs my hand to stop my incessant wiping; I can feel tears stinging my eyes. *Why am I freaking out?* Rex looks at me; his eyes are darker than Bell's but still green. They're beautiful.

"It's okay." He held my hand still. *"You are not the first drunk girl to spill a drink,"* Rex assures, his voice gentle but raspy. It's like Jay's, but more *"South Philly,"* the kind I've only ever heard in movies. It calms me a bit. He is looking at me quizzically. Probably to see if I'm a full lunatic or a partial one.

I stare at the spot on his hand where the drink splashed. He raises my face to his. *"You, okay?"*

I nod and look away, biting my lip. Rex holds onto my hand and reaches into his pocket for his phone. He says something else but I can't hear him. His words seem far away even though his hand tethers me to him. I don't even try to make out the words, instead I relax into him letting the party music wash over me.

I'm not sure how much time passes before I notice that there's a couple who are dry-humping on a pool lounge chair just a few feet away. I mean they are really going at it. Are they happy right now? Is anybody happy? I am so out of my element and I immediately think of Thena asking over and over if I was sure I wanted to go to a party tonight. I should call her and ask her to come get me.

"My older sister went to dinner for her business tonight. I need to call her and ask how it went," I blurt out to Rex, excusing myself.

Rex smiles but doesn't release my hand. *"Ask her at a normal hour."*

"Oh!" I say, nodding. *"What time is it?"*

"One."

Wow.

"Hey, Em." I look up, and Liv walks toward me. She smiles and kneels in front of me. *"What Cha drinking?"* She grabs my cup from me and takes a small sip. *"Oh f*ck,"* she whispers. She smiles at me and pours the drink on the floor; she looks me in the eyes. *"How many drinks have you had?"*

"Two."

"Three," Rex corrects. *"She grabbed one from a guy walking by."*

I did?

"Did she take something before she came?" Rex asks.

Liv shakes her head.

"There's something in the punch," Clara realizes. Liv nods and squeezes my hand.

"Liv, I don't feel happy anymore. Where'd it go?" I whisper. Tears burn my eyes so bad I just want to blink so they'll drip down my face, but they don't. They're stuck there.

"I don't know, but it'll come back, honey, I promise." She smiles, and I smile too. *It'll come back.* *"Let's go. I'm kind of over this party. Okay?"*

"Okay," I whisper. I look at Rex, who releases my hand I forgot he was holding. *"Bye, Rex."*

He waves, and I hold onto Liv. My feet and body are heavy. Before I know it, I'm swept up in someone's arms. I look up.

"Rex, you're back," I whisper, touching the ginger scruff on his chin. *"You're not Jay."* My words feel heavier as I speak, and I don't want to talk anymore.

In the car, I lay across Liv's lap, the smell of her soap and weed calming me down. Everything feels numb. It feels so much like the bottom of that pool, and it's comforting. Is it wrong that I like this? What would Dr. Young say?

We drove for a while. Liv strokes my hair, and I grip her thigh that I lay on. I can see Clara's blonde hair over the seat. Her hair is silky and bright. It looks so golden. I want to reach forward and touch it, but I feel molded to Liv and this seat. For a moment I think of Allison. I wonder if she was relaxed in a car just like this before the collision.

Wetness slides down my cheeks and down my neck, hitting my bralette. My cheeks are on fire, the wetness cooling them. I guess my tears figured out how to get out.

The door opens, and I feel Liv slide out. Two large hands pull me out, and I'm wrapped in someone else's arms. Their arms are warm, and they smell like Jay.

"What happened to her?" Jay asks, his voice cold. I want to tell him to be nice to Liv; she's my only friend.

"She drank something at the party. She should be fine in the morning. She's probably nauseous and she is really out of it, so yeah. Tell her to call me when she wakes up." Liv sounds so worried. Why is she worried? Jay doesn't respond.

"Bye, Liv," I say, but I don't think anyone hears me.

Jay carries me inside, the warmth of the building hitting me. A door opens and closes with the sound of a lock clicking. I feel a bed under me and melt into it. My shoes, socks, and jeans are removed. Blankets cover me.

My eyes are heavy. I can feel something pulling my consciousness, and I feel something Jay's hard and warm body pressed against my back.

"Sleep, Em."

He says something else, but I've already closed my eyes and fallen into the inviting darkness.

Chapter 24

James Averell

I need to find something to do. I've been watching Emi sleep for the past hour. After she woke up at five in the morning, clutching her stomach, I stayed up. She threw up, still half asleep. I made her drink some water, and she just went back to sleep without a second thought. I shower and get ready for the day. Knowing Emi, she could sleep the rest of the day away.

My dad calls me as I'm pulling on a pair of sweats. I answer it because he'll keep calling me if I don't. He likes doing annoying shit like that.

"What?"

"*Is that how you answer your phone?*" His voice is gruff, cold.

"*Just for you, Pops.*"

He huffs, which is basically a chuckle for him.

"*You're going to that meeting tonight, aren't you?*"

"What meeting?" I ask while rolling on deodorant and reaching for a pair of socks.

"Do you not listen to anything I tell you? The meeting with the head of the game programming department."

I roll my eyes.

"I'm not about to go to a meeting for something I'm not even interested in just because you used your connections." I haven't decided what I want to do, but I know I want to do it alone.

"If you would listen to me, you would know this is just an opportunity to keep your options open. You will go and see him tonight. Earl will be outside of your place. Text me when you want him to show up. Don't be an asshole to him. He'll be at the Christmas Gala."

"Fine," I grit.

"Oh, and tell Emi I said hi." He hangs up.

Why does he know everything about my life? Part of me isn't even surprised. He's always been ahead of the curve. Except for the whole parenting thing, he's never gotten the hang of that.

I text him.

Me: Tell your assistant to bring a box of my usual order from *Patisserie d'Artisan.*

Eric: They're downstairs.

I roll my eyes. Whoever told him where I was staying deserves to be evicted from my life. I left the dorm very quietly and pulled out cash for the deposit just to avoid his detection. He's basically the CIA. I go downstairs and get the pastries. The box is still warm, and two black coffees are sitting by it. At least he doesn't know my coffee order. A small comfort.

The apartment building isn't shabby. There's a doorman who's only asleep about half the time. My apartment is on the fifth floor at the end of the hall. The door is painted olive green with a gold painted number reading '**508**'.

Emi is still asleep when I come back inside. Her hair spreads across my pillow. I lay down the pastries, open the curtains, and crack a window open.

She groans, and I look over my shoulder. She rolls over, presses her face into the pillow, and slowly pushes herself up. She looks around the room, and her eyebrows furrow into the classic *"I have no idea what's going on"* look.

"Hey," I say, trying not to spook her. It doesn't work; she still jumps up. She looks at me and wipes some of the sleep from her eyes. I bring her the glass of water I'd poured earlier before my shower.

"Here, drink."

She drinks the whole glass, wiping her lips with the back of her hand.

"What happened?" Her voice is scratchy, and I can see a hidden level of panic and fear in her eyes.

"You got sick at a party last night, and your friend Liv and this blonde girl dropped you off."

"Clara."

"Who?"

"Clara. She was with Liv at the party last night. You don't remember her?" I get up and bring the pastries and coffee over, climbing into the other side of the bed.

"Why would I remember her?" I grab a scone and take a bite out of it.

"You made out with her your junior year."

I freeze, staring at Emi. She's never brought up that year or the summer after that year.

"Huh? Don't remember that."

She grabs a donut and takes a small bite. *"You did."* She exhales a deep breath. *"I-I don't know why I brought that up. I'm sorry. I'm sorry for coming here."* She waves around the room, dropping her bitten donut back into the box.

She climbs out of bed, my shorts reaching her knees.

"Wait, where are we? This isn't your dorm."

"It's a loft I bought for alone time. Got tired of listening to Caden complain about his girlfriend and Ireland." I finish my scone and grab a croissant from the box. *"There's a Danish in here; they're warm too."*

She checks the box out, biting her lip. She grabs one and takes a step back, not eating the Danish.

"I need to shower and use the bathroom."

I stood up and grabbed her a towel I ganked from my dad's place. I stole towels, soap dishes, kitchen utensils, and a pot that Rachel had to act like she didn't see me taking. I throw Emi the towel. She can't catch, so it hits her in the face, and she takes a step back, almost tripping.

"Thanks!" She yells through the towel as she walks to the bathroom, shutting the door behind her.

I go through the stack of papers I'm supposed to have read and annotated by my class on Monday. It's fifty pages, front and back, in size ten font. It's about the origin and transformation of cryptographic coding.

By the time Emi comes out of the shower, I'm only on page 17 and have finished my coffee. She stands across from me in a towel wrapped tightly around her body and one on her hair. She clutches the towel, keeping it close to her.

"I need clothes, please," she says in a shaky voice, looking everywhere but me. I nod and grab some clothes for her from the box of Emi stuff. I've accumulated over the years.

I hand her a pair of sweats, a T-shirt.

"Here."

She takes them and rushes back to the bathroom.

I read another page until she came out, her hair pulled up into a messy dripping bun. I put my work down and look at her. She sits on the edge of my bed. The sheets are messed up, and the apartment smells like my soap and her perfume. The smell of vomit and alcohol is gone.

I'm tired of her running from me and both of us ignoring what happened two years ago. We'll never move forward if we don't take a step in the direction, we've both been avoiding.

"I'm sorry about Clara. I'm sorry about all of the girls I've already forgotten that I was running through sophomore year. I was...looking for something. Well maybe burying something?"

She shakes her head. *"Yea you were burying something alright."* She rolls her eyes and I try not to laugh at her terrible pun. I stand up and walk towards her.

"You started it Em. You started dating. You had started talking to and spending time with douchebags. I was so angry that I took it out on everyone." Her breathing hitches. *"I don't remember any of their names and don't want to or care to. I was angry and worried about you, Em, so I went out and did*

159

anything to forget about you." I chuckle. It's brittle and forced. *"It has always been us, and then suddenly I wasn't enough so I tried to replace you. It obviously didn't work because I ended up at your house every night, even when I was fall-down drunk."*

I can still see how she looked every night when I showed up—always worried, always happy to see me, and never mad. One night it was so late the sun was starting to rise, and when I came to her room, she ran into my arms and hugged me. She'd been up worried about me; I'd lost my phone and had to walk to her house from the train. She had called me over fifty times that night.

"Do you know why I hated that you were dating Em?" I'm standing right in front of her. She has to look up to meet my eyes.

"You said it was because those guys were assholes, and you hated them, but that wasn't it. Was it?" I shake my head. *"Why?"*

"You know why, Em. Why would someone get so angry that their best friend's dating other people? What makes someone that angry and irrational? You know what, Em."

She knows. She just doesn't want to admit she does. Because then she'd have to admit so much more.

"You liked me? Like, as more than a friend."

I shake my head, taking a small step forward, her knees touching my legs.

"More than that, Em, you know." She shakes her head. *"I want you as more than a friend. I always cared about you more than anyone. I don't want anyone to be with you, Em, but I want you to be happy more than anything. Tell me what that is."*

She opens her mouth but closes it. She won't say it. I smile and take a deep breath.

"*Tell me why you've been distant since I went to college, and be honest.*" I push a piece of her hair out of her eye. "*Please.*" The "*please*" is what does it for her. Her body sags, and she sighs.

"*My mom told me not to be a burden and to give you space since you're moving forward with your life. She told me not to box you in like a selfish child. And I listened because it's been something I've thought about for years. I don't want to be the reason you're missing parties, and I don't want to be the reason you're missing all these experiences. I don't want to be a burden, not to you.*" She says it all in a few breaths, forcing it out in quick succession. I lean down and become eye-to-eye with her.

"*You could never be a burden to me, Em. You're it. You're all I need. I never wanted you to leave me alone. And I never wanted to stop coming to see you.*"

"*Then why did you?*" She grasps my hand and squeezes it. Her eyes are glassy as tears fill.

"*My dad told me to. He told me to get my shit together and grow up, before I could expect a Van der Berg to be with me, and I did. I don't know why I listened to him about dating advice when his only relationships are one-night stands. But I did. I don't know why I keep listening to him…*"

"*Because he's your dad,*" she whispers, a soft smile on her face. "*I'm not mad at you for listening to him. I can't be. I did the same, but I just want to tell you that you didn't need to change for me. He's wrong, Jay. You don't need to become a different person to be with me. You know that, right? Please tell me you know that.*" Her eyes and voice plead with me to believe her.

"I *know, Em,*" I whisper, wiping a tear from her face. This is a lot more emotional than I thought it would be. "*I don't want to be friends anymore; I don't want to keep pretending not to want you. I want you.*"

Her breath hitches, and she stares at me, her eyes flickering all over my face looking for any sign that I'm lying. But I'm not, I wouldn't, not about this. And not with her.

"*You want to date? To be boyfriend and girlfriend?*"

I laugh.

"*Yeah, Em. We can even make bracelets and change our Facebook status if it makes you feel better.*" She smacks my chest. "*I know you don't have Facebook.*" She rolls her eyes and huffs.

It goes silent, and I can see her getting lost in her thoughts. Her eyes are more distant. "*Tell me, what is it?*" I whisper.

A tear falls down her face, and I wipe it, just for another to fall.

"*Break up with me the second I start feeling like an anchor. Promise? Please Promise?* " she pleads, her voice cracking and more tears clouding her vision. I want to tell her she'll never feel like an anchor, but she doesn't want to hear that.

"*I promise, Em.*"

She relaxes, and I do what I've wanted to do since we last kissed. I kissed her deeply.

Chapter 25

Emillie Kate Van der Berg

I have a boyfriend. James Averell, my longest crush and my best friend, is my boyfriend. I can honestly say that the person who's taken all my firsts is my boyfriend. I can't stop smiling at the idea of it. I'm lying in his bed, in his super-duper secretive loft, while he grabs the food he ordered from downstairs. We spent the day eating pastries while watching season 12 of *The Simpsons*. I look around the loft. The only furniture is the bed. There are a number of boxes and maybe three large trash bags filled with stuff by the front door. all the curtains are drawn. I like it.

Jay comes back in, a bag of food in his hand. He slides his slippers off and climbs back into bed, handing me my food: a plate of spicy tuna rolls and salmon lover maki from our favorite sushi spot in Brooklyn.

"You got me sushi?" I gush, smiling at him. He rolls his eyes, and a soft pink tint forms on his cheek.

"It's no big deal. I just clicked a few buttons and ordered it."

"Yeah, but you know my order." I lean over and kiss his cheek, pulling back before it escalates.

I'm six rolls in when he says, *"I told your sisters you were staying here, and I have to take you to Thena's at seven. She probably wants you to spend the night."*

"You told them I was here? With you?"

Jay shrugs.

"Yeah. They kept calling, so I told them. They are covering for you with your mom. You want some more wasabi?"

"No, I have enough wasabi," I answer. I haven't been on my phone all day. I told Mom I was sleeping over at Liv's house. I already had planned to be hungover and didn't feel like hiding that from her, plus Lucille always worries too much when I'm hungover. *"Why were Thena and Bell worried?"*

"It might've been because I called them after you threw up while still half asleep and weren't responding when I called your name or shook you. Thena wanted to come over, but God knows I'm not giving her my address." Jay shakes his head like the idea is the craziest thing in the world.

"What time is it?"

He pulls his phone from his pocket.

"Six. We'll leave after we finish."

I nod and continue eating my sushi.

I like this—lying in bed eating sushi, watching cartoons with Jay. I don't have any bad thoughts or doubts here. The party seems like a distant memory. I lean on Jay when I can't eat another bite, and he leans back so I can be more comfortable. I listen to the steady beat of his heart and smell the soap on him and me, the smell that's overtaken the small loft.

###

164

His pickup truck is parked separately from everyone else's cars. The parking garage is mostly empty. I climb into the car, the light brown leather seats cold. He turns on the truck, and the engine's roar makes me smile. Jay always drives with one hand, mainly using only two fingers to steer and one hand to turn. That's how he always drove, even when he was just learning. I don't know how he passed his test.

"*What part of the city is your loft in?*" I ask him as we exit the garage. He turns right into a lane at the traffic light. The light turns green, and he presses the gas easing us forward.

"*Hell's Kitchen.*" He turns the radio down and grabs my hand, pulling me closer. "*It's twenty minutes from campus, and it'll probably take us twenty-five minutes to get to Thena's neighborhood. It's still in Manhattan, just not as downtown or uptown. I like it. More than I thought I would,*" he admits. I smile.

"*I'm glad. You think you'll move here full-time when you graduate?*"

He glances at me for a second, then looks back at the road.

"*I'll move wherever you want to. Even if it's with Thena, I'll be there with you.*"

"*I want to be close to you. I'll go where you go.*"

We stop at a red light.

"*Me too.*" I say, because what else do you do when someone says something like that?

###

"Em, we've been sitting outside for fifteen minutes," Jay reminds me. I look at Thena's white brownstone. She painted it white when Rick bought it. The giant Christmas reef she has on her door sparkles. I want to take a picture of it so I can see it all year round.

"I *know, but maybe just five more minutes."* I look at Jay, and he rolls his eyes smirking; he says nothing. Instead, he just opens his door and gets out of the truck walking over to my side to do the same. He opens it and waits for me.

"Come on, Em. There's nothing to fear. They're your sisters, not your mom."

I smile and climb out of the truck; Jay grabs my hand and leads me to the door.

When we get outside, before I ring the doorbell, he pulls me into him, his hands going to my waist and his head dipping, his lips meeting mine. More hungrily than before. I run one of my fingers through the hairs on the back of his neck, squeezing them and pulling him closer. He bites my bottom lip, and my mouth opens, our tongues tangling. I can feel myself losing air, but I don't pull away. I've thought about making out with Jay for a couple of years, and now I can do it.

The sound of a door pulling open causes me to pull away in surprise. Thena stands on the other side, a bored look on her face. She looks between us and purses her lips, her arms crossed over her chest.

"Goodbye, James."

Jay chuckles and let's go of my hand.

"Bye, Em. I'll text you when I make it back to my dorms."

"Wait!" I call after him. I jog down the three steps and stop in front of him. I don't know how to ask or tell him that I'm scared this won't work. Our lives are too different now, and we'll never see each other. I don't want to tell him these fears because if I tell him he might worry about them and overcompensate, our chances of breaking up are much higher.

He smiles, puts his hand on my cheek, and rubs his thumb along my soft cheekbone.

"Em, we'll see each other. No more ignoring, no more distance. We'll be fine. I promise. You gotta believe in us. This is years in the making."

I smile and nod. *Years in the making.* I turn around and go inside. Thena waits for me to come in before slamming the door shut. Bell lays on the couch, a wide smile on her face. I slide my shoes off and squeal, letting all my excitement show.

"I'm dating Jay!!" I yell. Thena rolls her eyes, but I see the smile on her face. Bell sits up and cheers and claps for me. I run into her and jump on the couch; she falls backward while laughing.

"Do not break my couch," Thena says as she walks past us, heading to the kitchen. I squeeze Bell, and when we pull apart, she's still smiling.

"How'd he asks you?"

I tell her what happened, everything besides the part about me asking him to break up with me if I feel like an anchor. Bell listens the whole time, gushing when appropriate. Her eyes even begin to glass, and I feel her happiness seeping into me.

By the time I finish telling them what happened, Thena has brought over a box of brownies and a miniature bottle of whole milk, like the ones you buy at bakeries.

"*Mom told you not to be a burden?*" Thena asks. Her eyes narrow, and I can already tell she's angry with Mom.

I wave my hand.

"*It doesn't matter anymore. I'm happy!*"

I take a bite of one of the brownies. They're still warm, powdered sugar sprinkled all over. There's so much powdered sugar on them that they resemble beignets.

"*I asked them for extra powdered sugar,*" Thena tells me. I smile at her and tell her thank you.

"*What happened at the party? Are you okay?*"

I take a sip of the milk.

"*I feel better. I just wanted to try something new. But I'm okay now. I promise.*"

I don't know how much of that is true, but I want it to be. I like the way life is going right now. I don't feel the weight of pushing myself from Jay. I'm spending the night with my sisters after spending the day with Jay. How long can this be feeling last?

I asked Thena about her business dinner, and she told me she has a meeting scheduled for the beginning of the year. I clap and cheer for her.

Chapter 26

Emille Kate Van der Berg

I can do this. I can do this. This therapy session will not be like the last one. I can feel it. When I walk inside, Dr. Young is watering her plants. Her hair was braided into a thick Dutch braid going down her back. Her long flowy, pastel pink skirt sways as she moves around the room.

"Hi," I say. She spins around and smiles at me.

"Emi! How are you?" She waves me in, and I close the door behind me, taking my winter coat off and sitting on the couch. She sits in her throne chair and smiles at me.

"I'm good." I can't stop the smile from spreading, and she smiles even bigger, anticipation filling her eyes. *"Jay and I are dating, and I told him why I was distancing myself, and he told me why he stopped coming over. It was good; we talked, and he told me why he did the things he did my sophomore year."* I rushed out.

"So, you admitted you liked him too?"

"*Well, not exactly, but it was implied. I think. I don't know. There's probably more to discuss, but we're good for now.*"

"*That's good. I'm happy for you, Emi. Anything else?*"

"*My finals are next week, and I'm pretty scared. I have to keep my C in Biology, but I turned in my art final, and I think I did pretty well. I like art and my creative writing class, but I think I like my creative writing class more.*"

She nods, urging me to continue.

"*Most of the stuff we've done this semester has been analyzing different works of fiction and comparing or contrasting them to our favorite books. A lot of the people in my class hate it, but I like it. I know I'm good at art—I've always been good at art—but in writing, I can feel myself getting better each time, and I don't know…it's like art in a way that just makes sense.*"

I've always been good at drawing and making things, and as I've gotten older, I've improved just by watching and seeing other artwork and artists. But my writing has always been private, just like my sketchbooks. There's always writing on the left-hand side, and on the right side, there's always some kind of sketch. The words and pictures go together; they always have.

"*If you want, I can help you with applications to art school,*" Dr. Young suggests, an excited look in her eyes.

I shake my head.

"*I don't think I want to do that.*" I twist one of the rings on my fingers, playing with it. "*I'm going to Brown this weekend with my mom. Thena and maybe Bell are coming. Rick insisted it should be a girl's trip, but I'm pretty sure my mom told him to say that.*"

Mom has already sent me an itinerary and a list of things I should pack. She even scheduled us for a meeting with a few of the sororities she wants me to consider. I read the itinerary to Jay last night on FaceTime, and he started laughing after the third wardrobe change. I couldn't even get through Saturday before my anxiety made my head spin.

Jai suggested that I just tell her you don't want to go. He left it at that. I didn't know what to say. We both knew I wouldn't tell my mom that, and we both knew early Saturday morning, I'd be in the car on the way to Brown University.

"Where did your parents go to college?" Dr Young asked.

"My mom went to Yale, where she met Rick, and my dad went to Harvard, but both my dad and mom and their parents were from Louisiana, and their parents were friends, so that's how they knew each other."

Every Yale vs. Harvard football game, Eric, Rick, and Mr. Yates drive up to see the game.

"Jay's dad went to Yale too. He wanted Jay to go there, but Jay chose Columbia instead."

I smile. Jay and his dad fought for months about it, but Jay didn't budge, not even when Eric threatened to cut him off.

"The Yates' both went to Yale too. That's where they fell in love and met Rick and my mom. They all went to college together."

"And the Yates' are Nick's parents?"

I nod.

"Tell me about him," Dr. Young says.

I never talk about Nick; it doesn't feel right, not after the way Thena reacts and how she feels. But Thena's not here.

"He was four years older than me and only three years older than Jay, but he and Thena were only a grade apart. They were best friends, liked the same books, and kept up with politics and stuff like that. She really cared about him, and when it was time for Thena to go off to Yale with Nick, he left. He just disappeared. For a few months after that, his parents stopped coming to country club brunches, and everything felt dead. Jay lost one of his best friends, and I know it hurt him, but he didn't talk about it. Then one day, he was a little better, I guess. But Thena? She just kept going. No one brings him up, and when they do, it's not good for Thena."

"Have you ever tried to talk to Thena about what happened?"

I shake my head.

"She acts like he never happened. I don't like the way she looks when someone brings him up. And I don't want to be the one to put her back in that place."

Maybe I'm weak for not being able to even help my older sister with something that happened almost three years ago.

Chapter 27

Emille Kate Van der Berg

"Alright, folks, your papers are due next Wednesday at 11:59 pm. If you have any last-minute questions, please feel free to reach out. I'm always able to help!" Mr. Fields announces as the class ends. Everyone rushes out, but I take my time putting my notebooks inside my bag.

Liv skipped halfway through class and was waiting for me in the parking lot.

"Emi, wait a second." Mr. Fields walks over to my desk, and I try to think of what I may have done wrong for him to speak to me. He smiles, and I force one back, but I can feel how stiff it is. *"I read your paper."*

"Already?"

I turned it in last night. I finished it at the beginning of the week. I'd been working on it little by little ever since it was assigned.

"It was good; a few grammar mistakes here and there, but it was organized beautifully. The whole thing flowed really well, and I liked the metaphors you used throughout the piece."

"Oh, wow! Thank you so much! I didn't expect that." I didn't. I expected a B and a lot of feedback about the lackluster vocabulary and, maybe, repetitiveness.

"Is this your first time writing something with that length?"

I nod.

"I usually just journal stupid random thoughts."

"Why are they stupid?" Mr. Fields asks, his eyebrows furrowed, a curious expression on his face. I open my mouth, but nothing comes out. *"Just because your thoughts may not be the same as others or written as if they were from classics doesn't mean they don't hold value."*

I nod.

"You should write more," he adds as I stand up.

I nod again.

"Thank you, Mr. Fields. Have a great weekend."

"You too. I'll see you in class on Monday and tell Liv I said to have a good weekend."

I have to bite back a laugh.

Liv waits for me in her car, parked in front of the school. The second my door closes, she pulls off. The sound of Chase Atlantic fills the car. This isn't her usual music taste. I haven't brought up her and Clara since last week's party, but art class has been quieter.

"Are you and Clara friends?" I ask. Liv takes a hit off her joint and holds it out the window.

"Not exactly." She looks at me. *"You can keep a secret, can't you?"*

I nod enthusiastically, and Liv chuckles.

"Sometimes, when her boyfriend's not paying attention, we hang out."

"Oh. What do you guys do when y'all hang out?"

"Wouldn't want to betray my Ice Queen's trust now, would I?" She smirks. *"But you're my best friend, so let's just say when it's just us two, Clara Lukov isn't who she portrays herself to be."*

I don't ask anything else. When Liv is ready to tell me, she will. Besides, there's only so much I need to know.

Liv and I eat at Pepe's. Halfway through our meal, Clara, her boyfriend, and a few of their friends arrive, sitting at a larger table behind us. Clara walks by us; she looks between us and huffs.

Liv smirks. *"Are you ready to go?"*

I nod. I grab two twenties from my wallet and set them on the table.

"You know you didn't have to pay."

I wave her off. *"They were just sitting there collecting dust."*

Liv laughs while shaking her head. *"Does cash usually collect dust around the Van der Berg estate?"*

I keep a straight face. *"No, we need it for valet."*

Liv burst into laughter.

"Rick insists we all should keep cash on us so we can tip people or give it to people who need it more than us," I add seriously. I've always liked that about Rick. He has this ability to be self-aware about his money and status. He tries to help others without having a savior complex.

"Let's get you home. You have to be up bright and early for…Brown University." She finishes her sentence in a posh British accent. I roll my eyes and groan, falling dramatically backward.

Liv cranks up her car and pulls out of Pepe's parking lot, more cars coming in as we leave.

"What time do you guys leave?" Liv asks me as we pull onto my street.

"Six in the morning, so we can beat traffic and get there before nine."

"I don't even get up that early for school!"

Mom texted me to be home before seven so she could go over everything she packed for me and what I needed to do to prepare. I don't want to do this, but fighting against it would be a waste of energy.

"Emi! Is that you?!" Mom yells from upstairs. I sigh and head upstairs.

"Yes."

Lucille and my mother are in my room. A large suitcase sits on my bed, half filled with clothes. Lucille sends me a sympathetic look as she folds a pair of black jeans. I look at the clothes that are packed so far.

"Mom, we're leaving tomorrow and coming back Sunday night. I don't need this many outfits."

She hasn't stopped moving. She ignores me and gets a skirt from my closet; one I didn't know I had.

"Your dress for the gala came in, and I have it hanging in my closet. It will stay there until the day of. I don't need you or your sister to find another option."

"*We wouldn't have to if you respected her requests,*" Thena announces, rounding the corner from the hallway. Her hair's pulled half up in loose waves, and she looks like she just came from class. Her oversized, white sweater has a few gold necklaces stacked over it, and a black pleated skirt goes just to her mid-thigh, with black tights underneath.

"*Thena, don't come in here and make this more difficult,*" Mom says, a hint of frustration already present.

"*I would never!*" Thena drops her designer tote bag on my bed and looks through the suitcase. "*Emi can pack her own bag. She's seventeen, not seven. Besides, you'll already be controlling how she looks next weekend. She should be able to be comfortable on her college tour.*"

Mom sighs and drops the skirt by my suitcase. "*Fine, but next weekend I want both of you at the hotel bright and early, and I don't want to have to remind you,*" Mom warns before leaving the room. Lucille hurries after her, closing the door behind her.

"*Thank you so much!*" I exclaim, hugging Thena.

I empty all the clothes from my suitcase, filling it with underwear, two bras, T-shirts, leggings, two pairs of ripped jeans, and three hoodies. It takes me less than ten minutes. The whole time while I'm doing it, Thena sits on my bed, her legs crossed, as she looks at her phone.

"*I went on a date on Wednesday.*"

I freeze. "*Oh really?*" I try to sound casual.

Thena sighs. "*No, not really. But I did chat up a guy next to me at the coffee bar.*"

"*It's okay. No one is pressuring you to move one. Well, no one but Mom. Do you think you're ready?*"

She thinks about it briefly, and I climb onto my bed, sitting across from her. Thena and I never had these talks when she was a teenager; I was too young. I think she told Bell, though.

"I don't think so. It doesn't sound desirable at the moment; maybe in the future." I can hear the doubt in her voice. I don't want her to lose all hope. Thena has always wanted a family—after figuring out her career. She's always wanted kids. Nick really did a number on her.

"Maybe. You never know. Prince Charming is just around the corner." It's something Bell would say, and she can tell. She rolls her eyes, a hint of amusement glimmering in them.

"I've never cared much for Prince Charming; he's always been a little too predictable. I've always liked the Dark Knight, though." Her full lips twitch, and I can't help but smile.

A Dark Knight. I can see it.

Chapter 28

Emillie Kate Van der Berg

I overslept; I was supposed to be downstairs with everyone else twenty minutes ago. It's selfish, but I still get into the shower, taking my time doing my hair into two braids. That alone takes thirty minutes. When I finish, I'm close to being an hour late.

Jay couldn't talk last night since he had a meeting with one of his professors and was just going to bed when he got back to his place. I tried not to be too sad about it but failed miserably. I distracted myself by eating cold pizza and watching whatever cartoon was on.

I walk downstairs. Rick waits for me by the door with a coffee in his hand.

"*Where are you going?*" I ask him. He is wearing khaki pants and a light blue polo shirt.

"*Golf trip.*" He smiles, and I resist the urge to groan, fall dramatically to the ground, and act injured.

"Have fun," I grumbled, pushing past him. He takes my suitcase, his chuckle echoing in the empty foyer. Outside, Mom, Thena, and Jay wait.

Jay!

I instantly smile and walk towards him, walking into his arms and hugging him. He must've come to tell me goodbye.

We pull apart, and I look up at him. His hazel eyes focus on me. He cups my cheek, pulls me forward, and kisses my nose.

"Come to tell me bye?"

He shakes his head, pulling me into his side. I look around and notice Mom and Rick talking by the trunk. I also spotted a simple, faded black suitcase that belonged to none other than James Averell.

"You're coming?"

He nods. *"Of course. I couldn't miss this."*

Thena's arms are crossed. She's wearing oversized round sunglasses as she looks around. I can tell she's not too happy about Jay coming, but she doesn't say anything.

"And he's sleeping in a separate room," Rick says from the back of the car. I look at him, and he's staring at Jay pointedly.

We all say goodbye to Rick and load up into the Escalade. Bell couldn't make it because her photoshoot got pushed back a day. So now it's just us four for the weekend. I spend the drive sleeping, waking up when we're fifteen minutes away from campus. Mom booked us a room at a hotel in town.

The first thing on the itinerary is a tour of the campus. It's currently thirty degrees, and most people are heading home for winter break but why not. The tour around campus is boring. Beautiful, but boring. Mom and Thena argue about whether they need to tour the library. Thena thinks we should because it's part of the campus and should be taken into consideration, and Mom says it's a waste of time because we all know I wouldn't be in the library. *Ouch!*

I stand by Jay, holding his hand and looking around the trees and students. Some girls stare at Jay with wide, lustful eyes, but he doesn't notice. He looks bored. His shirt is wrinkled, and he has a half-chewed straw behind his ear. Evidence that he is trying to quit cigarettes again.

"*Wanna look around?*" he whispers in my ear; I look up at him and see the mischief in his eyes. I nod, and he leads me toward a large building. We wait for a student to leave before we slip inside, running up the stairs until we reach the third floor.

A large studio comes into view. There are paintings and different works of art all around the room. The walls are a bright white, and most of the artwork has been removed, probably due to students taking their work home for winter break. Their finals have finished.

"*You could be painting or making stuff in here this time next year,*" Jay says somewhere behind me.

I could. I could be one of the students grabbing their work before heading home for the holidays or running across campus to do something before they leave. All of those are possibilities of things that could happen to me. Maybe I'd make friends in my art classes? Or maybe I'd be at the easel in the corner, isolated from everyone.

Jay's hands grab my hips and squeeze. He turns me around, and I can feel my whole-body flush. He stares down at me, his hazel eyes a little darker. He smirks before leaning down and kissing me, his mouth not giving me any time to adjust. His tongue presses against my lips, and I must not react quick enough because his hand travels down to my ass, and

181

he squeezes, causing me to gasp. His tongue invades my mouth, and I feel lightheaded. James Averell is a fantastic kisser.

He walks me backward until my back hits the wall, and his hands drift further, squeezing the underside of my ass.

"*You are so stressed, Em. Ever since we stepped on campus your shoulders are tight, your jaw is clenched. Let me help you relax.*"

I can feel my whole face warm, thankful he can't tell.

"*Thank you,*" I awkwardly muttered. Jay chuckles and leans down, kissing my neck. I bite my lip, keeping all sounds to myself. His hand comes to my front and goes right *there.* I gasp. He holds me in his hand like it's nothing and lightly squeezes. I squeeze his arms.

"*Yes?*" He questions. I nod. "*Words, Em.*"

"*Yes,*" I whisper, searching for his lips. He kisses me, moving his hand inside my leggings and staying above my underwear. His fingers trail down my most sensitive area, over and over again, I pull my mouth away from his, a soft moan escaping.

This should not be happening. I should *not* be grinding against Jay's finger in Brown's art room. My stomach tightens, and I put my face into his chest, smothering all sound from escaping. When the sensation explodes, I almost collapse against the wall. Jay kisses me as I return to Earth, my whole body cooling off. When I relax, he removes his hand slowly, and I gulp.

He smiles down at me, leans forward, and kisses my nose. I adjust my leggings and panties and push my braids behind my shoulders. Now that I am back from my euphoria, I am mortified that we could have been caught and a nervous wreck.

"Don't be shy," he teases. I smack him in the arm and look around the empty room. I don't think I could ever come back here with a straight face.

I walk out of the studio, and Jay follows me. Thena stands by a coffee shop and sips a small coffee. I smile and wave at her.

"Where were you two?" she asks, taking in my smile and me and Jay's post-makeout lips. She sighs and takes off her sunglasses, glaring at Jay. *"Please don't tell me you had sex with my sister on her college tour."*

My eyes widened.

"I did not have sex with your sister." Jay delivers this technical truth with complete confidence.

It's not a lie. I like how Thena keeps referring to this as *my* college tour. It doesn't feel like it, but she keeps reminding me it is.

"I'll be right back," Jay whispers in my ear. I nod, and he kisses my cheek.

"What did you two do?" She asks as soon as he's gone. I get in the two-person line to order myself a coffee. Thena stares at me, patiently waiting for me to tell her. When I finish ordering, I go stand by her.

"We kissed, and uh…messed around a little." My face is flushing hot, and I am worried that she can read my mind. Thena blinks and tilts her head to the side like she's trying to figure out what she got herself into.

"How romantic," she drawls. I roll my eyes and bite back a smile. *"Have you and Jay had sex since you two started dating?"*

"We just started dating last week, so no," I remind her. Again, a technical truth. My coffee order is called, and I thank the barista and grab it, sipping the iced coffee. It's cold, and getting an iced coffee wasn't the most intelligent decision.

"Do you think you're ready to have sex?"

"With Jay, yeah," I say, surprising myself. I mean, he's not some guy off the street." He is one of the few true constants in my life. He single-handedly dragged me back from the deep end of depression. And technicalities aside, Jay and I have already done what Thena is worried about.

Thena nods, looking away. Now that I think about it, I don't know if she's ever had sex. She and Nick spent long hours away on trips and studying together, but I don't know what they were doing. Maybe she met someone in college, or perhaps she's the queen of one-night stands. I only know what she shows me, and Thena has never shown me her love life.

Jay comes back fifteen minutes later, ten minutes before my mom. He has a breakfast sandwich in his hand and a small brown bag with grease stains in the other one. He hands me the bag, and I brighten.

"Egg and bacon bagel. It's not Sal's, but it's decent." He pulls a carton of orange juice from his pocket, and I see another brown bag in his other hand. I didn't see that one at first. He hands it to Thena. *"Oatmeal, cinnamon, and green apples on top."*

"Thank you," she swiftly replies, taking the bag and opening the oatmeal. We sit and eat outside in the cold. The hot food warms us. The sandwich isn't bad. It's not as good as Sal's, but it's good.

Mom arrives while we eat, her long fur lined trench coat buttoned tightly against her. She looks at all of us and narrows her eyes on my sandwich.

"Emille, do not get grease stains on your shirt; you have a meeting with a sorority in less than five hours." Five hours?

I take a sip of my orange juice, heat rising to my cheeks in embarrassment. Thena already finished her oatmeal. I could tell it wasn't her favorite, but it wasn't bad.

"You're meeting with a sorority?" Jay asks in disbelief; I can't blame him. I've never brought up the idea of joining one.

"Yeah, a group of presidents are coming to an early dinner with us." I look at the time on my phone. It's only 10:48 am. I know I have to change outfits before I go, so getting a grease stain wouldn't really matter all that much.

I don't know what Mom's been doing for the past hour, but none of us say anything. We merely follow her back to the car, so we can do whatever else she says. We're all her puppets for the day. Jay distracts me, and so does Thena, both not letting me fall into the trap of anxiety and dread that's slowly building. But when it's time for dinner, they can only do so much.

Chapter 29

Emille Kate Van der Berg

The dinner is at an upscale steakhouse off campus. Thena has changed into a conservative black dress with black and gold Prada heels, and her hair is still in the high slick bun she had it in this morning. Jay changed into a button-up shirt and dress pants, and I put on blue jeans and an oversized sweater I got on sale in Aspen last year.

When I come downstairs, I can see the disdain in my mom's eyes at my outfit, but she doesn't say anything. Jay distracts me from her looks by kissing me until we have to walk to the car. His arm stays wrapped around my shoulder, pulling me into him. Thena looks so tense. I want to reach across and squeeze her hand and tell her it'll be okay. But I don't know what it will be.

The hostess leads us to our table. She's a pretty blonde girl who is maybe in her early twenties, and she keeps checking Jay out. The girls are already waiting on us. I walk inside first. Mom is right beside me. I stop and take all of them in. All dressed in dresses, all white, and all pretty. They stare at me, pageant smiles on their faces as they take me in. Jay gently nudges me, and I walk inside, forcing a smile. I sit across from them, Mom at the head of the table, Jay to my right, and Thena to my left, closest to Mom.

"*It's a pleasure to meet you, Emille. Your mother has told us so much about you. I'm Nicole, senior president of...*" she rattles off a Greek alphabet combination I don't recognize. I nod.

"*And I'm Bethany, senior president of....*" I examine Bethany and she identifies the Greek alphabet combo that she belongs to. Her hair is a lighter shade of blonde than Nicole's, and her eyes are a darker brown. She has more arched eyebrows, and her lips look too perfect to be real.

I turn my attention to the last girl.

"*I'm Lainey Daniels...*" My dad's last name was Daniels. That simple fact makes me take her in more closely.

Lainey's hair is strawberry blonde. She has pale, freckled skin, with wide seafoam blue eyes that are more prominent behind her mascara-coated eyelashes. "*So, Emille, tell us a little about yourself,*" Lainey softly suggests.

"*Uh, it's just Emi.*" They stare at me, waiting for me to say something else. "*I'm still in high school, almost done with my first semester. I'm from Louisiana but live in Connecticut and enjoy dystopian novels and fantasy movies. I have three older siblings—two older sisters and one older brother.*"

I wrote that down in one of my sketchbooks to say in case I ever got asked. The idea of thinking of something on the spot made me anxious.

"*And who's this?*" Bethany asks, her eyes focused on Jay, a coy smile on her face.

"James Averell, her boyfriend." Jay introduces himself with a dry smile on his face.

"Oh, and that's my sister, Thena. She goes to Yale," I say it with a touch of pride. They nod, obviously not as impressed as I am. "Oh! And Jay goes to Columbia." I smile at Jay, and he just grins.

"Emille, it's hard for freshmen to join a sorority and stay in a committed relationship. I'm sure James can attest to this. There's a lot of temptation: new people, parties. A lot of times, the last thing people are focusing on is their significant others that are miles away," Nicole says, her voice calm and casual as she puts some of the salad on her plate.

I won't be tempted to cheat on Jay. I know that. But has he been tempted to cheat on me? My mind goes back to that picture of him and that girl, the tall, beautiful girl he was smiling with.

"I think if it's important to someone, which it is for Emi and Jay, two people can stay in a committed relationship. It's not that hard of a concept. Don't sleep with someone who isn't your partner, and break up if you're not happy. But I'm having trouble putting together what that has to do with joining a sorority at Brown," Thena adds, grabbing her glass of water and taking a sip. Nicole's face heats in embarrassment.

"I agree with Thena. Her relationship status isn't really relevant to her potential sorority duties and service commitments." Lainy chimed in.

A group of waiters and waitresses set down the same meal before each of us: steak, potatoes, and asparagus. I take a bite of one of the asparagus.

"Now, let's talk about appearances. Sororities are a brand at the end of the day. When joining, there's a certain route and…changes you sometimes have to make, like wearing your sorority's colors and trying not to associate with other

sororities' colors as much. More importantly, you have to attract the sorority you want. Looking at you now, I can't tell what sorority you want." Bethany looks me up and down. Her eyes narrowed in on my sweater and my French braids. I know

I look like a child. I can feel Thena bristling beside me.

"*My understanding is that a sorority is only as valuable as the integrity and commitment of its membership. I didn't realize that these were just expensive fashion shows and petty popularity contests. Are there any more passive-aggressive insults you'd like to share?*" Heat was rolling off of Thena and this dinner was taking a dark turn.

"*They are not insulting her, Thena. They're preparing her for the process she'll go through next year. If she can't handle this, she shouldn't join a sorority,*" Mom interjected, her voice strained.

I can't look at her. I can't look at anyone. I just stare at the food.

"*Emi, do you have an idea of what you'll major in?*" Lainey asks, trying to redirect the conversation.

I shake my head.

"*She doesn't know yet, but she's interested in art and creative writing,*" Thena answers for me.

"*Have you seen the art studio on campus?*" Lainey asks.

My eyes widen, and Jay chuckles.

"*We went inside and looked around. It's nice. I think Em would like it. Did you like it Em?*"

"*I did. I thought all the natural light was good, and it was positioned in the middle of the campus. I liked it.*"

Lainey smiles.

"I'm a film major, so I've been inside the art studio a few times. Some of the creative writing teachers are really amazing. They're all progressive thinkers and super down to earth, so even if you weren't one hundred percent sure, they would accept you with open arms."

"That's good," I murmur, grabbing another piece of asparagus and forcing it down. My stomach feels heavy, and it's all tied in knots. *"So, do you guys' host lots of parties, or is that just another sorority stereotype?"* I try to joke.

Lainey laughs.

"We host a few. A lot of times, the fraternities or other students host them. Some are on campus, some off. It just depends, really." I nod. That sounds cool.

"And what are the academic requirements?" Thena asks. Lainey seems to be the only one still interested in the dinner.

"A 3.0 to join, and after that, we don't really watch, but don't tell anyone." Lainey winks at me, and I chuckle. I could do a 3.0 if I don't get distracted and don't allow myself to have any bad days… or weeks… or months.

"That's good to know. Very good to know. Well, I don't really have any other questions. Thank y'all for answering them. It was very considerate of you guys to come here and tell me all about your club— I mean sororities!"

"Thank you for inviting us. It was a pleasure to meet you, Emi," Lainey kindly says. She stands up, waves goodbye, and leaves.

Bethany and Nicole stand up and say goodbye, but no one responds. When the sound of their heels clicking quiet, I relax.

"Well, I think that went amazingly well," Mom says with full sarcasm.

I laugh in disbelief, and Thena scoffs.

After dinner, Jay and I walk around the small town off campus, looking for something sweet to eat. We found a small restaurant that serves pie and ice cream, so we got one slice of apple pie and two scoops of vanilla ice cream with whipped cream on the pie. We sit on the curb outside of a random large building. Brown is a beautiful campus, and I think anyone who goes here would be lucky.

"You know Allison thought about going here, but she hated the cold, so she went to Florida State University," I told him in a whisper. He looks at me, the pie still warm in my hands.

"You never talk about her."

I shrug.

"Don't have much to say."

That's a lie. There's always something to say. But sometimes, it's just not anything good.

"I think if you went here, you'd be happy."

"We'd never see each other," I argue, leaning against his arm. This day has felt so long. *"Brown and Columbia are three hours away."*

"I know, but if you wanted to go here, I'd be happy for you. You know that, right?"

I nod. I do know that. It's one of the few things I'm certain of.

"You'd be less than two hours from Thena, though."

"For one semester," I reminded him.

I take a bite of the apple pie. It's warm and sweet. The apples are soft enough that you don't have to chew them, but they are not mushy. It feels like baby food. The food has been good most of the day.

"*Tell me something. Tell me something real.*"

He doesn't even look at me; he looks straight ahead. The cold causes his cheeks to flush.

"*You're my favorite person Em. And you don't deserve to be told to change or that our relationship won't work. You don't deserve that shit.*"

"*I know,*" I whisper too quickly.

After a moment, he says. "*Tell me something real.*"

"*I don't want to go to college, not even a little bit.*"

It feels so good to say. It feels even better because I know it's true.

Jay smiles and kisses my forehead. "*I know, Em. It's okay. I promise you it's okay.*"

Chapter 30

Emillie Kate Van der Berg

Last day of finals. Ms. Han has us write a small reflection on our semester before we can have free time, and then we are free to go. Today is Friday, so it's a nice end to the week. Clara finished her reflection first, then Liv, and then me minutes later.

"How'd you do on your AP Bio Emi?" Clara asks me as Ms. Han collects my paper.

"Oh, pretty good. Our teacher wasn't there, so Bryce and I may have worked together."

Bryce finished his test, and without even asking, he slid his paper over and started working on something else. When our scores were in the next day, I hugged and kissed him on the cheek. He deserved it.

"*That's good,*" Clara adds, the whole exchange awkward. She's been trying to be nice to me, but it doesn't feel as natural as her mild annoyance. "*So, are you going to the gala tomorrow?*"

"*Yeah. My mom is forcing me to. Are you going?*"

"*Nope. Plans with my dad. One of his associates is coming back to town, so we're meeting him for dinner. I'm just glad my mom's not coming.*"

Liv chuckles. "*What'd she does now?*"

"*She announced to her group of Botox friends that I would be going to Dartmouth with Chet next fall.*"

"*Dartmouth with the boyfriend. What's so bad about that?*" Liv asks, hiding her smile.

"*I don't know, sounds a little predictable, doesn't it?*"

Liv raises an eyebrow. "*I thought that's what you wanted.*"

Clara shrugs, her eyes locked on Liv's. "*Maybe it is, maybe it isn't.*"

Liv smirks and looks away. Clara pushes her hair behind her shoulder and focuses on Liv. They play a game of looking between each other and then away, not saying anything, a steady tension slowly building. I'm just here to third-wheel witness it all like a creep. *How exciting.*

I arrive bright and early at Yates Hotel. It's a ten-minute drive from the Met and usually where we get ready. I go up to the penthouse. It's been taken over as our room to get ready. I knock twice on the door, and Bell opens it, her glasses on, her hair frizzy in a high ponytail, and she is dressed in thick sweatpants and a thin T-shirt.

"*I like your glasses,*" I compliment her, walking inside the room and throwing my satchel on one of the chairs.

"*Thank you! The sales lady said the frames were called Boston.*"

"They fit your face really well and go with your eyes."

I walk further into the room, and the smell of shampoo and perfume hits me. Thena sits with a plastic shower cap and black hair dye on her roots. I sit next to her, her skin paler than usual.

Ever since I was fourteen, Thena has been getting her hair touched up to be black. It was always as close as it could get, but now there's no denying it. She did it after I dyed mine black, and Mom said I looked horrible, so Thena did it and dared her to say something. Ever since then, Thena's hair has always been jet black. She gets it touched up once a year.

She has a textbook and notebook in her lap as she writes down notes. Her handwriting is neat and concise. It kind of resembles a font.

"Where's Mom?" I ask. Bell lounges on one of the lounge chairs, her UGGs swinging back and forth.

"Talking on the phone. You-know-who is running late as usual."

I nod and take out my phone. Jay dropped me off. He had to pick up his tux and find something to keep himself busy for ten hours.

Jay: About to go back to sleep. Do you need anything?

Me: No, I'll see you tonight.

The room door opens, and Mom comes in, dressed in long sleeve silk pajamas, her hair natural and pulled into a low ponytail. She doesn't wear her hair naturally often, most of the time having it straightened or in slick buns or ponytails. She barely gets in two steps before a knock at the door.

Mom turns around and opens the door. The smell of fresh Louisiana irises overwhelms the room. We all stand up and walk over. Marie LeFleur stands in all her five-foot glory, wearing a flowy green dress, thick colorful necklaces, and bangles moving up her frail arms. Her hands are wrinkled, but they're the only parts of her body that shows her age. She pushes her sunglasses up onto her head, her long white hair moving back with the push.

"Où est Faye? Est-elle toujours en retard?" Marie says with an annoyed look, her pale pink-painted lips pursed. *Where's Faye? Is she always late?*

Thena and Mom both laugh.

"Vous êtes en retard. Quarante minutes de retard," Thena tells her, a growing smile on her face, her dimples showing on either side. *You're late. Forty minutes late.*

Marie shrugs, pulling a suitcase behind her as she enters the hotel room. She sweeps over the room and chooses the large table Mom had brought up and the salon chair that was also set up before setting her stuff down.

The bathroom door opens, and Faye steps out. *I didn't even know she was in there.* She wears leggings and a simple crewneck, drying her hands off on a towel. She walks over to Thena and checks her hair. Faye has short red hair, the pieces barely reaching her chin, and a serious yet soft expression. She's pretty, very quiet, though.

"Ten more minutes."

"Aurore, prends un café et des croissants, je ne travaille pas le ventre vide. Vous ne me payez pas assez pour ça" Aurore, get some coffee and croissants. I don't work on an empty stomach. You don't pay me enough for that. Everyone laughs because we all know that's not true.

Marie lives in Louisiana, and Mom flies her up here a couple times a year just so we can all get our hair cut, straightened, and colored if we need to.

The food comes up a few minutes later, and we all sit around and sip coffee, no one eating much.

"Has everyone already showered this morning?" Mom asks, taking her ponytail out and running her hands through her wavy hair.

Bell and I both shake our heads. Marie sighs, standing up and taking everything out of her suitcase. Two blow dryers, three different straighteners in different sizes, rollers, a crimper, and a whole bag of sprays and serums.

I shower first, and when I come out, Bell is in long silk pajama pants, a white tank top, and her hair wet, her curls more pronounced. I wear the same thing, only a bigger T-shirt.

Another man is here, and I instantly recognize him: Stanford, Bell's favorite makeup artist and stylist. She hugs and kisses both of his cheeks. I think Stanford is one of the most *fabulous* people I've ever met. Of course, he's the one who told me to start saying the word "fabulous" to begin with. He wears a vest with slacks and a bright pink shirt underneath his vest, large round-framed yellow glasses. His face is round, and his thick brown hair falls perfectly.

"Emi! You look absolutely fabulous! Have you decided on a dress yet?" Stanford cries.

"There are options?" I ask, my surprise evident. He laughs and squeezes my arm.

"I already chose hers!" Mom yells over a blow dryer. I find her, and she's sitting in Marie's chair, Marie's eyes focusing on Mom's hair.

Stanford turns to me and rolls his eyes. I laugh. I sit down next to Bell and listen to Faye hum. She runs her fingers through Bell's hair and inspects it. Marie and Faye switch spots. For a second, Faye blow-dries Mom's hair.

"Je garde ce ton, puis je fais un traitement. The last thing we want is your hair getting thin." Marie softly tells Bell. *I'm keeping this tone and then doing a treatment.* Even when Marie speaks English, her voice is heavily accented.

"Trés bien," Bell whispers, winking at Marie.

"How often do you get your hair colored?" I ask Bell.

"I've had blonde hair for years now, so my natural hair has become a dirty blonde. Marie thinks it has something to do with my aura. I think she uses strong bleach. But I go once a season, except for summer. I let the sun do its thing since I'm outside so much."

"What about your curls?"

"When I'm not working, I keep it natural, but it's not as curly as it once was. I went from a 4a to a 3b, but now I try to take care of it."

I nod. I'm the only one out of all of us who wears her hair in its natural state most of the time. I don't like my hair when it's straight; I feel like someone else. I feel like an imposter at every gala as if I'm forcing myself to fit into a box that wasn't created for me or people like me. It's how I feel every year, without fail, even with Jay there.

"Emille, mon chérie, à ton tour! " Marie sing-songs from the bathroom. *Emille, my darling, your turn.* She waits for me by the bathroom sink, a wide knowing smile on her face. I sit in the chair in front of the sink and lean back. She begins washing, using my usual shampoo and her own unique mix. *"I see you've made an honest man out of James."*

My eyes widen, and I can feel my body flush. *"We're not married, just dating."*

"Ah, but marriage will come! Combien d'enfants? " How many kids?

"Marie!" I exclaim. *"I'm not even out of high school yet."*

"Yes, I know, but you can dream and talk about the future. You don't have to be so focused on the now that you forget about all the possibilities! What is the future if you have no dreams? You are not a cynical mon cherie," she scolds me.

I let her words sink in. She's right; Marie LeFleur usually is, and she knows it, so when she brushes through my hair, combing the conditioner through my strands, the bathroom is quiet.

"I want boys. Maybe two."

Marie smiles and nods. *"They'll be handsome. Beaux petits disables déchirants."* Handsome heartbreaking little devils. I laugh into a smile. *"What will you do for work?"*

"I don't know."

She nods, turning on the cold water and rinsing the conditioner from my hair. *"That is fine. You do not need to know everything."* She pulls me up, wrapping a towel around my hair. *"I cut your hair before I started washing."* I didn't hear or feel any scissors.

I sit in Marie's chair, the smell of smoke and heat-protecting spray hitting my nose. I let Mom do whatever she wants to me, my hair becoming bone straight and a light layer of makeup on my face. Thena and Bell look like they're both in their element. Talking and laughing, everyone's relaxed, even me.

When it's time for us to get dressed, Thena meets me in the bathroom before either of us slips on our gowns. She pulls it out of her handbag. *"Here."* She hands me a pair of Spanx, and I thank her. I asked her to secretly buy me some, and she agreed, promising not to tell anyone.

I get dressed in the bathroom with the door locked. I must suck in everything and do an awkward shimmy dance to get the Spanx on. Mom brought my dress into the bathroom while I hid my Spanx-clad body behind a large white towel. The long, silver-jeweled dress has thick straps and a conservative neckline, a slit on my right leg, tight on the top and loosening the further it goes down. It's beautiful, maybe a size too small, but beautiful. I slip it on and leave it unzipped, looking at myself in the mirror.

Too short.

Lose a couple pounds.

God, Emi, save some for everyone else.

A knock on the door drags me from my head.

"Come in." My voice is small, too small. Thena steps inside, a black ball gown on, strapless with an intricate jeweled design all around, her hair in old Hollywood curls. She looks beautiful, with soft red lips and a simple winged eyeliner.

"You look beautiful," I breathe. I spin around and look at Thena. Diamond earrings fall from her ears.

"Thank you, as do you."

I smile and turn back towards the mirror. *"Want me to zip you up?"* I nod. I suck in, and she zips. I run my hands down the dress, the pattern distracting me. I look at Thena in the mirror, her eyes piercing mine.

I take a deep breath. *"I'm ready."* She nods and opens the door for me, and we both leave.

Bell stands centered in the room. Her hair is piled into an updo, a few tendrils falling to frame her face. Her pastel blue tulle dress is simple with a u-shaped cut at the top, the dress ending mid calves, with white flowers on the top, and her white high heels showing. She catches me looking and spins, the dress spinning with her.

She resembles a fairy gumdrop princess. Her whole body and face are glowing, the dress complimenting her bronze skin.

"You look amazing!" I compliment her, and she bows and winks at me.

"So do you, Emi. Like a silver princess."

Mom comes from the separate bathroom, Rick appearing with her. When did he get here? Mom's dress is a deep red, a simple conservative gown that's tight against her thin frame.

She looks over all of us with a small smile. Rick smiles at us, walks over, hugs Marie, and waves at Faye.

"Belles filles! Aurore, ma voiture est là? J'ai un rendez-vous ce soir," Marie announces, her bags packed up. Stanford has disappeared, and Faye is fully dressed in her winter coat. *Beautiful girls!! Aurore, is my car here? I have a date tonight.*

I look for the small purse Mom told me to use. I walk through the bathroom, my heels slowing me down. I found the purse in the front living area on one of the couches. I put my phone, charger, ticket, and Chapstick inside.

"*Un rendez-vous! Avec qui? Marie, tu ne peux pas courir dans la ville à des heures étranges de la nuit,*" Mom stresses, her voice rushed and louder. *A date? With whom? Marie, you can't run around the city at strange hours of the night.*

Marie rolls her eyes, throwing her scarf around her neck. Marie sighs and plants her hands on her hips. "*Aurore, je suis trop vieille pour courir n'importe où. Je vous verrai bientôt. Au revoir mes amours!*" *Aurore, I'm too old to be running around anywhere. I will see you soon. Goodbye, my loves!*

We all say goodbye, and she and Faye leave, leaving all of us scattering around for our last-minute items.

Mom, Rick, and Bell go on the first elevator downstairs, and Thena and I on the next. Thena checks her hair and makeup in her small mirror in her clutch and combs through it. The chances of there being paparazzi and different photographers are high, which brings me a whole other wave of anxiety. People like seeing Rick Van der Berg and Aurore Van der Berg, and more people like seeing my sisters just as much, if not more.

Jay waits downstairs, his tie loosened in his suit; he's supposed to wear a tux, but of course, he didn't. He smiles and walks over to me. One of his rare full smiles, his pearly white teeth shining at me. His brown hair is slicked back, and the closer he gets, the more I can smell his cologne.

"*Wow,*" he breathes, pulling me into him. I almost trip because of my heels. "*You look beautiful, Em.*" He runs a hand through my hair and cups the back of my head. I lean forward, and he captures my lips in a kiss. It's soft and swift.

I smile against his lips and kiss him again. He seems happier today.

"*Come on,*" he urges.

A limo waits outside the hotel; Thena is already inside the car, waiting for us. Eric sits inside, a cup of brown liquor in his hand. He smiles at me, and I smile back. Eric's always scared me a little bit. I know how much he and Jay argue and how he speaks to Jay, so I've always kept my distance, much to Jay's agreement.

"*You two look very beautiful,*" Eric compliments, nodding at Thena and me. We both say thank you. "*Emi, I've heard you've finally put my son out of his misery. About time. I was getting tired of the moping and carrying on about his unattainable love.*"

Jay scoffs. "*I asked you for advice one time, and it was shit, by the way.*"

Eric smirks. "*She's dating you, isn't she?*" A beat of silence passes. "*Exactly. Emi, how'd you like Brown?*"

"*It was alright.*"

Eric nods. "*You didn't like it, did you? I don't blame you; I didn't care much for it either. You have time to figure all that shit out anyways. What do people call it now when you don't do anything after high school?*"

"*A gap year,*" Thena answers. She unlocks her phone and texts someone.

"I think one of those would be good for you. You could figure out what you want without wasting time at college," Eric explains. He throws back the rest of the liquor, refilling the cup afterward.

If only my mom was as agreeable about a gap year as Eric. But I know Eric would rip Jay apart if he took a gap year. He's only okay with the idea of a gap year when it comes to me and not so much his son.

We arrived at the event.

"Let me find my checkbook. That's all I'm here for," Eric mutters, rummaging through one of the compartments. *"Emi, go left, and you won't have to take any pictures."*

I nod.

"I'll meet you inside; I'll be by our table. Okay?" I leave before Jay can respond, following Eric's instructions. There is always an extra exit or entrance for staff, big celebrities, and anyone really.

I show the security guard my ticket and slip inside. The lighting is slightly dimmed, and the theme is more contemporary than historic. There's a lot of gold and more unknown paintings and art pieces. Servers walk by with trays of champagne, and I grab one. No one even bats an eye. I sip my drink, finding our table. I sit down and wait for everyone.

Jay comes in with an annoyed expression. I stand up and meet him halfway.

"What happened?"

"I just got badgered for not having any posts on Instagram. What the hell is wrong with people?"

This would be a good time to ask him about that girl. *"Speaking of Instagram..."*

"No, you shouldn't get one just because everyone else has one."

I narrow my eyes. *"I wasn't going to say that. I was actually going to ask you who someone was. I saw a picture of you with them on Bell's Instagram account one time and was curious."*

"Who?"

I pull out my phone and find the post. I show Jay the picture, and he glances at me.

"That's Alia. I had to work with her on one of my projects. She's in a few of my coding classes. She's cool. I think you'd like her."

"Oh, you guys are just friends?" I casually ask. I don't know how subtle I'm being, though. Jay stares at me for a beat, his eyes narrowed, and I can see wheels turning in his head. But, of course, I don't want the wheels to turn in his head. *"They have champagne!"*

"They always do." He stands up straight, causing me to look up. *"You thought I was with her?"*

"I wouldn't say it that way. I thought you liked her as more than a friend." He tenses. *"B-but not anymore. I know now,"* I stress, grabbing his arm and squeezing.

"I never liked her, Em. She's just a person in my class. There are a lot of those people. Most of them piss me off." He sounds frustrated, and when I grab his hand and squeeze it, some of it seems to release.

"I know," I breathe. He nods and takes a sip of my champagne. A server passes by, and Jay finishes my drink and grabs two new ones. *"Are you getting drunk tonight?"*

He chuckles. *"No, not in the mood. Are you?"*

"Maybe a little tipsy, nothing too bad." He nods and hands me his champagne. He reaches up to his collar and pulls his tie off, loosening it. He takes it off and puts it around my neck. As always, a giddy smile comes

to my face, which in turn, makes him smile. He gently pulls me by the tie and pulls me into him. His lips locked on mine, his tongue entering my mouth in one swift motion. I quietly moan, and he squeezes me tighter.

A throat clears, and we pull apart. I keep my eyes shut. *Please don't be Rick. Please don't be Rick.*

"*Damn*," Jay groans. I open one eye, and Bell and Tristan stand across from us. Tristan wears a smug smirk on his face, and Bell an embarrassed sheepish expression on hers. They're the same height when she wears heels. He's barely 5'11, and she's almost six feet with four-inch heels on.

"*Hi*," I say to Tristan. He looks at me and nods. Tristan Danvers, Bell's boyfriend of maybe two years? He's not ugly, but he's also not outstandingly handsome. Everything about him is average, which is kind of rude to say. Tristan's soft blonde hair is slicked back. He has normal brown eyes and an average-looking facial shape. But when he smiles, it's always a little...sinister. And not in a good way.

"*Hello, Emi*," he pauses and stares at Jay. "*Jay.*"

Jay rolls his eyes. "*The dramatic pause was not needed. Nice to see you, Danvers. Now bye.*" Jay pulls me back into him, and I elbow his ribs. He can't be rude to Bell's boyfriend. It makes Bell uncomfortable.

"*So, how are you doing? I heard you got a promotion!*" I beam, the excitement somewhat fake. Jay wraps an arm around my shoulder, and I wrap one around his waist.

Tristan looks at Bell, and a smile forms on his face. "*Yeah, a few months back. It's been good so far. So, how's high school been?*"

Something about the way he says high school is just a tad condescending, and I'm not the only one who noticed. Jay tenses.

"Uh, it's good. Same old same old."

Tristan nods. *"How's Columbia? Still making trouble for your dad to clean up?"* Tristan chuckles, and Bell forces the same. It sounds shaky and scratchy.

"No, but I bet I could make some right now, and I wouldn't even need him to clean it up. Tell me, how much do you think I would have to pay someone at this gala to make it look like you punched yourself in the face?" Jay smiles darkly.

"Oh my! Time to eat!" Bell cries. I drag Jay to our seats. He finishes another champagne, and I do the same.

"I hate that guy. How does your sister put up with him?"

I look at Tristan and Bell. They speak in a whisper to each other, Tristan's face flaming red.

"I don't know, but promise not to say any more mean things. Please?"

"Promise," Jay promises.

###

Our large round table sits somewhat in the middle of the large ballroom. The announcer begins, first thanking everyone for coming, then thanking the donors and saying whatever else he's supposed to say. Rick's honored as *"Man of the Year,"* and he goes up to give a speech. He thanks his team, his beautiful wife Aurore, and his amazing and beautiful daughters; in his words, not mine. By the time dinner is finished, I'm on my third glass, and I've reached the tipsy level.

Rick has completely ignored Tristan even when Tristan tries to add something to the conversation. Eric finds the whole thing amusing, and Mr. Yates tries and throws Tristan a few bones. Thena doesn't even try to hide her smile every time Tristan is ignored, and Bell looks ready to dance her way out of here.

Music starts playing from the speakers, and the dinner and ceremony have concluded.

"*Dance with me,*" Jay whispers over my lips, all the parents besides Eric gone. I smile, bite my lip, and nod.

As he pulls me onto the dance floor, I feel the night has just begun.

Chapter 31

Emille Kate Van der Berg

I feel so light and free that my feet have gone numb. Maybe it's the laughter, the happiness, or the champagne. Jay gave me his jacket to wear after the third song. Thena dances near us, Bell is in front of me, and Tristan is off somewhere.

I don't remember galas being this much fun. Maybe it was because I would try to keep a distance from Jay so he wouldn't know I had a crush on him or because I'd be too scared to drink champagne, so I was the only sober person in our group.

It starts to get louder in the ballroom. The music has quieted, but everyone's talking more. I stop moving and start feeling lightheaded like everything is catching up to me. The champagne has begun to weigh on me. Thena and Jay both stop and look at me.

"You, okay?" Jay asks. I nod, a smile still on my face.

More people are talking, and there's a growing buzz coming over the crowd. Bell turns around, and her eyes are wide. She looks stricken, like she just saw something she wasn't supposed to. Did someone cheat on their spouse in front of everyone? It's happened before. Jay had to leave because he couldn't stop laughing.

"*Thena,*" Bell says, then she stops. Bell's eyes fill with sympathy and pain.

"*What happened?*" Thena asks, taking a step forward. She looks so beautiful. Multiple people have complimented her tonight, and she's already had her photo taken at least a hundred times.

"*Oh shit,*" Jay breathes, a wide growing smile on his face like he's getting the biggest Christmas present ever. Thena must follow his eyesight because she freezes. I don't think she breathes.

I finally see what everyone's talking about. Walking towards us with a gorgeous smile on his face is none other than Nicolas Lincoln Yates IV, dressed in all black.

"*He looks like-*" Jay starts.

"*A dark knight,*" I whisper, so quiet no one can hear me.

"*Same old Nick,*" Jay finishes.

Nick approaches us, standing maybe three feet away. I think I've forgotten how tall he is. Everything about him is grand; it's hard to look away or not cower. His brown hair is slicked back, a small part on his left side. Hazel eyes that are always glazed like stone appear to almost glow the more you look at them, sharp cheekbones, and a nose that looks as if it was sculpted by the Greeks.

He looks over all of us, and his smile is present with each flicker.

His eyes land on Thena, and he looks her up and down, his eyes landing on hers. She doesn't look away from him. His eyes shift to me.

"*Still wearing Jay's clothes? Some things never change,*" he notes. Jay chuckles. He looks at Jay. "*You look good. Columbia fits you, not as good as Yale fits me.*" Jay laughs, and Nick chuckles. *Fit.* He doesn't go to Yale anymore.

Tristan joins our circle, and I can feel people watching us. Nick scans Tristan with mild disinterest. "*Isabel, congratulations on your success with your career,*" Nick tells her. Bell beams and says thank you.

Then all that's left is Thena. Nick moves over so he's right in front of her. He's taller than Jay, so even with her heels on, she still has to crane her neck to look up at him. His eyes seem to sparkle with something that wasn't there before.

"*Elénore.*" He says her name in a softer yet more forceful tone, like he really means it. "*You look beautiful. Did you design the earrings?*"

Thena doesn't say anything for a while. Her glare seems to intensify, but Nick's smile doesn't waver. Finally, someone clears their throat, trying to fill the silence, and Thena turns around and leaves people moving out of her path as she does so.

Nick chuckles. "*I'll catch up with you guys later.*" He smiles and then leaves, following after Thena. Everyone's eyes follow them as if they know they're witnessing something they'll be reading online later. Nick Yates is back.

Chapter 32

Emille Kate Van der Berg

Christmas is in four days; Nick has been back for four days. Four days and everything has slightly changed. Thena and Bell have both come home for the week since we all leave for the Hamptons the day after Christmas, not coming back until the Saturday before I return to school. Thena's been 'working' on stuff for college and sketching in her sketchbook, while Bell has been tagging along with Jay and me.

Mom and Rick have been working and getting stuff ready for the holidays. I texted Liv and asked her if she wanted to come over, but she was at her grandmother's house in New Jersey. Bell lays in bed with me, and we watch Christmas movies. I eat sugar cookies, and she nibbles on them, not eating much. When Jay comes over, he lies on the other side.

###

Every Christmas Eve, we have our annual Christmas party. I wear a red sweater dress with high white socks and a Santa hat. Bell wanted me to wear matching Santa hats with her. The party is in full swing when we come downstairs. Bell successfully convinced Rick to invite Tristan, so he's in attendance.

I go into the kitchen and pour myself some eggnog. Dad always liked making and eating cookies and cakes during the holidays. It was his favorite part. Eggnog with cinnamon, and sometimes when we weren't looking, he'd add a splash of bourbon to his. I sometimes wonder how he would feel about this, the galas, the parties, the catered food… all of it. How did we go from being surrounded by people that looked like us, sounded like us, laughed with us, to being outsiders expected to perform like marionettes? Always picture perfect. Show no weakness. Take no risks.

Christmas was his favorite holiday, his favorite time of the year; the music, the sweets, the clothes, and all the traditions. I think we all kept pretending to believe in Santa for him. Now he's gone, and so are the traditions.

"Em?" I look up, and Jay stands next to me, his hand on the small of my back. *"You, okay? You looked lost there for a second."*

"I'm fine." I refocus on him and smile at his ugly Christmas sweater. *"You look very handsome, Mr. Averell."*

"Thank you. I'm glad you think so. My girlfriend bought me this sweater for my birthday in May." His smirk is devilish and dry.

"She sounds like she plans ahead. What else is your girlfriend like?" I turn around and lean against the counter.

"Oh, she's gorgeous, shy, sweet, a little awkward, and has one dimple in her left cheek. You want to hear how wonderful she is?" He looks up and checks who's next to us. I nod; his eyes darken and heat as he stares at me. "She has a smile that could light up any room no matter how dark, a heart too sweet and pure, and an ass so perfect I'll never get enough." His hands move down further, and he squeezes, causing me to rise on my tippy toes.

"My innocent ears are ruined," I breathe against his lips as he leans down.

"I've said worse to you," he huskily whispers, kissing my neck.

"I don't remember. Have you?"

Jay leans into my ear and whispers a thought so raw and uninhibited that my eyes widen in exhilarating surprise, and I have to laugh. Jay is very flirty tonight, and I love it. "Don't worry, Em. We'll try that soon."

I nod and kiss his lips, wrapping my arms around his neck. I like the way I feel in his arms, like everything will be alright, and I don't have to think about anything. He squeezes me against him, and I breathe in his cologne and soap. I love the way he smells. I love how he holds me without question.

"Is Nick here?" I ask him. I know he and Nick have been spending time together catching up.

Jay shakes his head. "No, he's coming later. He had to do something for dad."

Makes sense. I think Nick's been pulled in every direction since he got back. Spending time with his family, Jay, catching up on work, etc.

There's already been an article in the paper about him returning. They labeled him a *"Golden Boy."* Jay told me Nick found the article amusing and kind of flattering. Thena burned the paper in the kitchen sink setting off the smoke detectors. Bell documented the monumental meltdown on her iPhone. *"When we watch this later, I'm sure it will be funny,"* she whispered to Thena as we hugged her.

"Christmas lovers!" Bell yells, coming into the kitchen. I pull a little bit away from Jay, my arms still wrapped around his neck and his hands sliding up from my buttocks to a more respectable resting place. Bell has a Polaroid camera in her hand. *"Smile, you two! And no hiding!"*

I smile a full and genuine smile, and I can feel Jay do the same. Bell snaps a photo, the flash temporarily causing my eyes to have a dark spot.

"Okay, now come out of the kitchen. No more groping and kissing," Bell *sternly* tells us. We pull apart. I grab his hand and lace my fingers through his, leading him to the living room.

"Are you coming over tomorrow?" I ask. He sits up straight on the couch, and I sit turned towards him, my whole body angled at him.

"I don't know. We might, but probably not since we're leaving for the Hamptons the morning after." I nod in understanding and survey the room.

Gifts are already under the tree, always the same wrapping paper and a different color bow for everyone. I got Rick a tie, Mom a cashmere scarf—Thena picked it out—Bell a dress I found in a boutique before therapy with Liv one day, and a piece called *"Thena, the Lion"* I made in art class. I think I did pretty good. Jay and I don't usually exchange Christmas gifts, and I told him it didn't have to change now that we're dating.

Thena comes downstairs an hour into the party. I smile and walk over to her. She wears a dark green dress, black stilettos, and silver jewelry. Her hair is straight and pulled half up in a black hair clip. Always perfect.

I hugged her. I haven't hugged her in a few days. I can tell she's still trying to adjust to Nick returning, but I think she's struggling more than she's letting on. He left without saying goodbye. Now he's back without warning.

"How are you?" I ask her, my voice quiet so no one can hear us. Then, I noticed a glass of champagne in her hand.

She sighs, her posture straightening. "I'm feeling better, just annoyed that everyone's tiptoeing around me. I'm twenty, not five. Yes, Nicolas is back. But, no, I'm not going to turn to ash and blow away. That was an interesting example considering her baby arsonist moment with the paper, but I don't say anything. I just nod in understanding.

"Have you talked to him?"

"Yes, he's still annoyingly cocky and has a response to everything. Sometimes it's like I just want him to acknowledge how much he hurt me, but no! He has to respond and interject. I can't stand him; I simply can't stand him, Emi. He had the audacity to ask me to go with him to the new diamond exhibit in a few weeks at the Met."

"Are you going?"

"Of course, I'm going. I don't have my own invitation and I need to see what other designers are doing and get more inspiration from old classics they will pull from the archive. I'd be a fool not to go. But it's just one more way that magnifies that even when I hate him, I need him to get things done. And I think he enjoys that. It's like he gets off on..."

"Helping you?" I try to finish her thought.

"Upstaging me!" She finishes, cutting her eyes at me. *"Why are there so many people here? Ugh! I just wanted to watch movies and eat cookies, but instead, I have to converse with Rick's business partners while he and Mom make out in his office."* Aside from us, the Yateses, Eric, and Jay, everyone in the house today here is invited for business purposes.

"You saw them make out?" I ask making a gagging noise/

She sips her champagne. *"They're probably doing more now; it was heating up when I walked past."* I grimace, and Thena nods in agreement. I know she and Rick are married, but I try not to think about them doing anything - you know. Sexual. *Blech.*

"Are you having fun?" I ask her. She surveys the party a few times and then focuses on me.

"Ask me when I'm on my fourth glass, and I'll answer."

"What glass are you on now?"

"Second," she answers, walking past me and entering the kitchen.

Five minutes later, Nick arrives. He and Thena spend time talking in the kitchen in hushed tense tones before mingling with everyone. Thena never makes it to her fourth glass or her third, her champagne flute long forgotten in the kitchen. Once the clock hits midnight, Jay pulls me towards him, and I sink into him. His lips meet mine in a firm kiss.

"Merry Christmas, Em." My eyes swept the room for Rick. I'm still not trying to get in trouble. I wonder what my dad would think of Jay. A wave of sadness washes over me. I can't stop it. I try to ignore it, forcing a smile and kissing him back.

"Merry Christmas, Jay," I whisper, close my eyes, and lean against his chest. Even now, with everything I can ask for right in my grasp, the sadness is threatening to swallow me.

Chapter 33

Emille Kate Van der Berg

The entire Van der Berg family gathers in the sitting room, opening gifts, the smell of coffee and candy canes thick in the air. Rick sits with a cup of coffee, wearing Christmas pajamas, while Mom sits beside him, overseeing everything.

There's always a game of finding the pickle in the tree to decide who picks first. I look for it, and so do Thena and Bell. I won one time when I was fifteen, the first Christmas without Allison. I never tried to look before; I always let Allison or someone else find it. No one has even mentioned Allison this year. Or dad.

"Found it!" Bell cheers from the other side of the tree. I sigh, sit down, and wait for her to open her gift. She opens a large box from Mom. It's a large thick gray fluffy blanket. It looks expensive and warm enough for the Arctic. Bell smothers her face in it. When she comes up, her smile is even brighter. "Thank you!"

Mom nods, sipping Rick's coffee. He doesn't even seem phased. *"Since you'll be traveling more, you can bring it with you on planes."*

Very thoughtful. I go next, then Thena. Mom got me a large acid gray custom hoodie with a list of superheroes on the back and a mocking jay over the heart on the front. The two things don't necessarily go together, but I love them. I can tell she got it customized, and by the stitching, it wasn't cheap. I want to put it on now, but I just thank her and put it in the box.

We do this until it's time for us, my sisters and I, to give gifts to everyone else. Thena goes first, giving Bell and me matching blue aster bracelets. I take a moment to admire it. A thin gold chain sits four blue aster flower charms on it. It's beautiful, dainty, clean, and has that new jewelry smoothness.

"*You designed these?*" I ask her, clasping mine on. It fits me perfectly, not too flashy but still enough to catch the eye.

Thena nods.

"*Yes, they took a month and some change, but I think it's worth it. Blue asters represent sisterhood.*"

She takes my wrist and flips one of the flowers over. Our initials are on it: *EIE*.

"*It's beautiful, Thena! It might be one of the most beautiful bracelets I've ever seen,*" Bell tells her, her eyes glassy.

Thena shrugs. "*It's alright, but I'm glad you guys like it.*" We both hug her; she pats our backs.

"*I love you guys,*" Bell whispers to us. "*Okay, now my gift!*" Bell reaches behind me and grabs two medium-sized boxes, floral wrapping strings tied over both.

Thena opens hers first, neatly peeling the paper and taking the box top off. It's a set of silk slate gray pajamas with Thena's initials stitched on the right breast pocket.

"I know Nick got you a pair a few years ago, but now you have them in gray, and you can wear them whenever you want. And if you don't like them, there's another gift under the tree."

Thena sighs, a small smile touching her lips. *"I love them."*

"Are you sure?"

"Yes!" Thena says with conviction. Bell's smile turns triumphant, and she can't help but squeal and shove my gift in my lap.

I tear the paper like a child and pull out a brown chest box. I open it, and inside is a fresh collection of paintbrushes and small bottles of acrylic paint in all the primary, secondary, and tertiary colors. I run my finger along the new soft brushes. They're not stiff or crusty; they're white, fluffy, and clean.

"Thank you," I breathe, looking up from them and at Bell. *"They're perfect."*

She nods like it's no big deal.

"Of course, I know you haven't gotten any in a while, so I figured, why not."

Before I can thank her again, Mom interrupts. *"Emi, your turn."*

I get up and hand everyone their gifts. Rick opens his first, and he chuckles. Every year, I get him a new piece of clothing, always with the word *"Berg"* embroidered, a play on what I first thought his last name was when I was young.

He stands up, leans in, and kisses my forehead. I hug him like I've always done and smile against his chest, always dimming it a little when we pull apart. He winks at me and sits back down. Mom opens hers next and smiles when she feels the soft nude scarf.

"This feels amazing! Thank you!"

"Of course," I responded, sending a grateful smile to Thena.

Bell opens hers next. It's the biggest box, and I had to have the boutique wrap it for me. They even sprayed a floral scent on it. She unties the box and takes out the paper, showing a white dress with lilacs and roses all over it, the sleeves short and puffy, while the front is a slight V-neck. It should only go to her mid-thighs, maybe a little longer. I showed the lady a picture of Bell from her Instagram, and the lady returned with the dress.

"You like it?" She has a few dresses like this, but this one is covered in flowers.

"I love it!" she proclaims. My smile is so full it's taking up my whole face. She hugs me and kisses both my cheeks.

The last person is Thena, and I have to go to my bedroom to get her gift. When I come downstairs, I yell for her to close her eyes. I peek into the room, and when I see her eyes closed, I walk in and set the lion down in front of her. The lion is maybe twelve inches high and another seven or so wide. It takes up a good amount of space. She opens her eyes and focuses on the lion.

"You're fierce and strong, like a lion, and always willing to protect me. When I made it in art class, I was thinking of you, and I knew it was yours. It belongs to you," I ramble. Her eyes keep flitting between me and the lion. *"Say something. Please?"*

She stares at the lion, and when her eyes meet mine, they're glassy and shine with so many emotions. So much love, mine begin to well. I didn't imagine her liking it this much. I figured she'd force a smile, tell me she likes it, and hide it somewhere in her house until enough time passed, and then she could throw it away.

"*Thank you! Thank you so much,*" Thena whispers to me as I hug her, smelling her signature Chanel perfume. Something tells me she needed the lion more than I did.

After the gifts are done, we clean up the wrapping paper and head to the kitchen for breakfast. Always cinnamon rolls, eggs, and breakfast meat. I sneak out to the backyard, a light layer of snow on the ground. I pull my phone from my pocket and dial his number.

"*Hey, this is Matt. Sorry I couldn't catch your call. Leave a message, and I'll get back to you.*" After a muffled "*bye,*" his laugh echoes until the machine beeps for me to start my message. I clear my throat.

"*Hey, Dad. I just wanted to call and say Merry Christmas, and I really miss you. I'm sorry I didn't call on Thanksgiving. I was just caught up in stuff.*" My voice cracks, but I keep going. "*I just wanted to say I miss and love you. Bye.*"

I hang up and pocket my phone, wiping the lone tear that fell. The weight of not calling Dad on Thanksgiving seems a little lighter now. I close my eyes, trying to be okay. It seems harder today. I feel myself actively trying to keep it together.

As I walk inside, I can still hear his voice and the muffled "*bye*" he let Bell and I yell when he created that recording. I sit down and eat breakfast with everyone, his laugh still echoing in my mind. It was deep and quiet, never taking up too much space and always making me laugh.

I know everyone would think I was losing it if they knew I still called and left messages. So, this will remain my secret.

I miss my dad. I think he'd want me to miss Alison too, so I miss them both for him.

Chapter 34

Emille Kate Van der Berg

The snow is thick and bright white. No one has walked through it. It's completely untouched for miles. The large traditional Hampton house comes into view, Bell's Jeep crunches through the freshly salted driveway. I can see the white columns of the house and the chairs on the front porch. Thena, Jay, and I ride with Bell; Thena in the front seat, and me and Jay in the backseat. Thena's bag couldn't fit in the trunk, so it's in Rick and Mom's car. Their black Range Rover is packed with their bags, any extra bags, and a few bags of groceries.

Bell parks the car in front of one of the garages. She turns her car off, and we all get out. It seems so much colder up here than it did in Connecticut. The air is crisp and frozen. I walk towards the house, Thena's heeled boots click against the cobblestone leading to the front door. Jay's cheeks are a soft pink, and he keeps his hands in his pocket with a pissed-off look on his face.

"*Open the door already,*" he tells no one in particular.

"*No, let's keep it closed so you can freeze,*" Thena snaps back. She and Jay argued in the car about where we should stop. Thena wanted to find a Chipotle, and Jay wanted McDonald's, so we got Chick-Fil-A. Bell ate a kale salad and sipped a lemonade. I felt awful for her, especially since it was my idea.

"*Emi would freeze, too. Probably before me. You want to kill me that bad?*"

Bell opens the door.

"*She doesn't want to kill us,*" I tell Jay. He grabs my hand and squeezes it. His hand is much warmer than mine, but he doesn't pull away. "*Right, Thena?*" I raise an eyebrow at her.

"*I don't want to kill the two of you, James,*" she deadpans. Jay smirks and pulls me further into the house. I know of no reason why they argue so much, and I don't think either of them knows.

I look around the large house. I love it here. The stairs are by the front door, and the banister leads through most of the downstairs area. The living room is right by the kitchen. The kitchen is bright white with a seafoam blue backsplash. Our rooms are hidden upstairs. I untangle my hands from Jay's and go find my room. It has a view of the ocean and the pool in the backyard.

I open my room door and walk in. There is a queen size bed with white sheets with blue patterned designs, a dresser, a desk, and two side tables on either side of the bed. It's simple and bare, but after a night of me sleeping here, I know it will feel like home again. I drop my backpack on the chair in front of the desk, slide my old boots off, and climb into bed, shedding my socks before getting under the covers.

I fall asleep before I can hear anyone's footsteps up the stairs. It's a rare deep sleep—no dreams, no nightmares—but I don't wake up feeling any more refreshed than before.

Soft kisses on my neck wake me all the way up, followed by a loud gagging sound. I open my eyes, and Thena stands across from me with her arms crossed and a firm glare directed at something behind me. "*Gross,*" she says, rolling her eyes. It takes me a second, but I know who it is before I even turn around. Jay kisses my neck again before sitting up and sighing.

"*Yes, Athena?*" I smile at the nickname Jay calls her that when she's upset.

"*You were supposed to wake her up ten minutes ago, not kiss her neck and grope her.*"

I raise my eyebrows, glancing up at Jay. He's very handsome from this angle, but I think it's because he's handsome from all angles.

"*I wasn't groping her. And Emi likes being kissed on the neck while waking up.*"

I duck under my sheets, embarrassment rising. Jay laughs and pulls the sheets down. Everyone can see me curled in a fetal position.

"*Get out,*" Thena says flatly. Jay kisses me on the forehead and then leaves, closing the door behind him. Once the door shuts, I sit up and look around the room. It's dark outside.

"*What time is it?*"

"*Seven,*" Thena answers, sitting beside me on my bed, her heels hanging off.

"*Where's Bell?*"

Thena shrugs. "*On the phone with Tristan, I think.*"

"Oh. What are they talking about?" I ask while yawning. I didn't see him at the Christmas party.

Thena looks momentarily disgusted, but then she composes herself and answers. *"I don't know. She doesn't tell me,"* she says, a hint of hurt swimming in her eyes.

"But you guys see each other all the time. You both live in the city."

"I see you more than I see Bell, but it's okay. She's busy with him and modeling. She loves her job, and I love…what I have going on. As long as she's happy, I'll be okay."

I realize then that Thena is lonely. She stays in that big house all by herself. Everything she does, she does by herself. All this time I have imagined myself to be the sister that's left out, but she is feeling it too. If that's the case, I'm happy that Nick has returned. Even if he has a lot of apologizing to do, now that he is back, he won't let her be alone.

He couldn't. They were inseparable before. And they will be again.

Rick waits with bags of takeout downstairs. Eric emerges from the bathroom, his usual bored and firm scowl on his face. He sits next to Rick and begins talking about something while Rick takes all the food out of the bag. He got Chinese from town. As soon as everyone's seated, we all start digging in.

I take small bites of the fried rice and lo-mein noodles, listening to Eric and Rick talk about a business trip they're trying to decide on taking. It's in a few weeks, and Eric wants to go, but Rick seems disinterested.

Eric sighs, his irritation becoming more evident. *"Fine! We'll let Yates be the deciding factor."* Thena has a smile on her face, and Bell looks out the window, lost in her own thoughts.

"What are you kids going to do these next few days?" Eric asks, his eyes focused on his food. *"Besides, of course, make out in public spaces,"* he finishes, with a dry smile and his eyes locked on Jay and me. Rick tenses and glares at Jay and Eric.

"Don't embarrass Emi," Rick warns.

Eric holds his hands up in a defensive manner. *"Emi shouldn't be the one embarrassed. We all know who initiates it. I was surprised the Christmas party didn't escalate even further,"* chirped, oblivious to Emi's discomfort. *People saw that?*

"I'm pretty sure every other couple that still liked each other at that party was making out," Thena refutes, shooting a pointed look at Rick, who chuckles awkwardly and rubs the back of his neck.

"Really? Still?" Eric asks in disbelief, staring at Rick.

Oh great! That's not Mom and Rick's first time making out at a party.

Rick shrugs. *"What can I say? I'm in love with my wife."* His eyes twinkle as he winks at Eric, who groans and scowls at the rest of his food.

Rick's always loved Mom, even when she was in love with someone else, even when she married someone else, and even when she had four kids with that same man. Rick has always been in the picture. I sometimes want to ask him about Dad and understand how he saw him. I know it isn't my business, but I don't want Rick to be uncomfortable.

All three Yatese's arrive early on New Year's Eve. Mrs. Yates smiles harder than she has in years. Everything about her seems brighter, and Mr. Yates seems to feed off that brightness. The Nick effects. She shivers when she walks into the living room, wearing a long cream trench coat with white flowy pants, a tight white shirt, and a cream-striped scarf. She smiles and greets everyone, setting her handbag on the couch.

Mr. Yates wears his usual business suit and enters after her, carrying a large brown bag filled with what sounds like bottles. Nick joins us a second later, and Thena groans audibly, only making Nick's smile stretch wider. Thena stands up and walks towards Nick, who looks at her expectantly.

"There's no more room for you here," she coolly tells him. He smiles down at her and nods.

"Don't worry. I drove one of my father's cars so I'll be able to go to our estate. It's only a few houses down."

Nick smirks and walks past her, going to speak to Jay, who's outside on the phone with someone, even though it's too cold to be standing out there. Nick sounded so posh that I couldn't help but grin at his words.

Bell and I curl up on the couch, blankets wrapped around us as we watch a Harry Potter marathon. We hadn't moved all morning. Rick brought us food while yelling at someone for calling him while he was spending time with his family, and Eric made popcorn, claiming he wanted some and would give us his leftovers. Instead, he gave us a full bag and didn't take one bite.

"So, what's the plan? Now that Yates and Mary have graced us with their presence?" Eric asks, sipping some of his coke. He sits on the other couch, acting like he's not watching the marathon.

"*Rory's making cornbread, corn pudding, chicken tenders, fries, and maybe some extra stuff, and I think we'll go down to the club closer to midnight,*" Rick answers from the kitchen.

The same country club we visited in Connecticut has another location up here. It's where Rick and Eric usually hang out when we're here during the summer. Therefore, we all spend a lot of time there. Some of us enjoy it more than others. I could live without forced, stuffy country evenings.

Eric stands up, looking excited for the first time since we arrived. "*Thank God.*" He claps his hands and goes into the kitchen.

Somewhere between the end of *Prisoner of Azkaban* and the beginning of *Goblet of Fire,* I fall asleep leaning against Bell's legs, the smell of her cherry blossom perfume and freshly cleaned blankets welcoming me into a deeper sleep. I wake to a soft shake. I slowly open my eyes, and Thena stands across from me dressed in a tight brown dress that extends past her knees. She's wearing makeup, her hair sweeps down her back, the ends perfectly bumped.

"*I tried to wake you for dinner, but Mom said to leave you alone. It's time to go to the club. Do you want me to wait for you to get ready?*" she quietly asks. I sit up and look around. No one else is downstairs. I missed dinner

I shake my head. "*I'll be fine,*" I croak, my voice thick with sleep.

She nods.

"*Okay. Jay's upstairs, and Bell is riding with me, so she'll leave her car here for you guys to use. Everyone else has already left.*" I nod.

"*You ready?*" Nick asks from the hallway. He smiles at me, and I wave. He's dressed in an all-black suit, no tie.

Thena doesn't answer him and just walks by. Nick chuckles and follows her. She's clearly going to make him work for it this time. I head upstairs to my bathroom and brush my teeth. I splash my face with water and try to wake up a little more. Jay sits on my bed; he looks me up and down, taking in my oversized T-shirt, his legs on display in his black shorts.

"*You seem more tired than normal,*" Jay notes as I walk further into the room, stopping when I'm a few feet away from him.

"*I guess finals finally caught up to me,*" I lied. I don't know why I've been sleeping so much, but I know it's not because of my finals. The only one I studied for was Calculus, and I barely squeaked out a C.

"*Mmh,*" Jay mutters. He opens his legs wider, his feet resting on the floor, and reaches for me, pulling me towards him. His body radiates heat.

I put one of my hands on his shoulder and squeezed. I don't know if he still works out like he did in school, but he's still toned, the muscles on his stomach defined. He has a small beauty mark on his shoulder. I've always noticed it. Seeing James Averell topless is not a new sight. He's never been ashamed of his body. But now that we are official, seeing him this way feels intoxicating.

His hands caress the back of my thighs and rise, moving my shirt up with his movements. He pulls me toward him until I'm in his lap. Our mouths are inches away, my breathing is labored like I've run a flight of stairs, and I try to slow it down to match his. He's perfectly calm, his eyes trained on me, studying my quickened breathing and flushing face. "*You know I've been thinking about our first time ever since we got here,*" he admits, raking his eyes over my face.

"Really?" I squeak. He doesn't laugh. He just squeezes my hip reassuringly and nods as he continues. He grabs me by my hips and rolls me over so I'm lying flat on my back against the bed, and he's above me. His arms cage me on either side of my head.

"Do you want to do this?"

I nod. He chuckles, leans down, and kisses my nose, causing my eyelids to flutter in anticipation.

"Yes."

"Seriously Em," he says with concern etched across his face. *"If this is too much we can go slower. I just. I just want to be with you. Whatever that looks like. I know I haven't always been the best version of myself for you…"* He lets his voice trail off, not bothering to finish the thought.

I know what he is asking me but I feel ready. I'm not scared, not even a little bit. On the contrary, I feel the most awake and present I've felt this whole trip. Being close to him pushes the fog away, even if only for a little while. And this is not the partying drinking Jay from the chaotic high school days. This Jay is fully here with me just as I am with him. So, I nod again. More enthusiastically this time, and add a *"please."*

He doesn't say anything. And for a moment I think maybe he's changed his mind. Instead, he just captures my lips in a firm kiss that softens as I respond. I run my hands up his chest, then grab his neck, pulling him closer. I want more—I want to feel every emotion and every rush tenfold. I wish I always felt this alive.

One of his hands reaches for my shorts, and I lift my hips so he knows that I am ready for him. His touch is slow and deliberate. I lift my head up and capture his lips in a kiss. His lips are warm and strong. We kiss while he strums me like a guitar, getting me closer and closer to the edge. I break the kiss, a low moan escaping me before I can stop it, and his lips find my neck. My senses are so overwhelmed that I have shed my self-consciousness. I am putty in his hands and he is molding me into the kind of girl that arches her back and presses into her boyfriend's hand without thinking about how it makes her look or sound. He kisses the soft hollow at the base of my throat, a sensation so intimate that a tear springs to my eye. I sweep it away quickly before he notices.

He doesn't relent, not when I squeeze his arm or moan his name in a plea.

"*Jay, please,*" I cry into his shoulder.

"*Em,*" he growls into my neck, the feeling sending another wave of pleasure through me. I'm close to the edge, and Jay can tell. My whole body tightens, and then a current pull me over, and I let go. He begins to undress. I grab his hands before he can reach for mine, and stops.

"*W-wait.*"

"*What's wrong? Did I hurt you?*" Concern is etched all over his face, his hazel eyes trailing over me.

I shake my head. "*No, I'm not hurt. I just want to turn off the lights.*"

He freezes, and his jaw tightens. "*Why?*"

I don't answer, but he doesn't let me escape. Instead, he stares at me, repeating the question. I can feel embarrassment rise.

"*I've gained weight since the last time,*" I say briskly, clearing my throat and keeping my eyes locked on his chest, "*it's more noticeable in some places. Places like...*"

"*Your ass?*"

I nod, a smile threatening to show.

"And my stomach. It's not flat, and I have stretch marks. I don't want you to see."

"Em, I know what you look like." His voice is husky and thick. *"I've been watching you for years. I know your insecurities and the things you think make you less beautiful. But they don't. I don't care about any of that. I love you the way you are."*

He leans forward and kisses me again, taking me by surprise. I'm still hoping the light bulbs explode and plunge us into darkness, but they don't. Instead, Jay moves to lift my shirt over my head, I let him.

He looks me up and down, and smiles at me.

"You're beautiful, Em. You know that, right?"

When it comes out of his mouth, every word sounds genuine. I nod because it's hard not to believe him.

I lean all the way back and look up at him, tears still pooling in my eyes. I don't think anyone will ever compare to him. Not in any way. He'll always be my best friend, my first love, my first everything, and the one who makes me feel the most beautiful.

Jay leans forward and starts working that slow magic he makes with his hands. It's tamer than usual, almost timid. I need more.

"More," I whisper.

He is more than happy to oblige and before I know it, my body responds on its own. In just seconds I can feel him pressed against me and a cold panic arrest my senses. My eyes fly open.

"Condom," I choke out. I feel like I should've said that earlier. I can't afford to make that kind of mistake. Not now, when my life is finally starting to make sense.

"Already on," He whispers.

I hold onto him and try to remain in my body. I don't want to float away; I don't want the sadness to creep in. I don't want to think about anything other than being here and feeling like we share one body. He leans down, and kisses me, and I realize that he had been holding back, but he's not holding back anymore. An involuntary gasp escapes me and Jay stills for a second, watching me. I know he is just making sure that I'm okay and that tenderness causes tears to sting at the back of my eyelids. I don't want to tell him that I am escaping into him. That the reason I love these moments most, is because they feel so eerily similar to the bottom of that pool - his weight pinning me down. His ragged breathing muffled all other sounds. Loving him is like drowning. I press my face into his neck as a sensation starts to build deep in my center. I feel my whole-body tense before a feeling so intense that I let loose a loud moan. Jay groans my name, and my senses return. He lays down next to me, both of us catching our breaths. When I catch my breath, I prop myself on my elbow.

"Did you like it?"

He laughs, his whole body shaking with laughter.

"It was pretty amazing to me. Did you like it?"

I shrug and pause, pretending to think about it for a second.

"It was alright," I lied, biting back a smile.

He doesn't believe me for a second.

The mindless glow begins to wear off a bit when I notice how much of my body is uncovered. I grab the blankets, quickly covering myself before running into the bathroom and locking the door. Without the blinding haze of emotions, my insecurities had come flooding back in as quickly as they left.

Jay waits for me downstairs, dressed in all black, his hair messy and damp. We leave and head to the country club. It's only fifteen minutes away. We used to bike when we were younger and had no one to take us, but like everything else that was easy, I guess we've outgrown that. A valet approaches us, taking the keys from Jay and wishing him a happy New Year.

Jay holds onto my hand, and we walk inside. The sounds of music, laughter, and voices increase in volume as we walk toward the ballroom. Thena approaches us, and I wave and smile at her.

"It's almost ten. What were you two doing?"

"Uh-" I didn't think of a lie to tell her.

"Em was still tired, so we napped," Jay smoothly lies, taking another bite of the chicken parmesan sandwich we, both got. I groan silently at the poorly fabricated lie.

"You didn't!" Thena exclaims as my eyes widen. Were we that obvious? Suddenly I feel exposed.

"Yes, we did. And no, we don't want to talk about it," Jay retorts. He flashes her a dry smile and shrugs when I elbow him in the ribs. Neither one of them are being quiet, and I'm growing increasingly *terrified* that someone would overhear them.

Nick, never known for his good timing, joins the group and looks between us with a knowing smile stretching across his lips. He tucks his hands into his pocket.

"I'm surprised you two even came. Jay's been desperate to get some alone time with you, Emi. I'm surprised you two didn't just stay home."

"Thought about it." He lowers his head and whispers to me, *"But you locked the bathroom door."* My whole body heats.

"How's the food?" I ask them, trying to change the subject.

"The fish was cold and dry, but the pasta was good, especially the Alfredo." There's alfredo pasta!? I make a mental note to swing back to the buffet for that.

###

Bell joins our group a little while later. She wiggled her eyebrows at me, and it was clear Thena told her what Jay and I did. My embarrassment deepens, but I shove it down and lock it away.

"Where were you?" I ask her, hugging her side.

"Mom wanted to ask me about my traveling schedule for the New Year and if Tristan was going on any trips with me."

"Is he?"

"God, no." She looks almost relieved but catches herself before I have a chance to press or question her. *"I might be going to London for a week or two though."*

My eyes widened.

"Why are you going out to London?"

"Shooting a campaign for Parka. It's a luxury winter coat brand. It's becoming really big, and they're taking a chance on hiring me instead of some big-name model. I'm really excited!"

I'm excited for her. I know nothing about fashion but try to ask a question that shows interest and support.

"Did the Parka brand start in London?"

She shakes her head.

"*No, it started in Aspen, Colorado. I've been following them for a while. I wear their coats when I go skiing. I was just surprised they reached out to me. If you want, you can come visit me.*"

The idea of being around Bell and all her perfect-bodied modeling friends kind of freaks me out, so I just smile and tell her maybe.

As midnight approaches, we all get a glass of champagne and move closer to the large windows to see the fireworks.

"*One minute!*" someone yells over the speakers.

"*Follow me,*" Nick says. We all do, and he leads us to a private balcony. Thena pulls Bell between her and Nick, and I stand beside Jay. We can still hear the countdown.

"*Are you excited for the New Year?*" Jay asks me.

"*Kind of. Are you?*"

"*I think it'll be a good one. Never know.*"

The countdown starts. It's cold, and when I look up, snow falls. Light flurries hit my face and get lost in my hair. Plumes of my breath float up into the chilly night air.

"*Five!*" The people inside yell.

Jay pulls me closer, one of his hands going to my waist.

"*Four!*"

His eyes meet mine. They're warm and soft and bright. Hope fills them. Hope for this year and maybe even for our relationship.

"*Three!*"

I can hear Bell's nervous laughter and sneak a peek towards her. Thena and Nick are facing off, and she's right in the middle of it.

"*Two!*"

"*You know I love you, right?*" Jay whispers, happiness twinkling in his eyes. My heart squeezes.

"*One!*"

He bends down, and his lips meet mine as everyone screams, "*Happy New Year!*" His kiss is firm, warming up my whole face. I smile halfway into his kiss. Then, he pulls away, a matching smile on his face.

"*Happy New Year, Em.*"

"*Happy New Year, Jay.*" I squeeze his hand and turn around to see Bell kiss Thena's forehead while Nick looks on, thwarted and frustrated... We all bring our glasses to toast, each taking a big swig of the alcohol.

I tell my sisters and Nick, "*Happy New Year,*" and Bell gathers us around for a picture so we can send it to Alexander.

This year Allison would have been twenty-seven.

Dad would have been fifty.

This year I'll graduate high school.

I'll move out of my parents' house.

Everything is changing, but around me all of the Hamptons it feels are celebrating, and I need to look like I am too.

I bury all my bad thoughts and memories and focus on the one change that feels good, Jay.

January

Chapter 35

Emille Kate Van der Berg

Back in Connecticut, I'm the first one at the country club. The waiters and waitresses freeze when they see me enter the room. One approaches me with a nervous look. He stops a few feet from me with his arms crossed behind his back.

"M-Miss Van der Berg, we didn't expect you this early. Will your family be arriving early as well?"

I shake my head. *"No, it's just me. I had nothing else to do, so I just came on over. Is that okay? I can wait downstairs."* I move towards the door, but he starts shaking his head and waving me in.

"You're completely fine. If you want, you can sit at the bar."

"Thanks." I sit at the bar and drink a virgin mimosa.

I didn't wake up earlier than usual. I never went to sleep last night

We returned from the Hamptons earlier yesterday. Jay went home to his dad's house. His absence was like being unplugged from a power source. I tried to distract myself. After I unpacked, I started on some of the reading my Comparative Government teacher assigned. Before I knew it, the sun had risen. I grabbed the golf cart from the garage and rode to the country club.

I talk to the barback, asking him questions while he prepares for the breakfast regulars. He's from a few towns over and works here during the year to help pay for some of his school expenses. I like him; he's funny and lighthearted.

"I'm Emi, by the way."

"Ryan. It's nice to meet you, Emi."

"You too. Now tell me more about your puppy."

He tells me all about his boxer named Sheriff, who farts in her sleep and likes to cuddle. He even sneaks and shows me a picture of the dog.

Ryan and I talk until a guest arrives. He grabs a crate of glasses, and goes to the back, tossing a farewell smile over his shoulder. I hear someone clear their throat close to me and jump to find Eric standing beside me in a tailored navy-blue suit and a crisp white button-up shirt.

"God, I must still be drunk if you're the first one here," Eric says, his voice hoarse. The bartender sets a drink in front of him, and Eric takes a sip.

"When did you get here? My son is probably already at your house."

"Oh, I'll tell him I'm already here."

"How did you get here, Emi?" Eric sets his drink down. He already asked that, didn't he?

"*I took one of the carts.*" I look at Eric quizzically. He seems...off.

Eric stares at me like he's looking at me more in-depth for the first time. Of course, I've known him for a while, but all our conversations and interactions have been brief.

"*Aren't you usually late just like I am?*" I ask.

He chuckles. "*When you have to get up to pee more than three times a night, you just decide to stay up at some point.*"

The door opens before he can say anything else, and someone comes in. I look over my shoulder and see Jay and my parents enter. Jay doesn't look happy, not at all. "*How'd you get here?*" Jay asks. "*Your parents didn't even know you left.*" His eyebrows are pulled together, and his jaw is clenched like he's trying to control everything he says.

"*Golf cart,*" Eric answers for me, his words a little slurred. Then, he finishes his drink, stands up, and walks away to talk to Rick.

"*Why didn't you tell anyone?*" Jay presses me.

"*Yeah, I didn't want to wait for Rick or Mom to wake up, and I didn't want to wake you. I thought I texted you,*" I explain, briefly glancing over his shoulder to see who just walked in. Bell and Thena!

"*Hey!*" I yell. They both look at me and Bell waves. Thena just briskly walks over.

"*Hello!*" Bell cries. She waves at me and Jay, who doesn't wave back. He's still in a sour mood.

"*Brunch!*" Mom calls, and we all head over and take our seats.

As we sit at the table, the Yateses arrive, Nick leading them. Nick unbuttons his jacket and walks to his empty awaiting seat next to Thena.

"*Bell, I read up on the company you told me about, and they're doing very well. This next campaign will be big. Congratulations, by the way.*" Nick says as he sits down. The corners of his lips curve upward as he nods at Bell.

"*Thank you! This is the shoot that will be in Bellucci's Top Three. It's just a matter of if my pictures will be chosen.*"

"*How many models are they choosing from?*" Nick asks. He picks up his glass of water and takes a small sip before setting it back down.

"*There will be ten of us coming, only two or three in the spread.*" I can hear the slight nervousness in her voice, but she doesn't add anything.

"*And when do you fly out?*"

"*I leave January 16th and come back on the 23rd.*"

"*If you want, you can use my jet; that way, you don't have to waste any time at the airport,*" Nick suggests, leaning back in his chair.

"*I don't*"

"*Just think about it. Let me know, and I'll have my assistant arrange it.*"

"*You've been back for less than a month, yet you already have an assistant?*" Thena asks flatly.

Nick shrugs his shoulders, his whole body at ease. "*Comes with the territory. Have you found any additional help for Elénore Co.?*"

Thena stiffens. "*No.*" she snaps. "*I refuse to hire anyone when I don't have a retail space or any solid investors. It'd be a waste of their time and resources, especially since the chance of me having to let them go in three or four months would be selfishly high.*"

"*It's a smart business move and a good move in general. I was just curious because I hadn't heard anything,*" Nick defends, his lips thinning and eyes focused on Thena. Her cheeks are flushed, and she looks ready to argue with anyone. Fortunately, Nick drops the subject.

The rest of the brunch passes in a breeze. I talk to Bell about my biology partner Bryce and how my creative writing teacher always wears cardigans and starts class with a riddle. I never get any of them. Halfway through breakfast, Jay turns to me.

"*Are you okay?*" he straight up asks, his eyes filled with concern and his hand cupping my knee.

"*Yeah, I'm fine. Better than fine, I promise. Are you okay?*"

"*I'm good. I was just worried about you.*"

I peck him on the lips. "*Don't be. I just didn't want to wake you, I promise. Nothing more, nothing less.*" I peck him on the lips again for good measure, and he smiles when he stares at me. His smile is so infectious that I feel it all over.

I lean forward and kiss his nose like he's done to me so many times. There's this lightness in my chest and brain, and I want this to last forever. It's so addicting. It feels like happiness but heavier and more potent.

Chapter 36

Emille Kate Van der Berg

"What are you doing tonight?" I ask Liv as soon as she sits down in art.

"Going to chill at Rex's place."

"Can I come?"

"You want to hang out with a drug dealer on a Monday night?" Liv asks slowly. I didn't know Rex was a drug dealer, but I still nod. He was friendly and kind of funny. So why wouldn't I want to spend time with him?

"How about we go see a movie?"

"What movie are we seeing?" Clara asks as she sits down, her hair in a high ponytail.

"Let's see the new West Side Story," Liv suggests. I look at the board where Ms. Han has a PowerPoint projected. It's the first day of a new semester. One more semester, and then I'm done.

246

Clara's cheeks flush, and she fails to hide her smile. "*I guess we can see that one.*"

After Ms. Han gives her presentation, I take out my sketchbook and begin sketching. I tell Liv about my Christmas break, and Clara stares at me when I glance up from my sketchbook. She doesn't say anything, just stares for a beat longer, then turns her attention to her phone.

"*I think I'm going to hang out with Jay tonight, so you and Clara can spend time together at the movie.*"

Liv nods. "*Cool. She's been talking about seeing that movie since she saw that preview.*"

They're kind of a cute couple. I like them together. I wonder if they'll ever publicly announce they're together or if Clara will ever break up with her boyfriend. Relationships are complicated, but I think there's a lot of hope for them, more than I'd tell either one of them.

Before I know it, I'm in the car and on the way to Jay's apartment. The whole car ride passes in a blink. One minute I'm leaving school, and the next, I'm outside his building.

I slip past his security, which is a problem, and get on the elevator. I knock on his door, and he opens it, a toothbrush in his mouth and his hair damp. He freezes in surprise and then takes his toothbrush out of his mouth.

"*Em?* "

"*Jay?* " I retort, pushing into his apartment. It's still bare, but it smells more like him. Plus, he got a TV. It sits on a little bookshelf thing, something Rachel definitely picked out.

"*Did you make bacon?* " Jay can't cook anything, really.

"Rachel came over and made breakfast with the groceries she brought over. She also cleaned my bathroom. I told her not to, but she started speaking French, and I just gave up arguing with her."

Rachel treats Jay like her own child. She practically raised him since he was a baby, and when he graduated last year, I caught her crying in the pantry. She shoved a box of cookies and a bottle of champagne in my hand and made me swear not to tell anyone. I didn't. Now she washes his laundry and makes him enough meals to feed ten people.

"When did she leave?"

He goes to the bathroom and finishes brushing his teeth. *"About an hour ago. She had to go back to my dad's for some shit. She invited me to lunch tomorrow."*

"Are you going?"

He peeks out from the bathroom door and looks at me like I'm crazy. *"When have I ever stood Rachel up?"* Very true. *"I'm trying to get her to go out and start dating so she can back off."*

I sit on the edge of his bed and swing my feet back and forth.

"What are you doing here? I'm surprised to see you."

This is unlike me. I've never surprised Jay since he's been away at college. He always comes and sees me, or we meet somewhere and go from there. I've never shown up here at his apartment. I didn't even really think about it; it started as just an idea, but then I just did it without telling anyone.

"I wanted to see you. Do you have somewhere to go?"

He shakes his head. *"I'm in for the night. I planned to eat the lasagna Rachel made and watch whatever was on."* He walks into his kitchen, takes the lasagna out of the fridge, and turns his oven on. *"You in?"*

"Of course."

We eat lasagna and watch *The Matrix*; Jay knows most of the words. When his favorite part comes on, he turns the television up, and a childlike smile overtakes him. When we finish the first two movies in the series, Jay gets ready to take me home, but I'm not ready to leave. I feel too awake. But I don't say anything. Instead, I sit next to him in his pickup truck, listening to old Drake songs. I preferred Drake before he started doing dancing challenges involving moving cars, though I was a big fan of his album, *Views*.

"I'll see you later, Em." Before I reach for the door handle, he grabs my hand and pulls me back. I almost fell over at the movement. Our lips collide in a sensual slow kiss, one of his hands on my neck. When we pull apart, he smirks. *"You know I love you, right?"*

A giggle escapes me. "I *know*."

I get out of the car, and when I'm standing, one hand on the pickup truck door, I say, *"You know I love you too, right?"*

"I know, Em."

Chapter 37

James Averell

Rachel picked an Indian restaurant located on the corner of 76th and 9th. The place smells like garlic naan—of which I've already eaten three pieces—and bleach from the recently cleaned table. Rachel always picks where we go out for lunch or dinner. I just show up ten minutes early so she doesn't have to wait alone. Rachel has always been kind of shy and reserved. For most of my childhood, she didn't leave the house unless it was for me, to go grocery shopping, or to do other chores. One time, I straight up asked her if she was ever going to date again, and she blushed so hard I thought she would faint and said, *"You keep me busy enough. I'm happy here."* She left my room after that.

Rachel walks in right on time, standing by the door frantically looking around the restaurant, her body tight and stiff. She always looks like this, like she's terrified I'm not here.

I hold my hand up, putting her out of her misery, and her eyes focus on mine. She smiles and walks over. She's wearing the coat I got her three years ago. I had to sneak it into her room so she wouldn't get mad at me for buying it. Underneath the coat, she wears a simple purple sweater and blue jeans. Her curly auburn hair is down, pushed back by a thin headband.

Rachel's smile is wide and kind of crooked, but it's always been like that for as long as I can remember.

"*How are you?*" she asks.

"*Good. You just saw me yesterday,*" I reminded her. "*How are you? Dating anyone?*"

Her cheeks tint. "*I'm fine. Your father keeps me busy, and you just got on your feet.*"

A waitress comes over and takes our order. I let Rachel order for both of us. I know she likes it; it reminds her of when I was little and we would go out to eat. Once the waitress leaves, I focus on what she just said. I pray to God that the only way my father keeps her "*busy*" is with house chores and *nothing* else.

"*Rachel, I don't need you to focus on me and the shit I'm dealing with. You need to go out there and live your life. You're thirty-seven. You should be having fun, not worried about me having toilet paper, clean laundry, or meals for the week. I'll be fine.*" Though my reasons for wanting Rachel might not be entirely pure, they're still valid.

Her baby blue eyes well with tears, and when she blinks, they run down her cheeks. She wipes her cheeks.

"You know why I always come over to help you with stuff and invite you to lunch?" She glances out the window and then refocuses on me. *"Because I don't want you to forget about me. I've helped raise you, and the idea of you forgetting about me…"* she sniffles. *"It hurts."* she finishes. *"I'm sorry. I know you hate tears."*

She wipes her eyes and cheeks with her napkin and tries to bite back her tears, but I can tell she's been holding this in for a while.

"Remember when my mom left, and I came crying to you? And you just let me cry in your arms until I stopped? I wasn't crying because she left. I was crying because I was so scared you were going to. I thought you wouldn't want to be in a house with just me and my dad." I clear my throat. *"But you stayed and pretty much raised me. So, there's no way I could ever forget about you. You're the closest thing to a mom I've ever had and probably will ever have."*

She smiles, and her eyes continue to fill with tears.

"So yeah, you're pretty much stuck with me," I tell her, flashing a dry smile. The waiter sets our food down. *"Now, can we eat, or do you want another heart-to-heart?"*

She laughs, her head tipping back. When her laughter fades, she serves me chicken tikka masala with white rice. She hands me a piece of garlic naan and then serves herself. I wait until she has fixed her plate before I begin to eat.

"How's Emi?"

"She's good. She seems happier than she's been in a while."

Ever since the Hamptons, she's been smiling more, flirting more, and laughing more. She doesn't get lost in her thoughts as much, and when she showed up the other day, I was so surprised I thought she was a figment of my imagination.

"That's good. I'm happy she's happy. You know, she should come to lunch with us next time."

I shrug. *"Maybe."* She wouldn't mind, but she would be too nervous to eat a meal with Rachel. *"You know she's shy, so she might be quiet."*

"That's fine. I like Emi; she's sweet and doesn't let you get away with anything. Plus, she always compliments my baking." She eats a spoonful of chicken and rice. *"Are you going to Aspen with your father? He leaves Thursday."*

I didn't even know he was going on a trip. *"Nope, got classes."*

"Oh, he invited me," she casually says.

"Are you going? You don't have to."

"I think I might go. I like the snow, and uh… your dad might need help, you know." She frantically scans the room instead of looking at me.

"Don't sleep with him." I'm deadpan.

Her eyes widen, and she looks around to see if anyone has heard me. Maybe they did. I don't care.

"I-I'm not. Your father is a very attractive man, b-but he doesn't see me like that," she stutters. *"I mean, he hired me when I was eighteen! We've known each other for eighteen years, and nothing has ever happened, so I don't think that will change,"* she rambles, her face flushing.

"Okay, Rachel. Relax. Eat your naan and breathe."

She's squeamish about sex. It's kind of entertaining, especially since she's the one who gave me the sex talk. She sat me down in my bedroom with a stern look and told me everything, using only technical terms. It was like anatomy 101. Halfway through, my dad came in and sat next to me, and when he tried to make jokes, Rachel glared at him and told him to stop.

All my dad said was, "*Don't get anyone pregnant. If she says no, she means it, so stop. Never go in without a condom, and always bring your own. The last thing I need is a grandchild and a gold digger daughter-in-law.*"

Rachel rephrased what he said in a more child-friendly way. "*Always practice safe sex for yourself and your partner's safety and always bring your own protection because you never know other's true intentions. And remember, consent is key; no means no.*" Then she nodded and left the room, hiding in her bedroom until the morning.

She never brought up sex again. I liked teasing her about it, though.

"*It's okay, I'm teasing,*" I say. "*I know you are an actual woman and my dad isn't a total troll.*"

She blushes.

"*Have you been active recently?*" she asks concern etched across her face.

I smirk and nod.

"*New Year's Eve.*"

She has to look away. It's strange the way adults want you to grow up but also stay a child forever.

After a moment of quiet, she places her spoon down. "*I miss you at home.*"

"*I miss you too, but I'm happy.*"

"*I know, but promise to come by the house more. I just want you to be okay. I need you to be okay. I can help you restock your food and send your laundry out. I just want to look you in the eye more than once a month and make sure you're okay.*"

I squeeze her hand, and she smiles weakly.

I didn't know it meant that much to her for me to be okay. For her to be there for me, I might've lied earlier. Rachel isn't the closest thing I have to a mom. She's it.

Chapter 38

Emille Kate Van der Berg

"*So, Emi, how was your New Year?*" Dr. Young asks me, her legs crossed with a genuine smile.

"*It was nice. My family and I went to the Hamptons, and we went to the country club on New Year's Eve for a party. It was fun. I'm pretty sure Jay and I told each other, 'I love you.' Well, in a way.*"

"*That's amazing, Emi! I'm very happy for you.*"

"*Thank you. How was your New Year?*"

"*It was good. My husband and I drove to the beach in New Jersey and watched the fireworks and ate tacos and enchiladas.*"

"*That sounds nice.*"

"*My dad didn't care much for tacos, but he loved enchiladas. He used to make them at least once a week and then grilled steak and cut it up for us so we could have steak tacos. The food was delicious, and every year for our birthday, he made us our favorite food and some variations of dessert.*"

"Did Allison like his food?"

I laugh.

"She didn't like it much. Every year for her birthday, she'd become crueler, to the point where she'd leave before dinner. It hurt Dad's feelings a lot, but he never got mad at her. She just went to her mom's or out with her friends."

"How was your mom's relationship with Allison?"

"Allison hated her, and Mom kept trying to take care of her and be there for her after Dad died. And even before Dad died, she tried to help." I tilt my head to one side, lost in a memory. *"I remember when I was eight, Allison came into the bathroom and weighed herself. Then she made me weigh myself. I didn't want to make her mad, so I did, but when she saw the number, she kept laughing and telling me to do everyone a favor and eat less and run more. I never thought anything bad about my weight or body until then. I cried for hours, and when Thena found me, she told me I was beautiful no matter what number the scale showed and that Allison was a shallow bitch. It was one of the few times I've heard Thena curse. We were all a little scared of Allison, though."*

Dr. Young sits up straighter.

"Emi, are you okay? You're more talkative than normal and usually don't bring up Allison or your dad. Has something happened? Are you okay?"

"I'm fine. I just felt like talking. I don't know why. Do you want to hear about something else?"

"You can talk to me about anything you want," she reassures me, her voice soft.

"Okay, well, Rick has always been in my life. Always. I can't really remember a time when he wasn't there. But when I turned nine, he started being there more. Like every day. And my parents divorced six months before my dad died. At the start of the year, I turned ten. And then Rick and my mom married a month before my 11th birthday, but we didn't come to Connecticut until my birthday."

It's one of my most memorable birthdays.

"When my parents divorced, it didn't change much, you know? Like I saw Dad, and I saw Mom, but Dad had been working more and traveling, so Rick bought a house, and we stayed there with Mom while Rick flew back and forth from Connecticut to Louisiana. It was all kind of quick. I don't know." Even thinking about it now, it's all a little fuzzy. "I remember the day before my dad died, Bell, Thena, Alexander, and I all spent time together. We were all at his house. It was one of the best days ever. Then he died, and there were no more weekends at Dad's. It was just Mom and Rick."

"Do you ever miss your Dad?"

"Sometimes," I lie. "But everyone misses people."

"How did you feel when your parents divorced?"

I have to think about it. They divorced almost eight years ago.

"I think I was okay because we still saw both of them, and if I ever missed him, I just called Dad and told him that. I think Allison handled it the worst. She resented Rick, so she got in more trouble. And when she got in trouble, she'd take it out on...."

I paused for a moment and decided to not finish that sentence.

"We started going on more trips, too. Rick took us on vacation and made random little traditions. The Thanksgiving 5k, spring break trips, New Year in the Hamptons, stuff like that."

"Did you have traditions with your dad besides the birthday cakes?"

"Saturday morning runs, cinnamon rolls on Christmas, and summer bike rides. Sometimes we'd just sit outside on the porch. He'd be silent, thinking about something, and I'd just be there keeping him company. I didn't want him to feel alone, you know?"

I look at the clock, and the hour has passed. *"Bye, Dr. Young. It was good seeing you."*

I leave before she can say anything.

When I get outside, I realize I just told her most of my life story, and I didn't even mean to. A slight panic passes through me, but I force it away, making it roll off.

Chapter 39

Emille Kate Van der Berg

Bell sends a picture of the London Bridge and another of her in her hotel room in a big white bathrobe.

Bell: Hellooo from London!!

Thena: How was your flight? Was there turbulence?

Bell: Smooth as butter. I'll call you both tonight. I have a movie to go to.

Thena. Bye, be safe.

Me: Have fun!!!

Last night, Thena and I drove Bell to the airport instead of having Tuesday night sister dinner. After we dropped Bell off, Thena took me home, and we talked about her plan to do an online shop for Elénore Co. Her goal is for the shop to be open for a few hours online, and then she'll close it and handle all the orders. I told her it was a good idea, and if she needed help, I would be happy to.

This morning, I went on a run around my neighborhood, came home, made breakfast, and got ready for school. I slept maybe two hours last night when I got home from school, did homework and art, and talked to Jay while he wrote a paper.

After school, Liv and I hang out. She drives us to a small, one-story house across the train tracks. A beat-up black pickup truck was in the driveway, and a swing set on the side of the house that looked twenty years old was covered in snow. We walked through the snow to the front door. Liv knocked while I held the screen door open. Rex opened the door, dressed in a plain white T-shirt and faded blue jeans. He stares at us briefly until he turns around, leaving the door open.

I follow Liv inside, taking in the cozy home. There's a coffee table covered in textbooks and papers with a few sippy cups and pacifiers on the stacks. Rex sits on the couch, cutting up food on a small pink plastic plate.

"*Ella!*" Rex yells. Tiny footsteps smack against the floor before a small toddler comes into view wearing a pink dress and a crown tangled in her brown hair. Rex stands up and walks towards a small table by a window, a stuffed animal in one chair and the other empty. "*Here. Eat. Your mama will be back soon.*"

She sits down and smiles as he places the plate before her. Then, he goes into the kitchen, returning a second later with a sippy cup he hands her.

"*Fanks,*" she says, her mouth full.

He smirks and comes back to the living room.

"*How have you been, Emi?*"

I smile. *"Pretty good. I finished one of my art pieces in one week and even passed one of my Comparative Government quizzes. I didn't even have to cheat! So, life's been pretty good. How have you been?"*

Rex stares at me, then turns to look at Liv.

"Why did you bring her manic ass here? Why are you here?" He thinks I'm manic?

"She's not manic; she just had coffee before she came here," Liv lies.

I didn't have any coffee before I came here. Maybe I've been too energetic recently? I should probably work out tonight or do some more writing or drawing, something to throw all my energy into for a little while.

Rex and Liv go talk in the back for a bit, and when they come back, Liv looks happier, and Rex looks a little angry. I tell him bye, and he nods and gives me a side hug, telling me to be safe and take care of myself.

"Was that girl his daughter?" I ask Liv when we leave.

"No, it's his sister's kid. She goes to college, and he watches her during the day. It's just them two, I'm pretty sure. When she graduates, they're moving, I think?" Liv tells me as she pulls out of his driveway and leaves the narrow one-way street.

After she drops me off, I go upstairs and decide to spend some time doing homework, then I work out and start a new painting, and before I know it, it's midnight. My phone rings. It's a three-way FaceTime. I answer, and Bell and Thena's faces come into view. Thena is in her pajamas, her phone propped up on her bed. Her laptop is in her lap, and her hair is piled on top of her head, with no makeup on her face. Bell sits in a yellow chair, a painting on the wall behind her. It looks like she's in a bathroom.

"I'm sorry that it's so late. I have to be at the shoot at 8:30, but it'd be too late there for you guys."

"*You're fine; I was finishing some homework anyway,*" Thena quickly reassures her. "*Emi, what were you doing?*"

"*Homework. I started a new painting, and I worked out earlier.*"

"*You need to make sure you're sleeping, it's good you're doing your homework, but you also need to make sure you're taking care of yourself. Mom told me she's been hearing you up at all hours of the morning and late into the night.*"

"*I'm fine. I promise I've just been feeling more productive lately. That's all.*" I divert the subject. "*Bell, have you met the people yet?*"

She shakes her head.

"*I met them today. I'm nervous but really excited. I just want this to go well, and if I don't get picked, that's okay. I'm just happy to be invited.*"

"*I'm happy for you. But I know you'll get it. You're super beautiful and super-duper kind. You're kind of the best,*" I genuinely tell her, meaning it more than anything. I believe Bell will get the spot. She might not have an extensive resume, and Mom might've been the reason she got most of her previous jobs, but she has a spark that makes you want to keep looking at her.

"*Thank you!*" she beams. She sets her phone down on the bathroom sink and brushes her damp hair, the strands curly with a few pieces of wavy ones mixed in. She's focused on her reflection in the mirror. "*They said to come as naturally as possible, so I think I will go like this.*" She stands up and shows us what she's wearing: a thin T-shirt, no bra, low-rise white sweatpants, and her hair down.

"*I like it. How do you think they'll do your hair and makeup?*" Thena asks.

"Probably up in an extravagant style or an intricate braid design, full face of makeup and airbrushed to make it look like I'm the perfect human." She throws her arms up dramatically.

"Wait! Why are you up two hours early if the shoot isn't until eight? How far is it?" I interject. I feel like she told me, but I don't remember.

"Jet lag," she quickly answers, detangling pieces of her hair. *"And it's fifteen minutes away."*

"What are you going to do after the shoot?" Thena asks.

Bell leans forward on her elbows and smiles at us. *"Go to the best Italian restaurant in London and eat a big bowl of pasta with warm garlic bread and alba truffle sprinkled on top."* She wistfully sighs.

"Send lots of pictures when you get it!" I exclaim.

We talk for another hour or so until Bell insists, she needs to shower again to condition her hair and let her socks warm up in the dryer she asked housekeeping to use. Thena agrees, saying I need to get up for school in a little bit and to get a few hours of sleep.

I don't fall asleep for a few hours, though. I finish the drawing I started and get ready, sitting outside on the icy step waiting for Liv to pull up. She rolls down her window and smiles at me when she sees me. I get into her car, and she hands me a burrito.

Chapter 40

February

Chapter 40

Emillie Kate Van der Berg

If I wait any longer for Rick and Mom to be ready, I might pass out. I haven't slept in 48 hours, and if I sit down for a second longer, I'll crash. So hopefully, after brunch, I'll sleep for a few hours, then get up and eat whatever Lucille makes.

"I'll meet y'all there!!" I shout upstairs, my voice ringing through the foyer and up through the banister. I leave the house dressed in thick black plain jeans and a thick black sweater, with black Doc Martens, my jacket wrapped around me, and a beanie flattening my hair.

I start the walk to the country club, passing by people walking their dogs and babies in strollers, all with contemptuous looks on their faces. When I make it past the second street outside my neighborhood, I see a matte black Audi pull up next to me. I keep walking. *Please don't kidnap me.* I don't think that'll be good for anyone.

The window rolls down. I can hear it because of the snow and ice falling to the ground. *"Emi,"* Nick says as I look at him, *"you want a ride?"*

He phrases it like a question, but we both know I'm getting in. He rolls up the window when I get in, his car seat's warm, and the whole thing smells new. I've never had a problem with the *"new car smell,"* but I prefer cars that smell like their owners or something else.

"How are you?" he asks, pulling back into the lane.

"I'm good. You?"

"I've been good. Trying to talk to Thena, and, well, you can imagine how well that's going." He says it with a smirk like the whole thing is a challenge that he's been mentally preparing himself for, for years.

"How's Jay been?" he asks me.

"You haven't talked to him?"

"I have, just probably not as much as you have. Does he like Columbia?"

"Yeah, he does. He likes his roommate and respects his teachers, which is all he cares about. Did he tell you about his apartment?"

Nick smiles and nods.

"In Hell's kitchen. He told me about it. He bought it a week after he started Columbia, and Rachel helped him pick it out. I'm pretty sure she handled everything, and he just signed the papers."

"Jay bought that place?" I ask incredulously.

"Yes. He has a private parking lot in the building and complete privacy on his floor, except for a few houses down." Nick pulls into the country club, and the valet jogs over to take his keys. Nick smiles as he hands them off.

We walked inside together. Everyone besides the parents waits by the bar. Thena walks towards Nick, and they go speak in a corner. Bell sits across from Jay, both drinking orange juice. Jay opens his arms and hugs me, and I lean into him, his hands wrapping around my waist. He stands up, and I take a step back.

"How long have you been back?" I ask Bell as we walk towards the table. I don't remember her telling me she made it back.

"A week now. Tristan and I drove down to Boston and spent a few days in the city. It was really nice. He got me fresh flowers, we ate dessert, and we went out to my favorite place," Bell gushes, her face lit up with a smile.

"I'm so happy for you! That sounds amazing! Did you guys make up for lost time? " I wiggle my eyebrows to let her know what I'm talking about, and she laughs.

"Yes, we did. I love your all-black outfit, by the way."

"Thank you." We sat down. *"Did you like the heads of the company? "*

I don't know their names, and I don't know if she told me them. Maybe she did.

"Dakota and Jamie Phoenix." She supplies their names, and I nod, trying to remember them. *"They're really cool. They're twins from Santa Reese."*

Santa Reese is a small beach town in California right on the coast. I've never been, but I think Nick and Jay have gone together a few years ago. Jay said it was a popular spot for surfers and children of nepotism.

"Boy and girl? " I question, grabbing a buttered croissant from the tray.

Bell nods.

"I saw the girl in passing, but she was really sweet and chill. She kind of reminded me of you." Bell winks at me and starts to butter up a piece of toast. I remember Thena mentioning she doesn't have another shoot for a while. She told her manager she wanted a break.

"Nick gave you a ride?" Jay whispers. I look at him and nod, taking a generous bite of the warm croissant. *"He picked you up?"*

I think about it for a second. *"In a way, yes."* I yawn, wiping my eyes with the back of my hand. Now that I've had warm food and have been sitting down, my exhaustion suddenly hit me like a bulldozer. I know I won't be able to fight it, but it's the good kind of sleep that'll knock me out for a few hours, not the deep sleep that leads to everything going wrong. Then, when I wake up, I'll be as good as new. I kind of resent people who don't understand the different types of sleep or who do understand but don't care.

"How's therapy been?" Thena asks me, and I pause. She usually doesn't ask me about therapy at brunch in front of everyone. Of course, they all know I go, but it's never a topic of discussion.

"Good," I lied. I haven't been since I spilled my guts to Dr. Young. I've missed two appointments and don't plan to go after my birthday either. Jay must sense my unease because he changes the subject, bringing up one of his professors.

I grab a cup of coffee, not adding any cream, and take a generous sip. I just need it to keep me up for a bit longer, then I can sleep Sunday away and wake up sometime tonight. I don't participate in the rest of breakfast; Jay sends me concerned glances, but I just smile, squeeze his hand, and distract him with kisses. I don't think Mom or Rick ever pay attention to us during brunch; it's why I kiss Jay so much. I know they're not looking; they're caught up with their friends and their own personal shit, and I like it better like that. Better than them hovering.

Jay offers to take me home, and when I climb into his truck, it feels like we're already there. Jay's truck feels like home. I lean on him the whole ride, and before we even leave the country club grounds, I've fallen asleep. He wakes me when I get home.

When I wake up, it's midnight, and I still feel good. How much longer can I keep this up? I want this to stretch forever.

I call Dad and leave him another voicemail about everything going on, and how little I understand what's going on. Talking to him helps me feel better. Everything makes a little more sense.

But even when I start painting, the question still stays in my head: how much longer?

Chapter 41

James Averell

There were a few places I never considered going on a Friday night, and Thena's house is in the top five, especially without Emi. I've been inside her home a handful of times, never long enough to really look around but long enough to know everything was perfectly put together.

Nick, Bell, Thena, and I are in attendance. So is *Tristan*. Tristan sits on Thena's gray couch with Bell, a smug, annoying look on his face. Nick sits in the chair across from me. Thena stands up, looking at something. She has pieces of paper scattered across her coffee table and a binder full of party planning shit. Thena's planning Emi an 18th birthday party, and she wants it to be perfect.

"*She's turning 18, not five,*" Thena snaps for the fifth time. All of Tristan's ideas have been shit.

"Doesn't she like those superhero movies and shit? Just get her a cake with Iron Man on it, and I'm sure she'll be happy," Tristan says. He chuckles at his own failed joke.

I ask Tristan the question we've all been wondering, *"Why are you here?"*

"My girlfriend invited me." He smiles, but it looks more like a grimace.

Nick looks up from the paper he was looking at and redirects his attention to Tristan.

"Yes, but you could have rejected the invitation seeing as you know nothing about Emi and have no relationship with her besides the simple fact, you're Bell's boyfriend. One would think it'd be the smart thing to do, seeing as your company wasn't exactly wanted." Nick smiles his golden boy smile, and I can't help but laugh.

Tristan's fuming, and Bell looks ready to jump out of her seat.

"Can you guys please be nice?" she pleads.

"I have been nice; I didn't kick the shit out of him when he insulted my girlfriend."

"Yeah, and why didn't you?" Tristan barks.

"Emi doesn't like when my knuckles are busted; it makes her sad. Unlike you, I don't like making my girlfriend sad," I dryly answer.

Thena sighs loudly. *"Let's focus. I have a party to plan and only eight days to do it."* She focuses on one of the fifteen sheets of paper in her hand. *"I'm getting her favorite Mexican restaurant catered,"* Thena announces, leaving the living room before anyone can respond.

I don't even know why I'm here. All she asked me was to not fight inside her house, or she would tell Emi *every single detail*. Telling someone like Emi "*every single detail*" of a fight is never good. Her imagination will soak it up and make it look like a scene from *Fight Club*.

Nick takes out his phone and makes a call; it sounds like he's speaking to a bakery. I get up and go to the kitchen, pouring myself a glass of water. A large bouquet of flowers is sitting on the kitchen island.

"*Bell or Nick?*"

Thena purses her lips and stares at the flowers. "*Bell. But those are from him*," she sneers, glaring at a large red and blue bouquet on her kitchen table. Thena turns her back to everyone and faces me, staring at me expectantly.

I sigh and focus on her. She and Emi look nothing alike. They share some of the same features but mixed with all the other ones, the similarities tend to fade. Thena's eyes are a cold sky blue, Emi's brown with specks of green. Thena's cheekbones are sharp and defined, and Emi's face is round and soft. Emi's skin is a dark golden brown and Thena's is a pale brown.

"*Yes, Athena?*" Her glare intensifies, and I hold back a smirk. I've called her that for years and still get the same reaction.

"*Is everything okay with Emi? She's been more energetic, sleeping less, making unsafe decisions, and I don't think she's telling me everything. Is she okay? Has she told you anything?*" Concern etches Thena's brows, and she speaks low so no one can overhear.

"*She hasn't told me anything, but she's been going to therapy and talking to me more.*"

Last night we talked for an hour, and she wasn't skittish or distant.

"*Are you sure? Because last time-*"

"It's not like last time." I cut her off. It can't be. Last time something horrible could've happened, the worst thing imaginable could've happened, but it didn't. Thena looks at me for a second longer, then nods, hesitantly leaving the kitchen.

It's not like last time. I keep repeating that to myself.

I pick her up from Pepe's and pull her against me, her eyes sparkling like I'm the best thing in the world. She rises on her tippy toes and kisses me. Her lips are soft, and they taste like pink lemonade.

"I missed you," she breathes against my neck.

"I missed you too."

I drove us to my dad's house. Emi opens the door and yells over her shoulder, *"Last one there is a dead rat!"*

She runs towards my house. I chuckle and follow her, running past a smiling Rachel, Emi's laughter ringing through the house. Finally, I catch up to her just as she reaches my room. I pick her up, my arm going to her waist and lifting her to me.

"Cheating!" she cries through spurts of laughter. I slam my room door and throw her on my bed. She laughs as she bounces, and I stare down at her. She's never looked more beautiful, her hair wild and messy, her whole face filled with happiness as she laughs, her skirt from school still on with no tights underneath.

Her laughter fades, and she looks at me. She kicks her shoes off and looks me up and down. I smirk and lean over until I'm hovering over her, our lips meeting as one of her legs wraps around my waist, urging me forward.

I lose myself in her, and with each rush of pleasure that goes through her, she loses herself in me. I look into her eyes and promise myself she's okay. Emi's right here with me, not somewhere locked in her head. She's with me.

And once that realization sinks in fully, I let myself go fully.

Chapter 42

Emillie Kate Van der Berg

My 18th birthday is on Saturday. Today is Allison's. I haven't had a full night's sleep since last Friday when I spent the night with Jay. I told Mom and Rick I was at Bell's, then told Bell I was with Jay, and when Eric saw me in the morning, he simply said, "*Good morning,*" and kept walking, not even phased. That was four days ago. I took a three-hour nap yesterday and woke up to Mom banging on my door, telling me she and Rick were attending a musical in the city.

Now I wait at the train station; the next train heading into the city comes in seven minutes. The train station is filled with people dressed and ready for work, and a few kids from Greenwich huddle together, talking and laughing. The air is crisp, and there's a slight wind hitting me from under the small safety of the station. The bench is cold under my thighs.

The train comes ten minutes later, the sound echoing through the station. People rush towards it and climb inside. I find a seat by the window, and the smell of exhaust and morning coffee hits my nostrils in a wave. The train squeaks and jolts into a start.

It's a one-hour train ride from Old Greenwich to New York City.

I lean my head against the window and watch the houses we pass and the stretches of highway traffic. I wonder if Thena is sitting in traffic right now, trying to make it home, or if she's in class. I know Bell isn't working today. She's meeting with her agent for lunch, then she'll be free. I could've asked her to hang out with me, but why bother? Before I know it, the day will be over. It's just a regular Tuesday.

The train comes to a screeching stop, shaking me as I stand up and approach the doors. People rush off, pushing each other on their way out. I follow the flow of traffic up the stairs and am immediately greeted by the cold chill of the air. I keep walking. You can't stop in the middle of the sidewalk in New York, or you'll get pushed forward and be the butt of someone's conversation.

I keep walking, ending up at The Met. I pay for one ticket and walk around the museum. I find a bench and sit in front of a painting of a group of sisters all gracefully lying around and smiling together. It reminds me of the March sisters from *Little Women*. It makes me smile.

Someone sits next to me with the thick scent of perfume and butterscotch. I don't look at them and just focus on the painting. Their breathing is labored.

"What brings you here?"

I turn my head, and an elderly lady sits a foot away, a small smile on her wrinkled face, her cheeks slightly flushed.

"It's my sisters' birthday."

"How wonderful! Is she here with you?"

I focus on the painting; the sisters look so happy. Their dresses fall around them, some of them lying on the others. All of them intertwined as one. They look like a real family.

"No, she passed away a few years ago." It'd be easier to say she's dead, but it's not as nice to hear. *"What brings you here?"* I cheerfully ask, changing the subject.

"Oh, it's my granddaughter's birthday, and she loves museums, so we all came out. But I'm kind of tired. I think I walked up one too many stairs!" She laughs and takes another deep breath.

"How old is she turning?"

"Six. She wanted to come here and then eat Subway for lunch, so we'll go eat when we're done here. It should be fun."

"I think it will be," I murmur in agreement.

"Did your sister like art?"

"Yeah, she loved it," I lied. Allison hated art mainly because I loved it. A small girl with brown pigtails, a pink hat, and a pleated dress with stockings underneath stops in front of our bench. Her face is soft, and her eyes are big and bright.

"Granny, we're leaving," she says in a rushed voice, her cheeks flushed from running.

"Okay. Well, it was nice to meet you, dear. Sorry for your loss," the elderly lady sweetly says, sending me a sympathetic smile as she stands up.

"Thank you, and happy birthday!"

"Thanks!" The young girl calls as she and her grandmother leave.

I sit on the bench for a little while longer. Then, when I can't look at the sisters any longer, I get up and leave, not looking at any more paintings. I'm over The Met.

I start heading down an unfamiliar street, still thinking about the sister painting. The only time my sisters and I have been like that—laying together like we're intertwined—is when it's just been Thena, Bell, and I, never with Allison. The guilt feels heavier today.

I decided to go see a movie. I bought one ticket, a jumbo tub of popcorn, and a large slushie. I'm the only one in my section, sitting in the top row. I don't even know what the movie is playing; I just went to the first available showing. It's not even 11 yet, so I don't expect anything spectacular. Ten minutes into the film, I take my phone out of my backpack. I have five messages.

Liv: Where are you?

Liv: Are you okay?

Thena: If you need anything today, let me know.

Bell: Movie night tonight? I'll bring snacks, and you can pick?

Dr. Young: Just wanted to let you know if you need anything, I'm here. Call or text anytime.

I ignore all of them, pocketing my phone and turning my attention back to the screen.

It's a crappy old-time romance movie. I know it's older than me, but I'd say it's around 25 years old if I had to guess. Right now, the couple are dancing in the rain to a cheesy love song. Jay would hate this; he probably would've already fallen asleep. He still would've come, even though he'd cringe at almost every scene. Maybe I should've invited him.

###

It's true what they say: time indeed passes in the blink of an eye. The blink you take when tears threaten to spill, and you just give in and shut your eyes, opening them a moment later as the tears stream. That's how Allison's birthday feels. When it's too late to just keep walking around, and the cold has begun to numb my hands and cheeks, I find a diner to go to.

It's small in a questionable part of the city. A table of businessmen sit in the back, their bodies big and their faces cold. I don't look at them for too long; I just sit by one of the windows and order a coffee.

The waitress pours me a cup, and I give her a shaky smile. She looks me up and down and smiles. She can't be over forty, her bright red hair piled on her head and her dark brown eyes running me over.

"Are you coming or going?"

"Excuse me?" I don't understand her question. Going where?

"Into the city. Are you coming or going? Only time young pretty girls like you come in here, you're either heading into the city or escaping it."

"Oh, well, I don't know yet, but I think I should be going. I have my parents and school waiting for me."

She nods.

"Then you better start preparing yourself. It's 1:00 in the morning." I nod, and she winks at me before going to another table to refill their coffees.

280

Jay called me today, but I rushed the phone call, then hung up. And I texted Liv and promised I'd see her tomorrow. I know I'm going to school tomorrow; I only took today off for Allison. That's what sisters do, right? You find ways to celebrate their birthday instead of sitting in your room getting lost in memories.

The last time I hung out with Allison before she died was the day before the first day of my sophomore year. Mom insisted it'd be a girl's day, so she forced all of us to spend the day together. Thena had tried to convince her to just go with Allison by herself or for just her and Allison to go, but Mom didn't want to hear it. So, we all met Allison in the city at Neiman Marcus, and when Mom went upstairs to try on clothes, Allison focused her attention on me. Allison made me try on a dress I knew wouldn't fit. And when it didn't zip up, she stood behind me, staring at my reflection in the mirror with disdain.

"You know, I think this might be the year Jay stops pitying you and just leaves you. Then who will you have?" She tilted her head to the side and narrowed her eyes on me. Then, she turned around and left the dressing room.

I held back the tears, and when she came back in, she grabbed my shoulder, squeezing it almost tenderly. *"Try and drop twenty pounds. The last thing we want is for you to end up like Dad."* Her voice was soft. A stranger would've thought it sounded loving.

I barely made it home before I went into my room and sobbed into my pillow. I didn't hear Jay when he came in. I couldn't tell him what happened. I just cried into his shirt, and he held me.

That was the last time I saw her. A month later, she was dead.

I used to wish we could've had another moment so that wouldn't have been the last one. But the truth is that it reflects the relationship I had with Allison.

I finish my coffee, and the same waitress comes over to refill it.

"Do you guys have any pie or cake?"

"We got cherry pie, apple pie, key lime pie, and chocolate cake."

"Can I get a slice of apple, key lime, and a slice of chocolate cake, please?" She nods. *"Oh, and a glass of milk, please!"* She smiles and nods, returning a minute later with three plates and a large glass of milk. I read her name tag: Cherry.

"Thanks, Cherry." She gives my arm a motherly pat and goes back behind the counter.

I take a small bite of each dessert, and my favorite is the apple pie. It's warm, the crust has a crispiness that makes me think a baker made it, and the filling tastes like cinnamon and brown sugar. The worst one is the key lime. Cherry returns a few minutes later, takes away the clean apple pie plate, and sets another apple pie slice down.

"Don't worry, I won't charge you for the key lime. Not many people like it. And those that do think the hashbrowns aren't salty." She takes the key lime plate away and winks at me.

I look out the window. There are people still walking around. Cars fly down the street, some running the stop sign, and food delivery people on bikes go almost as fast as the cars following the speed limit. *Mmh, I guess the city doesn't sleep.*

"Emille," a deep accented voice says. I snap my head to the sound, and a tall, pale man stands in front of my table wearing a suit and a black trench coat. His hair is blonde and short, his eyes the same icier and more clear than Thena's. Stubble pricks his jaw and his upper lip. I know him.

"M-Mr. Lukov?"

He nods jerky and stiff. *"Hadeon Lukov,"* he fully introduces himself, "I'll take you home."

I look at the desserts. I'm only halfway through my chocolate cake and haven't even touched the apple pie.

"Cherry will pack it up for you." He tells me.

Cherry comes over and does just that, and I just sit there frozen. Cherry sets down the check, and I open my backpack and get my wallet.

"I got it. Let's go." He pulls his wallet out and sets two twenties on the table.

I stand up and follow him out. I'm embarrassed. I didn't expect anyone to find me here; it's 1:00 in the morning! Mr. Lukov's footsteps are brisk and quiet. For such a big person, his footsteps are light. He leads me to his Mercedes, and I climb in. His seat is almost as far back as it can get. He starts the car and pulls out of his parking spot. The ride is silent and tense.

"You know me?" I blurt. I only know him because I've seen him and Clara at galas.

"Yes, you have classes with Clara and Liv." He says Clara's name with a hint of an Eastern European accent and rolls the 'r.'

"Plus, I know your stepfather. You are the youngest, yes?" It's not a question; he knows the answers.

"Yup," I squeak out. *"Clara told you about me?"*

"Yes, you and Liv are close." I don't think when Clara told him that, she meant it as a good thing. He switches lanes, glancing over his shoulder. *"I know everything about my daughters. You do that when you care—discover things they don't even want to tell you."* He glances at me, his eyes knowing.

Does he know Clara and Liv like each other? The thought rattles in my head, bouncing around in a strained continuous echo.

"What else do you know?"

He sighs. We're stuck in a bit of traffic; everyone trying to merge and get on the highway. *"Clara wants to go to Brown in the fall to play lacrosse. She is concerned I want her to stay close to home, but I do not care where she wants to go. She can go anywhere. She is also scared about something else, but I will not say that."* His lips twitch, and he speeds forward, cutting someone off. *"Why were you at a diner at 1:00 in the morning, Emille?"*

Something tells me not to lie to him because he'll see right through it, and everything said here will stay between us unless he chooses to tell someone else.

"I didn't want to be home alone, so I stayed there and distracted myself." He knows about Allison. Everyone does, but I doubt he knows that yesterday was her birthday. *"Why were you there?"*

"Business," he grunts. I nod.

The conversation ends just as quickly and awkwardly as it started.

We drive through the city and eventually enter the suburbs; everything is familiar. Once we reach our community, Mr. Lukov enters the gate code and slows down his driving.

When he pulls up outside my house, I look at our large stone colonial mansion from an outsider's perspective. It features a secluded wraparound driveway where Rick parks his Range Rover, though it is barely visible from where I am sitting. Large trees surround the circular driveway. Not one light is on inside, only the porch light.

It looks like a family home. When I first saw it, I was amazed, and looking at it from inside Mr. Lukov's car, I still am. I open the door and step into a small patch of snow.

"*Thanks for the ride,*" I told him. I didn't know how I was going to get home. I think I would've just stayed in the diner until the sun came up.

Mr. Lukov nods in response, but before I close the door, he says, "*Emi, don't ever do that again.*" The force of his words causes goosebumps to rise on my arms. I nod and close the door and walk toward my house. Unlocking the door and stepping inside with light steps, the house is dead silent.

He doesn't pull off until I'm all the way inside.

Chapter 43

Emille Kate Van der Berg

I successfully parked Jay's pickup truck in front of one of the garages. We spent the entirety of my birthday at the DMV. Jay left once to get us food while we waited for me to take my driver's test. I am now a licensed driver in the state of Connecticut. I didn't want to drive his car back to my house, but he asked me, *"What's the point of getting your license if you're not going to drive?"*

In response, I took his keys and moved to the driver's seat, adjusting my seat as high and close to the steering wheel as possible. He told me *"Happy birthday"* once, but besides that, we've treated today as a regular Saturday.

"Are you in the mood for Lord of the Rings, Harry Potter, or Hunger Games?" I ask him, digging through my jacket pockets for my house keys. He leans against the door frame and stares at me languidly.

"Mmh, how about something you haven't seen a million times?"

I pause and narrow my eyes at him before turning the key.

"We watched The Matrix twice last week, and I even watched Die Hard with you during Christmas break."

"Die Hard is a Christmas movie. You know that, Em," he teasingly scolds. I roll my eyes and push the front door open. I don't know where anyone else is. I'm pretty sure Bell has a date with Tristan, Thena has a meeting with her friend, and Rick and Mom are spending time together.

"Did Lucille make any more of those coffee cakes?" Jay's voice calls. I spin around and find him walking towards the kitchen and larger dining room we only use for special occasions. I catch up to him and grab his arm, squeezing it.

"I think she might have this morning. I smelled something before we left," I answered. His hand lingers on the door handle.

He smiles at me as he opens the door. The lights are off, but as I come inside after him, a chorus of *"Surprise!"* fills the air, the lights flash on, and the whole room is completely different.

Party decorations were set up all over, with a pinata hanging in one corner and posters of superheroes and scenes from *The Hunger Games* on every wall. Nothing matches, yet it all seems to fit. A large sign reading, *"Happy 18th Birthday Emi!"* in what looks like Bell's handwriting. I look around the room, and almost everyone I care about is here: my sisters, Jay, Nick, Mom, Rick, Mr. and Mrs. Yates, Eric, Rachel, Lucille, and even Liv. She wears a party hat with a small, easy smile. She looks tired, but I'm happy she's here.

Thena and Bell come to my side, and both hug me and wish me a happy birthday.

"Don't tell me you actually thought we'd made plans on your birthday," Bell playfully scolds. I laugh and shrug my shoulders. I didn't want them to feel like they had to celebrate my birthday. It's just a regular day, another year I've been here.

I go around and thank everyone for coming, and when I get to Liv, who sits at a table with Rachel and Mrs. Yates, she waits for me with a smirk.

"Your house is fucking huge!" It's the first thing she says to me all day, and I can't help but laugh.

"It's not mine. It's Rick's, but it is pretty big. You've been here before, though."

"I know, but I forgot how big it is inside. Plus, I've only seen your room."

I nod in understanding and look around the large room decorated to fit all the things I love. There are tacos, chips and guacamole, Spanish rice, *and* Italian food.

"Are you having fun?" I ask Liv.

She nods. *"Yeah, your sisters are cool. I'm happy they invited me."*

"Of course! You're like one of the only friends I have." She and Jay are my only friends, but I'm not even sure he counts anymore now that we're dating.

"You're a cool person, Em. I like being your friend."

"I like being your friend too."

She chuckles. *"Clara's going to be pissed she wasn't invited."* Liv takes a sip from her can of Sprite.

My smile falls, and my eyes widen. *"Oh shit!"*

"Don't worry about it. You didn't plan the party. I'll tell her about it and then distract her, and she'll be over it."

I don't want to know how Liv plans on distracting Clara. I just nod and take another sip of the canned soda in my hand.

I look around the room. Everyone was smiling and talking. Nick speaks to Jay at one of the small party tables. Nick wears a party hat, and somehow, he doesn't look childish like everyone else. Thena walks around scanning everything, looking for any faults. She's not wearing a party hat, but her hair is in a braid like Katniss Everdeen, and she has a gold mocking jay on her shirt. Bell is wearing the same braid in her hair, only she wears a *Scarlet Witch* costume instead. Mom and Rick both wear Supergirl and Superman colors, both wearing capes. The Yateses have props from *Thor* and *Wolverine*, and Mrs. Yates looks like this is the best party she's been to all year.

Rachel looks nervous as she speaks quietly to Mrs. Yates and Lucille, who is on her second margarita.

"Cake!" Thena shouts. She moves towards my table with a large, perfectly decorated cake. The blue icing reads, *"Happy Birthday, Emillie! Big 18! "*

Thena lights the number 18, and everyone begins signing. All their eyes were on me, the warm flame of the candle heating up my face. I look around at everyone, and they're all smiling. Mom's eyes are glassy, and Rick squeezes her shoulder, his eyes equally as glassy.

Bell sings the hardest, her smile stretching across her whole face, and even Thena can't hold back her smile, dimples appearing on her cheeks. Nick has his usual self-assured smile, and when we lock eyes, it feels like he knows *everything*, and I have to look away. Jay sits on the other side of me. His smile is small and calm as he sings, *"Happy Birthday."* I really love him.

He squeezes my hand, and I blow out the candles when the song ends. I make one small wish: make this feeling last forever.

After Mom and Thena hand out a slice of cake to everyone, we all sit down and eat, conversation and laughter filling each table. Liv takes an extra piece to go, and I walk her to the door. I hugged her goodbye.

"Thanks for coming!"

"Of course! I'll see you on Monday."

I nod, and she leaves, walking down the driveway and getting into her car.

Rick meets me by the party's entrance, and I stop a foot from him. He's been at every one of my birthday parties, never missing one, not even if he was in the middle of a big business deal.

"I've wanted to give you this since you were sixteen, but you never wanted to get your license." He chuckles. *"It's simple, and it's pretty reliable."* He hands me a pair of car keys, and I stare at them. Then, after a moment of stunned silence, I hugged him.

"Thank you!"

He nods and kisses my forehead, and I rush past him, looking for Jay. I show him my car keys and jingle them.

"Rick doesn't know what he's unleashed into the world," Jay says, shaking his head. I smack his arm, and he grabs me and pulls me towards him, pecking my lips. His lips hover over my ear as he whispers, *"Reach into my left pocket."* I do as he says and pull out his phone. Using his face to unlock it.

"Now go to Instagram."

I furrow my eyebrows in confusion but do as he says. I found his Instagram and opened it. His timeline shows a picture of Bell in her London hotel room, leaning against a bed with a large smile on her face. It got thirty thousand likes. I like it.

"When did she post this?" I ask him, clicking on her profile. She has 654k Instagram followers. There's a picture of her and Thena a few rows down, both dressed for the gala. It has almost half a million likes.

"Go to my account."

I do as he says, and he has one post.

He's never posted before. I click on the post, and before even reading the caption, I scroll through and see pictures of us: the first one from the Christmas party, the picture Bell took, a picture of me sleeping with the covers bunched up around my waist, one of us reading books in the Hamptons, us at his high school graduation, one of us with my face illuminated by a candle at dinner, the one of me at the gala smiling from ear to ear as he stands behind me with an equally bright smile, and the last one of us on our first day of school when I first moved to Connecticut.

"Seven years of friendship in seven pictures," he whispers. My eyes water, and a smile pulls on my lips. *"Read the caption, Em."*

I read it out loud: *"Happy 18th birthday to THE Emille Kate Van der Berg. Love you more than life, this one and the next. I love you, REAL."*

Tears slide down my cheeks, and I sniffle, wiping my snot with the back of my hand.

"You referenced the Hunger Games!"

He rolls his eyes.

"It was the only reference I knew you'd get."

I know he's lying. He did it because it's my favorite movie.

"I love it! Thank you!" I wrap my arms around Jay and hug him, burying my face into his neck.

"Em, that's not the only thing I got you," he chuckles. He stands up and walks me toward the table with all the gifts on them. He reaches forward and grabs a small box, handing it to me. I open it, and it's a necklace with a Louisiana iris charm the size of a quarter.

"I know you always talked about the flowers you used to have at your house in Louisiana, and you don't have any jewelry like that, so I wanted to get it for you. If you don't like it, I can exchange it for something else."

It's one of the most thoughtful gifts I've ever received. All I can do is hug it to my chest, wipe more happy tears from my cheek, and hug him. I don't know what I did in a past life to deserve James Averell, but I'm eternally grateful.

"Want me to put it on for you?"

I nod and turn around, handing him the box. He puts it on me, the cool jewelry touching my chest. He bends down and kisses my nose, my eyes fluttering at the warm touch.

I don't open any more gifts for the night. Instead, I stay downstairs with everyone else, the party going well onto the night. I say goodbye to Mom and Rick. Mom hides her surprise at my help cleaning up. Usually, I would have snuck up to my room by the time everyone left. After Jay, Eric, and Rachel go, Mom and Rick head upstairs, and I pat myself on the back.

I've been able to successfully ignore the truth that's been hanging above me like a pinata, waiting to be smashed.

Lucille catches me before I head upstairs, her hands crossed in front of her. "*I have a gift for you.*"

I follow her to the kitchen, the light dim. A small, round cake with bright white icing and fresh-cut strawberries sits on the island.

"*I know your dad used to make you tres leches, and I know how much you loved it.*"

I stare at the cake, one lone candle on it. Lucille lights it and sings "*Happy Birthday*" in Spanish, her voice smooth and her accent thick and comforting like a heated blanket on a winter day. I stare at the cake the whole time, and when she finishes, I tell her thank you. She cuts a piece for me and her, then heads upstairs, her footsteps light.

I look at the cake, then at the slice cut for me, and close my eyes as a sob escapes my body. I clutch the island for support. I sob, watching the candle wax burn all the way down. I didn't make a wish because the one from earlier didn't last. I can feel the happiness and lightness escape me with each cry. My dad's not here for my 18th birthday, and that single truth rakes and pulls more sobs from me, each one feeling heavier and stronger than the last. Eventually, I sit down on the ground and just cry, the cool kitchen tiles greeting me as I fall onto them. The house is eerily quiet as my cries fill the kitchen until it's all I can hear and feel.

Why can't I stop crying?

I can't even bring myself to call him. Not tonight.

Chapter 44

Emille Kate Van der Berg

"Emi, you good?" Liv asks me.

I look at her and force a smile and nod. We're sitting outside in the freezing cold, eating our lunch, even though our lunch period ended twenty minutes ago. Neither of us is in a rush to get back to class.

"What happened last week? The day you ditched."

Oh, that day. It feels kind of long ago.

"It was my half-sister Allison's birthday. I didn't want to be here or in my room, so I went to the city and just walked around until time passed. I met Clara's dad in a diner that night, and he took me home," I told her. My voice is mechanical, and even though what I'm saying is the truth, it sounds like a lie.

"You met her dad?" Liv's voice is filled with shock, and her eyes look twice the size they usually are.

"Yeah. He's nice, I think. He and Clara are closer than I thought they would be. He knew about you." Liv's eyes snap to mine. *"That you and Clara are friends, I mean,"* I quickly clarify.

She nods, taking a bite of her sandwich. I know it's cold by now; we got it at the start of our lunch period. She's been smoking a joint the whole time and not eating much. I finished my food ten minutes ago.

"Do you love Clara?" I ask her, I've been curious for a while, but I've been too worried about how she'd react. I'm not as scared right now. I've been skating around their whole dynamic, but I don't feel like it anymore.

Liv shrugs.

"I like Clara, probably more than most people, but Clara and I are… we're too different. She's too scared, and I'm too messed up. Clara will go off to Brown in the fall, and I'll be here and do God knows what. When she comes home for breaks, we might see each other, but eventually, I'll just be the girl she tried to fix in high school. And she'll just be my Clara… and someone else's wife and Mom."

"You're not messed up, Liv." Liv is one of the most consistent people I know. She's never betrayed or hurt me. In fact, she's never intentionally hurt anyone.

"I'm glad you think that, Emi. I really am." She smiles, puts out her joint, and trashes her sandwich. We both stand up and walk toward the large school building. *"Do you plan on sleeping anytime soon?"*

"I don't know. Probably." I don't like lying to Liv, I don't want her to think of me as a liar, and I know she wouldn't tell anyone. So, everything I tell her stays with her.

I can feel it coming, but I'm too tired to fight it. Today is the last day of February. I've been 18 for thirteen days, and I've spent those days fighting sleep, chugging espresso, writing in my journal, and doing anything I can to keep feeling alive.

I don't think I like being eighteen.

March

Chapter 45

James Averell

"*Where the hell is she?*" I ask anyone. I've asked this question four times already. And the answer has been the same each time I've asked; no one knows.

We're twenty minutes into brunch, and Emi is nowhere to be found. She's not answering anyone's calls, and Rick has been trying to reach Lucille, who is at church, to see if she saw Emi leaving the house before she did. Rick is hiding his worry horribly; he's practically staring at the door and checking his watch every minute. Emi's mom looks annoyed with the whole situation, her face and body stiff and her eyes cold.

"*I'm leaving,*" I announce, standing up and throwing my napkin on the table. Thena, Bell, and Nick follow me.

"*Where are you going?*" Thena asks me before I get into my car.

"*Her house,*" I grit. It's the only place I imagine her being at. I texted her friend Liv, and she said she hadn't heard or seen Emi since Friday when they were at school.

It takes me maybe eight minutes to get to Emi's house, going at least twenty over the speed limit. My whole head is filled with worst-case scenarios. Even when she's all over the place, she still lets someone know she's okay. This isn't like her, but in a messed-up way, it is. She could be sick, breaking down , on her deathbed, and no one would know.

Thena, Bell, Nick, and I all make it to the house at the same time. Thena beats me to the door unlocking it.

"*Emi!*" I shout, running up the stairs, taking them two at a time. My whole chest feels tight, and I am trying to prepare myself for the worst. I swing open her bedroom door, and my entire body slacks when I see her.

She's lying in bed, her eyelids closed with the sheets covering everything but her head. There's one bottle of water on her bedside table, and her television is still on. The curtains are shut. I move closer and sit on the edge, softly shaking her awake.

Her eyelids flutter open, and she looks at me with a blank and distant look in her eye. She doesn't smile or lean closer like she usually does. She just stares at me.

"*Emi, you missed brunch, and you weren't answering your phone,*" I explain so she understands why everyone is in her room surrounding her.

"*Oh,*" she mutters, bringing her hands under her head.

"*You want to go get some food? We can ditch the rest of brunch,*" I suggest, rubbing one of my hands along her arm.

"*I'm tired,*" she weakly says. Her eyes glass, and I don't push. I just nod. She closes her eyes and turns over, giving us all her back.

I watch her for a second longer before standing and leaving her room. Everyone is already waiting for me outside. I close her room door, and Nick leans against the wall, his arms crossed and his whole face a mask of calmness. Thena opens her mouth to say something, but I hold up my hand and stop her, cutting her off.

"*She's tired. She's not fucking dying. Haven't you been complaining about her not sleeping? Now she is, so just drop it!*" I bark at her. She purses her lips and shakes her head before leaving, her heels clicking against the ground as she stomps away. Bell follows her.

Nick stares at me impassively. "'*Facts do not cease because they are ignored.*'"

I know who it is before he can even tell me—Aldous Huxley.

Emi would tell me; I know she would. Her sisters may not understand, but she made me a promise that when shit got bad for her, she'd tell me. I keep telling myself that as I head downstairs.

She doesn't come downstairs the rest of the day.

Chapter 46

Emille Kate Van der Berg
Three years ago

I stared at my reflection in the pool. I knew the water would be warm; Jay's indoor pool was heated. Rachel let me in on her way out. No one was home, and Jay wouldn't have been home for another hour or so. He was at a coding club meeting. Everything I'm wearing, except my shoes, is a size too big—the lavender knitted sweater, the black jeans, and even the fuzzy socks.

Allison had been dead for three months. There was snow on the ground outside, and everything looked dreary. I wanted to go swimming. I wanted to do something to distract myself from whatever was happening inside my head. Everything felt so long, but not long enough for me to remember.

I took a step towards the edge of the pool, and before I could think about it, I fell in. I stayed under with my eyes open. The water heated my whole body; I stayed under until my lungs started to burn, making my chest feel like it was being set on fire. Eventually, I began to slowly pull myself up. But before I could reach the surface, someone yanked me up. I gasped for air, and right in front of me was Jay, his eyes wide and his face a mask of horror.

He carried me out of the pool and sat me on the edge next to him.

"What the hell, Em?" I figured it was the only thing he could think of to ask.

"M-my socks are wet." It was the only thing I thought of to say. I knew how it looked, but it wasn't like that. I just wanted to feel something. And I think I did. For a second, I felt fear. Fear of not being able to come up in time and fear I wasn't as good of a swimmer as I thought.

"Why weren't you coming up? I waited for you…but you just stopped moving." His voice was frazzled and rushed. He kept moving his hands up and down my arms to warm me.

"I was holding my breath."

He stared at me; his eyes locked on mine as he rubbed his hands rhythmically over my arms. I wanted to tell him I was warm, but I liked his hands on me. They were big and warm and so comforting.

"You can't do shit like that! You can't just stay under until you can't breathe! You can't keep running from me and lying to me, and you can't keep lying to your sisters." His eyes glazed over, and the unshed tears thickened

with each word. "*Promise me, Em. Promise me you'll tell me when you feel down or when you want to stay underwater until you can't breathe.*"

I spoke before even thinking.

"*Promise,*" I whispered. His body relaxed, and he held me for a little longer, not letting go until the front door opened and the sound of Rachel's steps and voice filled the house.

Chapter 47

James Averell

Most—if not all—of my best memories have Emi in them. She's been there through pretty much everything. If she's not there, the memory is already five times less important. She doesn't have to do much; most of the time, it's just her presence and everything that comes with that. Her smiles, her jokes, her honesty, and her compassion. It's all a package deal.

I've been going to her house for a few nights, and each night she just sits there. We watch television, and sometimes she eats; other times she doesn't. She doesn't say much, but she'll respond if I ask her something. There are no random thoughts blurted or questions asked.

She lays on me, her head on my chest and one of her hands clutching my shirt as she stares at her television. We're watching *The Great Gatsby*, and the most she said the entire time is, "*I like Gatsby.*"

I draw shapes on her back and halfway watch the movie, and the other half I spend watching her. Bell told me she hadn't been to the dinner they usually have at Thena's house since before her birthday. Which means she's missed two already. I refuse to talk to Nick about it. He'll say something I don't want to hear; I can feel it.

"*Em?*" She makes an "*mmh*" sound in response. "*When was the last time you left your room?*" I think she's been to school.

"*I went to school yesterday.*"

"*Besides school?*"

She shrugs her shoulders and sinks further into me. She pulls her covers over her, and I know she's about to go to sleep. "*Promise me you'll leave your room for something else, anything. I'll even go with you.*"

She looks up at me and forces a shaky smile. "Promise."

"*You know I love you, right?*" I need her to know. It's one of the few things she can't forget.

A tear slides down her cheek. "*I know,*" she whispers, her voice so soft it's barely audible. She lies back down against me, and a few minutes later, she falls asleep. I slide out of her bed and leave through her window.

I drive back to the city and make it to my dorm room. Caden is fast asleep. I turn on my lamp, log in to my computer and do homework. It's the only thing I can do to distract myself from the fact the girl I love is trapped in her own head, and she's not letting anyone in.

Chapter 48

Emille Kate Van der Berg

I open my eyelids; my curtains are closed, and all my lights are off. The only light coming in is from the television. Everything feels stale, like a sterilized doctor's office, but this staleness has no useful purpose. It's just there, living inside of me. I sleep, and each time I wake up, I hope I feel better, that I feel something to make me get up and keep going. And each time, a wave of disappointment and nothingness washes me over, trying to pull me into another bout of sleep. If I'm not sleeping, I'm watching television. If the show or movie is good or easy enough, I don't have to think. I've watched most of *The Real Housewives of New Jersey* and a few cartoons.

I don't know what day it is. Time passes like a strained exhale; it goes by fast but still hurts. Sometimes I get up and go to school, usually after being yelled at by my mom, and other times, I just sleep. Then I wake up to messages from Liv, my sisters, or Jay.

I remember my promise. I need to get up and go somewhere… anywhere. I can't stay stuck here because when Jay comes back, and he always does, disappointment and concern will fill his eyes. And I won't be able to take it away. I'll be the cause of it.

Getting up seems like one of the most challenging tasks I've ever done in my life. I'll have to sit up, get off my bed, walk to my bathroom, shower, brush my teeth, get dressed, walk downstairs, and go somewhere. And from there, another impossible list of things. I need to, though, for him. I have to.

Just move.

Each step feels strained and heavy, but I make it to my bathroom. I know I won't make it if I shower, so I just brush my teeth and get dressed. My room is messy, but it's been worse, which is a good thing. I slide on gray sweatpants, a sweatshirt probably from Rick's closet, and UGG slippers. It takes me at least ten minutes to walk downstairs, and when I do, Rick is on the phone, his back to me. I grab my keys, jacket, and bouquet of flowers from Bell and leave.

I drive for a while, the music loud enough to drown out thoughts or words. I end up at the cemetery and park my car as close as I can. I trek up the hill and plop down on the ground when I reach my destination. I look around, and it's mostly empty; not many people here, just an elderly man a few rows ahead and a middle-aged woman across from me.

I stare at the tombstone.

Matt Daniels

Loving Father.

July 30, 1975-January 17th, 2013

It's clean. I lay down the flowers and look around. There's no snow on the metal plaque where the grass should be. It's just cold. Everything's cold, though.

"*Hey, Dad,*" I begin, my voice cracking. I look away, and tears fill my eyes. I can't even say anything meaningful without crying. I wonder what Dr. Young would say about this.

"*I really hate the way I feel right now, and I kind of hate you for not being here. Which is even shitter.*"

My chest seems to cave in, and I start to cry before I can control it.

I cry at my dad's grave. A grave that's been here for eight years that I've only visited a handful of times, none of them alone. What kind of daughter disregards her dad's grave? Never visits it, never makes sure there are flowers, and only calls him on holidays. Even when he was alive, I was a shitty daughter, and I'm pretty sure Mom would agree.

Guilt. It's all I can feel; it's worse than nothingness. I bury my face in my hands and cry, repeating "*I'm sorry*" until my voice is hoarse.

"*Emi?*" My head snaps up, and Liv stands a few feet away. I wipe my face and force a smile. She walks closer and sits down next to me. She looks at the tombstone.

"*Hey,*" I say with a sniffle, wiping the snot from my nose with the back of my hand. Liv doesn't say anything. She just gets a cigarette from her pocket and lights it.

"*My mom died four years ago. Cancer. She tried to fight, but she lost. I remember when she first found out she was sick. She kept saying, 'I'm going to win,' but I heard her crying in the bathroom one night. That was when she started losing her hair, but she never let me see her cry. She fought for one year. Then one day, she just didn't wake up.*" Liv takes a deep inhale of her cigarette and holds it for a while before exhaling, blowing the smoke to the side. Her eyes focus on mine, and they're not bright.

"Liv, I'm so sorry."

She waves me off.

"Don't be. You didn't ask for her to get cancer, and you didn't ask for your dad to die. You have nothing to be sorry for, Emi." I nod. I wish I could believe her words; that'd make everything so much easier. I'd feel so much better.

"You guys buried your dad up here?"

I nodded. *"Yeah. Dad wanted to be buried close to us, so we could visit. I guess he knew we'd eventually moved up here with Rick."* Guilt pushes down on me even harder.

She stands up and takes another hit of her cigarette. She holds her hand out, and I take it and stand up.

"Liv, what day is it?" I ask her as we walk towards my car.

"Saturday, Em. It's Saturday." She wraps an arm around my shoulder and hugs me to her side. We climb into my car, and I pull out of the parking spot.

"How'd you get here?" I ask her, following the GPS directions to get to her house.

"Rex dropped me off. Clara and I hung out this morning, but she had a lacrosse meeting, so I asked Rex to come pick me up."

"Has she already decided about Brown?"

"Nah, she's taking her time. She keeps saying, 'The deadline's not until May 1st.'"

The whole college thing has completely slipped my mind. The only thing I've been focusing on is making it to school and back home without any meltdowns or anyone noticing anything.

Liv lives two blocks away from the train station in a large two-story house painted a dark gray, with a simple wrap-around porch and wooden steps covered in snow leading to the front door. I park in the driveway and follow her inside. She unlocks the door and flicks on one of the lights. I don't have a chance to look around; I just follow her up the stairs.

Her bedroom door is at the end of the hall. There are clothes thrown all over the room, a full-size bed with simple white sheets, four pillows—two with silk pillowcases—and a desk in front of a window. She has a TV on the other side of the room, and her desk has textbooks, sketchbooks, and a Brown University pamphlet. I pick it up, and she quickly grabs it from my hand, hiding it underneath her textbooks.

"Clara left that over."

"Clara's been here?"

Liv nods, taking off her winter coat and throwing it on a chair in the corner.

"She likes coming over more than she likes me going over to her place. Her parents might ask questions. Plus, she doesn't mind if I smoke as long as it's here." Liv moves to her bedside table, takes a small pill, and lights up a joint. She moves to her window and cracks it open.

"Hold this." She hands me the joint, and I take it from her fingers. She removes her shoes and throws her hair into a high ponytail, the pieces frizzy and slightly dry. She takes off her hoodie, and she's left in loose brown mom jeans and a thin white tank top.

She takes the joint from me, climbs into her bed, and pats the spot beside her. I take off my shoes and winter coat and climb in next to her. We lay in silence for a while, the smoke from the joint filling the bedroom and making her sheets smell like Chanel perfume and weed. It goes well together..

"When my mom got sick, like really sick where all she could really do was sleep, I started taking her meds. And when she died, I kept taking them."

"You got addicted to them."

"And other shit." She puts out the joint, hiding it inside a wooden box. When she stands up, she moves slower and more languidly. *"But I'm not anymore. I got better."* That's good.

"You, okay?"

"Yeah," she mumbles. She brings out two canned sodas and climbs back into bed. *"Rex bought me a mini fridge and came over one day and installed it. Clara keeps it restocked."*

"That's so cute!" I gush. I'm definitely second-hand high, and I think Liv knows it.

"She's pretty cute. Half the time when she comes over, I can't keep my hands off her." Liv smirks, and my eyes widen.

"Do you think she cares that you tell me this stuff?" I ask with a laugh.

Liv shakes her head.

"I read her messages once, and she told her little sister every detail of us…together. Her sister couldn't even make eye contact with me for a week after that!" Liv laughs a full belly laugh, and I join her.

"Jay and I had sex one time for two hours. I'm pretty sure Rachel heard," I admit.

"Who's Rachel?"

I laugh and look at Liv.

"She's the cook, the person who does the cleaning, and the woman who basically raised Jay." Liv nods in understanding.

"My dad heard one time. Clara was so embarrassed she hid in my bathroom for thirty minutes, but she eventually came out, and I introduced them. He was just happy I wasn't getting pregnant."

"I can't imagine Clara being embarrassed."

Liv rummages through her nightstand, pulls out a tray and a small bag of weed, and begins crushing it up and placing it in a paper, using the pad of her fingers to smooth it out.

"She doesn't get embarrassed often. She did the first time we had sex and when Rex caught us in the act." She licks the paper and rolls another one. *"Pass me that lighter."* I turn over and grab the blue lighter from the other nightstand. I hand it to her, and she lights up, coughing softly at the first hit.

I watch her take lazy puffs and eventually pass out. The last thing I see is her winking at me.

###

When I wake up, Liv's standing in front of her window, smoking another joint, maybe the same one from earlier. Her window is still open, and the wind sends a crisp breeze throughout the room. Her face is a closed-off mask, her eyes locked on her window. She's lost in her own thoughts. *Is she okay?*

Liv must feel my eyes on her because she looks at me, smiles, walks over, and sits on the edge of her bed.

"How long did I sleep?" My voice is hoarse and thick with sleep.

"Five hours; it's almost nine. I washed some clothes and found an extra toothbrush, soap, and shit."

"You want me to spend the night?" I can hear the shock in my voice. I've never slept over at a girl's house, not by myself.

Liv chuckles.

"Yeah, if you want."

"I want to," I confirm in my most determined voice.

"You're such a dork." She laughs and stands up. She goes and grabs water from her minifridge and hands it to me. When she climbs back into her bed, I take a sip of the water and set it on the nightstand beside me.

"Can I take a hit?" I hesitantly ask her; she stares at me for a second, contemplating if she should.

She takes another hit before narrowing her eyes. *"It's strong, so go slow."* She hands it to me, and I do as she says, taking a small inhale before exhaling. I cough, and my lungs burn. But after a few seconds, the burn fades, and I pass it back to Liv.

We do this a couple times until I'm sufficiently buzzed. She keeps going, and I just sit across from her laughing, everything lighter, and the nothingness from the past week gone.

"I feel so much better," I tell her, a satisfying smile on my face.

"That's good. How'd you feel before?"

"Like I was nothing. Sometimes it's all I feel, like everything is just stuck, and I can't move forward…it's just not something I'm strong enough to do." I force a laugh and look away from Liv. *"But I'm fine now!"*

She chuckles.

"I'll tell Rex you like the weed," she jokes, and we both laugh. Her light is dim, and the space between us is maybe two feet. Probably less. The whole calculating length thing isn't going too well for me right now.

Liv's smile fades. *"Some days, I wish I could be a different person. I don't like who I am sometimes,"* she admits, her voice small and vulnerable. I think the worst part is I can hear the honesty in it.

That's so sad to hear, to listen to one of your best friends tell you they didn't like who they were. You want them to see themselves how you see them. I want Liv to know she's amazing, sweet, always there for me, and filled with so much light. Being around her is as easy as blinking.

"Me too," I whisper, both our smiles pained and fragile, our eyes glassy as we blink away tears, not letting one fall.

Maybe that's the saddest part. We both feel that way, yet we both hate that for each other.

Chapter 49

Emille Kate Van der Berg

There's nothing enjoyable about school. Not today. I have art next period, so I've gotten through most of the hard shit besides AP Bio. I haven't done an assignment since the week of my birthday, and I know Bryce has just been putting my name on it. Our teacher knows but hasn't said anything.

I open my locker, remove all my textbooks, and replace them with my sketchbook, AP Bio folder and notebook, and creative writing notebook. I feel someone brush past me, but I don't even bother turning around.

A body presses into me, and I freeze. The person is maybe a few inches taller than me, but I know it's a girl. The smell of Chanel perfume and the softness of their front against my back confirms it.

"Imagine my surprise when I woke up and found out you slept over at my girlfriend's house." Clara lets her venom-filled words sink in. *"You can imagine the anger, the frustration, the annoyance I felt. Can't you?"*

I nod.

"*Next time, invite me, or don't have one!* " she barks at me. I nod, and she takes a step back. I spin around and face her as she gives me a tight smile.

"*You and Liv are dating now?*"

"*Tell anyone, and I'll slam my lacrosse stick up your nose,*" she calmly threatens as we walk inside Art together. "*But yes, we are.*"

"*Good. I'm happy for you guys.*"

Liv comes in a few minutes later, her eyes barely open and a small smile on her face. Clara narrows her eyes then scoffs before turning around. She and Liv don't talk for the rest of the class, and I know they're in a fight before I ask Liv. With all of the tension between the theme of us, the rest of class is a bust; I just stare at the work I finished a few weeks ago and decide to turn it in for my midterms.

"*Before you all go, I just want to remind you guys the art competition is still underway, and if you want to be considered, you have to turn something in before May 16th! If you need any help, I'm always here!*" Ms. Han shouts as we all pack up.

I completely forgot about it, and the way things are looking right now, it looks like I'm out of the running. I don't see myself winning, not with the lack of inspiration and my lack of energy to do anything.

I sit in my car and nibble on my lunch. Lucille packed me an Italian sandwich with sugar cookies and a Coke. I can only take two bites of my sandwich before my stomach starts to feel like acid, and I'm on the verge of vomiting. I've stopped checking my messages. It feels like each time I look at them, I have to think of another lie to respond with. Occasionally I'll let my sisters know I'm fine, and that's enough.

During creative writing, we discuss Sylvia Plath and mental health in the twentieth century and how often people suffer from mental illness but keep quiet. Liv ditched, so I'm sitting with a group of students I don't really associate with.

After Mr. Fields finishes his lecture, a girl at my table turns to me and says, *"People who commit suicide are so selfish."*

I'm momentarily stunned that she's even speaking to me. *"What if they're really depressed?"* I mumble.

"So?" She stares at me like I'm an idiot, and my question is the dumbest thing I could've said. *"It's not any less selfish. It doesn't change the fact that they upend the lives of everyone around them. The same people they could have just asked for help!"* She huffs and shakes her head turning away from me. I feel like someone let all the air out of my lungs and consider walking out of class.

Mr. Fields comes over when the bell rings, stopping me from rushing out.

"Emi, I just wanted to say I loved your short story! If there's any more writing you want me to look at, please send it my way."

"Thank you. Wait…when did I send you a short story?" I try to shake off the girls words from earlier and put some pep in my voice for Mr. Fields.

"I believe the week of February 12th. Sorry it took me so long to get back to you."

I forgot I even sent him that. I thank him again and leave. I catch Liv and Clara slipping out of the locker room, Clara's cheeks flushed, and her usually silky straight blonde hair tousled. Liv looks cool as a cucumber.

They both notice me, and Clara glares at me, so I guess she and I are still doing this dance. But then her face softens a bit.

"Emi, are you okay? You look a little bit…tired." A hint of concern is in Clara's voice.

I must look like shit if Clara's is expressing concern. I tell her I'm fine and leave them where they stand to rush to my car.

I don't even take off my school uniform before climbing into bed. I bury myself under my covers and do the one thing that seems to shut off the constant drone of life: sleep.

Sometimes when I sleep, I dream, and the dreams last as long as I want them to. Sleep calls to me because sometimes the sun shines in my dreams, and I feel its warmth. The only problem is that I can't sleep forever, and the second I open my eyes, the warmth is gone, replaced by reality.

So, I force myself to sleep or watch television as much as I can. I try to stay checked out. I try to remember all the sayings like *"pain is temporary,"* but each hour, each day, it seems less and less believable.

I wake up to someone softly shaking me. I open my eyes, and Rick stands in front of me, my lamp on and a concerned look on his face that he hides with a smile.

"You gonna come down for dinner?"

I shake my head.

"I'm tired, really tired," I answer, my voice cracking. Before Rick says something else, I lie and tell him, *"I think I have the flu. I feel sick."* I should feel bad for lying to him, but I don't.

He nods.

"I'll have Lucille bring something up for you." He leans down and places a kiss on my forehead, and I watch him leave, closing my room door after him.

Lucille comes up 45 minutes later with a tray of food and medicine. She sets a water bottle on my bedside table and a tray next to me on my bed.

"Any sleeping pills? Something to knock me out for a while?"

She pauses, glancing at me briefly before handing me two pills. I take them with the water, and the last thing I hear is, *"Your favorite: broccoli cheddar soup."*

Chapter 50

James Averell

Rick opens the front door. He frowns when he looks at me and doesn't move to let me in; he just stands there with a weary look in his eyes.

"She's sick and doesn't want any visitors. She has the flu." He sounds like he's reading a script.

"The flu?" I repeat. He nods. *"Where the fuck would she get the flu? She doesn't leave the house."*

"Language!" he warns before continuing. I always forget how different Rick is than my dad. And make a note not to curse around him like that again. *"She had a sleepover with her friend, Liv, last weekend and went to school on Monday."* Rick continues/ It is flu season, you know.

It sounds to me like he's trying to convince himself as much as he is trying to convince me.

"Just let me see her. Uh, please."

He shakes his head.

"She's sleeping right now, and Lucille said not to wake her. I'm sorry." He closes the front door. I stand there for what feels like ten minutes, and once it's clear he's not opening it. I think for a moment about whether her window is likely to be unlocked. I circle around to peer up at it and see the outline of Lucille moving about. I curse under my breath and leave.

I drive back to the city to my apartment, my music so loud I can't even think. Caden is preparing to go home for spring break, and all he can seem to talk about is his girlfriend and their plans. He's also not-so-subtly told me he's excited to get laid. I can't listen to another one of those conversations. I unlock my front door, and Rachel stands inside my kitchen, which isn't surprising. I gave her a key, and she *frequently* uses it.

"How is she?" Pretty much everyone's been worried about Emi. She went from being all over the place, laughing and smiling, to sleeping and trapping herself in her room.

"Rick wouldn't let me see her; she has the 'flu.'"

"It is flu season…"

I glare at her, and she stops talking, biting her lip as she takes the pie out of the oven. *"I looked at your planner, and you still have two papers to write before you go on spring break next week. Lucky for you. I made plenty of food, so you have the energy to do it,"* she rushes out, forcing an excited look.

I give her a blank look, but she looks at me the way she did when I was little when I didn't want to go to bed or get in the bath. With a determined and fiery look that matched her hair, she always won, and this time was no different.

"I'll make you a plate," she tells me, her voice triumphant as she turns around and makes me a plate of chicken, corn, mashed potatoes, and gravy. I sit down at the table and begin outlining my essay.

I can't get Emi off my mind, though.

Did something happen to her?

Was she really sick?

Had her sisters seen her?

Was Lucille the only one taking care of her?

Did she do something she thought she couldn't tell me?

Was she going to keep her promise?

I know she hates that I worry about her, but I can't help it. When a person becomes ingrained in your heart, your mind, and your soul, they stay there. There's no way to erase them. You're stuck with them. So, when they fall, you try your hardest to catch them and pull them back up. When they're on top of the world, you feel it too.

And something told me, Emi wasn't on top of the world right now. And she wasn't going to tell anyone.

Chapter 51

Emille Kate Van der Berg

I can see the sunlight peeking through the windows. It's spring. My curtains are drawn, and my television isn't even on. I turned it off after I went to the bathroom last night. I count the books stacked on my floor and try to think which one I dislike most. It's hard, and I haven't decided yet.

My bedroom door swings open, and the sound of a loud scoff hits me.

"How can you live like this? This room is disgusting!" My mom snaps. *Who said anything about living?*

Once she realizes I'm not going to respond or get up, she leaves, slamming my room door after her and muttering words like *"lazy"* and *"dysfunctional."*

I miss Jay, but I don't want to be around him when I'm like this. I feel like I'll suck all of the happiness and love from him.

Last night I tried to get up and write something—anything—but I couldn't. It seemed like every creative bone and every meaningful thought in my head slipped, and I just stared at the page until my frustration won, and I threw my notebook against the nearest wall.

Lucille visits me every day with food and water. Yesterday she stopped bringing the sleeping pills, and I was too embarrassed to ask for them, so I just took a few bites of the soup and bread she made for me and washed it down with water and Gatorade.

She came in earlier for breakfast and suggested that I shower so I would feel better. I lied and told her I'd think about it. We both know I'm not sick, but every day she comes in and checks my temperature and feeds me, then goes downstairs to my parents and delivers the newest update about my *"illness."*

I turn over and turn on my television. Some random reality show is on, and I distract myself by watching. Five minutes into the show, my thoughts wander to Allison. I can imagine her standing in the corner of my room, looking at me with a smug smile, like she knew this would happen all along.

I can hear her voice, her shrill laughter taunting me, and I want to get up and tell her to leave me alone, but I can't. I'm lost in memories now. Memories of hiding in my bedroom so she couldn't find me, hiding behind Dad and Thena's legs so she wouldn't bother me, memories of listening to her yell at Mom and Rick until she was blue in the face, and memories of her reminding me we weren't real sisters.

I feel warm tears sliding down my face when the door opens. I open my mouth to tell Lucille I'm feeling queasy and she should leave, but I stop when I hear heels. I turn my head, and Thena and Bell come in, closing the door behind them. More tears fall as they enter.

I shake my head. *"I-I'm sick. You guys should go,"* I croak, trying to wipe the fallen tears.

Thena shakes her head and comes forward. She sits on the edge of my bed, leans forward, and pushes a piece of my hair stuck to my tear-stained cheeks off my face.

"We're not leaving," she adamantly tells me.

"Please," I croak, more tears sliding down my cheeks.

"No. Nothing you can say or do will make us leave."

I can tell she means it with everything in her, and that makes me break. I start to sob, and eventually, I sit up and wipe my face, but the tears keep coming.

"I- I don't like who I am anymore. I hate m-my thoughts," I cry. Thena moves forward and hugs me, and I cry into her white blouse. She doesn't say anything. She tells Bell to do something, but I can't hear them.

Thena pulls away from me and holds my shoulders. I look at her. My cries have quieted, and I'm trying to control my breathing.

"You're going to take a bath, and when you get out, you're going to eat something, and you'll feel better." She doesn't make eye contact with me. Her eyes keep scanning my room, looking at the piles of clothes, the sodas, the plates of food I won't let Lucille take out, and the journal on the ground.

I get up from bed and follow her into the bathroom. She fills the tub with hot water, sprinkles in some bath salts, and grabs towels and extra clothes. Bell doesn't come in, and Thena turns around as I strip, the water burning me in as I sink in.

Thena bathes me, and I sit there and let her brush through my hair.

I look at her, and her movements stop. Her eyes focus on me. They are red-rimmed and glassy.

"*I don't want to be here anymore,*" I tell her quietly.

She stares at me, and her jaw clenches.

"*We're going on spring break next week, and the fresh air will be good for you. You'll be able to relax without school or anyone pressuring you, and when you come back, you'll feel better.*" She rubs shampoo through my hair and begins washing it in sections. "*You will get through this. You're the strongest person I know.*"

Tears fall, and they make small drop sounds in the water, and I don't know if they're mine or hers. When she finishes, she stands up, washes her hands, and I catch her wiping her eyes. Thena braided my hair, and when I got out, I dried myself off and put on the pajamas she picked out for me: pink and white striped silk shorts and a matching large button-up shirt.

Bell cleaned most of my room, changed my bedsheets, and all the food and drinks were gone. My journal sits neatly on my desk, and I know without a doubt she didn't read it.

"*You didn't have to; I was going to clean it up. You guys don't have to clean up my messes, and I'm sorry for missing dinner. That was really shitty.*"

Bell walks towards me and hugs me, and I squeeze her back. She smells like cherry blossoms, and her hair is silky and straight down her back.

"*Don't worry about it. We just want you to be okay.*"

Thena joins the hug, and I'm pressed in between them. "*We'll always be here to clean up your messes. That's what sisters are for.*"

"*I love you guys.*" I do. I really love them, maybe more than anything.

We eat, and they distract me until I fall asleep. I wake up halfway through the night and find Thena facing away. Her hair is down and hiding her face.

"What day is it? " I ask her, still half asleep.

She sniffles. *"Friday."* She clears her throat. *"Go back to sleep, Emi."*

I do as she says.

April

Chapter 52

Emille Kate Van der Berg

A loud whistle fills the jet, and everyone quiets and focuses on Rick, who stands in the front with a bright smile. It's six o'clock in the morning, and the jet is scheduled to take off in fifteen minutes. All of us are inside, the Yateses, the Averells including Rachel, and all of us Van der Bergs. Bell told me that Alexander is currently in the Maldives, so he's unable to join us. None of us are surprised. It would be a surprise if he showed up.

"We are about to take off, so if you need anything, get it now!" Rick announces. He gives us a moment to let his words sink in, and when no one makes a move to go, he sits back down by Mom, who talks to Mrs. Yates.

Thena helped me pack my suitcase last night. Actually, she did it herself, and I'm certain we didn't forget anything. Jay and I sit beside each other with a blanket on our lap; I have the window seat. A table separates us from Bell and Thena, who sits across from us. Thena has a textbook and notebook out and is taking notes. It's a sixteen-hour flight, and she looks like she will spend at least half of it working.

"*Are you excited?*" I ask him, peeking up at him. He looks down at me and smirks.

"*Are you?*"

"*Kind of.*"

"*Then I'm kind of excited too.*"

I roll my eyes, hiding my smile, and press my face against his chest. I'm tired. I want to sleep, but I don't want to miss anything that happens on the flight.

Bell took a sleeping pill before we even got on the plane, and she stood up and stretched, gesturing towards the bedrooms in the back and disappearing inside. I fall asleep to the feel of Jay's lips on my forehead.

###

"*Pasta or chicken?*" The flight attendant asks me as I walk back to my seat from the restroom.

"*Pasta,*" I answered. She smiles, and we both brush past each other. I slept for five hours, and when I woke up, Jay was writing on a legal notepad; a thin paperback book was in his hand. Sticky notes and annotations are all on the pages.

He stands up, and I slide into my seat. Before I sit down, he pinches my ass, and I yelp. Thena's eyes snap to me. I force a smile and nervously sit back down, glaring at Jay, who just stares at his book. I grab my laptop from my bag under my seat and open it, putting on a television show.

The flight attendant brings our food, and I eat my spaghetti while watching *New Girl*. I've rewatched it at least twenty times.

330

I finish my spaghetti and slide my slippers off and get comfortable. I'm wearing Jay's sweatpants; I stole them from him maybe a year ago. Schmidt and CeCe are getting married, and I can't help smiling. I think they're one of my favorite couples of all time.

Jay leans over and kisses my neck, a soft kiss that momentarily distracts me. He eats the last bit of fries off his plate and adjusts the blanket so we're both equally sharing it. His hand drifts to my thigh, squeezing it before moving it further down until he reaches the back of my thigh. His hand moves between my legs, and I gasp. He begins rubbing before giving me a squeeze that makes me clench my thighs around his hand.

He chuckles and leans forward, kissing my lips.

"Bathroom. Five minutes." He kisses my nose and gets up, and walks to the bathroom.

I wait three minutes before standing up.

"I-I'm gone go check on Bell, make sure she's okay and still breathing, you know?" Thena just stares at me, and Nick doesn't even look up from his book.

I look over my shoulder, and Rick and Mom are watching a movie. Mrs. Yates is asleep, and Eric and Mr. Yates are in a heated discussion about baseball.

I knock on the bathroom door before entering. Jay leans against the counter, and before I can even say anything, he kisses me, his lips attacking mine as I try to keep up. I wrap my arms around his neck. He spins me around until my back presses against the sink. He detangles his lips from mine and trails kisses down my neck. *"I missed you so much Em. Please don't ever go dark on me like that again."*

He presses his body against mine and I can tell he plans to do more than kiss. *"Jay, we can't! Our parents are right outside!"*

"We'll be quiet…unless you don't want to?" He raises an eyebrow, and I bite my lip. You have barely smiled today and I can't take seeing you like this. I just want you to feel good. Tell me what you need. Please My heart swells at the sincerity in his voice. He is presenting me with a chance to unplug from the endless thoughts in my head and just feel our connection instead. I nod.

"*I do want to.*" I whisper. A slow smile stretches across his face that makes me laugh. The laugh surprises me. It's like Jay is the only sliver of joy that can always break through the fog of my brain. What is more evident is that he knows it.

After we both catch our breaths, and straighten our clothes we make eye contact in the tight space of the cabin bathroom and booth dissolve into laughter. "*SSShhhhh.*" I try to warn Jay to keep it down while my own giggles overtake me again. A shuffling outside the door causes me to clap a hand over my mouth and then Jay's. He licks my palm which makes me snatch my hand away and more giggles escape. "*We have to get out of here.*" Jay laughs trying to compose himself. I try to pull myself together also in time for him to open the door. A little bit of sadness is already creeping along the edges of this bright moment as I realize we will be stepping out of our little cocoon.

Jay opens the door, and Nick stands there with his usual self-assured smile, his arms crossed the expression on his face clearly amused.

"*Uh….*" I'm try to find a fast lie to explain why we are in the bathroom together, but I don't know how long he has been standing there or what he's heard.

"At least you won't be grumpy when we land," Nick tells Jay, who rolls his eyes and leans in to tell him something. I sneak past them as they talk and return to my compartment.

Thena greets me with a raised eyebrow. Apparently, everyone who was awake has managed to put two and two together about Jay and I.

"How many more hours?" I ask, avoiding eye contact.

"We should be landing in ten hours," Nick answers returning to the section and checking his watch. Thena crosses something off her to-do list and sits up more straight before pulling out her laptop and closing her textbook.

"What are you doing now?" I ask her, trying to peek at her to-do list.

"Writing my business ethics and law paper. I've gotten all the research down. Now I just need to write it. It should take me less than two hours, probably one if some people shut their mouths." She shoots a look at Nick, but the fire of previous weeks is gone. She is softening toward him.

"I think I'm going to crash with Bell in the back," I say. I know when I am being a third wheel.

Plus, I'll need all the sleep I can get; I can't go into a dark place on this trip. I can't. I won't ruin this trip for anyone. My family deserves that.

Chapter 53

Emille Kate Van der Berg

The second we step off the jet, the heat hits me like a slap in the face. My sweatpants feel damp from the humidity, and I'm thankful I took my sweatshirt off before we landed. I slept the rest of the flight, Bell cuddled up to me, and her tall warm frame was comforting. When I woke up, though, one of her legs was thrown over my hip, and her hair was in my face. She is still i wild sleeper, just like when we were kids.

Two black Escalades are waiting for us on the tarmac. Jay grabs my hand and laces our fingers together as we walk towards the second Escalade. Bell, Nick, Thena, Rachel, Jay, and I climb in. We pull off as soon as our suitcases are in the trunk.

"How far is the resort?" Bell asks.

"Thirty-three minutes," Nick answers. The top two buttons of his shirt are unbuttoned, and he sits with his legs crossed as he looks out the window.

"I think we should get food and then decide what to do something, but food and check in first," Thena announces. The air is on full blast, so she talks a little louder than normal.

Murmurs of agreement fill the car.

The resort is large and has a wooden hut structure. The whole resort is open concept with trees lining the path towards the entrance. Car's unload, kids run inside, and nannies and mothers run after them, calling their names.

It's warm, and the sun is high in the clear sky. It's only one o'clock here. I follow everyone inside, holding Jay's hand and looking around. We've been here before. It's not my favorite place, but I really like it here. Rachel stands timidly by Jay. She looks around with a big smile, her cheeks tinted. This is the first time that she has traveled with the whole group of us for fun and not as anyone's caretaker. I can't help but wonder if we've ever really made her feel like a part of the family or if we all treat her like the help.

Eric, Mr. and Mrs. Yates, Mom, and Rick all stand by the check-in desk. Mom and Mrs. Yates stand back, talk, and smile, making plans. I can see them on these trips as two young college students going on vacation together. They look younger and a little brighter. I like the way Mom looks on these trips. I also don't mind that she seems to take a break from micromanaging me when we are out of the country.

They all head over, and we make a large huddle.

"Mary and Linc," Rick passes them their key card. *"Emi, Bell, Thena, and Rachel."* Thena grabs our room key *"Eric,"* he always gets his own room. *"Nick and Jay."* Nick takes their key, and Rick holds onto his and Mom's key.

Rick checks his watch. *"Meet back here in half an hour."*

The walk to our villa is less than five minutes. It has two bedrooms with a king-size beds and a pullout couch. The bathroom has two separate sinks; by one of the windows, there's a desk and the living space opens right out to the water.

Our suitcases are dropped off a few minutes after we make it to our room. Bell goes outside on the little balcony area and takes a video for her Instagram, showing off the view. She uses her social media more than any of us. It seems like she's never really unplugged from it. But we understand that its required for her job.

"I think I might make one," I tell her, leaning against the railing and looking at the clear blue ocean and the white sand.

"Make what?" Thena asks, her heels clicking as she comes to stand by me.

"An Instagram. I'd like to document this trip."

"Are you sure?" Bell asks me. I nod.

I'm not as scared anymore; I think I can handle it. What people say about me is probably nothing compared to what floats around my head.

###

336

Forty-five minutes later, we leave our villa. Thena took a ridiculously long thirty-minute shower. Rachel changed in one of the closets, and Bell and I changed in the main bedroom. Bell slid on a short floral dress, and I found a pair of denim shorts with an oversized T-shirt to put over my one-piece swimsuit. Thena wears a simple and short blue dress with wedges, her hair, usually bone straight was starting to wave up from the island air and it felt like a good sign. If she let her hair revert to its curls, she would probably relax in other ways as well. The island really was good for everyone.

"*Where are you originally from?*" Bell asked Rachel as we walked back to the lobby.

"*A small town about an hour outside Austin, a military base.*"

"*Oh, cool! You're a military brat!*" Bell pauses and looks at Rachel. "*I'm sorry. Is that rude to say?*"

Rachel laughs and shakes her head.

"*No! No, not at all. I've been called one my whole life and told people I was one too. I lived in Germany for two years, Georgia for four, and once we got to Texas, we stayed there.*"

"*Do you miss Texas?*"

Rachel shakes her head, her face set. "*No, not really.*" By the tightness of her voice, she doesn't like talking about Texas.

Everyone waits for us in the lobby, too distracted with talking and making plans to be annoyed at our tardiness. Both Jay and Nick changed into shorts and collared shirts,.

"*You and Nick are twinning,*" I tell him with a big smile, looking between them.

Jay rolls his eyes. *"Yes, it was planned, and no, we don't have time for pictures,"* he sarcastically replies, standing up and stretching.

"Where are we going?"

"Lunch by the pool or something. I wasn't listening." Jay wraps one hand around my shoulder, and I lean against his chest, wrapping an arm around his waist. We stand like this until everyone starts heading to the pool for lunch. As we walk, he keeps his arm wrapped around me.

Before we eat, Bell takes off her dress and runs into the pool, her black bikini the last thing I see before she dives in. She swims and laughs, dunking herself underwater one last time before joining everyone at the table.

After we eat, we swim and lay in the sun, and for a little bit, I feel warm. I smile, my face tilted towards the sun. I smile because I *feel warm*. I soak up this feeling and try to commit it to memory because I know it can't last. I wish I could bottle it and access it again when things feel gray in my mind.

Chapter 54

James Averell

Rachel looks like a fish out of water. She keeps nervously glancing at my dad, and she's been sipping the same mojito for twenty minutes now. I'm already on my second, and Nick hasn't even touched his cognac.

Emi sits next to me at dinner, her brown skin already a little darker and glowing from the sun. I openly check her out. Her body looks amazing in the tight green tank top. She's quiet but her sisters sit across from her chatting away.

"What are you going to have in your bio?" Thena asks Emi, trying to pull her into the conversation. I turn to Nick and realize that he is openly admiring Thena as she talks. As she sips her drink, Nick stares at her lips. When she laughs, a smile instinctively appears on his face also. I shake my head. The guy is smitten.

"I don't know…maybe 'live love laugh'?" Emi mumbles while sipping something from an open coconut. *"Bio for what?"* I ask turning back to Emi. She looks at me with a nervous expression on her face.

"Instagram. I want to make one."

"You do?" She's used my account for the past two years. *"Yeah, I want to document this trip, and I'm not scared anymore."*

"Alright, well, let's make one!"

She smiles and grabs her phone from her back pocket, unlocking it and going onto the Instagram app. She signs out of my account and starts to create her own. She makes her username: emi.vdb.

"It's a long name," she says while she creates her account. She writes Emi Van der Berg in her name spot, though. She turns to look at me. *"How corny is it to use a quote from Harry Potter?"* Before I can answer, she adds, *"Or what about Dark Knight Rises? But people probably won't get that one."*

"Just do what you want. Who cares what everyone else thinks?" I told her. She stares at me and then looks at her phone, typing something I can't see.

"What are you going to do for a profile picture?" Bell asks, dipping her truffle fries into ketchup.

"I don't know. I don't take a lot of selfies."

I'm pretty sure the only selfies Emi takes are the ones she sends me when we text, and most of the time, those are pictures of her just waking up. *"What's yours?"* she asks her sisters.

Thena pulls her up. It's a photo of her in black and white, her face set with no smile and her hair down. She's had it for maybe three years now.

Bell pulls up her account which showcases one of her baby pictures. She doesn't look older than six. Her hair is in two pigtails as she cheekily smiles at the camera, wearing what looks like a dirty white tank top. Thena and Bell really are total opposites.

Emi searches through her favorite pictures, and the picture she chooses is one of us. I look over her shoulder, and when I see it, I whisper, "*Yes.*" It's my favorite picture of us. We're in the Hamptons, smiling. She sits on the arm of my chair, and I have an arm around her waist. The picture is from before we started dating, but even then, I knew I loved her as more than a friend.

"*I like that one. Or this one.*" I scroll to a picture of her smiling, the sun shining on her face, and her hair wet from the water. Her brown skin is glowing, and her brown eyes are so much brighter, the flecks of green more prominent.

I'd be happy with either one. Emi lets her sisters choose, and they both pick the picture of her smiling by herself. She sets it up, and she officially creates her Instagram profile.

"*I have an Instagram!*" she cries! She starts texting Liv and sends her the profile, and in a matter of minutes, Emi has ten followers.

Her excitement over her account is palpable over dinner, and I sip my drinks and put an arm on the back of her chair as I watch her. For the first time in a while, she looks connected to us, as if she's in the moment with us and not lost in her head. I want her to stay like this for the rest of the trip and even longer, not for my sake but for hers. She deserves it.

Chapter 55

Emille Kate Van der Berg

We've been in Fiji for three days now, and each day has been a little better than the one before. Bell went surfing yesterday, and she could barely stand up, but she was enjoying herself. Her hair hasn't stayed dry the whole trip. Thena, Nick, Jay, and I went swimming last night, and I'm pretty sure I saw a few heated glances between Nick and Thena. Which is progress. She wouldn't even look at him a week ago.

We go to a local restaurant for dinner. Six of us cram into a booth, and the others sit at the two extra tables added to the end.

"Are you hungry?" Jay asks me as we sit down.

"After all that swimming and napping? Starving." He chuckles and opens his menu. I do the same and try to find something to eat.

"I think on our last night here, we should have a private chef come by and cook dinner," Mom suggests, running her hand over her hair. All of us Van der Berg girls have been wearing our hair completely natural, not putting any heat on it. It doesn't happen often, but when it does I savor

it. I have a moment of realization that a lot of what I felt separated me from my sisters was really just a lot of carefully crafted styling and heat manipulation. This many days into the trip, Thena and Bell were sporting real curls and the sun had baked them much closer to my complexion. Not mom though. She was slathered in sunblock and wearing the most absurdly wide-brimmed hats everywhere she went.

"*That sounds good,*" Mrs. Yates agrees, her hair in a high ponytail that reminds me of something a cheerleader would wear.

Throughout dinner, Jay and Nick talk about a club or something, what Jay should do since his second semester is almost over, and his plans for the fall. Bell, Thena, and I discuss Bell's potential project in California towards the end of April. I feel myself trying to go inside my head, but I don't. I hang onto their every word and participate.

By the end of dinner, I'm exhausted. I do the same thing on repeat until our last day. Then I allow myself to break out of my routine.

THE LAST DAY

I sit on the beach, far enough from the water. The sky is dark as the sun rises. I watch the sky become a soft cotton candy pink, the clouds meeting the water's far edge. They look intertwined, becoming one. My feet are buried in the cold sand. I hear the sound of footsteps trekking through the sand, but I don't want to look away from the sky. I'm scared I'll miss all of it.

"*You've always liked the sunrise,*" Thena softly says next to me. I'm glad it's her.

"*I read The Bell Jar,*" I told her after a few minutes of silence.

"What? When?" Her surprise hides her excitement.

"A little bit before my birthday. I liked it. I can see why it's one of your favorite books."

I did like it, and it wasn't too hard to understand. Thena's copy of the book has post-it notes, highlights, and scribbles in the margins, so I bought my own, not wanting to mess up hers. I read it one night, and when I finished, I scribbled notes in my journal about the writing style and pacing. I do that sometimes when I finish a book—take notes about the writing more than the story.

"I'm glad you liked it," Thena whispers.

The sun is fully up now, and it's high in the sky, a few bright white fluffy clouds in the blue sky.

I look at Thena and take in everything about her: the clearness of her sky-blue eyes, the tightness of the curls in her wavy black hair, the golden tint of her brown skin, the fullness of her lips, and the sharpness of her cheekbones. She's beautiful inside and out. She's the one who's always there to help me back up after I fall, but I don't think she can help me now.

I hug her, warming my arms around her frame and squeezing her. She showered this morning. I can smell it in her hair and soapy fresh skin, her Chanel perfume heavy on the surface.

"I love you. You're one of the best sisters anyone could ever ask for," I whisper into her neck. She squeezes me tight, and when we pull apart, her smile is small, and her eyes are glassy. I stood up and asked her, *"Breakfast?"*

We walk back to the resort and pass Jay and Nick sitting on their balcony, both smoking. Jay is shirtless in swim trunks, and Nick wears a long sleeve light blue button-up shirt and black swim shorts.

"What are we doing today?" I ask them over the railing.

Jay does a smoke trick, blowing smoke in the shape of an 'o.' He lazily inhales another drag and then blows it upward. I wish he would quit, but he doesn't ask me to change so I've stopped asking him to either...

"Boat. We leave after breakfast, which starts at 9:00. Pack a bag," Nick says, typing on his phone. He takes one last hit and puts his cigarette out. Nick walks back inside their room, and Jay puts out his cigarette, leans over the railing, and kisses me. He tastes like smoke and mint toothpaste.

"I'll come get you from your room." I nod, and he kisses my nose.

Eric walks with us to breakfast. He stands by Rachel and Jay, and I stand behind them. They don't talk, but occasionally they glance at each other before looking away. Something is being communicated between the two of them that feels covert, I check to see if anyone else notices but they don't seem to.

"Does everyone have sunscreen? The last thing we need is one of you getting sun poisoning," Mom says loudly from the other end of the table. She puts sausage links, fruit, and some eggs on a plate and then hands it to me. She kisses the top of my head and hands another plate to Thena.

"Everyone eat up. We've got a boat to catch!" Rick calls. He shoves a pastry into his mouth and winks at me, frosting on his lip. Mom groans and rolls her eyes. Rick just smacks a kiss on her lips, frosting ending up on hers. She licks it off and wiggles her eyebrows at him.

When we board, excitement courses through my veins. We anchor far enough out where we can't see the beach, and Bell grabs Thena and me. Before I can talk myself out of it, we jump off the top deck.

I'm submerged in the warm water before I can even freak out. I immediately swim to the surface and take a deep breath, gasping for air. I look and find Thena coming up for air, a smile on her face, and Bell floating on her back, laughter spilling from her mouth. I look up at the boat. Rick takes a picture, and Jay smiles at me.

"Jump in!" I yell at him. He shakes his head and disappears. A few seconds later, he stands on the boat's edge, his shirt off, and jumps in. The splashes of water hit my face. He stays under, and I frantically look around and don't see him.

Something brushes both my legs, and a scream escapes my lips. Jay comes up to the surface, his hands touching my waist. I smack his chest, water hitting him in the face.

"You scared me!" I exclaim.

We both tread water, occasionally going under. We swim back towards the boat, climbing the ladder and returning to the deck. Mom and Mrs. Yates rub sunscreen on themselves and lounge on chairs in the sun.

I check my phone and see that Bell uploaded the picture of us in the ocean on her Instagram story with a caption in thick white lettering that reads *"Perfection."* I repost it to my story and power off my phone. Nick sits on one of the chairs alternating between typing on his phone and reading.

Jay sits next to him, and when I make eye contact with him, he waves me over. I walk over and sit right next to him, my legs tucked underneath me.

"I have to tell you something," he starts, one of his arms wrapping around my waist. *"I got offered an internship at Riniva Tech. It starts in October and goes until the end of the year."*

"Oh my God! Did you take it?! Please tell me you took it!" I squeal. I wrap one of my arms around his neck and scoot closer.

"I told them I'd think about it. I don't know what life will look like in October; they gave me until the end of July to decide."

"Jay, that could open so many doors for you! Why didn't you take it immediately?"

He nods, his expression thoughtful.

"I'm trying to figure out what I want to do, and I know it isn't working for someone else's million-dollar tech company. But the connections could pay off down the line. I gotta figure it out."

"What do you think you want to do?"

"I don't know, but I want to create something. Something that isn't a fitness app or another social media platform. It'll come to me eventually."

"Then just be patient because when it comes, I know it'll be amazing." I lean forward and playfully pepper kisses all along his cheek and jaw, making loud kissing noises. He laughs and tries to shrug me off, but before he can, I lean forward until we're face to face and press a kiss against his lips. He puts one hand on the back of my head and deepens it.

When we pull apart, I glance at Nick, and he's still reading his book.

"Jump in with me?" Jay says standing up and dragging me along. We look at each other, our toes over the edge of the deck's edge.

"Close your eyes."

I do, and I feel everything tenfold: the wind, the deck rocking beneath our feet, and the water slapping against the boat. Jay grabs me and jumps.

I open my mouth to scream, and a sound barely escapes before the cold fills my lungs. I open my eyes, and all I see is foggy burning blue.

I swim to the top, kicking my lungs and paddling my arms, my mouth half filled with water and my lungs beginning to burn and spread. I gasp for air. And look around, the familiar sting of the water in my eyes. Saltwater is brutal.

"I hate you! I wasn't ready!" I shout at him as we swim toward the ladder, and I climb up. He catches up to me by the third rung and wraps me in his arms. *"I'm sorry, Em. I thought it would feel like a thrill. You're such a strong swimmer."* If I wanted to be honest, I would admit that it was a thrill. But I was happy to let him feel bad a little while longer. An apologetic Jay is a very generous Jay.

We docked and showered and were getting dressed for dinner. Jay sits inside the bathroom while I do my hair, already dressed in a white linen shirt and blue jean shorts.

"Jay, I promise you they're not having sex," I assure him for the fifth time. I focus on my reflection and straighten out my part. *"Is this even?"* I point at the part in the middle of my head.

He glances at it. *"Yes."* He runs a hand through his hair. *"Em, he was standing so close to her. Neither one of them noticed when I walked inside the kitchen. I had to clear my throat and slap my hand against the island, then they nearly jumped out of their skin. I mean, I've told him a million times not to touch her, and the first family trip she comes on, he tries to flirt with her."*

"*Maybe she wanted to flirt with him,*" I suggest. He stands up and stands behind me. I freeze, my brush in hand. He glares at me, his jaw clenched. "*What?*" I ask.

"*Rachel would not flirt with him; she's half his age and I've seen guys hit on her, and she's completely oblivious.*" He lowers his voice. "*Em, I think she's a virgin.*"

My eyes widen and I stifle a laugh before it can escape and antagonize Jay. "*She's not Jay. She's an adult; she probably just doesn't discuss it with you.*"

He shakes his head.

"*Em, she hasn't been on a date since she moved in with us. I've tried to set her up, and she just makes excuses.*"

"*What would be the big deal if he was flirting with her. Maybe she likes his company.*" I refocus my attention on my hair, grab the large hair tie, and tighten the ponytail. My arms are burning from being up in the air for so long. There's a knock at the door. I say, "*Come in,*" before even thinking about it.

Thena walks in with her makeup bag and hair bag in both hands. She sets them down before noticing Jay sitting on the toilet.

"*Emi, why is your boyfriend in our bathroom?*" she asks; I look in the mirror, avoiding both of their eyes. I grab another hair tie and tie my hair's ends into a bun.

"*Uh, he had to pee.*"

"*Why is he still here?*"

"*He likes our bathroom.*" I shrug and put a bobby pin in my mouth, using my teeth to open it, and I start pinning flyaway from my bun. I finish my bun and start to brush my teeth.

Thena begins combing her hair while spraying some serum onto her hands. She puts on a headband and begins doing her makeup. She finishes her makeup with expert precision in ten minutes before moving on to her hair.

"Pass me that hair clip," she says. I do. She clips half her hair back and uses gel to slick it. She looks herself over in the mirror before nodding. *"James, go back to your own villa. Is there any location on the planet where you will not push up on my sister?"* She leaves before he has time to respond.

We lock eyes in the mirror, and Jay's eyes sparkle. He looks me up and down.

"Nope." He says before leaving.

Thena comes back in and changes into a navy blue dress with white wedges. She puts on her jewelry and then looks me up and down. *"You look beautiful, Emi."* She holds out her hand, and I take it. *"Come on."*

Bell and Rachel talk while they wait for us by the door. We walk to the boat, and Mom and Rick meet us on the way there. Rick hugs me to his side and kisses my forehead.

"Have you been having fun?" he quietly asks me.

I nod.

"One of the best trips in a while. Did you have fun?"

"Yeah, it's been fun. I'm happy you've enjoyed yourself, Emi. As long as you and your sisters are happy, I'm happy."

Rick is a good guy, maybe one of the best. He's always been there, and he always will. But giving him another burden, a burden he never asked for, isn't fair. I can only tell him so much. When I look at him, I can see how he and Mom worked out so well, but then I wonder if Mom and my dad ever worked out to begin with. Rick opens so many questions, some I never want to be answered.

###

A long table with white tablecloths and small candles aligned in the middle sits on the boat, taking up most of the deck with six chairs on each side, with a plate in front of each chair. Mr. and Mrs. Yates lean against the railing and sip their drinks, quietly talking to each other.

Jay and I sit down towards the right end of the table, and Thena and Bell are across from us, Rachel next to them, and Nick next to Jay. The staff serves drinks and appetizers meant to be shared. Everyone is talking, and I listen to Bell talk about the trip she took a few weeks ago and the date she had with Tristan when she came back. It sounds romantic and exciting. They went to her favorite restaurant, and he took her to the movies to see the latest romantic comedy and finished it off with a walk in Central Park. I know Tristan is not perfect, and Jay and Thena really dislike him, but I think he loves Bell. And that's all that matters to me. Maybe one day we'll see him the way she does.

"*Thank God he's not here*," Jay says when Bell gets up to go to the bottom deck. "*I think I would've thrown him overboard while the boat was moving*." Nick chuckles but hides it behind his drink.

Bell comes back with a waiter carrying stacks of packages; she carries some, too. They're all wrapped in black wrapping paper with pastel pink ties, bows, and large notes with each of our names. She passes them out, and the conversation quiets as she hands each of them to us. All the same size. My name is written in thick cursive.

"Wait!" She grabs her phone from the table and turns it on, holding it up to record all of us. *"Everyone open their package when I say go. Three…two…one! GO!"*

We all start opening our packages. Inside is the latest edition of *Bellucci's Top Three.* On the cover of the silky, shiny magazine is Jamie Phoenix with two other models, one male and one female. Bell sits right in the center. Both the male model and Jamie Phoenix have a composed straight face while Bell is beaming at the camera, wearing a Parkas brown winter coat with a white shirt underneath.

She looks beautiful like she's on center stage. I go to the page where the shoot is featured, and most of them are shots of Bell, some of them just her alone and others with the male model standing with her. In one of them, he stands alone.

"Who's the other model?" someone asks. I'm still looking at the page; her name is listed on the cover page.

"Daniel Ueda. He's from California, but his parents are from Japan. He's really sweet. He was only in town for the shoot, so he flew out that night. We only took those pictures together, no more than that. He's the one who saw the magazine first. It won't be out in stores until tomorrow."

Bell is on the cover of one of the biggest magazines in the world! I read the little excerpt written about the Parkas brand.

The company Jamie and Dakota Phoenix started focuses on creating effortlessly chic winter coats and clothes. The brand has taken the country and—and soon, the world—by the hand and has guided them through its vision. The one thing this brand brought to the table that others lacked or missed the mark on is the feeling of a new era being awakened, with fresh faces like Isabel Brigette Van Der Berg and Daniel Ueda captivating viewers. Every great thing must have a beginning, and this is theirs.

Wow. *Wow!*

"*Oh my God! This is amazing!*" I squeal. I'm pretty sure my reaction is probably a few minutes delayed. "*They called you captivating! You're part of a new era!*" I jump up and hug her. "*You want this, right?*" I ask her. She nods, her eyes filled with tears and her smile breathtakingly wide.

Thena stares at the picture.

"*You wore my ring. You wore the ring I made for you. You didn't have to do that, you know?*" Thena whispers to Bell, who's still smiling.

"*I wear it everywhere. It's beautiful. Thena, I did it for you, not for your business but just for you,*" she whispers back. Bell and Thena hug, and I smile, watching them.

"*I'm so happy! We need champagne to celebrate!*" Mom cries. She rushes to the bar, Rick follows her, and they pop open a bottle of champagne. The waitress pours champagne into flutes and passes them out. We all take one and cheer, congratulating Bell on her success. Happiness hangs in the air over us.

"*Speaking of brightened futures, Emille, have you decided what you're doing in the fall?*" Mom asks me. I don't want to dim Bell's night, and I know telling her the truth will do that. Mom looks so happy, her eyes bright and her face softer. She reminds me of how she did before Dad died when I used to lay in her arms and when she used to kiss me "*good morning*" and tell me stories in French.

"*I've decided to go to Brown in the fall. You were right; it's a good fit for me,*" I lie. I know she wants to hear all this, so I tell her. Eventually, I'll have to tell her the truth or someone else will.

Her face brightens, and she hugs me, her thin arms wrapping around me. "*Crotee, I'm so proud of you. This is what I want for you. For you to be happy and have a good future.*" She wipes under her eyes. "*Come, let's take pictures.*"

She positions all of us together, and I smile as wide as I can, thinking of all the unknown and sweet nothings while hugging Jay and my sisters.

My family deserves pictures, so they know it wasn't them. It was me, and they couldn't fix me.

Chapter 56

Emille Kate Van der Berg

The second we got back home, every weight I'd shed in the tropical waters returned ten times stronger like a monster that had lain in wait for me. I missed the first few days of school after the break. I try to get up, to make myself feel or do something, but I can't, and I feel so *weak* because I can't.

I can't continue like this, but I don't see anything changing. Each day feels like another step into the same dark path. But after a while, it starts to feel okay, like a horrible swallowing blanket. Part of it feels good. I shower and stare at myself in the mirror. Even after the shower, I still look asleep and lost.

Maybe it's been a few days since we've been back, but my room door opens, and it's Jay. He comes in with a bag of food, his eyes filled with concern. I wonder how much easier his life would be if he didn't have to worry or come visit me.

355

I sit up and smile at him. He slides his boots off and crawls into my bed. We eat, and I listen to him talk about his classes and how his midterms went.

He makes me laugh, and I make him laugh. I always want time to speed up, but at this moment, I want it to stand still so I can stay here and soak it in a little while longer. But time never does anything I want.

When we finish eating, I look at him, lean over, and kiss his neck, the smell of his cologne and soap prominent. I move closer and kiss again. He pulls away, looks down at me, and squeezes my hand. I lean forward and kiss him once more.

"Can we?" I ask him. He doesn't say anything, just leans away from me. I cannot handle a rejection from him at this moment so I wrap my legs around his waist and grind against him.

"Em, no," he protests. I find his lips and kiss, my tongue tasting his.

I want to get lost in this feeling because I know it'll feel better than whatever I was feeling before. I reach down between us and he grabs my hand and stops me. He pulls away. *"Em, when you are hurting like this, I don't feel comfortable..."*

I groan and squeeze my legs tighter around him. *Please don't make me think, don't make me feel anything but the distraction of pleasure.* He puts a hand gently on my stomach and pushes our bodies apart. I can feel the hot tears sliding from the corners of my eyes, but I am not ready to give up trying yet. *"Please,"* I beg. *"I feel so empty. Please just for a little while."*

Jay looks down at me, his own eyes glistening with tears now.

He raises his head and kisses me before I hear the sound of his sweatpants sliding down. He doesn't want to do this but he doesn't want me to be in pain. I want to tell him that it's okay, we can stop. But I am selfish and right now I'm a coward, so I don't. He squeezes his eyes shut and then opens them to peer down into my face. I can feel all the love he has for me, all the pain he is trying to hold for me and I know it's not fair to ask this of him but I just want to feel good, even if it is only for a little while - and Jay feels good. A sob escapes me. He stops moving.

Before he can ask what's wrong, I choke out a whisper, "*I really love you.*"

"*I really love you, Em,*" he whispers back, kissing my neck. I hold his head and kiss him, the saltiness and warmth of our tears mixing.

He stays the whole night holding me, and when he falls asleep, I sob.

How much longer can I keep this up?

How much longer do I have to go through everyday fights to stop myself from drowning just for little moments, or nights like tonight, or trips like Fiji?

I understand my dad now more than ever and that scares me.

Chapter 57

James Averell

"So, James, why should you be accepted into our brotherhood? What makes you worthy?"

Is this guy serious? I look at Nick, and he looks amused like he knows what I'm thinking. My dad forced me to meet with one of the *"societies"* he wants d me to join.

The president is sitting across from me with a smile and posture filled with entitlement. He looks at me like I'm prey or like he's in on some big joke. I can't stand him, and I've beaten up guys like him for messing with Emi. And once in a while just for speaking.

"I'm only here because my dad asked me to, and seeing as he makes sure I don't go broke and fire one of the few people I actually care about, I decided to listen. Now this stupid ass club you have going on sounds like the competition for the most entitled ass, and seeing as I'm richer than you, I don't think there's a reason to join. Tell my dad I turned you dipshits down or I'll key your car and punch you in the face until my knuckles bleed. And just to warn you, I have

strong knuckles." I flash him a dry smile before standing up. He and Nick both stand up. The guy smiles, buttoning up his jacket.

"*Your father and Yates were right. Follow me.*" I follow him, we go inside a dark common room with leather seats and a thick black desk with a brown leather chair. I shoot Nick a questioning look over my shoulder, but he ignores it.

A tall guy in a black tuxedo—no bow tie—with slicked-back thick brown hair and a smooth face stares at me. I look around the room. Above the fireplace is a school crest for Welton Prep. Black and white pictures line the fireplace and the walls. That guy wasn't the president; he was just a test and I probably just failed it.

He stands up from behind the table and walks over. He's two inches shorter than me, so probably 6'1.

"*James, it's nice to meet you. I'm Patrick Kane, chapter president. We've been asking your dad to get in touch with you for a while now,*" he explains, a poshness to his voice I can't quite place. I've seen him before.

"*You play professional hockey, don't you?*"

He nods. "*In my rookie season right now.*" It clicks now. I think he was a first-round draft pick. If not the first, then the third. He went to Yale and led them to a championship two years in a row. Emi and I went to one of their games with Thena.

"*Well, have you considered everything?*"

I don't know what to consider.

"*What exactly do I have to do to stay in one of these things?*" I ask him straight up. I'm not about to be someone's errand boy for six weeks or kiss someone's ass for a year.

"Well, there'll be a quarterly chapter meeting; a lot of people telecommunicate to join it. There will be galas and events that you are required to attend, but not often, and most of the time, you'll probably have planned on going. Your dad already paid the two grand entrance fee, and everything else is up to you." Patrick clears his throat, taking a step back.

"We're mostly here for networking or to provide a place for people to go if their family's shit. There are thirty men allowed per year. This year, we've only found fourteen; you'd be the fifteenth if you accept. During Yates's year, we found twenty-eight, and most of them joined because he was there." Patrick chuckles, and Nick shrugs unashamed.

"Any hazing or pledging phase?" I ask.

"For some, yes, but not for you. And before you ask, it has nothing to do with your parents. To get in, you do have to have money. I won't lie about that. But once you're considered, everything from there is based on character."

I nod, taking all of it in. They wanted me, not my last name. I know joining would please my dad, but I also know that in order for me to do what I want to do—whatever that may be —I need contacts. Contacts that aren't his.

"So, are you in?" Patrick asks. I can see the urgency he has swimming in his eyes. I like seeing that. Maybe that's fucked up, but I like knowing how bad he wants me to join this little club.

"I'm in."

His shoulders sag with relief, and he shakes my hand. Nick claps my back and winks at me.

Chapter 58

Emille Kate Van der Berg

I need to shake this feeling, shake myself out of this cycle. I need

something that can remind me that I'll be okay and that I'm not spiraling

toward something permanent. Or tragic. I look around my bedroom. There

are the same posters that have been here for years, old worn paperbacks, a

few comics shoved in between some of them, and my journals are thrown

throughout, some hidden, some not. Just depends on the year they were

written in. My room has colorful chairs and random trinkets, a closet with

clothes peeking through the door frame, and a large television mounted

on a wall.

There is also trash, clothes worn so many times they belong in last

month's wash load, and a layer of comfort underneath it all. I'm the only

one who could change this. It's one of the few things I can control.

I lay on my floor, the feeling of clothes and shoes underneath me. It feels like I'm lying on a rocky hill, a shoe wedged between my shoulder blade and clothes elevating my hips. It's not exactly comfortable, but at this point, I don't think I deserve that.

Can I go any lower?

If I think hard enough or pray hard enough, maybe this sinking desperate feeling will disappear, and I can take a deep breath and breathe. Maybe if I were not me, this wouldn't be happening. It seems like I'm paying the price for something, but I don't know what. Why, why can't I just be *normal.* I don't want to feel like this anymore.

I'm exhausted, and if I was around me, I think I'd be exhausted just talking to me.

It kind of feels good to be alone, just a little bit. I know I'm not draining anyone else. I'm just slowly rotting inside. Not quite visible enough for anyone. I can fake a smile long enough for Rick and Mom to leave my room. And lose myself inside of Jay long enough to take a deep breath and not break.

But when they leave and go back to their lives, I'm here with the same problems, the same brain, and the same insecurities and uncertainties. I close my eyes and do the one thing that hasn't failed me yet, sleep.

Eight years ago:

Bell and I ran through the living room, laughing while Alexander sat on the couch eating pizza and drinking a soda. Dad was upstairs, and he and Mom were talking.

Allison went out with her friends, so I knew the zoo would be fun. Everything is more fun when Allison's gone, but I haven't told anyone that.

Dad comes downstairs, his footsteps thudding on the wooden steps. I squeal and run to him; the smell of smoke and soap fills my nose. He picks me up and kisses my cheek.

"How you been, Emi girl?" he asked, his voice raspy and deep. I look at him, smile, and nod my head. His eyes were hazel with big green specks, and his face was slightly scruffy. His eyes were hollow, and it's no wonder Mom told us that he didn't sleep well. In her words, *"He works so much and travels all the time, so the time zones catch up with him."*

"How have you been?" I asked him back, and he smiled and chucked me on the nose. Bell ran into his legs, and he hugged her side.

"Where's my little beast?" he asked, his voice louder. Thena came from the kitchen with a playful glare on her face. Dad winked at her. *"Y'all ready to go to the zoo?"* We all nodded, and Bell squealed with excitement and anticipation.

"Xander, you good here?" Dad asked. Alexander nodded and smiled. Xander was at the age where hanging out with his sisters just wasn't cool anymore.

"I'll take the girls, and we'll meet you and Rick there," Dad told Mom. Everyone had adjusted so well to Rick being in our lives, but even as a little girl, I could see the pain in Dad's eyes when he watched Rick father the family he built.

I climbed into his car, and then Dad got in. He asked us about our day and what we did before we came. He asked us if we were going anywhere with Rick soon. Thena told him about a museum trip she was going on soon. He listened attentively as he always did. Even when we didn't make sense, or our words were incoherent, he listened. He was good like that.

We met Mom and Rick at the zoo. Rick had just returned from his trip to New York City with a guy named Eric. I waved at Rick, and he waved back, a small smile on his face. Bell hugged him, and he kissed Thena on the top of her head. I held onto Dad's hand and walked into the zoo with him. I didn't let go of his hand the whole time.

He always wore long-sleeved shirts, even in the heat of the summer. Mom wore shorts and a plain T-shirt, her hair curly in a low bun. She did all our hair and let us pick out our outfits this morning.

"*Emi girl, you ever get sad and don't know why?*" Dad asked me as I ate ice cream. He sat next to me. I shook my head. Allison made me sad, and leaving Dad made me sad, but that was it. "*Good. If you ever do, you'll tell your Mama, won't you?*"

"*I wanna tell you,*" I told him with a mouthful of ice cream. He wiped the corners of my mouth with a napkin.

"*I know, but your mama might be able to help you better.*" He could help me; I knew he could. He always helped me. I told him everything. Dad was my best and probably only friend besides Thena and Bell. "*Promise you'll tell her?*"

"*I promise.*" We pinkie promised, both bringing our thumbs up to our lips to kiss.

When I finished my ice cream, he grabbed my hand and led me back to where everyone was waiting. Rick had his arm wrapped around Mom. He watched Bell ride a horse while Thena stood on the fence.

Dad picked me up for a piggyback ride, and I rested my head on his shoulder. I was getting too old for this. I was ten, and he was still carrying me around, but sometimes he picked Bell up and threw her over his shoulders.

"Emi girl, are you staying for dinner or going back with your mom?"

I didn't even think about it. *"You!"* I yelled. He chuckled and lifted me into his truck. All three of us were going back with Dad. We spent the last two nights with Mom, and I missed him. He had chocolate chip cookies, and his house was small and cozy. If I had a nightmare, his room was two doors down.

"Daddy, I want to go to the bookstore tomorrow," I told him. As he unlocked the front door, he looked down at me with a sad look.

"I'll have Xander take you. Hopefully, he's not too hungover." He mumbled the last part.

We had his favorite food for dinner. All of us sitting at the small dining room table, I remember him looking thinner than he usually did. His smile was still bright, and his arms were still covered with his plaid button-up shirt. He looked like he had always looked: like my dad.

He tucked each of us in one at a time. While I took a bath, he talked to Thena. When I saw Thena brushing her teeth, her eyes were red. He talked to Bell next while I waited in bed; I shared a room with Thena and Bell. Thena always stayed up later than me, and Bell sometimes slept on the couch or in Alexander's room.

Dad came to tuck me in next and sat on my bed next to me. I stayed put and smiled at him, and he smiled back, tapping my nose with his finger. He leaned forward, angling his body towards me, one of his legs bent on my bed and the other on the floor. His hands intertwined with each other.

"You know, I wasn't close with my dad. He was always working, and my mom hated him. She kind of hated me too, so I was always alone. I've been alone most of my life until your grandma introduced me to your mom. Then she wouldn't leave me alone." He chuckled. His eyes were bright and filled with love. *"Then she had you guys, and I never want you guys to leave me alone."*

"I won't," I promised him.

His smile had fallen.

"I want you to promise me that you'll always be sweet and you'll always be there for your sisters. And even when you don't want to, you'll keep going. You'll never be alone, Emi, not like I was. Okay?" I nodded. I didn't know why he was telling me any of this, but I listened. *"There's a lot of things I can't tell you right now, a lot of things I wish I could, but you'll have Thena, your mom, Bell, Rick, and maybe even Xander to help you."* He stood up and walked towards my room door.

"I love you, Daddy," I told him before leaving. He smiled at me over his shoulder.

"I love you too, Emi girl. You'll always be my favorite girl." I smiled, and he winked at me before flicking off the light and leaving.

I had a dream about swimming in the ocean. Thena was floating on her back while Bell swam with a dolphin, and Xander made sure I didn't drown, holding onto the back of my swimsuit if I was starting to sink.

When I woke up, everyone was downstairs. Allison was still gone, Xander and Thena were talking while making breakfast, and Bell sat on the kitchen counter eating chips. I held out my hand, and she gave me some.

"Where's Dad?" I asked them. Xander looked over his shoulder, smirking at me.

"Morning, smelly." He made a scrunched-up face, and I smacked his back. *"He's still sleeping. He asked me last night to make breakfast for you guys."*

I ate chips with Bell and watched cartoons while Thena and Alexander argued over which school was more prestigious. Thena was obsessed with her *"five-year plan,"* and Alexander was obsessed with nitpicking her. The front door burst open, and Mom came running in, still dressed in pajamas. Rick followed her, fully dressed. We all watched them. After a few moments, though, Xander went upstairs. He came back down a second later and told Thena to call 911.

"What happened? Where's Dad?" I asked. I started to jog towards the stairs, but Alexander caught me by the waist. I squirmed in his hold.

"He's not feeling well and doesn't want you to get sick, so wait down here with Thena and Bell, okay?" I nodded. *"Promise me you'll wait down here, Emi."*

"Promise," I whispered, turning to join Thena and Bell.

Thena was crying, and so was Bell. Why were they both crying?

An ambulance arrived outside of our house, and they went upstairs. When they returned downstairs, they walked slowly, a body on the stretcher inside a black bag. I stood between Thena and Bell, who were both crying, both holding onto me. And I was patting their hands.

Mom came downstairs, her eyes red and tears falling down her face. Rick stood behind her, his eyes filled with tears. I looked over their shoulders to see Dad, but it was just Alexander. He wiped his face with the back of his hand.

"*Girls,*" Mom eased down onto her knees, sniffling as she did so, "*your dad, well… he had an accident. Last night when he was sleeping, his heart stopped, and the doctors couldn't bring him back. I'm so sorry, mes amours.*" My loves.

They cried louder, and I just stared at her. I knew what she was saying, but I needed it to click. They were carrying *my* dad out on a stretcher. He was a body inside of a zipped bag. He wouldn't have his favorite food anymore or listen to us tell him stories. He wouldn't go on walks or wear his favorite shirt. He couldn't do anything anymore.

Allison came back later that afternoon, and she just went to her room. Mom and Rick stayed at Dad's house and made funeral arrangements. Rick did most of the planning, and I just stayed in my room. I could still smell him, and I could still hear his voice.

I guess he wasn't really gone. Just halfway.

We had the funeral three days later in Connecticut. He wished to be buried close to his girls so we could always visit him. His wish was entirely ignored.

I didn't speak at the funeral, but Mom did. She talked about how amazing of a dad he was and an even better friend. They weren't together, but Dad still called Mom his best friend. More people spoke, and I froze when it was time for him to be buried. I couldn't look, so I turned around and buried my face in Rick's leg. He held onto me, and when it was time to go, Alexander carried me to the car. Everyone had been crying, and I had a few tears fall, but mostly out of fear he'd hate the ground and never be able to get out of it.

When we returned to Rick's house, I went upstairs to one of the bathrooms.

Allison came in, and my whole body stiffened.

"Tell me. Do you think your dad offed himself because he couldn't handle how much of a crybaby you are? Allison fixed her hair, and I could feel anger surge through me."

"He didn't off himself!! He was sick! He's not gone! You're a liar! A liar!" I yelled at the top of my lungs. She turned around and looked at me with a look of surprise.

"Aww, don't tell me you believe that." A look of fake concern on her face.

"He's not gone!! You're a liar! Liar! " I screamed, my throat tight and hoarse. I pushed her with everything I had in me, and she hit the countertop. *"Go away!!!"*

The door opened, and Thena and Mom came rushing in. Thena pulled me away, and I tried to squirm and push Allison again. I couldn't stop fighting until my screams turned into sobs. I cried into Thena's chest until Rick carried me into an empty bedroom.

When I woke up, my eyes were puffy, and everything felt weird.

"Hey," Thena's voice came from the right. I looked at her, and she smiled. *"Any time you miss him, you can call him. His number is on the post-it note."* I took it and clutched it in my hand.

"Thanks," I whispered.

"Go back to sleep."

I did.

Less than six months later, we moved to Connecticut.

But I had his number so I could always call him, and he would listen.

###

I jumped up from my dream, my breathing labored and sweat sticking to my skin. *He's not really gone.* I keep repeating it to myself. *I don't have to do this. I'm okay.*

I start looking around for my phone, throwing pillows off my bed, and putting them back. I went through my bedside table and searched under the heap of clothes I had just napped on. It's under my bed, by *three* condom wrappers. I find it and take a deep breath, forcing a feeling of ease to spread through me. I find the number and click on it.

A shaky smile spreads across my face.

"Sorry, the number you have reached is no longer in service. Please check the number and dial again."

What? No. That's not right. They wouldn't turn it off. They couldn't. I call it again.

"Sorry, the number you have reached is no longer in service. Please check the number and dial again."

No, this can't be happening! I keep calling and keep calling. The same answer over and over again. I repeat this process until I feel insanity blurring the lines of sanity.

Why is this happening to me? This can't be happening. There has to be a way for me to call him. I have to be able to hear his voicemail. I can't just stop. I pace back and forth, my hands running through my hair and gripping pieces from the root, pulling them to distract me from the panic and desperation filling me.

There'll be no end to this; I can feel it. I'll always feel like this. No number of trips and no time spent with the people I love can fix this. I can't use them to make me feel better. It's selfish and draining. I'm drained.

I'm so exhausted. I'm so tired. I want to stop. Stop the sadness, stop the anger, stop the memories, and stop this. I'm eighteen. *Only eighteen.*

Everything I do next seems like I've been planning on it for months, and maybe I have.

No one should be home for a few hours, so I go into the bathroom, squat down, and find a bottle of pills hidden underneath all the hair products and the extra shit. I hid it so Lucille couldn't find it. She does a lot for me, but I know she'd tell people about this. Everyone has a limit to secrets, and prescription pills are Lucille's.

Things have never been this bad.

I open the bottle and find a can of Coke and begin taking pill after pill. I stop counting.

I shouldn't do this. I'm breaking so many promises to Jay and to Dad. Do I want to do this? How many days can I wake up feeling s miserable though? I sit against the counter in the bathroom and try to think through what I'm doing. Try to think of the suggestions my therapist made for when I feel low. *But if I don't do it today, won't I just do it tomorrow? I should stop this*, I think. I drop to my knees and start to gag myself, but before anything comes up, I feel a calmness pulling me under.

I feel warm, and I feel....

I stop feeling and let go, or maybe something snaps like a tether, and I fall. There's no chance to look back and no place for me to land. There are just flashes of faces and silence that screams so loud everything hurts.

Until there's nothing at all.

April
Part Two

Chapter 58

James Averell

Em is going to flip. I drove to Jersey this morning and got her favorite donuts. Her car is in the driveway, but both of her parents are gone. Just as I pull up, so does Athena. She looks like she just came from school or a meeting with the way she is dressed. She narrows her eyes at me and the box of donuts in my hand.

"*You're such a good puppy,*" she tells me. I flip her off. Sometimes her insults come from out of nowhere. All I can do is just flip her off and try not to say something too bad.

Thena unlocks the front door, and I walk past her. She scoffs when I bump her shoulder. I yell Emi's name, and Thena groans in response.

"*Must you scream down the house?*" Thena catches up with me, and I realize Emi must not have answered her calls. There's a stiffness in her body and a tightness in her jaw like her worst fear can come true at any moment.

"*Em!*" I shout. I entered her room. It's messier than usual, but I don't say anything. I don't see or hear her. There's no shower running, and it's too quiet. I look over my shoulder, and Thena is looking around the room. She walks a step behind me.

Em's bathroom is a foot in front of me. I walk inside, and instantly the life is sucked out of me. I'm frozen. The box of donuts falls to the floor, but I can't move until I hear Thena gasp. I run towards Emi's body. She's lying on the floor, a bottle of pills on the bathroom counter, and a can of coke spilled on the floor. She's not moving, her eyes are closed, and her lips are parted, but there's no rise or fall in her chest. Her chin is wet from drool or vomit.

A guttural sound rips from me and I don't even know I'm screaming until I feel the rasp in my throat. "*Em!*" I cry. I check her pulse; it's faint and so weak that I might only be imagining it. She's limp in my arms, her head slumping to her side.

"*Choke her! Make her vomit!*" Thena tells me. I turn to look at her. She's on the phone, her eyes focused on Emi.

I do as she says, pushing my finger back into Em's throat and turning her on her side. Em's throat reacts and spurts of vomit come out, some of it getting on my hand. I pull a trashcan over to her, and more comes out, but she doesn't wake up. She doesn't even blink. She just lies limp in my arms. She's not warm. She's cold and clammy. She's not supposed to be cold.

"*What do I do? Tell me what to do?*" I beg Thena. I can't see anything. My eyes are blurry, and my heartbeat sounds like a drum in my ear. Thena has to know what to do.

"*You're going to carry her out of this bathroom and downstairs so when the ambulance comes, they can take her to the hospital. If they don't show up in two minutes, we're driving her to the hospital.*"

I shake my head. "*We can't wait! Let's take her. I'll drive, and you can ride in my truck,*" I frantically tell her. Maybe I'm imagining it, but Emi seems to be getting colder.

I carry her downstairs, and Thena follows me while on the phone with someone else. When we get outside, Nick is there, on the phone, a black G-Wagon parked right in the front.

I walk towards my car.

"*You are not driving my baby sister! You can barely carry her!*" Thena snaps at me. I pause and look at both of them. My hands are shaking, and I can barely control my breath.

Nick walks towards me and grabs my shoulder. "*Get in the backseat with Emi, and I'll drive. We'll be there in three minutes.*" His voice sounds stoic and rehearsed, and I want to yell at him and ask him how he can be so calm while Emi withers away in front of us while her life hangs in our hands. But I don't. I can't get myself to open my mouth. I'm scared if I do, I will start sobbing and drop Emi. *I can't drop her.*

I do as Nick says. I hold her head in my lap, and we make it to the hospital faster than we should. As soon as we arrive, a group of nurses and doctors rush to us and take Emi. They have her on a gurney, a nurse climbs on straddling her and starts administering CPR, while others call out numbers, instructions and vitals, and we follow them inside as far as we can. Finally, a nurse redirects us, and we stand alone, waiting.

Our family arrives, and I don't pay attention to any of them. Rachel comes in and hugs me. I can't hug her back. I go outside and bum a smoke from a guy who looks as frazzled as I am, only coming inside when Rachel comes out to tell me she's in a room.

She's not awake.

Chapter 59

Emille Kate Van der Berg

I know I'm not dreaming. I'm just floating through two realities. One pulls me toward an uncertain fate, and the other a familiar warmth. It's a choice between two sides. I open my eyes, causing a wave of exhaustion to roll over me as I blink my eyes against the unexpected fluorescent lights.

The room is bright and white. The sheets are thin and scratchy, and a consistent beeping sound fills my ears. Hushed voices surround me, and I can smell Thena's perfume. I blink a couple of times, and the pictures get clearer and wider each time. I'm not in my bedroom.

"Emi! Emi, you're in the hospital. You're okay," Thena says, moving closer.

"Do you remember what happened?" A nurse asks. She puts a light in my eye and moves it back and forth.

My throat's dry, but I answer. "*Uh, I took too many pills, I think…
Accident.*" My unconvincing words hang in the air.

"*The doctor will be here in a few minutes to talk to you,*" she tells me
before leaving the room.

Thena, Bell, Mom, Eric, Nick, Rick, and Jay are in my hospital
room. I can't look at Jay. I don't want to look at any of them, so I settle on
looking between Thena and Bell. My eyes well with tears.

"*Hey you,*" Bell whispers, her eyes red and her cheeks stained with
tears. She smiles, and it's shaky. More tears fall.

"*Hey,*" I whisper back. This is bad. This is really bad. "*How have
you been?*"

She shrugs her shoulders. "*Worried, crying, the usual stuff. You?*"

"*I'm okay.*"

She shakes her head, her lips trembling. "*You're not okay, Emi.*"

Tears fall, and I wipe them with the back of my hand. "*I*"

I don't know what to say. I don't know what to do. I did this and I
don't know how to fix it.

"*Emi, your therapist is here. She wants to talk to you. Do you want to
talk to her?*" Thena asks, taking the weight off me to think of something
to say.

I nod. I've been ignoring Dr. Young for months. Everyone gets up
and leaves. And for a second, I have the opportunity to gather my wits and
catch up. I look out the window. It's cloudy. The clouds were thick and
gray, like a storm coming.

"*Emi,*" Dr. Young says. I turn, and she's sitting in the chair by my
bed. She smiles at me, and I smile back.

"*Hey,*" I whisper.

"*Hi.*"

"*I'm sorry for ditching you. That was really shitty, and I promise I'll start going to our appointments,*" I rushed out, not looking at her.

She grabs my hand and holds it. "*Emi, it's okay. It's not the first time a patient has skipped out, and it won't be the last.*" I nod. "*Talk to me,*" she urges after a minute of silence. I look at her, and my lips quiver, and tears feel my eyes.

"*M-my dad didn't die of a heart attack.*" I sniffle, a small cry escaping. "*He killed himself!*" I cry, and she squeezes my hand and passes me tissues. "*I-I'm sorry for not telling you…and I'm sorry about all this. I'll be better, I promise.*"

I look into her eyes, and they're teary. She gives me a sad smile. "*Oh Emi, you will get better, but Emi, you need help.*"

I shake my head. I don't want that kind of help. She wipes a tear that's fallen, and she squeezes my hand, sitting up straighter.

"*I'm the head psychiatrist at an inpatient facility about forty-five minutes outside the city. I want you to check yourself in and stay for a little while. I want to help you, Emi, and a therapy session every other week won't do that.*"

I shake my head. "*No, I can't. No,*" I answer. She has to know I can't do this.

Thena steps closer to me. Her eyes are blood-shot red.

She sits next to me on the bed.

"Dr. Young told me about the inpatient program her practice offers and what it can do to help you, and I think you should do it. This isn't okay, Emi. You can't keep living like this. Harboring all these secrets and all this grief." She pauses, her eyes drilling into mine. *"You need help, and that's okay."*

"She doesn't need it. She's fine. I'll find her a new therapist, and she'll start going once a week," Mom interjects, the first thing she's said the whole time. *"I won't allow her reputation to be marred by an inpatient stay! What will people think? This could ruin her chances at..."* Her voice trails off as she realizes her daughters are staring at her mortified. She appeals to Thena with pleading eyes. Thena's own gaze has hardened

"Emi is 18 years old. She can decide for herself," Dr. Young adds, her eyes on me.

I look at Thena, and she nods.

"You'll leave tomorrow morning."

"So soon?"

She nods, squeezing my hand. I know I can't do this again, and I also know if I go home, I'll be doing the same thing in a few weeks. I'll probably be successful next time.

"I'll go," I whisper.

I have to, and when Thena nods and Dr. Young stands up and squeezes my hand encouragingly, I know it's the right choice.

Chapter 60

James Averell

Emi is talking to her therapist while we all are in the private waiting room. Her mom made sure Emi was put into a private suite so no one would recognize us. We stood far enough from her room so she couldn't hear us. I don't know where my dad is. It's the first time I've noticed his absence. I remember the last time Emi and I were in a hospital together. She had broken her arm skateboarding with Bell, and we sat in the emergency room. She was doped up on pain pills, eating popsicles while I held her hand. I bite back the tears that form at that memory of simpler times. Now she's in the hospital because she overdosed. And how much of this was my fault? I've seen every tear, every sniffle, and every forced shaky smile. I've watched as she turned to me more and more as an escape. I hid her secrets, helped her avoid the concerned prying of her sisters and mother.

Substituted my love for the type of help she actually needed. Truth be told, Em has unraveled on my watch.

Dr. Young comes from down the hall, and she smiles at all of us. None of us return the smile. She doesn't falter; she just keeps walking.

"Emi and I haven't talked about anything in a while, and I wanted to ask you guys if there have been any major changes in her life?"

I shake my head. No one says anything; I can see everyone trying to figure it out.

"Dad's phone is turned off," Bell supplies. She clears her throat, *"I tried to call it, and it was turned off. I think it was turned off two weeks ago."*

Dr. Young sighs and nods, everything sees to click together. I close my eyes and release a deep breath, running a hand through my hair.

"This whole thing escalated when Allison died. When she misses them, she does drastic things." Her mom sighs. Rick grips her arm and shakes his head.

I can't let that comment stand. *"Don't you get it?! She's not depressed because she misses Allison! She's suicidal because she doesn't! She felt relief when Ali died, and she hates herself for it! She's depressed because it's been eight years, and she still hasn't grieved her dad! She's living in a continuous loop of pain and guilt! How don't you understand that?!"* My voice rattles and shakes the hallway. Aurore and Rick stare at me, both shell-shocked and completely frozen. Rick's eyes water. Fuck their tears.

"I'm going to go pack her a bag."

I leave all of them and walk toward the elevator to go downstairs. When I head outside, I see Rachel and my dad talking to each other. His hand rests on the small of her back. I don't have the time or energy to keep him from being inappropriate with her.

"Jay, you shouldn't be driving," Rachel tells me, her voice soft and her big eyes giving me a pleading look.

I brush past her, and my dad grabs my arm, spinning me around.

"Get the fuck off!" I coldly tell him.

"You're not driving. Give Rachel your keys. "

"I'm not doing this with you right now. Rachel doesn't go above the speed limit. I don't have time to take a lazy parade route."

"If you get behind that wheel, I'll have you banned from this hospital. Try me, son. Let's see who's the biggest asshole," he threatens, his voice low. I know Rachel can hear us.

He lets my arm go, and I hand Rachel the keys. She adjusts the seat for a minute and a half, then takes another ten minutes to get to Emi's house. Nick's car is already in the driveway. The front door is unlocked, so I go to Emi's room and see Thena frantically cleaning. Her bed is stripped, and her clothes are separated into piles.

"You need to breathe; you can't spend the whole day cleaning. She'll notice you're gone," Nick tells her. I look around and find Emi's suitcase, setting it on her bed. I open it and start putting pajama pants inside when I hear Nick tell her to: *"Stop!"*

I go inside the bathroom, and Thena's scrubbing the floor even though the floor is already clean. Her heels are outside the bathroom, perfectly lined up by the door.

"Thena! Athena!" I bark her name, and her head snaps as she looks at me. *"Stop! It's clean. Scrubbing the floor isn't going to erase what happened."*

She drops the sponge and breathes, her chest rising and falling in a quick pattern. Her cheeks are red, and her nostrils flare. She still sees Emi's body lying there. We both do. We'll never forget that image, but now we have to move forward. If only you could scrub your memories as hard as you could scrub floors.

"Help me pack?" She nods and I leave her to get herself together and go back to Emi's bed. I don't know everything she needs for her... trip. I just know the things she'd want with her: hoodies, hair products, blankets, and her favorite books.

"I'll start with her undergarments."

I help Thena count out the right amount of clothes and then fold them. Anything she'd need, we packed.

"Don't forget she needs clothes for tomorrow to travel."

I nod and grab black leggings and one of my gray sweatshirts.

"I'm going to take these to the hospital. I'll see you there," Thena tells me. She must realize I'm not ready to go back yet. Nick follows her out.

I sit on Emi's bed. I've laid in it so many times, but right now, it feels different. Lucille comes in and takes another load of laundry. Neither one of us speaks. I know Em is alive; I've seen her talking and breathing, but part of her feels gone. Maybe the part that was holding onto everything so tightly it was beginning to pull her under.

Rachel comes into the room and sits next to me. She doesn't say anything; she just sits down. Her hands are in her lap as she looks around the room. I can feel myself crumbling. Emi was slowly dying inside, and no one knew. I sat with her, laid with her, had sex with her, and I didn't know a fraction of what was going through her head.

I choke on a sob. Rachel rubs my back like she did when I was little, and I break down, crying into my hands until she pulls them away from my face and holds them in her lap.

"*She w-wanted to die.*" The realization settles into the room. They had to pump her stomach. Her pulse was so faint in my hands.

I cry into Rachel's lap. She rubs my hair and back, and I cry in the bed of the girl I love, in the lap of the woman who raised me.

Chapter 61

Emille Kate Van der Berg

The crowd of family begins to thin. Bell sits with me for a little bit. We don't talk much, and that's okay. I'm happy she's here. She's still smiling even after everything. Her brave face has always been the most convincing of any of ours.

Rick knocks on the door, and Bell excuses herself as he enters. He sits in the chair next to me, and silence stretches between us.

"I'm sorry, I know what I did" He grabs my hand, cutting me off.

He shakes his head, tears welling inside his eyes. His hands shake as they hold mine. *"I'm just happy you're okay,"* he assures. More tears fall, and seeing him crying makes me cry. I squeeze his hand. *"I don't know what I would've done if…"* he swallows, unable to say it.

"I'm sorry for not noticing and picking up on the signs of what you were going through. You've just always been so shy and introverted. I figured if something happened, you would tell Jay or your sisters. I'm sorry."

"There was nothing you could've done; I didn't want to tell anyone. It's not your fault. It was never you."

He nods, and he wipes his eyes. *"I'll always be here for you, Emi. I know I'm not your dad, but I've loved you like a daughter."* I sniffle and wipe my eyes.

He stands up and kisses my forehead before he leaves. I tell him something I've wanted to say for years.

"I've always seen you like a dad. I'm sorry if I haven't shown it to you."

"You have, Emi." He leaves, and Bell rejoins me.

She sits with me, until Thena walks in with a large suitcase—my large suitcase—and her purse in her hand. She looks around the room.

"God, I should've bought flowers or candles." She scrunches her nose in disgust, looking around the room.

I laugh. *"My hospital room isn't up to your standards?"*

She purses her lips. *"It's alright."* She sits in the other chair and crosses her legs. She's out of her element, and she knows it. *"I talked to Dr. Young, and you'll be able to have visitors once a week. And you can call us as much as you want, but you can't have your phone."*

I nod. That makes sense. *"At least I'll be able to see you guys."*

Thena nods. *"I'll be at every Visiting day,"* she promises.

"So will I !" Bell excitedly adds.

I won't be completely alone. I'll have my sisters. I'll call and see them, even when things get really dark, and things will get dark. They always do.

Jay comes in carrying a large bag of food. He has Chick-Fil-A. Rachel carries the drinks inside, and Nick enters, closing the door behind him. Jay passes everyone's food out and sits on my other side. I eat and talk with them. I'm surprised when no one shows up and tells us visiting hours are over.

It's close to nine when we finish eating, and I can see the exhaustion and worry from the day on everyone's faces.

"You guys can go home and come back in the morning. I'll be fine. I'm literally being monitored as we speak," I assure them. None of them move. *"Guys, there's one extra bed here, and you all need to sleep. Only one of you can stay here."*

Jay doesn't say anything; he just looks at Thena and Bell. Bell stands and hugs me before leaving, and Thena glares at Jay.

"I'll be here at seven," she tells me. I nod and force a smile. Thena leaves, and then it's just me and Jay.

I can't look at him. I can't face him.

Nick walks into the room with a calm look on his face. *"You have a visitor."* It's all he says before turning around and leaving. I sit up straight, adjusting the hospital gown. I hope it isn't Liv or anyone from school.... Who knows I'm here? Did anyone see me? Has Mom or Rick told anyone? I doubt Mom told anyone her daughter overdosed.

All my thoughts are stopped when I see who walks through the door. The last person I would've guessed.

"Xander," I gasp! He smirks and walks further into the room, dressed in a black peacoat, black dress pants, and brown dress shoes.

He sits down across from me. Xander looks around the hospital room and nods at Jay. Jay returns the nod before leaving me and my older brother alone. I haven't seen him in almost a year. He looks the same. His brown skin is radiant and his hair is cut in a low tapered fade.

"*I didn't know you were coming.*"

He looks at me with an irritated expression while reaching into his pocket. "*Yeah, 'cause I wouldn't come when my baby sister tries to kill herself.*"

He's the first person to just say it.

"*Where were you?*" I ask him.

He smiles. "*Places.*" I narrow my eyes. "*I'll tell you where I'm going next.*"

"*Where?*" I've never known any of his travel plans. I don't think anyone does. Bell always knows where he' been, but sometimes she wonders if he just sends her old photos.

"*San Marino.*"

"*What are you going to do there?*"

He shrugs his shoulders, pulling something from his pockets. "*Smoke, work, whatever I feel like.*" He lights up a cigarette. My eyes widened. I don't think this is the place to smoke a cigarette. "*Relax, it's not weed.*"

I laugh, and he blows cigarette smoke above his head then notices the smoke detector and quickly stubs it out against the metal arm of the chair, but continues to hold it.

"*Dad and I used to drink a cup of bourbon with a splash of coffee together. I think it really hit me that he was gone one late night, and I was going to get something to drink and saw the bourbon.*" He leans forward until his arm is resting on his knee. "*I threw the bourbon against the wall and cried like a baby.*" He inhales slowly like the memory had winded him.

"*I'm not saying all of this,*" he waves his hand with the cigarette around the room, "*is right, but it's understandable. When he died, he was gone, and no one talked about it. Mom made it impossible to talk about him. I'm sorry for being a shit brother.*" I open my mouth, but he just holds up his hand, smiling at me. "*I know I was; I left the first chance I could. I hated America.*"

"*The whole country?*" I ask with a smile on my face.

"*The whole fucking country.*" He smiles and nods. "*But mostly the way i had to exist in it and this family, with a million stereotpyes and expectations forced down my throat. Okay, well, I told you my sob story. Time to talk about you.*"

"*What do you want to know?*"

"*College in the fall?*"

"*No.*"

He nods. "*Understandable. You've never liked school. How's art?*"

"*Good, going through a dry spell.*"

"*How are you and Jay?*"

"*You know?*"

"*Bell sent me a picture of you guys in Fiji. I don't think she realized he was grabbing your ass in the picture, but she sent it.*" I heat in embarrassment, but Alexander doesn't even seem phased. "*So, how are you two lovebirds?*"

"*I think we're good. I love him a lot, but I've been a lot for him to carry. He's off at school now and I want what's best for him. And I don't think that's me when I'm like this.*"

Alexander leans back in his chair and places the cigarette back in his mouth before remembering it wasn't lit. Then he slid it back into it's metal case and dropped it into his coat pocket.

"Just talk to him, but remember you have to do what's best for yourself. Love can't fix everything. And I don't even think you love yourself."

"I do," I argue. Xander's face is blank as he waits for me to continue. *"I love parts of myself, different versions of myself. Not this version but other ones."*

"Can you really love something if you don't love everything?"

I don't know the answer. I just look at him as he lazily stares at me. Smoke from his earlier puff still lingers in the room. He is going to get us kicked out.

He stands up. *"You know you're my favorite sister, right?"*

I laugh. *"No, I'm not. Bell is."* And I'm pretty sure Thena is a *very* close second.

He smirks, *"Yeah, but you were definitely Dad's favorite. We all knew it."*

Chapter 62

James Averell

Alexander walks out of Emi's room. He smirks at me before he and Nick walk together, getting on the elevator. I head into Emi's room; Bell left to check on something, and Thena went back to her place to shower. Rick is still here somewhere with my dad.

Emi sits up straight, her eyes on the window outside. I sit in the bedside chair and look at her. She looks exhausted, which is more than understandable. I don't think; I just get up and climb into her bed, and take off my shoes. She scoots over and makes space; I can see her face clearly.

I can see everything start to break down, and her lips tremble. She bursts into tears, burying her face into my chest. I hold her to me, rubbing her back and consoling her. I knew this would happen, and I knew she wouldn't want it to happen in front of her sisters.

"*I'm so scared,*" she chokes out in between sobs. She hides her face in my chest, and I can feel the tears soaking through my shirt.

I have to be strong for her right now. We can't both be sobbing. She needs a boost of strength, not another thing to worry about.

"*Don't be. You need to do this for yourself,*" I tell her, rubbing her back. She clutches my shirt in her hands. "*You have to believe you can do this.*"

She shakes her head against my chest. "*I can't leave you. I can't leave.*" She's scared that when she comes back from the treatment center, nothing will be the same. She'll be forgotten like an old memory, and we'll all hold onto a different version of her.

"*You can and you will.*" I lift her chin up, and she looks at me, her eyes filled with tears. "*Because when you return, you'll be able to breathe and live a little easier. I could never forget you, Em, and neither could your family. Every visiting day I'll be there.*"

She shakes her head. "*I don't want you to come to see me.*" Pain slices through me, but I can't show it. "*Not in there. Not like that. Promise you won't? For me, please.*"

I look at her, and I can see the fear. She's terrified that I'll never look at her the same if I see her in there. Or that I'll stop loving her.

"*I promise, Em. That's what you want?*" She nods, and I force a smile. "*Then I'll do it.*" She relaxes a little, but tears still fall. "*But once you get out, you know I'm not leaving you alone, right? You'll never be able to get rid of me, not even when you're grumpy and smelly.*"

"*I'm never smelly!*" She laughs between cries. She must realize she's still crying because she laughs even harder. I laugh with her kissing her forehead.

When her laughs die down, she lays down on my chest.

After a few minutes of silence, she asks something, her voice meek and timid. *"Are you mad at me? For what I did today."*

Mad at her? No. Mad at myself and the world? Yes.

"No, Em, I'm not mad at you. Not even a little bit. I just want you to be happy, and not for me but for yourself. I don't want you to ever feel like that's the only solution."

"Me too." She sniffles.

I can feel her body filling with sleep. *"You know I love you, right?"*

I feel her smile against my chest. *"I know."*

Chapter 63

Emille Kate Van der Berg

Thena braids my hair in the bathroom while we wait. I've showered, gotten dressed, and am sitting on my bed watching Thena prepare everything. Rick came in and handed me a coffee while Eric stood by the door. He winked at me before walking away with Rick.

Someone knocks on the bathroom door just as Thena finishes my last braid.

"Breakfast is here, finally. I told him to be here twenty minutes ago. One would think he'd be able to tell time," she rants while we leave the bathroom. Nick stands near the table by the bed with a large bag of McDonald's. I smile as the smell of hash browns fills the air. I sit on the bed and begin eating.

Nick leans against the wall, sipping a coffee. He looks at ease, and I try to mimic his easiness about today. Thena even eats a breakfast sandwich and half a hashbrown. Bell is on her way, and Rick is downstairs. I haven't seen Mom since yesterday.

Breakfast is gone. I could only take two bites before my stomach turned into thick stone, unable to swallow any of it.

"*Are you ready to go?*" Thena asks. I nod. I'm not, but I can't stay in this hospital room forever. Bell waits for us outside, her hair in two thick pigtails. She's wearing leggings with a Parkas cropped jacket on. She leans against Nick's car and smiles, waving me forward.

Bell and I sit in the backseat, and Thena sits in the front while Nick drives. They argue about the fastest route and which roads to avoid. I think Nick is a good distraction for Thena. She's not as stressed about me and can somewhat relax.

We have one stop before we go to McCarthy's, the inpatient facility. It's not along the way. I'm pretty sure it's completely out of the way, but we need to go. We pull into the driveway of a Tudor-style mansion. A beautiful boy is sitting on the steps, smoking a cigarette.

I get out of the car and walk over to Jay; he stands up, flicking his cigarette out. We stand less than a foot apart, looking each other over like this is the last time. He wears a black hoodie, blue jeans, and dirty white Vans.

The front door opens, and Rachel comes out. Squeezing and rubbing my back in a comforting way, she hugs me like a mother hugs their child. The way my mom should be hugging me right now. And it brings tears to my eyes. She pulls away and holds me by my arms, smiling at me, her eyes glassy.

"*Take care of yourself, okay?*" I nod. "*And if you need anything, just call. I'll always answer. No matter the time of day.*"

"*Thanks. I'll miss you.*"

She softly laughs. "*I'll miss you too, but I'll see you soon.*" She hugs me one last time before going back inside the house. It's just Jay and me. So many words floating in the air, yet I can't open my mouth to say any of them.

"*Do you want me to call you while you're gone?*" he asks me, his hazel eyes soft. I nod. I can't go however long I will be there without talking to him, not telling him anything, or even hearing his voice. "*You'll be okay, Em,*" he assures.

"*Will you be okay?*"

He nods. "*I will. Don't worry about me. I'll be here waiting for you.*"

"*I'm going to be better when I get out. I want to feel better.*" I say it more to myself than to him, but he nods, confidence oozing from him. He believes in me more than I believe in myself.

I hug him, pressing my face to his chest. He squeezes me, and when I pull back, he captures my lips in a kiss, the hint of smoke and coffee filling my mouth.

"*Go, Em. Your sisters are waiting.*" I nod and walk back to the car. I get in and look at him through the window, my eyes watering.

He holds his hand up in a motionless wave, and I do the same, pressing my hand to the glass. We probably look like two lovesick fools, but it's how I feel—sick and like a fool. I keep looking at him until he's out of view.

Then it's just the soft lull of the music filling the ride. We drive through the city until the buildings and houses fade into trees.

McCarthy's resembles a large house from the nineteenth century. There's a darkness to it that makes it resemble a haunted house. The gates are metal with the sign rusted on it. It creaks when it opens and takes twice as long to close. The driveway leading is gravel. Rick is already waiting for us with Eric. Both of them have cups of coffee in their hands. Eric looks bored and slightly uncomfortable with all the emotions, but Rick's eyes are glassy, and his whole body is stiff.

Bell hugs me and says her goodbye first. She squeezes me and kisses both my cheeks. The smell of cherry blossoms and soap fills my nostrils as I clutch her.

"This isn't the end, just the start of a wonderful new adventure." I hugged her again.

"I'm going to miss you. You'll come to visit, right?"

She nods. *"Every week. I'll be there,"* she assures me. She hugs me again and takes a step back. I move down the line to Rick. We hug, and he kisses my forehead.

"Where's Mom?" I ask him.

His eyes look away for a brief second. *"She couldn't come."* I appreciate him not making an excuse for her.

"That's okay. Thanks for coming." I force it out, throat thick and heavy. I try not to let it bother me that she's not here.

"Of course, I would never miss this. I love you, Emi. Take care of yourself."

"I'll try." It's all I can give him without it sounding like a lie.

I stand across from Nick. He smiles at me, and I think he knew it'd relax me slightly. Nick knows his capabilities, and sometimes he takes advantage of them.

"Please, please take care of her. Make sure she doesn't go crazy worrying and thinking about me. Remind her of Elénore Co. and school. Just remind her that I'll be okay," I beg him. He listens to everything I say before nodding. *"And ma-"*

"I'll check and take care of both of them. I promise."

I nod, taking a deep breath before I turn around, and Thena walks me inside. The place is quiet, and it's not what I expected. It's bright, and the hardwood floors are shiny as we walk. The front desk lady is petite, blonde, and has a bubbly air about her.

"Hello! How can I help you all?" she chirps, a wide smile as she looks between us.

"Uh, I'm here to check in." Is that what I'm supposed to say?

She nods and stands up. *"Well, come on back."* She points to an opening, and we walk inside a large office. We stand in front of a desk where a plump lady sits typing on a keyboard, a wall of pictures behind her. I examine them. They're pictures of people who've attended. A lot of them are group pictures.

She must catch me staring because she says, *"Don't worry. Those are ones from years ago. Now mostly everyone that comes doesn't really want anyone to know."* She chuckles. *"It's funny. People want help but don't want anyone to know they need it. I don't blame them, though. Society has thoughts about places like this. Thoughts that probably won't change for a while."* She sighs wistfully and begins typing again.

Dr. Young walks towards us with a wide smile. She wears a flowy white skirt, a bright yellow long-sleeve top, and a big blue necklace, her hair up into a bun. She checks her watch.

"Right on time like always, Emi," she compliments. She grabs a clipboard and hands it to me. *"I wrote down most of your information, but some of it you need to fill out and formally sign yourself in, and when you're done, I'll walk you back."*

I nod, and she points Thena and me to a chair. Thena does most of the paperwork, and I just look around. Pictures, folders, and file cabinets are all confidently locked, and besides the two women we talked to and Dr. Young, there's no one else to be seen. I can see an elevator in the distance down the hall.

Thena taps me with the clipboard, and I look at her. *"You need to sign it,"* she reminds me. I nod and grab the pen from her. I sign my name, even my middle name. I know I'm only writing it to draw time out, but I don't care. When I'm done, I hold the clipboard in my lap. I stare at it.

This is it. I stand up, and so does Thena. We hand the clipboard to Dr. Young, who's making small talk with the bubbly lady at the front. She takes it, looks it over, and hands it to the plump lady who scans it before putting it into a white folder and writing the name *"Kate B."*

"Security purposes," Dr. Young explains. I nod, and we walk towards the elevator. The sound of Thena's heels fills the hallway, and when we're ten feet away, I stop, and so does Thena. Dr. Young keeps walking, looking over her shoulder when she gets on the elevator.

I look at Thena. *"You have to go now."*

Thena shakes her head. *"I'll walk you to your room and help you settle in."*

I smile and shake my head. *"This isn't a dorm room, and I won't be here forever. I need you to go."* Her eyes fill with tears, and I can see her actively trying to prevent them from falling. *"You have to go. You can't stay here with me*," I whisper to her; I wouldn't even want her to stay. She'd have to give up too much, put too much on pause for her to be able to.

I look over her shoulder, and Nick walks towards us with a look of determination on his face.

"*I love you; I'll see you in a week.*" I turn away and walk towards the elevator, each step heavier than the one before because if I break, so will Thena. Dr. Young presses the elevator button, and the doors open. Not even a second later, we get on. And Nick holds onto Thena, and she stares at me with a look of pure pain and agony. I wave and force a smile until the doors close. I feel my body fill with tears. I'm unable to get off the elevator until I grab Dr. Young's arm, her eyes filling with concern.

"*I-I c-can't do this. Please. Let me go back.*" I'm hyperventilating; all I feel is the heat of my tears.

"*Breathe, Emi. Just breathe,*" she coos, waving over a nurse who grips me with a firmness that eases some of the pressure.

"*P-put me to sleep, just for today. T-tomorrow, I'll be ready.*"

Dr. Young thinks this over, and finally, she relents. I feel a soft pinch until my body sags, and I breathe easier. A blanket covers me, and everything turns black.

Chapter 64

Emille Kate Van der Berg

Day 1

I wake up, and grogginess overcomes me. It takes me a few minutes to figure out where I am. I'm in a strange bed much smaller than mine, and the sheets are thicker and have a texture to them that feels as if it's gripping to me. My suitcase is against the bright white wall, and there's a desk on the other wall to my left. I rub my eyes, trying to wake up.

The door opens, and Dr. Young comes in wearing yellow pants, a yellow polka-dot shirt, and brown flats. She smiles and closes my room door, sitting in the chair by the desk.

"I slept the whole day," I murmured. I know I asked for it, but part of me wishes I could've just come in and started.

"Don't feel bad. Many people ask to be put to sleep on their first day. Sometimes you need to sleep to be able to restart."

401

"*I sleep all the time.*" Probably too much.

"*But you weren't sleeping to restart; you were sleeping to escape. It's not the same.*" She stands up. "*Breakfast ends at ten during the week and 10:30 on the weekends. I'll have Helen tell you the schedule after you eat.*" She walks to the door, and before leaving, she speaks over her shoulder. "Good morning, Emi."

###

The breakfast room has large windows with thin curtains, a buffet table, and three round tables. There are two tables filled with people. I load my plate with two sausage links and scrambled eggs with a plate of strawberries on the side. I sit at one of the empty tables by myself and eat. Loneliness is a feeling I've become acquainted with, but it still hurts each time. It's like a wound that continues to get stabbed and is never quite healed.

I eat and look outside. The trees are starting to fill with leaves, the property grounds are large, and the grass is cut low.

"*Emille?*" a stern voice questions. I look up, and a woman with dark skin and pursed full lips looks down at me. Her glasses are circular and thin.

"*J-just Emi,*" I correct. She nods and stands across from me with her hands crossed in front of her.

"*Come on.*" She waved me forward. "*Leave your plate there; someone will get it.*" I stand up, and we're the same height, but something about her makes her seem close to six feet.

We leave the room and walk through two large navy blue doors.

402

"This is the sunroom; this is where group sessions are held. This room is only used for group sessions." She closes the door, moves down the hall, and points to a green door. *"That is Dr. Young's office. You will meet with her every other day at 3:00 p.m. Do not be late."* I nod and follow her to an open room across from the eating area. *"This is the rec room where you can spend your free time. Dr. Young has not granted you grounds permission. She told me you could ask her, and she'll grant you access."*

I nod, and when we return to the eating area, she stands before me with a blank look.

"Breakfast is from 7:30 to 10:00 during the week and 7:30 to 10:30 on the weekend, lunch is from 12:00-1:30, and dinner is from 6:00 to 9:00. Snacks are always offered throughout the day. Group therapy is from 11:00 to 12:00. You must be there. Visiting day is every Sunday from 3:00 to 5:00, and you can call any time after 7:00 and before 9:00. You will be in your room every night before 9:30. Do you understand?"

I nod, but she continues to stare at me. *"Yes, I understand."*

"Good. Now do you want to change out of your pajamas, or is that how you want to look for your first group session?" She looks me up and down, and I heat in embarrassment.

"Um," I clear my throat, *"I'll change."* She nods like I made the right choice.

"Good. You have 40 minutes. There's a clock by your bed. I'll set it up while you change."

Thirty-seven minutes later, Helen walks me to my first group therapy session. She waits for me to walk in before turning around. The chairs are in three rows, and I sit in the back row. The room starts to fill up, and when the clock makes a loud ticking sound, an older man in a three-piece suit comes in and starts talking. He spends the whole time talking about the importance of a sponsor and the truth that goes into that relationship, and when he's done, he stands up and calls a girl's name, who walks over to him. Apparently, it's her last day in rehab, and tomorrow she goes home. She admits she's scared to go home, but she'll live with her grandma and move away from her old family friends.

When she's done, everyone claps and eats cake. I don't know the girl, so the whole thing is slightly awkward, but I'm happy for her. She's been here for three months, which makes me wonder how long I will be here.

I spend most of my lunch trying to figure out how long I'm going to be here. A month? Two? Six? A year?!

After lunch, I return to my room and go through my suitcase, seeing what Thena and Jay packed me. I found four journals, a pack of mechanical pencils and gel pens, and my three favorite books. I opened one of the journals, and one of the first entries was from my sophomore year.

March 2019

I think Jay and I might be in our first-ever fight. I've decided to call it our very own "Cold War." There's no yelling or ignoring each other, but there's a tension that's always with us. Sometimes it's gone like last night. We ate donuts in his dad's car, and it felt like old times. We laughed and talked, and when it was time for me to go home, he hugged me and kissed my forehead. But when he came over later that night, I could smell perfume all over him, and I just rolled over and kept a lot of distance between us. He didn't say anything; he just scoffed before passing out. I've had to wake him up a couple of times because he's passed out drunk. I hate how much he's drinking and how much time he's spending with all these other girls. Should I say something? Thena thinks I should, but Bell thinks I should just give him time. I'm going to go with Bell's option. It sounds easier.

The next page is a short story I wrote about a lady sitting in a cafe every night, drinking the same drink. It wasn't much, but rereading it now, and it doesn't look half bad. Most of my journals are a mixture of personal diary entries, book reflections, and stories I haven't finished.

There's a knock at the door, and it's Helen. She gives me a look.

"*Emi,*" she reprimands.

I look at the time, and it's 2:57. I drop my journal in my suitcase and walk towards the door.

"*Oops,*" I sheepishly say, brushing past Helen.

Helen leads the way to Dr. Young's office. It's time for my first therapy session here.

Dr. Young's office is very different from her office in the city. It's not as bright, more organized, and she has a brown leather sectional instead of her sofa. I sit on the sectional, and she sits across from me, a notebook in her lap.

"*I didn't know you worked here.*"

"*You never asked.*" She softly smiles at me. "*I've been working here since I moved to New York, but I usually just do sessions at my office in the city. I like the sessions at my office because they're more personal, but here I can see the growth more closely.*" She shrugs her shoulders. "*I like what I do. What can I say?*"

"*That's good.*"

"*For this to work, you must speak your mind and the truth. I just want to remind you.*"

"*I understand.*" I pause and lick my lips. "*How long am I going to be here?*"

"*I don't know, Emi. You can legally leave whenever you want. All I can do is help you, and I don't know how long that will take.*"

"*Six months? That's half a year.*"

She giggles. "*You'll be out of here before six months. I can feel it.*" I nod, relief coasting over me.

I spend the rest of the session evading her hard-hitting questions—the questions about the past and the thing that got me here. I avoid it all, and even though she doesn't say it when I leave, I can feel her disappointment. I don't even blame her.

I don't eat anything for dinner. I don't call anyone either. I have nothing good to tell them. I just go to bed and hope every day doesn't feel like this one.

Chapter 65

Emille Kate Van der Berg

Day 2

Helen wakes me up with a sound of annoyance, tapping her foot against the floor. She doesn't say anything until I'm completely awake.

"Bathrooms are two doors down. Bring your clothes with you," she tells me. I pick out a pair of leggings and a sweatshirt and leave for the bathroom.

Thankfully Helen doesn't stay and watch me get ready. She disappears for a while, and after a painfully boring breakfast, I sit in my room until group theory. I'm the first one in there again. The chairs are still in the same rows as before.

The whole day is a repeat of yesterday: another person leaves rehab, I eat by myself, and spend my rec time in my room. The only difference is Dr. Young isn't here, so I don't have to meet with her for therapy.

I decided to call Thena. If I keep waiting for something amazing to happen, I might not ever call.

She answers on the second ring.

"Emi?"

"Hey, it's me. How are you?" I ask her, sitting on the metal stool in front of the phone booth. There are five phone booths, and another girl and I are the only people inside the room.

"I'm fine. Busy. But how are you?"

"Fine."

"Emi," she warns.

It's a hard habit to break, trying not to lie to the people you love so they don't worry. I'm too late for that, though. I'm here, and they are not.

"Sorry. Lonely. I'm scared to say anything real to Dr. Young because I'm pretty sure she will make me stay here for years and give me so many medications I won't be able to feel anything," I ramble.

"One, I won't allow her to keep you there for years. I'll sue her and that whole building. Second, medications won't take away who you are as a person. Third, you must allow yourself to receive help before deciding it's the worst option. Fourth, you don't need anyone else; you're your strongest ally. You just need to realize it." I take in her words, and she's right. She always is; it's why I called her.

"Okay."

"Do you feel better?"

"Yeah, I do." I sigh and rub my forehead with my hand. *"I miss Jay. It's going to get worse, isn't it?"*

"Missing someone usually does, but eventually, it gets better. It starts to dull. But I don't know if that's any better," Thena softly admits. "I miss you, Emi."

"Miss you too. You'll visit on Sunday, right?"

"Of course, Bell and I'll be there. I promise."

Chapter 66

Emille Kate Van der Berg

Day 3

I successfully made it to breakfast on time, *all* by myself. Helen sees me making my plate and gives me a *small* but proud smile before leaving the eating area. I sit at my usual empty table and eat, looking out the window. I have therapy with Dr. Young today and a group therapy session. Something tells me there'll be no cake today.

I reach for another piece of bacon, but my plate is empty. I get up to get more, bringing it back to my table. When I sit down, I notice someone walking towards the kitchen. Mostly everyone is already here. I drop my fork, and the clatter echoes.

"Liv !" I scream. She smirks, and I run towards her, crushing her into a hug. When we pull apart, my smile stretches across my face. I grab her hand and lead her back to my table. *"Come! Come eat! How'd you know I was in here? Did Thena tell you? Today's not Sunday, is it?"*

Something hits me. It comes at me in full force. When I look into her eyes, it clicks. I drop her hand, shock and pain shooting through me. It's not a visiting day. Liv is not visiting.

"*Oh! Oh no, Liv,*" I whisper. She softly smiles, her eyes glassy as she looks at me. "*What happened?*"

She shakes her head. "*I'll tell you later, I promise.*" She grabs a piece of bacon off my plate and takes a bite. "*Now, tell me about these group therapy sessions.*" She looks at me with a pleading look in her eye.

"*Well, the last two have been kind of parties. The girls have been leaving and going home. So, there's cake, people congratulating them, and them thanking their sponsors and stuff.*"

"*Oh shit! So it's like graduation.*"

I smile. "*Kind of, just for rehab and not high school.*"

Why is she here? Did she try to kill herself too? Where's Clara? Does Clara know? Did she try to call me, and I didn't answer? How long has she been here?

The questions stay in my head until we go to group therapy. We're the first people in the room, and when we stand outside the threshold, I can already feel it won't be a party. By the way Liv groans as we walk towards our seats, she knows it too.

The chairs are arranged into a small circle. And there's one bright blue chair while the others are black. Liv and I sit away from that one. I have a feeling she's the leader of this whole thing.

The room starts to fill up, and when the clock chimes at 11:00, there are seven girls, nine including Liv and me.

"*I thought rehab had more people, like a lot of groups,*" I whisper to Liv before the group leader comes in.

"*Yeah, well, most people can't afford rehab this exclusive, plus it's only for teenage girls.*"

A woman with chopped black hair and tattoos on both arms walks in. She's thin and has a smile bigger than her whole body. She sits in the blue chair, and Liv and I look at each other out of the corner of our eyes. We were right.

She looks around the circle and smiles, nodding at each of us.

"*Good morning. I'm Kathy, and I'll be leading today's group session. I think I'll just jump right in today. Today we will go around the circle, and you guys will introduce yourselves and tell each of us why you're here. As always, I want to remind you guys that this is a safe space, and judgment ceased to exist at the door.*" She nods, letting her words sink in, and looks to her right.

A thin girl wearing black sweats and a black hoodie with short UGGS stands up, her hair is long and brown, and it hits her waist. She has a small face that's filled with small features.

"*Hi, I'm Sylvie.*" She shifts on her feet. "*I'm sixteen, and a few weeks ago, I didn't make prima ballerina in my studio show. I don't know; I kind of just flipped. I stopped eating and stopped feeling, so I just started doing things to feel. Things I shouldn't have done… I didn't eat for three days, and when my brother found me, I was passed out.*"

"*And how do you feel now?*"

"Alive. I feel things now, even the things I didn't want to, like the anger and disappointment, and I also feel slightly lost. Because when I get out of here, I know I will still want to dance, but I know it's not good for me."

"Thank you, Sylvie." Sylvie sits back down, wiping under her eyes. *"Sometimes the things we love bring us the most pain in return for an ounce of satisfaction or validation. Sometimes it's best to just walk away and work on you."* Kathy sighs. *"Who's next?"*

The girl next to Sylvie stands up. She's tall and kind of resembles a movie star. Everything on her looks designer, even her jeans. She has a smooth west coast accent. Her hair is brown, and so are her eyes.

"I'm Cleo, and I'm eighteen. I'm here because I got drunk and drove my dad's car into a tree." Oh. Very blunt, very straightforward, and with no remorse. Liv chuckles, and Cleo smirks, a look of pride flashing across her face.

"Why did you do that, Cleo?" Kathy asks the question everyone's wondering.

"He slept with a 20-year-old less than six months after my mom died, and when I found out, I flipped out on him and told him his money couldn't fix this. Because it couldn't. My mom is still dead. My dad is still dating a girl closer to my age than his, and I'm still angry. So, he sent me here, far away from his friends and mine." She sits back down, and her cheeks are tinted pink with anger.

"Do you regret it?" Kathy asks.

"Honestly?" Kathy nods. *"No. I hope he can never get that car restored."*

The room is silent for a while, and I can see Kathy trying to think of something positive to say, but instead, she just moves on to the next person.

The next girl that goes is named Barbara, and she's fifteen. She tried to kill herself after being sexually assaulted for the third time a few weeks ago.

"I'm tired of trying to trust people, trying to live, trying to fall in love, and being human and getting hurt in turn. Is there something about me that just screams no means yes, keep going?" She laughs humorlessly. *"No one believes me, and the one person who does is my housekeeper. I refuse to go back there."* Barbara shakes her head adamantly, and her choppy black hair hits her face.

"After you committed and woke up, how did you feel?"

"I kind of hated myself a little more because I felt like I let them win… all of them."

Kathy nods. *"Sometimes the only thing you can do is keep fighting and living, even when it seems impossible because eventually, you'll start finding moments of hope. Maybe in others, maybe in books, maybe in art. But you just have to look."*

Maybe I hadn't looked hard enough, or maybe it was all right in front of me, but I just didn't think I was worthy of any of it.

It's my turn, and it takes Liv nudging me in my side to stand up.

"Hi, I'm Emi. I'm 18, and I accidentally overdosed on some pills. I was having a bad day, so yeah." I sit back down.

"Was it an accident if you were having a bad day and took them?" a girl with short ringlet curls asks. She sits by Kathy on the other side.

"Yes?"

Cleo sends me a sympathetic look like she knows something I don't. I look around, and a lot of people are looking at me like they're all in on something I've yet to figure out. I ignore it and look at Kathy. She studies me before nodding and moving on to Liv.

Liv stands up. *"I'm Liv. I'm 18 years old, and I accidentally overdosed on oxy."* She sits back down, crossing her legs.

"Was it your first-time doing drugs?" Liv shakes her head. *"Did you want to overdose?"*

Liv shakes her head. *"No, but it happened."*

"Today is both of you guys' first day, isn't it?"

Liv answers yes, but I shake my head. *"Today's my third day."*

Kathy nods. *"Well, welcome."*

We both murmur thanks, and she moves on to the next person.

A petite dark skin girl stands up. *"Hi, I'm Raina. I'm 16, and I have an eating disorder. I've had one for a while, but I guess it just got to the point where people couldn't ignore it. I'd weigh myself every morning, night, and right after school. My best friend heard me…using the bathroom… and she told my dad, who told me I needed to eat. And when I couldn't, he sent me here. I'm not mad at him; he did the right thing. My mom left us a few years back, and it's just been us. I hate putting him through this, and he's all alone."*

I can feel my eyes watering, but I don't let any tears fall. Raina's clothes are drowning her, and her eyes appear sunken, but she still wears a small smile. I wanted to clap and cheer for her and for all of them for standing up and sharing their dark secrets. For not cowering or lying. For being *real.* I wanted to know how long it took them to be able to look strangers in the eye and tell them.

I don't hear anything after Raina. I'm embarrassed—borderline mortified—for not saying more. I stood there, said as little as I could, and sat back down, pushing the spotlight off me and onto someone else.

Once the group session ends, I run to my room and bury my face in my pillow. Liv comes in behind me and sits next to me. She doesn't ask what I'm doing; she just hums a melody. When I looked up, she'd let her hair down and put on a beanie.

"Want to go for a walk on the grounds?"

"I *don't think I'm allowed,*" I admit.

She stands up and shrugs. "*Well, let's go see and find out.*" I nod, put on a jacket, and follow her out.

Turns out, I'm allowed to walk on the grounds. The air is still cold and has a crispness that's poorly hidden by the sun. Liv and I sit on a bench facing each other. She smuggled snacks in her jacket, so we ate potato chips and sour candy and drank small cans of Coke. "Why are you here?" I ask her. I can't run from this. I won't.

She looks at me. *"Emi, I'm addicted to drugs and alcohol, really only hard liquor. I'm fine with a beer."*

"I thought it got better. You said you got better."

She shakes her head, shame filling her features. *"I lied, Emi. I'm an addict. I lie to do the shit I want. I'm sorry, Emi."*

I nod and let her words sink in. *"It's okay,"* I whisper.

"How long?" I ask.

"Since freshman year, and I don't mean 'I need weed to sleep.' Which I do. I need coke or pills to get through the day. I've tried going sober for Clara and my dad, but I always end up at Rex's house begging him for something. But a few weeks ago, Clara found me passed out somewhere, and she freaked

out. She said she couldn't do it anymore. She started crying, and I just stood there like a jackass. You know what she told me?" Liv clears her throat. "She said watching me get high is like watching the slowest suicide. Each time hurts a little more and a little less. I told her I loved her, and she told me it wasn't enough and then left. An hour later, I went to Rex's house. He told me 'No,' and I flipped. I walked home. Then I went to a party, found some pills, and took them, not caring what they were."

"How long has Clara known?"

"Forever. I stopped doing hard shit around her for a while, but I made Clara promise not to tell you, and she did."

"Why didn't you want to tell me?"

She squeezes my arm. "Emi, you're the only person in my life who doesn't see me as an addict or a failure. I didn't want that to change. I didn't want you to be up at night, worried if I'd get home safe or if I took something laced. I liked the way you saw me," she admits, tears falling down her cheeks.

"I still like you, even knowing everything. I don't hate you, and I'm not disgusted. I just want you to be safe, happy, and sober. I'm sorry I wasn't there for you, but I'll be here now. I promise." I will. I'll do whatever she needs me to do.

"I need you to get better and to stop lying to yourself and everyone else. You're not okay, Emi, and what you did wasn't an accident. You got to come to terms with that. One way or another."

After Liv and I return from our picnic, she has to meet with her sponsor. So, I go to my room and begin writing until it's time for lunch. We ate lunch together in comfortable silence. Liv and I sat in the rec room and watched television with everyone until it was time for yoga, then we hid out in my room until dinner.

We ate baked sweet potatoes with baked chicken and sweet corn for dinner. Liv told me about Clara accepting the offer to attend Brown. She was so happy for her when she found out, but she cried a little that night in Clara's bed. I teared up a little when she told me that, but I wiped my eyes before they could fall.

While Liv calls her dad, I call Jay.

The phone rings three times before he gruffly says, "*Hello?*"

I don't say anything for a minute, his voice washing over me. I didn't know I could miss his voice so much in three days.

"*H-hey, it's me.*"

He doesn't say anything for another minute, and I think he's doing the same thing I was.

"*Em?*"

"*Yup, the one and only,*" I tease.

"*How are you?*"

"*I'm okay. Liv is here, so I'm not completely alone, which is good. It was pretty lonely the first two days, but that's over now. I have therapy with Dr. Young tomorrow.*" I ramble everything out.

"*Are you nervous?*"

"*Kind of. I'm scared to, like, dive into my dark and weird secrets.*"

"*I thought you liked weird things.*"

I smile. "*I do, but I don't think Dr. Young wants to hear about my weirdness.*"

"*I don't know. Dr. Young seems pretty down to listen to anything.*"

"*Probably,*" I mumble. "*How are you? How's school?*"

"*It's alright. Caden's girlfriend came to stay for a while, so I had to stay at my apartment. I had to go and get some more clothes from the dorm, and I heard her moaning from down the hallway. I couldn't even make it to my door before the noises were too distinct.*" I laugh, and I can hear Jay chuckle.

"*Why don't you ask them to keep it down?*"

"*I did. That was them keeping it down! No wonder they used to hook up in abandoned barns back home.*" I burst into laughter.

"*How do you know this?*"

"*Caden overshares when he smokes.*"

Neither one of us says anything for a while.

"*I miss you,*" I tell him.

"*I miss you too, Em.*" He clears his throat. "*Everything will be okay. You will come home.*"

"*I know,*" I whisper. I don't want to get off the phone with Jay, but I have to. Liv has already left, and someone else has taken her place. "*I got to go.*"

"*Okay. I'll talk to you soon, yeah?*"

"*Yeah. Bye, Jay.*"

"*Bye, Em.*" He hangs up.

I put the phone back up and drag a hand over my face. I sit there for a while before getting up to take a shower. I go to bed, and when I lie down, I think about my first kiss. It was my freshman year of high school, and I was outside my house.

"You know, there's like ten parties we could be at right now," Jay reminded me. I carried a gallon of milk, and he had two boxes of donuts in his hand. His hair was longer then and a lighter shade of brown. I think Bell had convinced him to dye it, and he kept it.

"You'd rather be at a party than watch a Lord of the Rings *Marathon?" I asked him, slightly taken aback.*

He smirked like I had fallen right into his trap. "No, Em, this is what I want to do."

I looked away, hiding my smile. "Okay, good, because it starts in thirty minutes."

He grabbed my arm, and I froze, looking up at him. He hadn't hit his growth spurt yet but was still taller than me. I think my crush had just started to blossom. We had started hugging more and lying in bed together closer than before. Never doing anything more, but sometimes we'd end up holding each other. We held eye contact longer than necessary, and sometimes, when I felt like no one was watching, I looked at him, really looked at him. And sometimes, I swear I could feel him looking at me.

"You look really beautiful today, Em," he whispered. I laughed nervously and shrugged off his words. "I'm serious. New jeans?" His hand skimmed my waist, and my breathing hitched. I nodded in response.

"T-they're high-waisted."

He smirked and looked me in the eyes, rubbing circles on my hip. "I like em'. Do you?"

"Yeah, they're comfy. They have rips, which is a plus, and you know they're mom jeans. I mean, who doesn't love mom jeans, you know?" I rambled. He chuckled and leaned forward. His eyes flitted between my lips and eyes.

Is this about to happen? I didn't move; I just stood there and waited. Jay dipped his head down until our breaths were tangled. I didn't know if I was breathing in him or the air.

"You good?" he asked.

"Yup," I squeaked out, and his nose touched my cheek as his lips pressed against mine. His lips were warm, and mine were stiff. He squeezed my hip, and I loosened up. I moved my lips, and he moved his. When I felt his tongue, I pulled away. His cheeks were flushed, and both of us were breathing harder and more labored.

"Em-" he started, but I didn't want to hear the words 'I'm sorry' or 'This was a mistake.'

"We're gonna be late for the marathon, and you know how much we love the beginning." I turned around and walked away. He caught up to me, and we didn't talk about the kiss, but a year later, we had another one.

Chapter 67

Emille Kate Van der Berg

Day 4

"Are you excited for group?" I ask Liv as we finish the last of our breakfast.

She shakes her head. *"No, we didn't even get through everyone. We have two people left, then we'll do coping mechanisms, and something about that screams self-positivity on Pinterest posters."* I chuckle and chug the last of my orange juice.

"Has your sponsor given you tips?"

Liv nods. *"He mostly focuses on digging and figuring out the root of the problem and different triggers."*

"Do you like him?"

"He always looks at me with a blank look on his face, and I've called him an asshole three times already, but he just keeps talking and being nice to me." She says it with a hint of displeasure, but I don't push.

We sit in the dining room until it's time for group therapy. We sit in the same seats as last time, and I eat the rest of the blueberries in my hand as we wait for everyone to fill the room. Everyone sits in the same seats as last time. Kathy is the last person in, and when she sits down, she smiles at us.

"Hello, how are you guys today?" No one answers. I don't think we're supposed to. *"I want us to finish the circle. So, let's begin."* She looks at the girl two seats in front of her.

A tan, average-height girl stands up and shakily introduces herself. *"I'm Liza, I'm fourteen, and I tried to kill myself a few weeks ago."* She sighs. *"I got tired of being lonely, feeling like shit, and I did the only thing that seemed permanent. The only thing I knew would make…everything go away. My older brother found me, and he committed me as well."*

"Are you angry at him for it?"

"Kind of," Liza admits.

Kathy nods, and the next girl stands up before she can say anything. She kind of reminds me of Reese Witherspoon, just bright green eyes and a little taller. She has blonde hair in big curls and wears blue low-rise jeans and a hot pink strapless top with sandals.

"Hi! I'm Bethany Tisdale, and I'm 17 years old. I'm captain of the cheerleading team and in the top five of my class. I'm from Beverly Hills, and my favorite place to vacation is definitely St. Barts."

"And why are you here?" Kathy asks after an awkward moment of silence.

"Oh! Well, it's actually a funny story." She laughs, the sound high and soft. *"My boyfriend— well, ex-boyfriend now—slept with who I thought was one of my good friends, and she posted the video for everyone to see, and I*

accidentally drove his car into a lake. I stood there, watching it drown, in my favorite little black dress. My mom sent me here until the press cooled down. And as for the girl, well, I think she has something better coming for her." She smiles, and it's a warm, innocent girl-next-door smile.

"Do you regret it?"

She thinks about it for a second. *"I don't know, it felt good. Most of the time, I just let everything slide, but the anger and frustration had been building up for a while, so when I let it out, it felt like I could breathe."*

Bethany sits down, and Kathy nods.

"After listening to all of you guys' stories and the challenges you've overcome, I want to talk to you all about your past." Kathy shifts in her seat. *"You guys were able to stand up and be honest with yourself and random people you don't know, and it takes some people years to admit they even have a problem. In order to get help and to get better, you have to identify and know the problem. And sometimes, that means sitting yourself down and facing the truth. If you look at life with rose-tinted glasses, nothing will ever be real."* Her voice is calm and soothing, like she's reading from a book.

"What's the scariest thing about getting help?" Kathy asks us.

"Admitting you need it," Sylvie squeaks.

Kathy nods. *"But once you overcome that, what's the second scariest thing?"*

"Failing or realizing how deep the problem is," Barbara answers. She stares straight at Kathy.

"Is it worse to live in the prison of your thoughts and pain or to fail, trying everything you can to free yourself?"

The room is silent.

"Wouldn't the failure hurt more, though?" Cleo asks.

"It might, but you'd know you've given everything you had. The 'what if' is always more frightening than the repercussions." Kathy crosses one leg over the other. *"You can't go through life thinking about what if's from when you were teenagers. Do you want to wake up when you're forty and think, 'Man, what would life be like if I'd gotten sober when I was eighteen?' Or maybe when you're forty, you'll have lost everyone that loved you because you never even tried, or even worse realities."*

Death. When people refuse help or live in denial for most of their life, they usually end up losing everything, including their life.

"So, all you can do is try. Life is a game you keep trying. Even if you don't win, you keep trying."

"It's been a while since I've seen you," Dr. Young begins. She slowly sits down in her chair. It's been three days, but I don't say anything. *"How have you been, Emi?"*

"Okay." I need to ask her something, but I'm scared. *"Do you think I'm bipolar?"* I blurt.

I've been thinking about it for a day or two. I heard someone talking about the manic highs and depressive lows, and I think I experienced both this year.

"You might be bipolar, and that's okay."

I shake my head. *"I don't want my whole life to be categorized into a series of highs and lows,"* I admit.

"I understand, but people can't choose if they want to be bipolar or not. You can't control it; it's part of the cards dealt to you."

"Are they my cards?"

She purses her lips. *"Honestly, I don't think so. I think you were becoming overwhelmed with grief and sadness, and the fear of being sad and going into a dark place gave you the energy to run from it. I do think you suffer from depression, though, and you've had a few depressive episodes before."*

I shake my head. *"I'm not depressed. I just got sad, you know, and tired."*

Dr. Young writes something down in her notebook. *"How did you feel after your dad died?"*

Oh, we're just jumping right in today.

"I was really lonely. Like, I didn't know a ten-year-old could be that lonely. I had my sisters, but it wasn't the same. Thena was so focused on schoolwork, and Bell and Alexander would sneak off. It would just be me and Allison, and she'd make me wish I was with Dad." I clear my throat, my voice cracking through my words. *"I didn't have any friends; I think it was one of the reasons why we moved to Connecticut so soon after. It felt like nothing was keeping us in Louisiana."*

"And when you moved, you had Jay?"

I nod.

"I had Jay and Nick. Thena and Bell would tag along sometimes too. The hole where he was never quite filled, but I liked to think it shrunk or disappeared. But sometimes, when I'd be in bed without Jay or my sisters, I'd think of him and get so sad. I started calling him, so he wasn't really gone...I could convince myself he was still in Louisiana." I humorously laugh and wipe my cheeks.

"Did your mom talk to you about his death?"

I shake my head. *"We all just kept going, and when it was his birthday, we'd all get a little quieter, but on holidays we celebrated. I miss him sometimes."*

"It's okay to miss him," she reminds me. I know this, but sometimes I feel guilty for missing him and not missing Allison. I can't say this out loud, not yet. Because when the words leave my mouth, I'll feel even shittier. I'll feel the weight and pain of being a bad person.

"I know," I whisper. *I wipe the tears that have fallen.*

"Let's talk about Jay. How are things with him?"

"They're good. They're always good." I know she wants more; I can't skirt around this. *"He didn't know I was feeling sad. I tried to hide it from him, so I'd lay on him and distract him with movies and food when he came over. I didn't want him to worry or see me like that. I didn't want him to think I was...sick. I didn't want him to leave me, when he saw how bad I was."* I clear my throat.

"Do you think he had a feeling?"

"Probably. Jay has always noticed too much about me, even when we were just friends. I've never been able to really lie to him. I've tried, but it never lasts long, and I think he just goes along for my sake most of the time."

She smiles. *"Do you ever imagine yourself having a future with Jay?"*

I smile. *"Yeah, I do. I don't want to push him away because I've got shit to figure out. I want us to have a happy ending, and I want it to be with each other. It scares me, but I want to try."*

She smiles. *"That's all you can do."*

###

Liv and I eat dinner together. We eat spaghetti while watching the sunset. I tell her about my therapy session—well, the part about Jay—and she tells me about her sponsor's apartment in Malibu and the other in Rhode Island. Liv gave me an annoyed look when she said that. I think she likes her sponsor, but she's just moody since she's sober now.

"Have you talked to Clara?" I ask her as we sit down with our second bowl of spaghetti.

"She was in the hospital, but other than that, no. Should I call her?"

"If you want to, I think you should. You love Clara, right? Go for it."

"I might," she murmurs noncommittally. I nod, and we finish our spaghetti, cans of soda and glasses of water in front of us.

I don't call anyone; I just shower and get ready for bed.

Chapter 68

James Averell

Day 5

Five days. Emi has been gone for five days, and each day, I can feel her absence a little stronger. With her absence comes strong feelings I don't want to feel, anger being the strongest.

I've been staying at my dad's house for the past three days. I needed to do laundry, and I didn't have any food at my place, so I just came back home. Rachel has been cooking enough food to feed an army, and Dad's been home for dinner. So yeah, they're clearly worried. I've been driving my dad's car, it's less noticeable, and the windows are fully tinted.

I slide on my shoes, eating the last of the cinnamon-buttered toast Rachel made for me. She's washing the *three* dishes she used for breakfast. Dad came downstairs, got a coffee, and went back to bed.

I get up, finishing the last bite of the toast. *"Where are you going?"* Rachel asks me, drying her hands. She rushes to catch up to me.

"Club meeting or something." I shrug.

My days have consisted of school, club meetings, working out, and figuring out something to do to keep busy.

I grab his keys from the counter and go through the garage. By the time I pull out of the gates of our neighborhood, someone is tailing me.

I don't mind. It's just another reason for me to speed and cut people off. It takes me 28 minutes to get to the chapter house. I valet and tell them to park close so I don't have to wait with the paparazzi afterward. When I get out of the car, the sound of cameras flashing hits me.

"James, where's Emi?!"

"Did you and Emi break up?!"

Paparazzi shout strings of questions at me as I walk inside. I ignore them. Ever since Emi ended up in the hospital, paparazzi have been following all of us. They had been slowly increasing their presence around Bell because of the magazine cover, but now they follow her 24/7. And the rest of us whenever they can. Nick is the only one who doesn't seem surprised or phased by this whole thing.

By the time I get inside the room where meetings are held, it's already underway. Nick stands by the door, his arms crossed as he listens. The only reason he comes is because he knows I'll be here. The chapter vice president, this quiet kid named Todd, speaks about donations for the end-of-semester trip to Cancun. I'm not going, and I doubt Nick is.

I half listen, and when Todd adjourns the meeting, I walk over to Nick, who simply looks at me. This is how our relationship has been going since Emi overdosed. He doesn't say anything, and I get angry at his silence. I can feel his unsaid words; they're heavier than bricks.

"Are you going on the trip?" I know he's not.

"No, are you?"

"No. Emi wouldn't want to be in Cancun with a bunch of people she doesn't know for a week."

"You could still go alone, and Emi could stay with her sisters. I doubt she'd mind. She trusts you," he argues, his voice calm and serene. His composure is starting to piss me off. He didn't look phased at the hospital when she had to check in, and he doesn't look phased now.

My girlfriend, Emi, Thena's little sister, tried to kill herself, and he looks as cool as a cucumber.

"I wouldn't want to go without her. Maybe this is hard for you to understand, but some of us like spending time with the people we love!" I snap. I don't mean it, not really, but I want him to get angry or just say what he's thinking and move on.

Nick doesn't say anything; he just smiles and walks away. That's who he is. Nick doesn't pick fights or entertain childish games, he's the most composed person I know. He's the bigger, smarter, more talented person, and he knows it. In every room Nick enters, he's the best. Half the time, I think his confidence is what convinces people before he even opens his mouth.

I write a check for three grand and donate it to the club treasurer and leave. The paparazzi are still there, and the valet is actively trying to keep them away from my car so I can leave. I tip them each a hundred and leave.

Life is a lot lonelier without Emi. Even when she was ignoring me, she was still there. I could go see her, and she wouldn't push me away. Now, she's away, and I can't go see her. She doesn't want me to. I respect her decision, I always do, but this one hurt.

Today is visiting day, her sisters are seeing her right now, and I'll have to hear how she looks from them. They could be lying to me and I wouldn't even know.

I end up at the gym, and after running a couple of miles, I lift weights. Nick comes in halfway through my second set and joins me. We don't talk. I'm still pissed at him, but at least he's here. I'm not lonely with him there. I can feel myself slowly crumbling. I'm lucky if I get three hours of sleep at night, and each time I eat, I feel like I'm forcing food down.

As I leave the gym, Nick grabs my arm, and I look at him.

"You can't look like you're dying when she gets out. You know that, right? What good would that do either of you?" He turns around and goes back inside the gym.

Rachel and I eat lasagna and watch a movie together. After finishing my third slice of lasagna, I sprawl out on the couch and go to sleep. She doesn't question why I'm staying here again, she just covers me in a blanket. All I see is Emi as my eyelids close.

Chapter 69

Emille Kate Van der Berg

Day 5

In group, we talk and learn about coping skills. Kathy instructs us to practice our breathing and focus on that. She reminds us and shows us the feeling of weighted blankets for panic attacks. Kathy goes over tip after tip, and I listen to a few. She really emphasizes the importance of having something *healthy* to look forward to. We spent ten minutes meditating and practicing our breathing. She asked people to name a few triggers and had us repeat, *"I'm okay. I can feel like this. I'm okay."* We did those ten times.

Then she told us that it's okay to just walk away, even if you feel like people will look at you. It's okay to just walk away. Your feelings and your mental space are more important than what others think. It was a good session, very positive, very relaxing. I don't think Liv enjoyed it, but she hasn't enjoyed many things except the meals. We both thoroughly enjoy the meals.

Today is visiting day, so I spend a little more time getting ready. I pull out the jeans Thena and Jay packed for me and a random sweater. Liv takes time and irons her shirt, and during lunch, I can see her trying to hide her nervousness. She doesn't like the feeling; I think she used to get high instead of feeling nervous.

"You'll be fine. Is Clara coming?"

"I don't know. I could just be sitting there."

"You won't, and if she doesn't show, come sit with me. Bell and Thena won't mind," I assure her they won't. Bell likes Liv. She thinks Liv is effortlessly cool, and Thena is just happy Liv brought me somewhere safe when I got high. *"You ready?"* I ask her. She nods and runs her hand through her hair, and fluffs it.

We walk up one flight of wide stairs that creak with each step to get to the visiting room. We sign both of our names and go inside a room.

There's a handful of tables all separated throughout the room. Two tables are occupied, one with Bethany and a tall, muscular guy who has a shopping bag on the table.

"And you got me my favorite silk robe? ! " she cries, taking it out of the bag. She stands up and wraps her arms around him, squeezing him to her. He sits there stiff as a board as she hugs him. *"You're the best!"* She sits down next to him and pulls something else out.

At the next table are Clara and Mr. Lukov, both sitting there with glares and both impeccably dressed. Clara's face softens when she sees Liv. Clara stands up, walks over, and hugs Liv. Liv hugs her back, and when they pull apart, Clara's eyes are filled with tears.

Mr. Lukov stands up and holds out his hand. Liv shakes it.

"Nice to finally meet you. Clara has told me a lot about you," Mr. Lukov says. He tries to smile, but it looks even scarier. Only Liv would meet her girlfriend's dad at rehab.

"You too," Liv shyly says. Clara drags her down, and they sit next to each other.

"He invited himself. He wanted to make sure you were okay," Clara explains, loud enough for her dad to hear.

I watch them with a smile. Clara and Liv hold hands, Clara's hand occasionally drifting to Liv's lap. Eventually, her dad stands up and excuses himself. He looks at me and nods in greeting.

I go to use the bathroom, the sodas from earlier hitting me. I'm happy Clara showed up for Liv. When I leave the bathroom, Bethany and Liv are still at their tables, and another table is filled with my sisters.

I walk over and sit across from them. They look different. Bell has her hair in two braids with a baseball cap covering most of her face, and Thena has a black baseball cap on with one single braid, her hair straight and resting on her right shoulder. They wear large jackets and no traces of makeup.

"What's going on with you guys?"

"Nothing, we just didn't have time to get ready. Too excited to see you," Bell answers, a cheerful smile on her face.

I smile and relax. I cross my hands on the table. *"I miss you guys."*

"We miss you too," Thena responds, her lips twitching up into a smile. *"But how are you? Really?"*

"I'm okay. I've been sharing more and learning coping strategies. I promise I'm okay. I'm doing better."

Thena nods. "*That's good.*"

"*How are you guys?*" I don't just want to talk about myself. I need to hear about their lives so I can still feel like I'm a part of them.

Thena sighs, slipping off her baseball cap. "*Fine. Nick and I have visited three different locations for potential stores, and each one is horrible.*"

"*He picked them out?*"

"*No, I did. I'm letting Nick choose the next one, and we're seeing it on May 3rd.*"

"*Are you excited?*"

She looks at me like I'm crazy. "*For him to brag and flaunt his subpar pick? I think I'd rather move back in with Mom and Rick.*" Bell and I both laugh. I don't even think she knows how much time she and Nick spend together. Thena shot a glare between Bell and me. I try to bite back my laughter, but I fail.

"*Bell, how are you?*" I redirect the subject.

"*I'm good. I have a meeting with my agent in three days, so I'm excited and slightly nervous.*"

"*Why are you nervous?*"

"*I never know what she's going to bring up. She might yell at me for not doing any shoots, or she might have good news. Never know. I think that's why I like her.*" Bell likes surprises, so her agent is the perfect fit for her.

"*How are Mom and Rick?*" I ask them a minute or two later.

They exchange glances. "*Rick is good; he offered to come but didn't want you to feel pressured, and Mom is…*" Bell eases in.

"*In denial as usual. She truly feels that she can bend the facts to her will and rewrite our lives.*" Thena snaps.

I grab both of their hands. *"I'm not mad at Mom, I promise. And I'll call Rick tonight."* He would've come if I had asked, but I didn't know how awkward that'd be. *" "* I wave it off. I can't think about it for too long. I don't want to.

I change the subject and ask Thena about school and Bell about Tristan. Thena is doing well in school and is excited for it to be over within a few weeks. She's studying for finals and claims her house has become a study zone. She says it with a hint of disgust, like she'll need to deep clean it for weeks afterward.

Bell says Tristan is working more, and he's happy, so she's happy. That's all she says, and Thena and I exchange a look, but we don't say anything. She has a few pictures with him on her Instagram highlights, and they look happy. And she never tells us anything bad. But I'm pretty sure she didn't tell him why I'm in here or that I'm in here. Which is good; I don't really want him to know.

Thena checks her watch, and I know they have to go. I know I'll see them soon. I stand up and hug them, both of them squeezing me. Bell kisses my forehead, and Thena pats me on the back three times. Thena slides her baseball cap back on, and Bell puts on a pair of sunglasses. I appreciate them going through all this so no one recognizes them, but it seems a little extreme.

"I love you guys," I tell them.

"I love you too," Thena replies, her eyes watering. She wipes her eyes before the tear can fall, and when she notices I saw, she narrows her eyes at me, giving me a hard look.

"Love you, Emi cakes." Bell hugs me again, and then they leave.

Liv sits at a table with a tall, slightly muscular man wearing a blue shirt and blue jeans. His hair is the same ashy brown color as hers, but his skin is pale, and his eyes are light brown. They talk, and he holds her hands across the table, hiding his sobs behind a fist. Liv's dad came. I smile encouragingly at her and leave.

When I turn on the water to shower, sobs rack through my body, and I don't know how or when it happened, but I end up on the floor, my face to my thighs as I cry. The door opens, but I don't pick my head up. I feel a towel on me and look up. Helen sits next to me, her clothes getting wet from the shower. She has a stack of my clothes in her hand. She pushes my hair away from my face and gives me a soft, warm smile.

"L-Liv's dad came," I tell her, and when the words come out, another wave of tears skates through me. And I know it's selfish, but I can't stop.

"That's good, right honey?" I nodded, and she dried me off. I changed into pajamas. Helen dries most of my hair, putting it into two French twists. She shouldn't be doing this...

As she does my hair, the tears stop. She walks me back to my room and tucks me in.

"Sleep, honey. You need to rest," Helen soothes. I know she's right.

Liv's dad came, and I'm happy for her because she needs support while she gets sober. She needs people who love her so she can *stay* sober. Liv deserves to have all the love and hope in the world.

My sisters came and saw me, and they distracted me for two hours. They showed up for me, and I know if I had asked, Jay would've too. I don't know why I started crying or why I couldn't stop.

I just know I'm tired, so I close my eyes and fall asleep to the soft hum of Helen's voice.

Chapter 70

Emille Kate Van der Berg

Day 6

Helen helps me reduce the puffiness in my eyes and face when I wake up. It takes us thirty minutes, but it works. I leave my hair in the French twist, not caring if it's messy, and put on leggings and a hoodie. Helen even lets me wear fuzzy socks and slippers.

Before I leave my room for breakfast, I apologize about last night. She doesn't say anything for a moment; she just squeezes my hand.

"*I want you to get better, Emi. Don't apologize about last night; that's not needed. Apologizing because you broke down and felt things are rarely needed.*" Helen leaves, and after a moment of looking at the spot she was standing at, I leave too.

Liv sits at our table, a plate of eggs, toast, and breakfast meat in front of her.

"Where have you been? You overslept?" she asked me. I'm not hungry, so I just sit down.

"Yeah, I overslept. How's the food?"

"Good. Eggs are fried hard, just like I like them. Good meat too." She takes a bite of her sausage, and I force a small laugh.

"How was yesterday?"

"Good. Clara and I are good, I think. She didn't yell about the overdose; she was just happy I'm okay."

"That's good. How was the visit with your dad?"

"Good. I told him everything and made sure he knew it wasn't his fault. He said he promises to work less so he can be there for me." Liv smiles.

"That's good. I'm happy for you," I quietly told her.

Kathy is the first person waiting for us. She smiles and says hi to Liv and me as we take our usual seats. I didn't make small talk with Liv while we waited. I didn't know what to say, and I could tell neither did she.

Kathy begins group therapy by saying, *"Sometimes the things that save us or keep us off the edge are our coping mechanisms, even if they sound mundane or like they just came from a poster in a doctor's office."* Some people chuckle. *"But they work, and they might help you."*

Kathy goes over a few coping strategies and reviews some of the ones we talked about yesterday. She has us practice them. Most of them are for addiction, reminding yourself what you have waiting for you. She talks about the importance of relationships and figuring out if those relationships enable you or help you, and if they are enabling you, how you can fix that.

"A relationship built off of drugs and alcohol is not a relationship; it's a suicide pact." Her words hang in the air for the last fifteen minutes of the group, even when she brings up something else.

Liv and I eat snacks outside again after lunch until it's time for me to go to therapy.

"I cried in the shower last night, and Helen had to help me get to bed," I told her, my knees pulled up to my chest.

"Oh shit! Why?"

I shrug my shoulders. *"Happens sometimes. Does that ever happen to you?"*

"Yeah, when I feel like I've hit rock bottom, but it's not a daily or even weekly occurrence." She looks up from her bag of hot chips. *"Hell, I don't even know if it's a monthly occurrence, but in all fairness, I had drugs to distract me from my sadness."*

So maybe it is normal. Maybe you just cry until you can't stand anymore and have to sit down and bawl your eyes out until you have no tears left. People all over probably experience it. *Am I making excuses? Is this really normal?*

Maybe normal is just subjective to who you ask.

Dr. Young knows. I can tell by her gentle smile when I come in. I know she knows, but she still asks what happened last night.

"I cried, and Helen came to get me. She helped me into bed then I went to sleep."

"Why did you cry?"

"I saw Liv talking to her dad, and I just got sad. I don't know why. My sisters came, and I was happy when they left. And then I wasn't."

"Does that happen to you a lot?" I shrug. *"How often, would you say?"*

I really think about it, and the more I think, the more I hate the answer. I stand up and start making small steps going back and forth, trying to think. Sometimes I'll cry and not know I'm crying. Other times I don't cry at all, feeling so happy, and then other times, the tears blend into the fake smiles. Sometimes there are no tears at all, but I can feel sobs moving through my chest.

"I-I don't know. It depends."

"Depends on what?"

"I don't know." Why does she keep asking questions I don't know the answer to? Shouldn't she know?

"Emi." I stop and look at her. She doesn't mind that I'm standing up. She looks like she's been expecting it. "How old were you when you started feeling depressed?"

"I'm not depressed," I quickly replied. Dr. Young tilts her head to the side and closes her notebook, putting it on the coffee table.

"How do you know that?"

"I don't have a reason to be depressed."

"You think you need one?"

"Yeah, I think so. I just got sad last night."

"And before you attempted suicide, you just got sad?"

I flinch. *"It was an accident. People make mistakes. I had a few bad days and made a mistake."* My voice is flat and quiet, and I'm struggling to believe my own lies.

"Your dad suffered from depression. Did you know that?" I don't answer. *"Did you experience guilt, lack of concentration, hopelessness, or sadness after he died?"*

"Maybe."

I feel myself being sucked into the past, the crying I had even a year after he died, and the way Jay distracted me. The random pamphlets about child depression at the doctor's office. Random meetings with counselors. The stares and questions.

"What about with Allison?" I flinch at the name, but Dr. Young keeps going. *"Did you have any guilt, excessive crying, hopelessness, or sadness after her death?"*

I felt guilt, so much guilt I felt like I was constantly drowning and fighting against it. Not even Jay or my sisters could distract me. I run a hand over my hair and down my face, trying to distract myself. *Why is she doing this?*

I can see Allison's old room, how I never went inside it, and how it became haunted. I couldn't even cross the threshold. She had so much makeup, so many hair straighteners, so many Victoria's Secret bags, and bottles on bottles of perfume. She was vain. Her image was *everything*.

Allison was drunk at Dad's funeral, but someone kept her away from us, so I didn't have to see her. She didn't even want to come. Her mom made her.

"I'm not depressed," I grit. I know Dr. Young is reading symptoms. I've seen them a million times before.

"Because you don't have a reason?"

"Yes!" I look at her, tears straining my cheeks.

"You don't need a reason, Emi."

"Women who have lost their husbands and have to raise their kids alone; they have a reason to be depressed! People who are verbally, physically, and sexually abused have a reason to be depressed! People who have gotten the short end of the stick in everything have a reason to be depressed! I don't! I have parents who can buy me anything and everything I want! I have a boyfriend who loves me! Sisters who would drop anything and everything to be there for me! I don't have a reason to be depressed! Don't you get that?"

My chest heaves, and when I look at her, I have to stop myself from curling up on the couch and crying. Dr. Young sits up straighter and smiles at me. It feels like my voice is echoing through the room.

"Your parents' money and the people in your life don't make your pain or struggles any less real. When are you going to be able to accept help and know you're worthy of it?"

"I don't know," I admit.

"Are you going to keep shoving all these feelings down because you don't think your struggles are real? Because eventually you'll crumble, Emi, and I don't know if you'll be able to get up."

I begin to cry because I'm so tired. I'm exhausted.

"How can something invisible be so heavy?" I ask in a small cry. Dr. Young slides a box of tissues to me, and I take one.

"I don't know, Emi, but it's time to really feel and try to heal."

I nod in agreement. *"I'm sorry for yelling and dragging this out. I was just scared."*

I don't need to explain why. I love my dad, but in this aspect, I don't want to be like him. This breakdown has been years in the making, and I think she knows it.

She smiles. *"It's fine, Emi. I'm just happy we got here."*

Chapter 71

Emille Kate Van der Berg

Day 7

It's warm outside, the sun's shining, and there are a few clouds in the soft baby-blue sky. Liv and I sit on our bench, sandwiches, chips, cookies, and sodas between us. It's been warm almost every day, so more people have started coming outside and eating their meals.

Today marks a week since I've been here. How many more weeks do I have left until it's time for me to go? I have no idea. Raina told Liv she's been here for three weeks already, but she knows she's not ready to go, so she hasn't been in a rush.

Liv finishes her sandwich and opens her bag of chips. I've taken maybe three bites of my sandwich and eaten three cookies already.

"How'd your session go yesterday with Dr. Young? You kind of disappeared into your room."

"Uh, it went fine."

"Really? So, she told you that you're all good to go?" I look at Liv, and she gives me a blank look. *"No more hiding the truth from each other,"* she reminds me.

I sigh. *"I'm depressed, and not just 'oh my God, I have so much homework, I'm so depressed.' No, I'm like, 'go to therapy and keep a book of feelings' depressed."* I relent; I didn't plan on sharing this with anyone. *Not surprising at all.*

Liv laughs, and I join her. *"So, what'd she say is the next step?"*

"Getting to the root, talking to her more, figuring out how and when a hole in my life happened. I said the 'hole in my life' part; she didn't," I admit.

"Well, that's good you have a plan. Better than going in blind."

I turn to face Liv. *"Aren't you a little bit surprised by my prognosis or whatever?"*

Liv sighs and drops her cookie on the paper towel we've used as a tablecloth. She moves closer and grabs my hand. *"Emi, I knew you were depressed."* Oh. *"I knew, but I didn't say anything because it was so obvious you didn't want to know. Now you know, and you can't run from it."*

"Okay."

We don't say anything else. There's nothing else to say. We finish our food, walk back inside, and go to the rec room. There's a lady I don't know inside. She talks to the group about the importance of a hobby and having a safe space to distract yourself.

"Do any of you have any hobbies?" the lady asks.

Bethany raises her hand. *"I love shopping and planning parties; I like bringing a bunch of people together and seeing them enjoy themselves."* Something tells me I would enjoy one of Bethany's parties.

The lady nods, a pleased smile on her face. *"Anybody else?"*

"Emi likes painting and sculpting, and she's a really good writer," Liv casually says, her head propped up against a pillow. My eyes snap to her, and I give her a look that says, *"Stop talking."*

"She wrote a short story about this girl looking for the cure for the apocalypse or something in our creative writing class."

"How'd the girl find it?" Sylvie asks, a few seats over from me. She peeks up from her worn copy of *Ana Katerina*.

"She didn't; got eaten."

Sylvie nods like that's completely understandable and not a lack of laziness on my part.

"Is her work any good?" Cleo asks like I'm not sitting right here. Cleo and Liv talk a lot, usually in passing or when we're eating. Cleo will talk while she gets her food. She's kind of sarcastic but nice.

"Yeah, she sucks at grammar, but she's pretty good."

Cleo looks at me, her lips pursed in thought. *"Good shit, Emi."*

"Thanks," I mumble.

I don't say anything to Liv for 28 whole minutes. After the lady finishes her speech, I hide out in my room. I force myself to read a little bit, but I've been on the same page for at least ten minutes.

The room door opens, and Liv comes in. I put my book down and narrow my eyes at her. She sits down on the edge of my bed and stretches. She always looks so calm and casual, like this whole thing is right on script.

"Don't be embarrassed. Sylvie asked to read your story. I told her you probably had something she could read, but you didn't like sharing." Liv sits up. *"Do you ever get scared about your future, like shaking and panic attacks?"*

"Yeah, but most of the time I think about it, I'm usually terrified." I sit up straighter. *"I used to get so scared Jay would go off to college, fall in love with this beautiful girl, and forget all about me. And when that didn't happen, I was scared I'd be shipped off somewhere and be all alone. My mind always has a new fear or scenario to get lost in."*

"And now, what do you fear?"

"Kind of just everything after this. The 'after' is always scarier than the now. My dad used to say that."

"Emi." I look at her, her voice vulnerable and quiet. *"Do you think I can actually do this? Like the whole sober thing for the rest of my life? I'm 18, and thinking about doing this until I'm 60 or 70 years old is terrifying."*

"I think you can do this, but I don't think you should think about being sober for the rest of your life. I think you should think about being sober for today. And when tomorrow comes, think about being sober for that day. And then one day it'll be your one year, then your five years, and ten years, and eventually you'll be twenty years sober."

"Day by day," she whispers, a tear sliding down her cheek.

"Day by day," I agree.

"And if I relapse?" I can hear the tremble of fear in her voice, but she tries to hide it with a shaky smile.

"Then you start over."

"You really think I can do this?"

I smile. *"Yeah, I really do. I believe in you, Olivia Brunes."*

Her face breaks into a smile, tears sliding down her face. I know I'm not the first person to tell her that, but I think she just needed to hear it from someone in the same place as her.

###

As Liv gets up and leaves my room, I look at my journals sitting inside my suitcase, at least four of them right there.

"You really think I'm a good writer?" I blurt.

She pauses her hand on the doorknob and looks over her shoulder at me with her usual easygoing smile. *"Yeah, I really do. I believe in you, Emille Van der Berg."*

"You know we have to be best friends now," I call after her.

I hear her laughter as she closes my room door.

Chapter 72

James Averell

Day 8

"Push! You're almost done," Nick coaches me. He's been spotting me for the past thirty minutes. I finish the set and rest the bar on the rack. Nick just walks away and doesn't look at me or say anything.

Each day we see each other, I feel the passive aggressiveness radiating from him. I wait for him to say something, but he never does. He and Thena communicate by text or through me. Bell has been off traveling ever since she came back from visiting Emi. Everyone is off and distant but trying to act like we're still whole.

"Hey!" I yell at Nick; he stops, turns, and looks at me. *"Do you have something to say? The passive aggressiveness is getting old, don't you think?"*

"I have nothing to say to you. If I did, I would've said it. We both know being passive isn't my style." He smiles, making me want to punch him in the face that much more. I'd be smiling or bantering with him any other time, but not right now. Not when Emi's still not back, and he's acting like nothing happened.

"Are you sure about that? Cause ever since Em overdosed, you've been acting really cagey, acting like everything is fine when it's not."

"I haven't. I've been here for you and her sisters. I can't control what you feel and what you think my intentions are."

"Tell me, what do you want me to say? You want to hear that you were right?" I step closer to him; we're almost toe to toe. *"That I ignored the signs that something was wrong? Huh?! You want me to feel guilty!? Well, guess what. I do! Does that make you feel any better?"* I push his chest, and he takes a step back from the impact and just looks at me. "Say something!" I snap.

"You can't blame yourself for this. Emi won't want to come home and see you drowning yourself in guilt. It's not your fault. Look at me!" I look at him, and his eyes and words are genuine. *"It's not your fault. I don't blame you, and neither do Bell and Thena. You have to stop blaming yourself."*

"I don't know how," I admit in a broken whisper. This is not how I thought this conversation would go. I can feel tears welling in my eyes, but I don't let them fall. Even with Nick's words, I can still feel anger there. And it's not towards me.

"You need to figure it out soon, I don't want her seeing you like this." I shake my head and leave. I can feel Nick following me, but I don't look back until I'm in my car. He stands there watching me.

Rachel and my dad stand in the kitchen talking when I get home, too close to each other. Is this the day everyone's decided to piss me off? I throw his keys on the island, and Rachel jumps from the sound.

"Sorry, was I interrupting something?" I ask, glaring at my dad.

"W-what? Of course not! How was the gym?" Rachel rushes out, her cheeks flushed. I send my dad a dry smile.

"Don't you have a company to run? Why are you here?"

He chuckles, grabs his keys, and leaves. *"Drive your own car."*

I should've expected that. The front door slams shut, and it's just Rachel and me. She must sense my shit mood because she leaves me alone.

I know the address; she texted it to me one time. There's one Mini Cooper in the parking lot and two other cars parked right next to each other. I turn off my dad's range rover and get out of the car. I lost the paparazzi after driving through random neighborhoods for 40 minutes.

As I walk, my phone dings, a text message from Thena. Great. There's an attachment with a picture of me pushing Nick in the chest and my face making it clear I was not using my inside voice.

Athena: Are you mentally, okay? What makes you think this is what Emi needs to see? Please keep your fights private.

I don't bother responding. Nothing I could say would make her feel better. I've been getting along with her a lot less since Emi is not here to keep us in check. I don't know when it started, but Thena and I have never been friendly. I think we both just feed off the idea of pissing the other off.

454

I look in the directory; her office is on the third floor. The stairs are steep, and the place smells heavily of lavender and other essential oils. The door is ajar, and she reads a file behind her desk. All the lights are on, and the curtains are drawn. I knock on the door, and Dr. Young's head snaps up. She looks shocked for a second before her face melts into a smile.

"Jay! It's good to see you." I didn't know if she remembered who I was.

"You remember me?" I ask.

She laughs. *"Of course, I do! Emi has talked a lot about you, and well, that day isn't something you just forget, now, is it?"* She walks away from her desk, closing the file. *"Please come in. Take a seat."*

I slowly walk in, sitting on the couch across from her large, slightly weird chair. She sits down and smiles at me.

"So, what brings you in?" she asks after a few moments of uncomfortable silence.

"Oh, just wanted to come by and check the place out," I sarcastically respond. Dr. Young doesn't even seem phased. Maybe Emi told her that I'm kind of an ass. *"Emi. I want to talk about Emi."*

"So, talk about her. The floor is all yours."

"It wasn't an accident. I know it, and I hope you do too. Emi didn't accidentally take those pills. She didn't want to be here anymore and was looking for a solution. I don't know if I could've done something, maybe spent more time with her? Paid more attention to the signs? I don't know."

"You couldn't have done anything. Maybe by some odd chance, you could've walked in when she got the pills out, but even then, it would've just prolonged her decision. From what Emi has told me and what I've witnessed, your love and support kept her going for as long as she did. And it's what helps

keep her going." She crosses her arms. *"Don't blame yourself. She wouldn't want you to. Sometimes we can't save the people we love. Sometimes they have to save themselves."*

I let her words sink in. I lean forward, my arms on my knees, looking around the room. It's bright and a little messy but still organized. Dr. Young's personal touch is all around the room. There are flowers on her desk with a note peeking out from them.

"What else has been going on with you? How are you feeling?"

"How do you think I'm feeling?"

"Sad, lost, maybe even a little angry?"

I scoff. *"A little?"*

"Why are you angry?"

"I'm angry because she broke her promise. I'm angry because she won't let me see her. I'm angry because she felt like she didn't want to live, not once but twice. I'm angry at the world and everyone who contributed to Em's decision."

"That's understandable. You have a right to feel like that, Jay. Anger doesn't make you a bad person; it's what you do with that anger." Dr. Young clasps her hands and takes a deep breath. *"When a person is sick in a way you can't cure, they sometimes do selfish things to make themselves better. They don't consider how that affects the people they love."* Dr. Young clears her throat. *"And sometimes it's hard for us to move forward."*

"I wish she would've told me. I wish I could've seen the signs and saved her."

Dr. Young shakes her head. *"She needs to save herself, and she will. You have to heal in your own way. You have to recover."*

I nod. *"Is she okay? Does she look okay?"*

"Emi is doing better. She's sleeping a good amount and eating three meals a day. I can't tell you what she says during our sessions, but I can tell you she's opening up more. She's going to be okay."

I feel the tension slip from my body. I knew it was there, but I didn't know how tightly it held onto me.

"How are you handling the paparazzi?"

"They're annoying as hell, but they don't really bother me. I just hope they'll be gone by the time Emi comes home." I don't ask Dr. Young when she's coming home, and I doubt she'll tell me. I don't think I'd be able to keep it myself.

"Do you want to talk about anything else?" she asks with a look of patience.

I stand up and smile. *"Absolutely not,"* I answer with a chuckle.

She stands up and smiles. *"I figured. Emi mentioned you don't particularly care for therapy."*

"She told you that?" Disbelief fills my voice.

"No, but I'm correct, right?"

I chuckle. *"Yeah, you're right."*

Chapter 73

Emille Kate Van der Berg

Day 9

Kathy stands up, a wide smile on her face. *"Today, we celebrate a beautiful, kind, and resilient soul. Today we celebrate Liza! Liza has decided she's ready to go and make her own home and grow !"* Kathy releases a deep breath. *"So, stand with me and clap for Liza. We clap for hope, courage, and freedom. Freedom from our pasts and those who haunt it."*

We all stand up and clap. Liza's eyes welled up with tears. When we finish clapping, she says thank you so softly and quietly it's like we've all watched it come from her lips and just made the sound up.

Everyone hugs and congratulates Liza. After a brief moment of hesitation, I hug Liza, and she hugs me back.

"I'm really happy for you, and I hope…I hope you stay you." She smiles and nods and hugs me again.

I drift away from Liza and stand by Liv.

"I'm happy for her," I whisper. Liza has a whole life waiting for her; she's only fourteen. There's so much more for her to do. I just hope she experiences it all.

###

"What do you want to talk about today?" I nervously ask her. I'm not in the mood for emotional outbursts or declarations.

"Your dad and his suicide."

Oh.

"What do you want to know?"

"Tell me how you felt afterward, not leading up to moving to Connecticut but everything leading up to now."

I have to think about it for a second, to spot a pattern of the last eight years and if any of it connected to him. It probably did, and I didn't want to think about it. Denial and I are close friends.

"I didn't want to admit that I knew he killed himself, but after a while, it became clearer. I was so used to telling the lie that it kind of became true to me. I think my sisters and family thought I believed it, so they let me. They didn't want to hurt me. But I knew." I clear my throat. *"I sometimes felt like I was following his path, you know? Not asking for help, putting on an act for my siblings and mom, and eventually just…"*

"Letting go?"

I nod. *"Yeah, letting go."*

"So, I know about your dad's death and the effect of that, but tell me about Allison's." I flinch. I don't want to talk about her death and the things that followed. *"Take your time,"* she encourages me.

"After she died, I didn't feel anything for a while. One day I was at school, and someone said, 'Sorry for your loss,' and I said the usual thank you, and they kept talking, saying stuff like they couldn't imagine losing their older sister. And I felt so bad because I wasn't feeling anything, and I didn't miss her. I remember asking Jay if I was a bad person because I didn't miss her, and he told me I wasn't and that it was understandable because she was a bad person."

"But you still felt guilty?"

"I felt guilty, and then somewhere along the way, I started to hate myself for not even being able to miss the little things. That turned into sadness. And then, I stopped going to school and started sleeping and staying in my room. I didn't want to leave, but I did. I went swimming at Jay's house, but I stayed under too long, and he pulled me up before I lost consciousness. He was freaking out, and I hated seeing him like that more than I hated myself, so I forced myself to get out of that…" I look for the word. "Funk." I remember the promise I made to Jay.

"And then after you started to feel better?"

"I started dating and talking to people I would've never talked to before and just going to parties. I was kind of all over the place. Jay and I were basically in a silent fight, and Thena was away at college. Nick had left, and I was kind of lost. I wanted to feel something—something happy—and I tried to find it. I tried to stop thinking about her, and I kind of did."

"Allison wasn't a good sister or person to you, so when she died, it's understandable that you didn't feel the same thing you did when your dad died." Dr. Young leans forward. "Death is one of the few universal things all living beings' experience. And yet it doesn't hit us all in the same way. Death doesn't equate to sadness. Sometimes it means relief. You can't make it mean something you want."

I shake my head, tears leaking from my eyes. It should.

"She was my sister," I try to explain. *"Half-sister,"* I correct.

"And she hurt and ridiculed you any chance she got. She verbally and emotionally abused you, Emi. You have siblings who love and support you, and you know Allison wasn't that, half or not. You can't change the past, especially the past of someone else's actions."

"I wish...I wish I could miss her."

"And that's okay, but you can't hate yourself because you don't."

###

That night I called Bell. I hadn't talked to her since I saw her on visiting day, and I needed some of her endless optimism right about now.

She answers right as I think it's going to go to voicemail. *"Hello?"* Her voice rings through the other side, concern etched into it.

"Hey, it's Emi."

I hear her sigh. *"Oh, Emi! How are you?"*

"I'm okay. How are you?"

"What happened?" she whispers, her voice soft and quiet

"I talked about the past, like what really happened and my feelings."

"That's good. You're closer to getting to the root of everything, which means you're closer to your personal end goal."

"Yeah, it's just hard getting there."

"*I know,*" she agrees. She releases a deep breath, and if I close my eyes, I can see her face, her comforting smile on her face, and her eyes bright and welcoming as she speaks.

"All your wildest dreams will come true, Emi, but first, you have to weather the storm."

Chapter 74

Emille Kate Van der Berg

Day 10

Liv and I lay in the grass, our eyes shut as the sun soaks into our skin. It feels like the start of summer, but there's still a soft chill and dampness that lingers from spring.

I open my eyes and look at the sky. Dark gray clouds slowly take over the sky.

"It's going to rain."

"I know, but let's soak up the sun a little longer," Liv murmurs. I nod in agreement and close my eyes.

We lay until the warmth from the sun slips away and the coolness of the clouds takes over. A drop of water hits my face, and I jump up.

"I'm leaving," I announce. Liv grabs our small bag of trash and follows me. By the time we close the door behind us, it starts pouring.

"April showers bring May flowers," Bethany sing-songs as she walks behind us. Liv and I both crack a smile and watch the water pour.

"Clara called me crying last night," Liv mentions as we walk towards my bedroom. I open the door, and she slips inside.

"Why?"

"She misses me, and she's worried. She's never been in a real relationship before, so she's kind of freaking out. Then she felt bad that she was calling me crying while I'm the one in rehab."

"So what'd you do?"

"I calmed her down, told her it was okay, and just told her about laying in the grass. She thought it was corny, but she laughed and felt better. So that's good."

I can feel my face break into a giddy smile. *"You really love Clara, huh?"*

Liv rolls her eyes, but she can't stop a smile from spreading across her face. *"Yeah, I really love Clara Lukov."*

"Love is in the air," I dramatically cry, falling backward on my bed. Liv snorts.

###

"Do you feel a little better after our last session?" Dr. Young asks me. She sits with her legs crossed in her chair. Her mustard yellow flare pants catch my eye.

"Yeah, I kind of do. It felt like something was coming off my chest, and a little bit of the guilt from lying for so long slipped away."

"That's good, Emi. I'm really happy for you. Today, I want to talk about your family."

"Haven't we been talking about my family?"

"Yes, we have. Let me rephrase that. I want to dive into the way your family interacts today."

"Okay."

"How do you feel when you're at your mom and Rick's house?"

"Alone. Neither one of them bothers me that much, and we usually don't even eat dinner together. I'm able to trap myself in my room, and it takes them a little longer to notice. I'm grateful, of course, for everything they do for me and the house we live in."

"But you're lonely."

I nod.

"Everyone left," I rush to explain. *"I know my mom and Rick are still there, but Alexander left a long time ago, and he rarely comes back. Thena left, and her leaving really, really hurt...I know it's stupid. I knew she was going to college; she'd been talking about it all her life, but it hurt. No one made me breakfast in bed when I was having a bad day or helped me study before a big final. I really missed her when she left."* That was a hard year.

"Did you tell her?"

I shake my head. "She was so excited about leaving, and Nick had just left. She didn't need me crying and begging for her to come home. Plus, she visited close to every weekend, and we started sister dinners once she got her house in the city. Slowly, it got better, and Bell and Jay were still there, so it wasn't as bad."

"But when they left?"

"I was all alone. Bell's jokes and laughter were gone. I stopped waking up to bouquets of flowers and random stories about her job. I knew she was busy, and I was happy because the busier she was, the more successful she became. But I missed her. Bell was always there until she wasn't."

"And when Jay left?"

"I hated being home, and I hated being without him, but I hated the thought of holding him back even more. I missed him, I felt like I lost my best friend, but I kept pushing him away. I thought it was better for him to be fully gone than partially gone."

"But now that you're with him?"

"I'm happier, and even when he's away, I know he'll come back."

"Do you feel like your sisters might not come back?"

I shake my head. *"Not necessarily, but I feel like I miss so much of their lives, and they know only the parts I want them to of mine. I used to know where they were eating for lunch, and now, I don't even know if Thena still hangs out with the same people she did in high school."*

She nods, and after a few moments of quiet, she leans forward and clasps her hands. *"Where do you see yourself? What do you want in your future? It doesn't have to sound pretty or be up to your parents' standards. What do you want?"*

I think about it for a second.

"I want to be happy, like really happy and not just manic. I want to be close to my sisters and go on family trips with them and be with Jay. I don't know what I want to do for a living, but I know I want my own family someday. Is that bad? I don't know what I want to do for a living, but I know I want kids and marriage one day?"

She smiles. *"No, Emi, not to me. I knew I wanted to help people, but I knew I wanted kids and to be married one day. Just because your future isn't ideal to societal standards doesn't mean it's wrong."* I relax a little into the chair. *"Anything else?"*

I shake my head. I don't know anything else at the moment.

She looks at the clock. *"I want to talk about one more thing."*

I can already tell I'm not going to like it; *"saving the best for last"* hasn't been the norm in therapy. Well, I guess it depends on what you consider the best.

"How's your relationship with your mom?"

Oh.

"We've never been close. It was always me and my dad. Mom was there, and she loved me, but by the time I was born, she and Dad had started to drift apart, and I kind of clung to him. She never resented me for it, but it was just clear he was my person."

"Keep going."

"And when he died, I was lost, and she didn't say anything. We didn't talk about Dad or his death. She kind of pushed it away, and I kept it to myself. As I got older, I grew closer to Jay and my sisters, and I grew away from her. The endearments weren't said as much, and all the shopping and lunch dates turned into quarterly meetings. I love her. I do. She's my mom, and she's sweet, funny, and sometimes really fun to be around." I wipe my eyes. *"But she's not...the person I go to for anything."* I let out a small cry. *"S-sometimes I think about going to Rick before her."*

I bury my face in my hands and try to stop my tears. I reach for the tissues and wipe my eyes.

"Sometimes I want to ask her if she even likes me or what she sees when she looks at me...I-I'm so sorry."

Dr. Young moves to sit by me, rubbing my back. This is probably weird for both of us, but I appreciate it. I cry for a little while until I can control my tears enough to lift my head up.

"Don't be sorry. We can't control the actions of our parents, even if we want to. We can't make emotionally absent people present because we love them."

"She's there for Bell and even Thena. I've seen it."

"Just not for you," she finishes.

"She is in ways...she took me on a college tour, and she was so happy when I told her I was going to college."

"But what about when you told her what you wanted to do?"

"I-I don't know. I don't think I told her those things. I don't know myself, right?" I try to joke. Dr. Young gives me a sad smile.

"Oh, but you do. You know where you want to live, and you have passions, Emi."

I do. I never considered my paintings and journals passions, but they are.

"I started writing again," I told her. It's random, but I want to share it with someone. I don't know if I've ever even told her I wrote to begin with.

"That's good, Emi! How's it going?"

"Okay. Just been writing a random little story." I shrug my shoulders.

"You must decide what's best for you, even if it upsets others. You can't live for others because, at the end of the day, who will have to live inside your head?"

Chapter 75

Emille Kate Van der Berg

Day 11

Helen wakes me up with soft pats against my back. I roll over, and she looks at me with one of the brightest smiles I've seen. She's been looking at me like that a lot lately. I look at the alarm clock, and it's already 9:37. I stayed up a little later last night writing. I want a good ending to this short story and not something generic or lackluster.

I roll out of bed, go to the bathroom, shower, and get ready. I've worn most of my clothes, but it's okay. I'm a firm believer in wearing jeans multiple times before washing them, and if you just sit in the leggings and don't do any workouts, you can get away with repeating.

I beat Liv to the breakfast table. I make a plate with eggs, bacon, toast, and strawberries. I eat for a while, fully engrossed in my meal, when Liv comes in. She still looks half asleep, and she fills her plate up even more than I do.

"How'd you sleep?" I ask her, with a mouthful of bacon.

"Like a baby. Didn't want to get up," she mumbles while taking a sip of orange juice.

"You know, I thought I'd miss my phone more, but I haven't really missed it. I mean, I've missed texting Jay whenever, but I've called him every night the last few nights, so it's not as bad."

"I definitely don't miss it. Once I get it back, I'm deleting all my social media. It annoyed me before, but having to deal with that shit and be sober sounds like mission impossible." I laugh, and Liv smirks, downing her orange juice.

We talk about random stuff for the rest of breakfast before sitting in my room a little bit before group therapy. On the way in, Kathy gives me an even wider smile, which startles me for a second, but I return it.

"Okay, so today, I want each of you to say how you're doing and what you're struggling with. Just give everyone a progress update or just an admission. Whatever you're comfortable with," Kathy announces before sitting back down.

As she sits down, Sylvie stands up. *"I'm doing better. I still miss ballet. I think I always will, but I'm starting to come to terms with why it's not good for me. I've been talking to my brother more, and when I get out of here, I think I will stay with him and focus on graduating and helping him at his garage. I don't want to let ballet go, but I know I need to."*

Sylvie doesn't say anything; she just lets the next person go.

Cleo stands up. *"I feel great! I've been sleeping more and without my phone. I've been reading and doing yoga. I haven't apologized to my dad, and he hasn't apologized to me, but I leave in five days, and I've already had my housekeeper arrange a meeting with a real estate agent.*" Liv snorts, and Cleo smirks in return.

Barbara stands up and smiles. "*I've stopped having nightmares every night, and it feels good to sleep for more than three hours. My housekeeper, Sally, came to visit me, and it was nice to see her.*" She sits back down, and now it's my turn.

I stand up, and I can feel everyone's eyes on me. The last time I stood up in front of everyone, I said something everyone knew was a lie.

"*Fifteen days ago, I tried to kill myself. I was in a really bad place, and I felt like I had lost one of the people I loved most in the world. I didn't know what to do. My dad died eight years ago, but I always acted like he was just a phone call away. When that was taken away, I kind of just crumbled.*" I release a deep breath. "*I'm doing better. I've stopped lying to everyone, including myself, and I'm not terrified about leaving here. I know I have a lot of work ahead of me, and I'm not fixed or whatever. But I'm better, which is good, right?*"

Enthusiastic "*Right!*" s and "*Yes!*" s fills the air, and I smile and sit back down. Liv squeezes my shoulder before standing up.

"*I still sometimes crave a line of coke or a pill to take me away… away from all these thoughts and feelings. I knew the anxiety would be here, but I forgot how hard it was to handle. I know it'll get easier. Someday, I won't even think about relapsing, and I'm waiting for that day.*" Liv shrugs. Her honesty is like the first chew of gum: strong and consuming. "*I'm just taking it day by day.*"

I lean over and hug her as she sits back down, and she chuckles and gives me an awkward pat on the back.

"I ate a full plate of food today and didn't think about the calories. I ate, and it felt good when I was finished. I didn't feel stuffed or hungry; I felt just right and liked it. I've gained weight. I don't know how much, but I freaked out a little when I saw how I looked in the mirror. I calmed down and did the breathing and the words my therapist told me. So yeah, I ate a full plate of food today." I clap for Raina, and others join in. She gives me a shy smile and sits back down.

Last but not least is Bethany, who wears a cute spring dress with hot pink sandals and a hot pink scrunchie in her high ponytail.

"I'm so happy for you guys!" she exclaims, giving us a small clap. *"I, for one, am doing really well. Jack told me I could leave in four days which is so exciting! Right in time for summer and my finals! He also told me that no one has been in my room unless it was to wash my sheets, and he monitored the whole process."* She nods like that's the most important detail in the world, and for a split second, she reminds me of Thena. Bethany is a perfectionist, and I don't know if she's been hiding that or if I haven't been paying attention. By the way she runs her hands down her dress exactly four times, I think it might be the former.

"I'm really proud of all of you guys' improvement and your honesty with yourselves and each other."

###

Liv and I walk back inside. We ate lunch outside with Cleo and Bethany, who, apparently, have cabins in Aspen that are close to each other. They asked me if I skied or snowboarded, and I told them no, but Bell did. Bethany liked Bell's magazine cover and asked me to tell her.

When we open the door, Dr. Young stands on the other side with a patient smile, like she'd been waiting here.

"*H-hi, what are you doing here?*" I only ever see her when it's time for sessions.

"*Can we talk for a second?* " I nod, and Liv tells me she'll be in the rec room. Dr. Young and I walk until we get to the large sunroom. It looks different without the chairs, more open and a little brighter. "*Emi, tonight you're going home.*"

I don't say anything. I can't be processing this right. *I'm going home?* After two weeks, I'm okay to go home? It's only been two weeks? I expected to be here for at least a month.

"*Today?*"

She nods.

"*Late tonight, you're going home. I've already let your sisters know, and they've been planning it with me,*" she explains. I nod, hearing her but not letting the words fully register. "*Are you okay with that? Are you ready to go home?*"

I can't stay here forever. And I have to believe that when I go home, I won't completely unravel, that I'll be okay, and I'll be able to breathe.

"*I'm ready.*"

I run into the rec room, stopping in front of Liv with a giddy smile as she looks me up and down, examining my face and my heavy breathing.

"*You're going home,*" she states. I nod, and when she stands up, she cheers and claps her hand like we both just won gold at the Olympics. "*When are you leaving?*"

"*Tonight, sometime late tonight. I don't know. What should I do?*"

"*Have you packed?*"

I shake my head.

"I came straight here. It's too early to pack."

"Emi, it's 5:00! We got time to kill. Let's go pack." She pulls me back to my room, and we empty my suitcase and completely pack. Helen comes in halfway, looks at our progress, and refolds half of the items.

When we finish packing, it's time for dinner. While eating, Kathy whistled, causing the talking to stop and all attention her way.

"Today, we celebrate a beautiful, compassionate, and courageous soul. Today we celebrate Emi! Emi has decided she's ready. She's ready to go and make her own home and her own life in this world. She's ready to grow and fight." Kathy begins to tear up. *"So stand with me and clap for Emi. We clap for hope, strength, and freedom. Freedom from our pasts and those who haunt it, and freedom from our fears."*

Everyone stands up and claps, and I can feel the warm wetness of a tear slide down my cheek. I wipe it with a smile. People come up and hug me, and I tell them thank you.

Bethany squeezes me and does a little rocking movement exactly four times before patting my back twice. She pulls away and squeezes my arms with a breathtaking smile. *"If you're ever in L.A., call me, and I will throw a really good party."* She lets me go before I can respond.

Someone taps my shoulder while I'm talking to Liv. I look, and it's Sylvie holding a small piece of paper. She hands it to me, and I realize it's one of the loose sheets of paper I keep in my journal, a random jotting of the beginning of a story I never wrote.

"Liv wasn't lying. You're good! Good luck, Emi, and I'm happy I met you."

"You too," I whisper. She smiles and leaves.

After dinner, I go and shower and get ready to go home. It sounds weird. *Going home.* I knew it would happen, but not this quickly. Everything is mostly packed up, and the hours pass both achingly slowly and too fast. Before I know it, Dr. Young is knocking on my room door with Helen behind her. Liv stands up from her spot on my bed. Helen takes my suitcase and starts walking.

I look at Liv, and my eyes fill with tears. *"I don't want to leave you here."*

She'll be alone. She's better at making friends than me, but who will she lie in the grass with? Who will make her a plate if she's late or ask her if she's sleeping? Who knows about Clara? Will she be okay? She hates yoga and can only handle so many hours of pep talks before she bursts. Liv's my best friend—her and Jay but in two completely different ways.

"It's time for you to go home, Em. I'll see you when I get out. Tell Clara I'm coming, okay?"

"Okay," I whisper. She hugs me, and I hug her back, squeezing her gangly frame. When we pull apart, her eyes are filled with tears, and one falls. She smiles and gives me a nudge, and I walk with Dr. Young. I look over my shoulder, and Liv is still standing there in polo pajama pants and an old, faded T-shirt that's two sizes too big. She waves, and I smile before turning around.

Dr. Young and I walk down the elevator together, Helen already waiting for us outside. I can't see my suitcase.

Before we reach the door, I ask her, *"Who'd you call?"*

She doesn't answer. *"I'm really proud of you, Emi, and when you get home, call me so we can schedule our weekly appointments."*

I nod. *"I will, and I won't ditch you."*

She smiles and opens the door. We walk outside, but before I can see who she called, I grab her arm, and her face fills with concern.

"Can I call you Lily?"

Her smile stretches across her face. *"Of course, Emi."* She hugs me, and I hug her back. She smells like sunshine even in the dead of night.

I pull apart, and when I wipe my eyes, I see who is waiting in the parking lot. Illuminated by the moon and streetlights is a black beat-up pickup truck. Its owner leans against the side with a smile on his face. I don't think. I just run until I reach him. And when I make it, large arms engulf me and squeeze me. Our lips meet in a chaste kiss.

"Jay," I breathe, happiness filling every letter and every breath.

May

Chapter 76

Emille Kate Van der Berg

I've missed him. I've really missed him. He smells the same, and his lips and hands feel the same, but he holds me tighter. His truck feels the same, the leather cool as he speeds down the streets.

"*Where are we going?*" I ask him as he exits the highway. We're nowhere near Greenwich. He doesn't say anything. He just kisses the top of my head and squeezes my shoulder. He steers with one hand. I watch him, not noticing him pulling into a parking lot.

We're outside a diner. I climb out of the truck, and Jay waits for me on the other side, wrapping an arm around me. I look at him, and he's looking around, ensuring there are no cars or anything behind us. I saw him checking his rearview mirror a lot while driving, even though the streets were mostly deserted.

We go inside the diner. There must be parking in the back because there are more people here than I'd thought. Two people are at the bar, one person is in a booth, and two other booths are filled. Jay grabs my hand, shaking me from my examination. He walks towards the secluded side. A long table sits three people.

Nick, Bell, and Thena are all sipping what is probably burnt coffee. Bell noticed me first. She jumps up and walks over to me, pulling me into a hug.

"*Emi!*" She squeezes me, and I squeeze her back, rising on my tippy toes to do so. Thena comes in for a soft, quick hug before sitting back down. Nick just smiles at me. Jay and I sit on Bell's side.

Thena looks tired but happy, her shoulders slacked and her eyes looking me over like she's making sure I'm really here and all this isn't a dream. A waitress brings us two mugs and fills them with coffee. "Orders?"

Bell starts to order, asking questions about the pancakes. I open the menu and read it over. I freeze when I get to the third and fourth items on the menu.

My eyes snap to Jay. "*They have mozzarella sticks and fried green tomatoes.*"

"*Oh shit, this place must be trying to get on your good side. Which one are you getting? Sorry, stupid question. You're getting both.*"

"*And a vanilla milkshake. Three cherries,*" I add. He smiles. I can feel Thena's eyes on me, and I focus on her. "*You know I really missed you,*" I casually told her while Jay ordered my food and his. She's already ordered.

"*So I've heard.*" She purses her lips, trying to hide her smile. "*I kind of missed you too.*"

I smile. I knew she missed me. "*How's school?*"

"Good. Studying for finals, so I've been busy, but it's nothing I can't handle. Besides, I'm not the one who missed three weeks." I cringe. I did do that. I can't even imagine the amount of work I have waiting for me. *"Do you want my help with anything?"*

I shake my head. *"I'll figure that out tomorrow,"* I mutter. Oh shit! I have to go to Rick and Mom's house tonight. Well, this morning.

What are they going to say when I walk in? Are they going to be happy? Am I going to be grounded?

"Em," Jay says my name, *"You, okay?"* I nod.

"Just freaking out about school and everything else. Did anything else change?" I ask while running a hand over my face. I can't see their faces, but their silence is enough for me to pull my hand away.

"No, everything's been pretty much the same," Jay tells me. I nod, relieved, and lean against his arm.

"I'm happy I'm back with you guys, I really am, but I'm going to miss Liv," I admit. They all listen, and Bell rubs my arm in comfort. Before they can respond, I ask Bell how work has been.

She glances at Thena before answering. *"Busy. I flew out to the west coast for a few shoots last week and earlier this week, but I will be here for a while."*

I smile. *"That's good. Are you still happy modeling?"*

She thinks about it for a second. *"I am. I like traveling, and it feels natural. It's hard and sometimes stressful, but I like it, and it makes me happy."*

"I'm happy you're happy." She smiles at me, and we both dig into our food.

There are eight fried green tomatoes, all in different sizes, and eight mozzarella sticks with a small container of marinara sauce. We all eat and talk; it feels like old times like I was never away.

When I finish my food, I lean against Jay. I know how long I was away, but even before that, time seemed to blend and do whatever it wanted. It felt like I'd been in bed for a few days. I know we were in Fiji from the fourth until the eleventh of April. But everything after that is a blur of dates.

"What day is it?"

Jay releases a breath. *"Saturday, May 1ˢᵗ. It's two in the morning."*

Oh shit. Oh shit. *Oh.*

I look at Jay. *"Your birthday is in twenty-eight days."* I turn to Bell. *"Your birthday is in thirteen days. I graduate next month!"* I point a finger at Thena. *"You finish school in ten days!"*

"I know. I still have to edit my term paper," Thena sighs, running a hand through her ponytail.

"I could edit it for you," Nick suggests, sipping his coffee. He and Bell were the only ones who got breakfast. He got an omelet with sausage links, and Bell got pancakes with strawberries and bacon.

Thena completely ignores him, which seems to make Nick stare at her harder, a small clench in his jaw. No one else seems as freaked about as today's date, which relaxes me a little. At least I didn't miss their birthdays.

I yawn, catching the last bit of it with my hand.

"Tired?" Jay asks,

I nod against his shoulder. *"I've been asleep before ten for the past week or so. Are you tired?"* I peek up at him and notice the bags underneath his eyes and the paleness of his skin. He looks sick like he hasn't been sleeping for a while.

"Yeah, I am."

"Let's go to your apartment," I whisper, he nods, and we stand up. Everyone else is rising with us. *"I'll see you guys later."*

"Brunch is tomorrow," Nick tells me as we leave. I stop walking, and everyone circles me. Jay checks over his shoulder, and so does Thena. They're leaving this decision up to me.

"Oh, well, I'll be there. Are you guys going?" I ask them, looking around the circle. They all stand so tense and aware, none of them looking as relaxed as we were inside the restaurant.

"Yes, we'll all be there. Are you sure you want to go? We can all go somewhere private," Thena suggests, her eyes focused on mine.

"No, no, I'll be there. I want to go. I haven't been in a while."

Nick nods. *"Good. We'll wait for you by the bar."*

I nod. Jay opens his truck door for me, and I slide in. He turns on his car, and Thena, Bell, and Nick wait for us to pull out before they leave.

I fall asleep on the way to Jay's apartment, waking up to the feeling of my jeans sliding down my legs. I smile at him, and he rolls his eyes. He tucks me into his bed. I wait for him to slide in before I go back to sleep. My face pressed against his warm chest, the smell of his soap hitting me.

I'm home.

Chapter 77

James Averell

She's back. I watch her sleep as I sip the coffee I made earlier. I slept the whole night and wanted to stay asleep for the first time in two weeks. I already told Nick I wasn't going to the gym with him today. He responded, saying he had already assumed that and had made other arrangements. Sometimes his text messages are eerily similar to business emails.

I've finished all of my final projects except for one. I'm supposed to write a business proposal and some other shit. I didn't read the rubric yet, so I'll do that later tonight or tomorrow morning.

I go and shower. When I get out, I dress in sweats and a plain white T-shirt. Emi starts to roll over and make small stretches, letting me know she's about to wake up. I watch her curl into a ball, then stretch out. She blinks a few times, adjusting to the light coming in from the window and the light in the kitchen.

"Morning," I tell her. Her eyes search for me, and when she finds me, she smiles. I'm lazy and sleepy.

"Morning." She sits up and wipes her hand over her face. *"How long have you been up?"*

"An hour," I answered, walking over to her side of the bed and sitting beside her. She eyes the coffee in my hand before taking it from my hand and taking a generous sip. She relaxes and melts into the pillow like she just had the best coffee. *"You wanna talk about it?"*

She thinks about it for a second. *"Food first. You want to go find breakfast tacos?"* She climbs out of bed, heading towards the bathroom. She closed the door while she peed, then opened it to brush her teeth. *"Do you?"*

"Uh, let's get some delivered," I suggest, looking for my phone. She doesn't protest; she just finishes brushing her teeth and rinsing her face. Her suitcase is on the floor by the bathroom door, and Thena brought over an extra bag of hygiene products earlier this morning.

"How many do you want?" I ask her, pulling up the restaurant from which we usually get breakfast tacos. They're less than three blocks away, so it doesn't take them long to deliver.

"Three."

A few minutes later, our food is ordered, and Emi's face is pressed into my chest as she holds me. Her arms wrapped around my middle, I feel her inhaling my shirt, and I do the same to her hair and soft cheeks.

"I have to go to therapy every week," she mumbles into my chest. *"Every Tuesday, I'll be talking to Dr. Young. Oh, I almost forgot! She said I could call her Lily now."*

"You like Lily?"

She nods. *"I like her a lot. She helps me and listens, even when I don't make sense. I told her about Allison and my dad, and it felt good."* I hold her, letting her tell me what she's comfortable with. I never want to push her.

"I didn't know when I was going home. She kind of just told me and asked if I was ready, and I told her I was. Isn't that good?" She looks up at me, and I nod. She's never shared this much about her therapy sessions. I know what she's gone through but never this deeply.

A knock on the door interrupts us, and she pulls away to answer the door. The delivery driver looks her up and down, and I can tell by the smile on his face he's about to say something he shouldn't.

"Thank you," Emi sweetly tells him; I stand behind her wrapping an arm around her chest. She grabs the bag from the guy, and he stares at me. He opens his mouth, but I slam the door in his face.

Emi doesn't scold me or say anything, she just climbs into my bed, and we sit on top of my covers and eat our food, watching cartoons on TV.

"I missed breakfast tacos," she says, finishing the last bite of her three tacos.

"Was the food bad?"

She shakes her head. *"No, it was just healthier, really filling, and kind of had a home-cooked feel to it."*

"This is better?"

She looks at me and smiles. *"This is way better."*

We both know she's not only talking about the food, which makes me smile.

"You want to go and get dinner together?" she asked me. We've been lying in bed all day, eating, watching television, talking about random shit, and occasionally making out.

"Not really," I quickly answer, and she narrows her eyes at me, but I look away. I look for a book I was supposed to read a week ago. I find it and throw it on my pillow while checking my phone.

One of the guys from *"The Trie"* texted me. More and more of them have been texting me lately, always asking *me* questions about planning and fundraising. It's like none of these losers are in college for *business* or *marketing.*

Jason The Trie: Hey Jay, it's Jason. I was just wondering if there's any way, we could find a different location for the fundraiser and maybe invite a few more sororities.

Me: Invite whoever the hell you want. They pay the fee and keep it at the same location. It's in less than a month.

I click out of the messages and walk into the kitchen, grabbing water from the fridge.

"What if I make us pasta? And we watch all three of The Matrix movies."

"This sounds too good to be true, Em." She shrugs her shoulders, a mischievous gleam in her eyes. *"Don't tell me you're trying to get laid."* Her eyes widen, and I laugh. She's definitely trying to get laid. *"Em, all you had to do was ask."*

"W-we should," she clears her throat, her voice husky. *"We should wait until after dinner."*

I smirk. *"What do you need for the pasta? I'll go get it."*

"A pound of ground beef, crushed tomatoes, more heavy cream, onions, and garlic bread." I nod and kiss her lips before leaving, grabbing a baseball cap and my keys.

When I return thirty minutes later, Em is standing in one of my shirts, her hair damp in a low bun, and she stirs a large pot of boiling water, pouring noodles inside the water. She smiles over her shoulder at me and takes the ingredients out of the bag. She gets a large pot I didn't even know I had and sets it on the stove.

I watch her cook; she checks her phone, reads over the recipe a few times, and while the food cooks, she avoids my eyes and goes through her suitcase.

"I don't know what I'm going to wear to brunch tomorrow," she mumbles, walking into the kitchen and turning off the stove. She grabs two of the four bowls I have and serves us. My portion is significantly larger than hers.

I look at her out of the corner of my eye as we eat. I want her. She can feel it. She shifts and subtly squirms. Emille Van der Berg is the most beautiful person I've ever known, inside and out. There'll never be another her. It's one of the reasons I love her so much.

We finish our food, the silence and tension thick in the small loft. She clears her throat and shifts.

I grab both of our bowls and take them to the kitchen, not even bothering to put them into the sink. Emi sits in the center of the bed, her eyes wide with anticipation. Our sex life has never been consistent, even

488

when she felt good. But going close to three weeks with little to no physical contact has us both on the edge of our seats.

I stand by her side, and she looks up at me, her eyes flickering between my lips. She sits up on her knees so she's closer to my height. She leans up and kisses my lips. She runs her hands through my hair. I kiss her back, tangling my tongue with hers, and I moan.

I move my lips away, and she whimpers. I trail kisses down her cheeks to her neck, gently biting and kissing. She grips me tighter and tries to pull me toward the bed. I don't relent. My hands move down her body to her breasts, and I squeeze. She gasps and trails one of her hands down my back. I finally let her pull me onto the bed, and I rolled over so she's on top of me. I grab her ass, grinding her into me. I'm hard. My pants are tight, and I know she feels it. Her moan confirms that. She sits up and takes her shirt off. She's in nothing but underwear, and I groan at the sight.

"*Please,*" she whispers above my ear, grinding into me. "*Jay, now!*" she demands. I smirk and roll her off, standing up and grabbing a condom. I throw my shirt off, and when I kiss Emi, her hands slide down my chest and stomach.

"*I can feel your heart,*" she whispers. She leans forward and kisses me.

I slide my sweatpants off and crawl into bed with her. I grab one of her legs and wrap it around my hips. I slide her panties down, throwing them off to the side. I slide the condom on and pull her to the edge, her legs and eyes wide in anticipation.

Every time I look at her, I fall more in love. When she smiles, when she laughs, when she's happy, I feel it in me. I feel it light everything up inside me. She seems to reach all the good and bad parts.

I lean forward and kiss her as I rock into her. She moans and clutches me tighter. Our breaths tangle together, and I tangle our fingers together.

"Em," I groaned. She moans and kisses me, trying to stay quiet. I feel her tighten, and I know what's coming. She arches off the bed and moans. Our breathing is labored as we both calm down. I lay next to her, and she rolls on her side and props her face on her hands. Her light brown skin gleamed with sweat.

"Ready for the Matrix?" She asks me, a soft pant in her voice she's trying to control. I smirk and grab her hips, squeezing her.

"No," I whisper. I move down the bed and trail kisses down her neck and all the way down her body.

"Again?" she squeaks, a look of excitement and surprise glittering in her eyes.

I smile. *"Again,"* I breathe.

I spend the rest of the night getting lost in Emi, and when she passes out, so do I. Our bodies are sweaty and warm, tangled in our sheets.

Chapter 78

Emille Kate Van der Berg

If there were two words to describe how I'm feeling right now, they'd be sore and embarrassed. The former, for obvious reasons. The embarrassment came a few minutes after I woke up. Jay was already up and drinking coffee and reading a book when I felt a wetness. I looked down, and it was *red.*

I got my period on Jay's bed, and when the realization hit me, I jumped up, stripped the bed of sheets, and hid in his bathroom. The sheets were by the door, keeping me company. Jay knocked and asked what was wrong, but I couldn't bring myself to say, *"Hey! I bled all over your sheets, and I don't have any pads or tampons!"*

Instead, I asked him for his phone and told him it was an emergency. I called Thena and explained my situation; she assured me she'd be on her way. I slid Jay's phone back under the door and waited for Thena.

I sit in a towel, waiting for Thena so I can shower. I don't have my phone; I've kind of forgotten about it. I don't even want to open my computer because I know what awaits me: a million missing assignments and tests for me to make up.

I hear Jay's front door open, so I press my ear against the door.

"Where is she?" Thena asks, her heels clicking against the hardwood floor.

"Hiding in the bathroom," Jay answers, his voice louder than Thena's. *Did he do that on purpose?*

Thena knocks on the door. I open it and peek out. She stands with two large bags. The bathroom isn't large, but thankfully, it's not the size of a shoebox. She comes in, and I shut and lock the door before Jay can enter.

"Ha!" I scream in victory. Thena rolls her eyes and pulls out two boxes of pads, two boxes of tampons, wipes, and underwear.

She has a tote bag in her hand and puts it on the counter. *"I brought you extra clothes— just jeans and a T-shirt—and some hygiene products."* She wears a soft tight blue dress with the bottom half flowing outward and white heels. Half of her hair was clipped back.

I turn on the shower, strip, and climb inside. Thena tells me about studying yesterday and her mild annoyance with Jay. When I get out of the shower, I brush my teeth and wash my face.

"Do you have my phone?" I ask her.

She shakes her head. *"I'll tell Bell to bring it to you."* I nod, and Thena helps me get dressed. When I finish, I look at her. I have to be honest with her.

"I'm scared and nervous. Can we ride together?" Her eyes soften as she looks down at me and nods.

"Don't be scared, and don't be nervous. This is your family too, and nothing you do can change that. As long as Bell and I are here, you'll always have us."

I hugged her.

"I don't want to not know anything about you anymore," I admit while hugging her. I'm tired of hiding things, no matter how awkward, and despite feeling weird saying them out loud. I don't want to hide from her.

"I don't want to not know how you're feeling or where your head and heart are. I don't want to ever find you like that again." I look at her, and a tear has slid down her cheek. She wipes it.

"You won't. I don't want to be that low ever again. I promise."

She nods. "Good. Now let's go before you ruin my makeup."

Nick, Jay, Thena, and I all stand by the bar. We're waiting for Bell. She has my phone and had to stop to charge her car. I always forget she asked Rick to get her car redesigned to make it electric.

None of the parents have arrived yet, so I still feel fine, with no anxiety or the need to hide in the bathroom or on the golf course. I sit on one of the barstools, my legs crossed as I sip a Shirley Temple.

"When are you going back to school, Emi?" Nick asks, a drink in his hand.

"Tomorrow? I don't know, I haven't really thought about it."

"Understandable. If you need any help, I'm here." I nod and thank him.

Bell enters in a short flowy light green dress. She walks over to me and hands me my phone. I missed the feel of it in my hands. I squeeze it and press it against my chest.

"Thank you!" I gush. I look around, and no one else is as excited as me, which makes sense. I unlock it, and before I can pull up Instagram, someone taps on my shoulder. I look up, and everyone's heading inside. I follow them, sitting in my usual seat.

It feels weird but normal sitting here. Sunlight streams through the large window, the curtains drawn. The table is set with biscuits and bowls of fruit down. I watch Mr. and Mrs. Yates enter the room. They both smile widely at me and welcome me back. Mrs. Yates walks over and hugs me. I hug her back, and she kisses my cheeks.

"I'm happy you're back. It wasn't the same without you." She smiles, and I don't say anything. I just let her sentiments sink in.

Eric comes in a little while later, and when he sees me, he just holds up his glass of brown liquor and winks at me. I liked that he didn't make a big deal of me being back. He just sat down and ordered another drink, talking to Mr. Yates.

"French toast or crepes?" I ask Jay, looking over the menu. He keeps one hand on my knee.

"French toast, extra bacon," Jay responds, pouring cream into my cup, just the right amount. I take a sip and make an appreciative sound only he can hear.

I look up in time as my mom and Rick come in. They both look at me, two distinctively different looks on their faces. Rick looks happy and relaxed to see me, and Mom looks uncomfortable, like this wasn't supposed to happen.

Before they sit down, Rick walks over and kisses my forehead, squeezing me. It makes me smile. Mom gives me a stiff smile and sits down, focusing on her menu. Bell and Thena distract me with small talk.

"*What do you want to do for your birthday?*" I ask Bell, taking a bite of one of the strawberries on my plate.

"*Uh, just something casual.*"

Mom sighs, the sound exasperated. "*I still don't know why you don't want to have a party, Isabel.*" I thought Bell liked having parties.

"*Mother,*" Thena warns. There's something else going on.

"*What?*" Mom looks between me and my sisters. "*You two didn't tell her.*"

"*Tell me what?*" I try to keep my voice calm.

I think about how they've been acting, the speed with which we drove here, and how Jay wears a baseball cap and Thena wears big sunglasses wherever we go.

"*Go on Twitter, Emi,*" Nick calmly tells me. He leans back in his chair, sipping a cup of coffee. Thena shoots him a murderous glare.

I do as he says. I go on Twitter, and one of the trending topics is "*Van der Berg.*" I click on the first one.

Record company owner Rick Van der Berg's stepdaughter Emille has been reported to be committed to a psychiatric institute after attempting suicide. Sources say she's been in trouble in the past.

I click on another one.

Sister of rising supermodel Isabel Van der Berg has been sent to rehab. Sources say this isn't the first time either.

And another one.

The last one is from a local media magazine that focuses on gossip and socialites. I am neither. There's an article saying I'm a cry for help. None of them are from big news company names, but one is from a fashion company. There are so many pictures: walking to their cars, grocery shopping, a few of Jay and Nick going to the gym, and at least a hundred of Bell walking around.

"*Is the paparazzi following you guys around?*" I ask them. I look at Jay, and his face is etched with concern.

"*They were; they wanted to see Bell with us. They want to see Bell, and they want to see you guys together. Bell's success is rising faster than she or her agent expected. Thena has been all over Bell's Instagram. The mystery was just who you were. Now people know. Paparazzi won't follow or harass you,*" Nick explains.

Bell is the target. My decision boosted her even more. It forced her into the limelight, and she wasn't quite ready for that. She probably would've been at this level by herself, but what I did just hastened her path.

"*That's why you guys met us at the diner so late?*" They all nod. It makes sense. I go on Instagram and find Bell's Instagram. She has 997k followers; the last time I checked, she had somewhere around 660k. The last post was pictures of us in Fiji. She posted a mirror picture in her stories. The picture was taken in her bathroom at Rick's place.

Mrs. Yates has distracted the parents into a conversation about summer trips and lunch meetings she went on.

"Are you okay with this?" I ask Bell. She smiles, and her shoulders slacken.

"I knew this was coming; I signed up for this. I'm okay. Please don't blame yourself," Bell quietly tells me. I look at her, and her voice has no trace of sadness. She just wants me to be okay.

I nod, and she relaxes a little. Everyone else is still on edge, and I realize it's because they're all wondering what I will do or say. I've never liked attention, and this is a different level of attention.

After this, I'll have to go home alone with Rick and my mom. I'll be up in my room, Rick will keep my mom calm, and I'll tiptoe around both of them. I don't want to go back to their house. I don't think I'm ready to.

I look at Thena. She looks back at me, her eyebrows furrowed. *"Can I stay with you for a little while? I can sleep on the couch or wherever. I just want to stay with you."*

"Of course, you can." Her eyes water, and she nods.

Chapter 79

Emille Kate Van der Berg

After brunch, Thena practically dragged me back to her place. Mom was furious, but I needed to do this. I've never seen Thena so excited. Bell came with us. Thena pulls me upstairs and leads me down the hall to a guest bedroom. Windows fill one of the walls, and there is a queen size bed with thick fluffy white sheets, silk pillowcases, and nightstands on each side. It's beautiful, clean, and organized.

"Thena, this is beautiful!" Bell gushes, falling onto the bed. She barely bounces. Her blonde locks are bright against the white sheets.

"You have a TV?!!"

Thena rolls her eyes. *"Yes, I had it installed in case one of you slept over."* I climb on the bed and stand on it, my feet barefoot. Bell stands up next to me. She jumps, and I teeter over and laugh. I jump, and she becomes uneasy, almost falling.

"Please don't bust your heads open on my freshly mopped floor!" Thena calls as she rummages through the walk-in closet. She comes back out with a stack of blankets and a wide smile. *"Emi, you came just in time! I go grocery shopping Sunday nights, and I want both of you to come."*

I realize we've never done any of Thena's household chores with her, which explains her excitement. I've never even seen her change her trash.

"What do you do after you go to the grocery store?" Bell asks, plopping down on the bed.

"Takeout dinner, movies, maybe a face mask," Thena answers, folding a thick blanket and draping it on the bed. I plop down on the bed next to Bell and lay back. There are six pillows—four big ones and two smaller decorative ones.

"I'm down," I say, crossing my legs and relaxing. I could use a nap. That'd be good, but by the way Thena flits around the room and Bell dangles her feet off the end of the bed, I can tell I'll be waiting until tonight.

Thena, Bell, and I eat dinner at her kitchen island, Thai take-out boxes sprawled across the countertop. Bell sits on the counter, and Thena and I sit on her stools.

"So, are you going to school tomorrow?" Thena asks me, taking a bite of one of the spring rolls.

"I think so. I feel like I've missed too much already."

Thena contemplates it for a moment. If she thinks I shouldn't go, I probably won't. But I can't keep staying home. I have to finish my senior year. I need to graduate.

"Then you should go. I can drop you off before I go to Yale."

"Am I going to be here by myself this week? Are you going to be at Yale?"

She shakes her head. *"No, I have to get the last bit of work I need for my finals, but most of my classes are done."* She sighs. *"Though I do have one teacher who's teaching until the final. I don't care much for his class."*

Thena rambles on about her classes, how she's trying to maintain her grades, and everything else. She then talks about Elénore Co. Apparently, there hasn't been much improvement. The thing she needs most is a storefront.

I participate in the conversation, listening to my sisters tell me about their problems and struggles. I feel like I'm really here at this moment. Maybe it's because I'm temporarily living with Thena, but I feel a part of their lives now.

Chapter 80

Emille Kate Van der Berg

This is worse than I imagined. I didn't think it could be this bad. People are looking at me, like really looking at me, as if they're seeing me for the first time. And the one person I talked to and hung out with is still not back.

Calculus is a lost cause. I've missed two chapters, two-unit tests, and six quizzes. I will have to schedule a meeting with my teacher this week to see how we will handle this. The last chapter I was here for, I wasn't really *"here,"* so I got a D. I'm failing that class. And I definitely deserve that.

It was a slow month in AP Comparative Government. My teacher got sick and has been assigning video notes, and the note answers are on the internet, so I have five packets to copy before she returns next Monday.

When I get to AP Art, my table is empty, and I sit by myself, looking over my sketchbook, which is missing designs from the past couple of weeks. Ms. Han comes over as soon as she finishes addressing the class and smiles sympathetically at me.

"How are you, Emi?"

"Better. I'm doing better. You?"

"I'm good, I'm good. My cat is sick, which sucks, but it's nothing too bad." She shrugs her shoulders. *"Now, you didn't miss much but a check-in. I excused you because of the circumstances. I want to remind you about the school art competition that is still happening. This year we'll have three winners."*

I nod. I forgot about that competition. *"And the final?"*

"Oh! It's a completion grade because the AP Art exam is completely optional." I relax, and she must sense it because she smiles.

I spend the rest of class making sketches and passing the time with music and meaningless thoughts. This class is the fastest to go by and feels the most comfortable.

Bryce smiles when he sees me. I smile back and sit next to him. Bryce explained the whole unit we did and even let me review his notes. None of it makes sense, but I listen, and when our teacher begins our next lecture, I take notes even though everything sounds like it's in a different language.

"Have we had any quizzes or tests I need to make up?" I ask him as we pack up our stuff.

Bryce shakes his head. *"Nope, he's saving everything for the final."* Just by looking at Bryce's face, I know that's not a good thing.

Mr. Field's class feels like I never left. He welcomes me back and gives us ten minutes to decide everything wrong with our favorite novel. I do the dystopian genre as a whole and have written two pages by the time he tells us to stop.

The rest of the class is filled with talk about structure and allusion and how foreshadowing is supposed to be subtle and not a big blinking sign that says, *"THIS IS WHAT HAPPENS LATER."* He gives us examples, and I take notes. I enjoy his class, I always do, and when class ends, he smiles at me like I never left.

Chapter 81

Emille Kate Van der Berg

I sit on the floor in Thena's living room, doing homework until she gets home. She makes chicken, rice, and corn. We eat together at the island again, and I tell her about my schoolwork and the meeting they schedule for me.

"I'll be there. Add me to the email, and I'll be there."

The meeting is scheduled for the next day before my therapy session. My calculus teacher, Mr. Heath, sits on the other side of his desk with a small stack of papers.

Thena and Nick both came. I secretly invited Nick so they'd have a reason to talk. Jay told me the other day after brunch that Thena had been giving Nick the occasional silent treatment, and Nick never knows when it's coming. Now they both sit on either side of me, staring at Mr. Heath like he's nothing more than a speck of dust.

"So, what's your proposal?" Thena asks after the silence has stretched longer than it should have. Nick has his legs crossed, and he looks around the office with a calculated expression.

"Well, in most cases, the student must make up all their quizzes and test by the nearest date."

"Well, this obviously isn't most cases unless most students have a medical emergency and miss nearly three weeks of school. Now that we've established that, what is the latest date Emi has to do these tests and quizzes?" Nick interjects, his voice smooth and authoritative.

"Before her final, but honestly, it'd be best for her and other students if she takes the test and quizzes home with her. She can use her notes but nothing else. Her daily presence in class is fine, but seeing as she doesn't have a free period and I can't help her during her lunch since I teach during that period, there isn't any time for me to teach her without interfering with other students' learning. The test and quizzes will be adjusted as she has her notes."

"They'll be harder?" I ask, my voice laced with disbelief. They were pretty hard before.

Mr. Heath nods. *"Yes, probably twice as hard but less material. Quizzes will be fifteen instead of twenty-five, and tests will go from 45 to 30."*

He hands Thena a folder of tests, and she puts them inside her tote bag. "Thank you. If there's anything else she needs to complete, please let us know."

Mr. Heath nods. *"Your homework assignments will be excused seeing as how they're only five percent of your grade."* I nod, and we stand up and leave.

"*Well, I'll see you later. Thanks for coming,*" I tell Nick. He nods and smiles. Thena walks to her car, and I follow her.

"*Are you and Nick good now?*" I ask as Thena drives me to therapy.

"*Good,*" she says the word like she's tasting it, "*is that the word to describe how I feel? No, frustration is what I feel right now. Nick left, and he didn't say goodbye. He left when he was supposed to stay. Now he's back and I am having a lot of feelings. He is giving me space to work through them, but I am having a hard time letting go of the pain. He is working so hard to make things like they were before, but he still hasn't been able to explain why he left. He owes me the truth. Until Nick can give me that, I don't see how we can be good.*"

Oh, okay.

Dr. Young—Lily—stands in front of her window when I come in. I sit down and look at the fresh flowers on her desk. They look less full than the ones Bell brought over this morning.

"*Emi, how are you?*"

"*Good. Better. I'm behind in school, so I have to spend the next few weeks catching up and doing my assigned work. But I think I can do it. I might have to get a tutor before my finals, though.*"

"*Is all the work making you feel overwhelmed?*"

"*Kind of, but most of the time, I just think about something else and vent to Thena. She's good at managing heavy workloads. She made a to-do list and is looking for a tutor. I think she's going to nominate herself.*"

"Do you want Thena as a tutor?"

"I wouldn't mind, but she has finals to study for, and I'm pretty sure she and Nick are seeing a building tomorrow for her store. So, I'm going to look for someone else."

"Good. Do what you think is best. But I want to congratulate you and tell you how proud I am of you. You're speaking and being more open with your family. That's good, Emi."

"I didn't tell them what happened and what we talked about. I want to tell them all at once, so I don't have to repeat the same conversation, but I feel like that's awkward to organize."

Lily shakes her head. *"You might feel uncomfortable at first, but after you start talking, it'll feel even better. If you want, you don't even have to make eye contact."*

"I just have to get it out, right?"

"Right. Now how's school?"

I tell her about the loneliness and how I miss Liv, how Clara hasn't been there these past two days, and how I stayed up until three in the morning finishing the first two packets for one of my classes. She listens and gives advice, but what I appreciate the most is that she's quiet and accepting throughout the whole thing.

I know my sisters and Jay will be just as accepting, but talking to Lily is easier because she doesn't see me every day and hasn't known me for years. Sure, I've lied to Lily a few times, but I've been withholding the truth from my family for *years.*

Chapter 82

Emille Kate Van der Berg

Thena and I stand outside the Yates hotel, a coffee and donut in my hands and my backpack filled with books swung over my shoulder. Thena is in a black dress with matching high heels, and her hair is straight and down, her makeup done.

I saw her getting ready before we came. I asked her, *"Why are you doing your hair?"* It'd been natural the past two days.

She glared at me. *"Because it's getting hotter, and soon, I'm not even going to be able to go outside without it frizzing up. I'm taking advantage of it."* I made a sound of acknowledgment and watched her straighten the jet-black pieces until it was all silky straight.

We take the elevator all the way up to the top floor to a large suite at the end of the hall. We knock, and the door opens. The person who opens it leaves as we come in. The suite looks normal, but there are no suitcases or travel bags. Everything is unpacked; it looks like he lives here. Books are stacked by ashtrays. This is the most anyone has seen of Nick Yates's living arrangement. I've never been to the Yateses' house, and I don't think Thena has either.

Nick sits in the small living room, and I sit on the opposite couch. Nick has his legs crossed and stacks of paper by a legal pad on the table. The legal pad is filled with his handwriting, he writes small and neatly, and it resembles a font.

Thena stands, and they stare at each other like they're about to have a face-off. I eat my donut and put my backpack on the floor.

I look at Thena, silently telling her I won't be speaking for her. They need to talk. I want them to talk, and I'm pretty sure Jay and Bell do too. Probably Bell more than Jay, but Jay is not a romantic like Bell and me.

"I made her a schedule, and her finals are in three weeks, so she has to keep up with the next three weeks of work and make up for the last three weeks." Thena moves forward and hands Nick the paper. He looks over it and nods.

"We can meet here three times a week," Nick casually says. He looks at the schedule and then at his notebook.

"No, you should come over. It'd be easier, and I would be less likely to be late," I rush out. Nick smiles, obviously picking up what I'm saying, and nods in agreement.

Thena huffs but doesn't say anything. *"I liked the place we saw,"* she says resigned now that she realizes I've joined team Nick...

"I figured you would. I can give you the name of a contractor and interior designer to use. And yes, they can meet remotely."

"Good. Would you like to attend one of the meetings?" She looks away from him as she asks, and I realize this is how Thena looks when she's nervous. It's kind of unsettling to see.

"Of course. Send me the dates, and I'll put it in my calendar."

Thena nods, then turns on her heel and leaves. Nick and I are alone in the large suite with mountains of work.

"Why did you leave?" I ask him. It's the question that's been suspended in the air for years now. After what I've been through, I'm over dodging around questions I want answers to.

"I needed to. I had to." It's vague, and he knows it. Nick thinks about every word before he says it.

"Does she know that?"

He nods. "She doesn't know why. Jay knows parts of it, but no one knows the full story. And it's not something that will be easy for everyone to stomach. Thena can paint me as the villain in her story if she wants, as long as I am in the story till the very end."

"Very romantic," I mumble, a smile spreading across my face. Nick chuckles.

"You know, sometimes I wish I could be as strong as you and Thena."

"You can be whatever you want to be. Your story is still being written kiddo."

I don't have a chance to respond. He hands me a packet.

"Ready?"

I nod. "Ready," I whisper.

Nick spends the next four hours teaching me one chapter of pre-calculus. Each hour, I get a fifteen-minute break. And we end the session with one unit test. I got 78%.

Chapter 83

Emille Kate Van der Berg

Thena isn't home when I get back from therapy. I go upstairs into my *"temporary"* room and jump when I see Jay sitting on my bed. I drop my backpack on the floor by the nightstand, smile, and climb onto the bed.

"Hey! What are you doing here?" I ask him, but he doesn't smile or even look at me. He's been distant for the past two days. I can tell he wants to tell me something. *"What's wrong?"* I whisper.

"Nonthin'. How was therapy?"

"Okay. We talked about inpatient a lot and the whole making amends thing. Lily thinks it'd be good for me to reach out and talk to my parents and anyone else who was directly affected by my attempt." I put my hands in my lap and take a deep breath. *"I never asked you how you were after the whole thing. And I should've."*

He nods and looks away. I want him to talk to me, but I can tell he's scared to say what he wants.

512

"You can tell me anything," I whisper, my voice breaking. I clear my throat and keep looking at Jay. I have to be strong for him right now.

"You know, after all that stuff happened sophomore year—our fight, Allison's death, Nick leaving, and you trying to drown—you promised me that if you ever felt like that, you would tell me. And you broke that promise, Em." He releases a shaky breath. *"I know I'm messed up and selfish for focusing on that and not the fact you tried to take your life. I know."*

"You're not."

He shakes his head. *"I was angry, Em. When you were gone, I was angry, and a part of me was angry with you. For breaking the promise, for not talking to me, and for feeling like that for so long. I was angry, and I shouldn't have been, but I didn't know how to be anything else."*

I move closer and grab his shoulders, making him look at me. *"It's okay that you were angry; I broke a promise. I made a selfish mistake. I should've talked to you or my sisters…but Jay, you have to know that I wasn't okay. I hadn't been for a long time, and you couldn't have healed me."*

"I want to be there for you, Em. I want to be with you, but I need you to be honest with me. I'm not going to run the second you break down. You have to believe me. I won't leave you." His eyes glass, and tears stream down my face.

"I believe you. I believe you," I whisper. I put my face in the crook of his neck and breathed him in.

I'm glad he told me because if he can tell me this, I can tell my sisters how I've been feeling.

Chapter 84

James Averell

Emi and Nick's tutoring session doesn't end until 6:30, but Nick told us not to come down until 6:35.

Thena, Bell, and I wait upstairs in Emi's room. She's made it her own, a small level of clutter and clothes strewn about. Most of her books and journals are scattered around. Thena looks like she's ready to clean the whole room up. I lay on her bed, eating a pack of chocolate chip cookies.

"*She has something to tell us tonight,*" Thena says, brushing her hair into a high ponytail.

"*What?*" I ask.

"*Obviously, I don't know, or I would've told you or not have mentioned it at all, James,*" Thena replies. Touché.

"How's Mom?" Bell asks Thena. Thena sighs, turning around and looking at us. *"She wants Emi to go home. She's made threats about cutting Emi and myself off. She wants Emi home the day after Bell's birthday."*

"Well, what did you say?" I ask.

"Nothing. She hung up before I could. It's not up for discussion; she doesn't want Emi here with us, and I'm pretty sure she has the power to make sure that's accomplished."

"So, Emi's going home on the fifteenth."

"That Saturday morning, I'm driving her back. I just have to tell her."

"And if she doesn't want to go?" I snap.

"Then she can stay." Thena shrugs her shoulders and checks her watch. *"It's 6:37."* She leaves.

Emi hugs me when I come downstairs and rubs her head against my chest.

"I feel like I just became ten times smarter, but my brain hurts," she mumbles. She pulls me into the kitchen and opens up a pack of prosciutto. Leaning against the counter, she eats it, offering me a few pieces.

"You have something to tell me?" I quirk an eyebrow up at her.

"Not just you, everyone. I want to wait for the pizza to come. Pizza and sadness, a match made in heaven," she jokes. I don't laugh, and she frowns. *"I promise it's not bad. It's just the truth."*

What does that mean? She rises on her tippy-toes and kisses the corner of my lips.

"*You know I love you, right?*" she teases, her face in a forced, concentrated look as if she's unsure if I remember.

"*Yeah, I know.*" She turns and walks away, but before she does, I pull her against me and whisper above her ear, "*You know I love you, right?*"

She turns her head and smiles at me, our lips inches apart. "*I'll never forget it,*" she promises.

###

We all sit in the living room, Emi and Bell on the floor and the rest of us sitting on the furniture. Pizza boxes are on the coffee table, and cups of soda litter around us.

Emi takes a deep breath and begins. She tells us about the loneliness she felt after her dad's death and how it never went away; it just got smaller as she grew closer to us. She describes the relief she felt after Allison's death as the second source of the guilt plaguing her. She admits to her phone calls to her dad and how she broke when the phone got cut off. She tells us the truth.

"*I wanted to kill myself, and it wasn't an accident. I regretted it after I did it, but it was too late by then.*"

We all listen, and Bell and Thena hide their tears as best as they can, but after Emi uses the words "*depressive episode,*" Bell crumbles. Her cries are quiet, but her shoulders shake, and eventually, Thena has to wrap an arm around Bell.

When Emi finishes, a blanket of silence settles over the room. Someone sniffles, which must snap her out of her trance because she looks around. Sadness and worry fill her eyes. Before she can say anything, I call her name. Her eyes snap to me, and she gets up. I walk her upstairs to her room.

"Are they okay?" Emi asks, he hand flying to her face. *Thena* was crying rivulets of tear. *"Are they going to be okay?"* Emi is pacing, her eyes wide and frantic.

I grab her hands and hold them. *"Emi, they're fine. They hate that you went through that, but they're fine. Are you okay?"*

She nods. *"I feel better. I told Lily about telling them, and she thought it was a good idea, so I did. I wanted you guys to know."* She releases a shaky breath. *"I wanted to get it off my chest, and I did."*

I believe her. She speaks with so much conviction it's hard not to. I'm happy she told me. I feel lighter and at ease, like maybe there are no walls up for the first time in a long time. I really see her, and she wants me to. And I still love what I see. I knew that wouldn't change.

"I'm proud of you, Em. I really am."

She smiles and squeezes my hands tighter like she wants to use them to hold onto me. I lean down and kiss her, our noses touching and the tips of our tongues teasing each other. We kiss like children, timid and rushed, like her mom will come in and catch us at any moment.

"Let's go back downstairs," she suggests. I nod and follow her downstairs. Bell's face is dry now, and she smiles at Emi when we come down. They both rush over and hug her, telling her they love and support her.

When everyone is back to normal, we continue to eat pizza and talk. Nick takes a phone call, and when he returns, he looks satisfied with himself.

"What?" I ask him examining his assertive posture.

"Emi, how would you feel about attending a concert with us next Wednesday?" he asks.

Emi smiles. *"On a school night?"* Everyone laughs. *"I want to go! Who are we seeing?"*

Nick smirks, leaning back in his chair. *"The Carrols."*

Nick wants to take Emi to a rock concert? Emi yelps with joy and runs to him for a hug.

Chapter 85

Emille Kate Van der Berg

Nick is on the list to get into the VIP section, which isn't surprising to anyone. We go to a private section, waiting for the show to start. Bell disappears for a little bit, and I wait for her to come back before fully relaxing. Thena doesn't look like she's having fun, but in the band's defense, it hasn't started yet.

The small venue is packed, and people are laughing and yelling over each other. Bell returns with two drinks in her hand just as the lights darken. She chugs one and then takes leisurely sips of the other one.

Thena and I both stare at her.

"Did you guys want one?"

"Uh, no thanks," I answered, still staring at her. *What part of the model diet is this?* I wonder. She shrugs her shoulders and raises her glass as the concert starts.

The band starts, and the sound of drums and electric guitar fills the space. The beat continues, and then a raspy smooth voice starts singing. I don't know any of the songs until the last one comes on, but by that time, I've been cheering and humming. I feel like I'm a real fan. The last song, "*Jack and Coke,*" is a popular one about addiction feeling so good in the moment, but afterward, you feel like trash. He compares it to sex.

The lead singer is attractive, but I can't make out any of his features from the VIP section. After he finishes his last song and thanks the crowd, he leaves. By the time the rest of the band is off the stage, Nick is leading us backstage. The room reeks of weed, and there are girls everywhere, plus a few random, older guys. Jay and I stand by the bar. Bell sits on the couch, a fruity drink in a glass bottle in her hand. I don't know how many drinks she's had.

A tall, tattooed guy talks to Nick; his eyes meet mine. He smiles and waves. His hair is buzzed cut, and his dark skin has a sheen of sweat. He wears a T-shirt, both of his arms are covered in tattoos, and his smile is easy and warm. He finishes his conversation with Nick, and then they both come over.

"*Emi, this is Clay Joyce. He's the lead singer.*"

Clay Joyce is very attractive, his eyes an arresting gray. I can't stop looking at him.

"*Oh! It's so nice to meet you.*" He moves closer.

"*You too. Nick told me about you and what happened. And I just want you to know that I experienced the same thing a little while ago. If you ever want to talk, I'm here. I know what it's like to be at war with your own mind, and I don't want you to go through that alone.*" His voice is hoarse as he speaks, and his words bring tears to my eyes.

"T-thank you. That's really sweet, and if I ever feel that low again, I'll call. I promise."

He nods and takes a step back, and looks at Nick. *"I'll be in New York for a few days after the tour finishes."* Nick nods. I'm kind of starstruck. I've heard of Clay Joyce before. I've seen him on Instagram and Pinterest, paparazzi photos of him walking with beautiful women. He looks around the room, and when his eyes land on something, he tells us he'll talk to us later.

I watch him walk away. He grabs a water bottle and then sits by Bell. I can't hear what he says to her, but when he talks, she angles her body towards him and smiles.

"I like him," I tell Jay.

"He's good. I'm happy he performed stuff off his debut album."

"You listen to his music?"

"I like them. Good lyrics."

"And how do you know him?" I ask Nick, who's still standing next to us.

"We met when I was away. He's from California, but I think he'll be in New York a little while longer."

Nick and Jay look at each other and smile, clinking their glasses together. Uh oh. When Jay and Nick get a mischievous glint in their eye, it's rarely beneficial for the greater good. Thena returns from the bathroom then. She stares at Clay and Bell and then looks to me with a raised eyebrow. I shrug. There's no where to go but up for Bell in the relationship department.

Chapter 86

Emille Kate Van der Berg

Today is Isabel Brigette Van der Berg's 19th birthday. I skipped school to celebrate with her. All three of us slept over at Thena's house last night; we slept in my bedroom. We snuggled and squished inside my bed. Bell wanted us to recreate slumber parties from when we were younger.

We watched romcoms, gossiped, and ate junk food. Thena even participated. The next morning, we went to Bell's favorite bakery in the east village. The owner is a frail Ukrainian woman who hugged Bell when we came in.

Bell ordered a whole spread, and we sat at a small table away from the window. The coffee is burnt but sweet, and the crispness of it as it goes down is kind of addicting. She tells us each dish's name, and we take small bites of all of them. She decided on an old-fashioned Ukrainian honey babka. It's moist yet fluffy and not too heavy. Bell also eats Khrustyky, fried cookies the owner's daughter makes every morning. I try one and finish it in two bites, grabbing another from Bell's plate.

"*What do you want to do next?*" Thena asked, sipping the coffee. She was on her third cup.

Bell shrugged her shoulder. "*Maybe a movie, or we can go on an adventure.*" Bell wiggled her eyebrows, and Thena and I both forced a smile. I've been on a few adventures with Bell, and they've always ended with me doing something I was terrified of doing.

###

Three hours later, we're back at Thena's house. The adventure was mostly tame. We ran through a fountain and sipped soda while sitting in the park. Paparazzi watched us the whole time. Thena's dress sticks to her body, and her hair hangs in wet curls. We walk into the kitchen, and a large bouquet of flowers is on the island. Large pink peonies and white roses are arranged perfectly, crisp gray paper holding them together. A note sits in the bouquet, and I look over Bell's shoulder to read it. In small, neat scribble reads:

To: *Isabel Brigette*

From: *Clay Joyce. Happy birthday. X.O.*

"*X.O.! Kisses and hugs!*" I cry. Bell smiles but tries to hide the card.

"*Everyone says that. Besides, Clay knows I have a boyfriend. We're just friends.*" Her cheeks have tinted.

"*You told him about Tristan?*"

She nods. "*I told him the first night we met.*" Of course, she did.

"*And what did your boyfriend get you?*" Thena asks from across the island, staring at the beautiful bouquet.

"He's taking me out to dinner when he returns from his trip."

"What trip?" I lean forward and smell the flowers. They smell fresh, like they were picked this morning.

"He had to go on a business trip. He'll be back on Tuesday."

I peek at Thena, and her eyes are cold. Her neck tightens, and I can see her physically holding herself back from saying something. How long has he been gone? When did Bell find out? Is she alone in their apartment?

I hug Bell, and she laughs and hugs me back. She laughs like Thena and I are overreacting.

"Stay here until he comes back," Thena tells her. She doesn't frame it as a question, and Bell doesn't deny or say no. She agrees, and we both hug Thena, our wet clothes making the hug damp and squishy.

Chapter 87

Emille Kate Van der Berg

Bell chooses one of the best Italian restaurants in the city for her official birthday dinner. I stand behind Thena and in front of Jay. We have to rush inside. Paparazzi crowd us, and cameras flash. They're calling our names, but we ignore them. Bell waves and occasionally smiles, but she forces her way inside.

We're immediately taken to a large table in the back, where our parents wait. Rachel rushes over and hugs Jay and me.

"I'm so happy you guys came!" she exclaims.

"How many glasses of wine did my dad give you?" Jay asks her, staring down at her.

She fiercely blushes. *"Three. You know I love prosecco."*

"Yeah, and I also know he wants to fuck you," he mumbles. I elbow his ribs, and he sits Rachel next to us and away from Eric, who glares at Jay when he sees what he did. Jay shoots him a dry smile and hands Rachel a water.

Rachel sips and starts to stiffen up like she's getting lightheaded. Jay orders her some bread. I catch Eric watching her, but when we make eye contact, he looks away and joins Rick and Mr. Yates's conversation.

Bell has her hair done up in an updo, tendrils slipping from the top, and a few on her side. She's wearing a shiny gold dress, and Thena did her makeup. They both look really done up. Thena wears a tight black dress with red lipstick, and her hair slicked into a tight bun.

"Are you guys celebrating anything tonight?" the waiter asks. He gives all of us a friendly smile.

"My birthday! I'm nineteen!" Bell shouts over the music and voices.

"Well, happy birthday." He smiles.

"Thank you," Bell gushes like it's the first time she's been told all day. We ordered meatballs, bruschetta, and toasted garlic bread for appetizers.

When our appetizers are mostly gone and while we wait for our main course to come out, I go to the restroom. I freeze when I see my mom at the sink, washing her hands. Staring at the mirror, she looks me over and smiles.

"Emille, are you finished packing?" She must see my surprise because she shakes her head and sighs. *"Why must they always make me look like the bad guy?"*

"I have to come home tomorrow?"

"Yes. I told Thena to tell you to be packed and ready to go. I've let you do whatever you want for far too long. You had your fun with your sisters in the city, but now it's time to come home." She dries her hands with the paper towels and looks herself over in the mirror. She nods at me like she's done my whole life. It's the same nod she gave after my dad died and when I got myself ready for the funeral. She looks like she truly has nothing else to say, but there's always something to say. *Always.*

###

I don't tell anyone what Mom says. I try to enjoy dinner, taking pictures and videos for Bell, and getting in her pictures when she asks me to. I smile as wide and as full as I can because you only turn nineteen once, and when Bell is old and gray and looks back at these pictures, I don't want her to see my sadness and anger at my mom.

Bell, Thena, and I sleep in the living room, playing *Golden Girls* while we fall asleep. Bell is tipsy from champagne and happiness, and Thena is tipsy from white wine. Our stomachs are full of carbs and drinks that burn when they go down.

Bell is the first one asleep, and after another episode of *Golden Girls*, I join her. In the morning, I'll go to Mom and Rick's house, but I'm not staying home. If anything, I'll be leaving it.

Chapter 88

Emille Kate Van der Berg

Rick waits for me. He and Lucille are my welcome party. They both stand in front of the front door with wide smiles. I climb out of Thena's car and grab my suitcase from the trunk. Rick rushes over and takes it from me while also squeezing me into him.

"I've missed you," he genuinely tells me. I hug him back because I've missed him and his small acts that spoke thousands of words, like warming up my car before I got in, sneaking in and taking plates out of my room, and distracting my mom so I could be alone. Looking back and being away from him has made me see things clearer.

My room is cleaned, and by how my bedsheets are tucked in and my clothes are folded, I can tell Thena did it and not Lucille. Ever since she finished the semester five days ago, she's been throwing herself into her business and planning Jay and Bell's joint birthday party in a few weeks.

528

I close my room door and exhale a deep breath. It smells like Thena's perfume and cleaning products. I unpack my clean clothes, the room's silence causing me to work faster. When I finish, I sit on my bed, and for a while, I don't know what to do. I feel kind of lost here. If I felt alone at Thena's, I'd just go downstairs, and someone was always there. But I can't do that here. I could, but it wouldn't be the same.

I find one of my favorite books, turn on the television, crawl into bed, and begin reading. When the sun has set, and I've finished the book, I go downstairs for dinner. It's just me and Rick. We sit across from each other and eat twice-baked potatoes, baked broccoli, and sweet honey-glazed chicken. We talk about his trip with Eric and Mr. Yates soon and his gift for Bell's birthday. He always gives her a gift a little later. Mainly because they've been bigger gifts like a car, an apartment, or a trip for the past few years.

"*So, what are you going to get her?*" I ask him when we finish dinner and are cleaning our plates in the sink.

He smiles as he looks out the window, the backyard illuminated by a single light. "A place to escape to."

Chapter 89

Emille Kate Van der Berg

"James Averell, where are you taking me?" He blindfolded me the second I got in his car. He picked me up right after school, my sketchbook and journal in hand.

He stops his truck and gets out; I hear the familiar creak of the metal before the slam that shakes the truck. He opens his door and grabs my hand, helping me down.

We walk down a quiet hall that smells like fresh coffee. Jay slides open a door, and when he closes it, I stand still and wait for him to take my blindfold off. When he does, I gasp. I'm inside a large room with floor-to-ceiling windows, showing off a backyard with a small garden and a swimming pool.

I spin around, and the room has brown beams on the ceiling, a large wooden table, three easels spread out, and a rolling cart filled with paints and paintbrushes. Some of my old sketchbooks are stacked on a table. I've never been in this room in his house, but I'd recognize Jay's backyard anywhere.

"*Jay,*" I breathe, "*you did this for me?*"

He smiles. "*Of course! Rachel helped, but I wanted you to have a place where you could come and create art without anyone bothering you or making you uncomfortable.*"

I rush towards him, grab him and kiss his lips.

"*Thank you!*"

"*I expect you to have a winner for that art competition. Don't tell me you forgot?*"

"*I didn't.*" Ms. Han has brought it up every class and even comes over to my *empty* table and reminds me of it.

"*Good! Then get to work.*" He pats my ass and leaves the room.

I spend hours painting. Rachel brings me food, and I blast music from the speakers. Jay told me no one would care, and as long as I didn't start a fire, I was free to do whatever I wanted.

I finish half a painting, not knowing what I have planned when I start. The change of clothes Jay had stocked in the room were covered in paint. My fingertips are covered in paint, yet I don't even bother washing it off.

Rachel drives me home, and I take my clothes off and climb into bed. I fall asleep, fulfilled and blissful. Maybe this is what people search for, the feeling of fulfillment after doing something you love all day.

Chapter 90

James Averell

"Jay, we have to go outside now. The party started twenty minutes ago."
Emi tells me. We're currently inside Emi's bathroom making out like kids.
Since she got home from her inpatient care we have been exploring ways to
be intimate without crossing over into actual sex. Because it was one of her
unhealthy escapes, it's best if we do without it for now.

Last night she snuck out and slept over at my dad's house with
me. We stayed up until midnight to bring my birthday in. She gave me a
cupcake with a single candle and made me make a wish. In all of our years
of friendship, she's treated each of my birthdays with the same excitement.

I've had her three times already; it's all I asked for. She laughed
when I told her, and she just walked away when I didn't say anything. We
slip back downstairs. Rick acts like he doesn't see us, and we do the same.

The backyard is decorated with bright streamers and catering tables set up with my and Bell's favorite food. We've shared a party for a few years now. Neither of us wanted to be the center of attention nor invite other people, so we got dressed up and let Aurore do what she wanted.

She dotes on Bell and respects Thena, but she ignores Emi. Emi holds my hand as we walk around the backyard. Colleagues of Rick and my dad are here, people neither one of us cares for but act like we do. We stand by a table, sipping lemonade and watching everyone. A familiar-looking guy walks in, a small box in his hand. He's dressed in a white dress shirt and black jeans. His right hand is covered in tattoos, and the ones on his left wrist are peeking through. His skin is dark and smooth.

Clay Joyce. Bell walks over, and they hug. After a brief conversation, he hands her the gift. I watch them walk over to us, Clay following closely behind her.

"Hey, Emi," he says to her, and she waves in response. He gives me a curt nod. *"How have you been?"* he asks her, speaking at a low volume.

"Better. I've been going to therapy and being honest. Getting more sleep."

"Good. If you ever need a distraction, you can come help out in the studio. It's a good distraction, but it's not too consuming."

She nods. *"I'll keep that in mind."*

He nods and turns to Bell. *"Where's the boyfriend? Only reason I came."*

Bell laughs. *"Only reason you came? I thought it was for the tacos."*

Clay shrugs, trying to hide his smile. *"You, tacos, the boyfriend."* His eyes flit to hers.

"Oh well, he's not coming," Bell says after an awkward pause between them.

"Why?"

"I didn't invite him," I bluntly say. Emi presses further into my side, and I hug her.

Clay smiles, looking at me with a different look in his eyes. *"Mmh."* Bell gets pulled away by her mom, and Clay looks over her shoulder as she leaves. *"Nineteen,"* he murmurs, looking at the flower arrangement. The number nineteen stands up with flowers covering it.

Thena calls Emi's name, and she releases me and walks over to her sister.

"How old are you?" I ask him. By the way he said nineteen, he's not twenty.

"Twenty-five."

I whistle, and he chuckles and nods, knowing what I'm thinking. He and Bell are six years apart. *"Her and Tristan have been together since they were young. None of us really know when they went from friends to boyfriend and girlfriend, but it happened. And then we couldn't shake him."*

Clay nods. *"He still come around a lot?"* Clay's eyes meet mine. "Not much. Tristan got this big job, so we see him less and less. Hopefully, one day we'll never see him again." I flash a dry smile, and Clay laughs.

"Isabel and I are only friends, and I'm happy with what she wants." Clay shrugs and pours himself a cup of lemonade. I don't know if he realizes it, but it sounds like he's telling himself more than he's telling me. Nick comes over and makes small talk. I listen to Clay talk about California and his plans now that he only has one show left.

Rick walks over and smiles at us.

"Rick, this is my good friend Clay Joyce." Nick introduces them. Rick's eyes flit to Clay, and he doesn't even hide the fact that he looks Clay up and down.

Clay extends his hand, and Rick reluctantly shakes it.

"Nice to meet you," Clay says with a polite smile.

Rick nods. "How do you know Bell?" Rick gets right to the point.

"We're friends. I met her at my concert."

"You're a musician?" Rick asks, his shoulders slacking a little bit. Rick's warming up to his guy.

Clay nods. *"Lead singer of The Carrols."*

"I've heard of you guys. You're good. Your label is horrible, but you guys have a lot of potential."

Clay smiles. *"Our label is pretty shit, but we're done with them after tomorrow night's show. Then we'll be looking for some options."* Clay sips his lemonade, and Rick crosses his arms, fully immersed in the conversation.

"Are you looking out here or in California?"

"Doesn't matter. Whatever's best for the band, but I like New York."

Or a certain blondie in New York, I think but don't say. Rick looks between Clay and Bell and smiles like he has a million-dollar idea. He tells Clay it was nice to meet him and walks over to Aurore.

"Well, I'll be damned."

"What?" Clay questions me.

"You just got into Rick Van der Berg's good graces."

June

Chapter 91

Emille Kate Van der Berg

"Where's Clay?" I ask Bell after brunch. Everyone stands outside on the course enjoying the warm air. We've all been soaking up the private, quiet moments more and more lately, with the barrage pictures constantly posted about us online when we venture out.

"California. I think he's visiting his dad," Bell answers, her eyes closed as she looks up at the sun.

Last week he performed the last show of his tour, and there were pictures of Bell at the show, a smile on her face in every single one.

"Are you going to go see him?" I ask her, and she looks at me like I'm crazy.

"Of course not! He's spending time with his dad. Besides, that'd be weird. I can't go see him. He'll be back in three days."

"*You're counting down the days until he'll be back?*" I tease. She sighs and gives me a shaky smile.

"*I have a boyfriend, Emi, one I love very much. I would never cheat on Tristan.*"

"*I know,*" I whisper. I sometimes forget she's in a relationship, and that probably says more about me than her.

I look over my shoulder, and Thena and Nick are talking. They've been doing that more lately. Since Nick has been tutoring me and Thena's been helping out with my life in general, she has been forced to acknowledge Nick. They have made small, progressive steps: eating together, working together, and even yelling at each other. I consider any and everything better than the silent treatment at this point.

"*When are your finals?*" Bell asks me. I turn around and look at her.

"*Tomorrow. I'm ready for them.*"

I've never studied as much as I have this past month. If Nick had been here and tutored me for the SAT, I would've gotten a 1600.

After my third final, I can feel a slight tremble of exhaustion. When I get home, I eat and go to my room to study before going to bed for the night. I repeat the same process every day until the end of the week. My last class is creative writing, and all I do is hand him one of my journals, the one I started working on when I was an inpatient and have just been adding to. It's not about me; it's about a girl like me but stronger.

Mr. Fields looks at the journal and takes it from me. Opening it, he sees my handwriting and reads the date.

"*Emi, are you sure?*" He asks me, already holding it in both of his hands. His grip is loose, so I could take it back if I wanted to.

"*I'm sure.*" I grab my bag and leave before I can talk myself out of it. I drive home, the music as loud as I can handle, and all the windows down. I don't drive to Mom's house. I drive straight through the city all the way to Jay's house. A paparazzi van is parked outside, and I turn into the private garage as fast as possible.

I know where Jay and Nick are both waiting. I park inside Jay's lot. There's only one car in the lot, Jay's pickup. I ride the elevator up to Jay's and knock on the door. Nick opens the door, and I smile, pushing past him.

Jay is in the kitchen opening a beer. He holds his arms up in a look-who-it-is gesture and smiles, "*Emille Van der Berg has just completed her last high school final!*"

"*Wooo!*" I cheer, walking over and grabbing the drink from his hand. I take a large sip and then kiss him. The taste of beer is on his lips. I chug some of the beer and wipe my mouth with the back of my hand. "*What have you two been doing?*"

"*We went to lunch with Clay, and then we came here to wait for you to get out of school,*" Jay explains, taking a long sip of his beer. I wrap an arm around his waist.

"*You guys hung out with Clay?*" I look between him and Nick. Jay nods.

"*Yeah, he's cool, plus he took us to this small burger place. I invited him to your graduation dinner. You like him, right?*"

"*Yeah, he's cool. I listened to his new album.*" I pause for dramatic effect. "*It's really good. He's an amazing singer. He has like one sad song on there, but, it's so good!*"

"*Don't tell me you're fangirling,*" Jay deadpans blankly.

"*No. Kind of. Maybe.*" He rolls his eyes and kisses my forehead. "*Where's Thena?*" I ask Nick. He always knows where she is.

"*Meeting with Rick,*" Nick answers, walking into the kitchen. He throws his beer into the trash. "*She wants everyone to come over tonight for tacos and movies. We're celebrating you for finishing your finals.*"

"*What time?*"

"*Six,*" Nick answers, and I nod.

Clay is not at Thena's when we get there, and before the movie's opening credits are over, I'm fast asleep against Thena's lap, my feet in Jay's lap.

Chapter 92

Emille Kate Van der Verg

The art competition announces the winners on the last day of school. Everyone is gathered in the gym, papers thrown around, and yells and cheers fill the air. Seniors gather in groups together, talking and smiling and posing for pictures. My last day of high school. I've been waiting for this day for years.

I remember Jay and Bell's last day. I was so sad; I didn't even want to go to school, but they both made me. Bell ran the halls and did all the traditions, and Jay kept me right next to him the whole day.

We took pictures in the gym together, and when we left, I had to hide some of my tears from both of them. Their excitement was so tangible. They'd both be in the city together, and at that moment, I thought they'd be together. Bell and Jay. They'd go together, both beautiful and full of life.

The principal steps out onto the stage and begins a speech, his voice silencing the students. He talks about everything we've overcome and the hope for our future. The speech is long and, at times, generic, but we all listen, and when he finishes, cheers and claps fill the gym.

Ms. Han moves towards the mic, three pieces of artwork covered by a white cloth. She smiles and clears his throat.

"Every year, we have a school-wide art competition. Usually, we have one winner and two second-place winners, but this year we are recognizing three winners. There was just too much talent to pick from! So without further ado, here are the 2022 art competition winners!" Ms. Han moves out of the way, and the students remove the cloths from the art pieces.

People gasp and make sounds of awe, and I freeze. In between one painting and one sculpture is my painting. I painted two headstones, one filled with flowers and vines, life sprouting from it, and the other dark and clear with one lone flower sitting in front of it. I painted myself between them, and my hands are in the grass before the one with life. I painted Dad and Allison's headstones. I can't change what happened with Allison or how I felt after she died, but I can learn to forgive her. But I don't think I'll ever miss her, and if Dad knew everything, I think he'd understand.

The other painting is Liv and me, lying in the grass, our personal things around us—my spread-open journal and Liv's favorite Converse. Our hair is touching and tangled into one. She has a smile on her face, and mine is hidden by my hair, my smile barely peeking through. There's food on a blanket towards the bottom of the painting. Liv painted us. She painted that! And she won! Tears sting my eye, and I can't help but smile.

I've never had a best friend like her; someone to see me, be with me at my lowest, think of me the same, and even love me more. That's friendship. I may not have many friends, and I probably never will, but Liv is more than enough. She's the jackpot.

The sculpture is an intricate face made of different materials and fine angular lines. It looks like a sculpture from Roman or Greek mythology. The man looks godly. Part of me wants to go up and drag my fingers along the lines to see if I'll bleed or cut myself.

"This year's winners are Ana Wu, Emi Van der Berg, and Liv Brunes, who couldn't be here with us today. Please come up and get your trophies, and if you want to say a few words, feel free." I slide from the bleacher and walk down the steps, feeling all eyes on me.

Ana takes her trophy first, makes a short speech about her inspiration, and thanks the judges for voting for her.

Ms. Han hands me my trophy. *"Amazing, Emi! I'm really proud of you!"* She hugs me, and I hug her back.

"Thank you," I whisper. I stand in front of the microphone. *"Thank you, judges, for voting for me. And I want to thank Liv for being such a good friend. Thank you to my dad for doing the best he could for as long as he did. Bye."* I leave the stairs, and applause follows me back to my seat.

I won the art competition with Liv. We both won it.

Chapter 93

James Averell

We're all cramped inside the large building that the school rented out. Paparazzi followed us all the way to the building's entrance. Emi's name is coming up. Her row is standing by the stage, and three people are in front of her. All of us sit up straight and get ready.

The principal takes a breath and reads her name, "*Emille Kate Van der Berg.*" We clap and holler. I'm pretty sure Rick whistles, and she looks at us from the stage with wide eyes. A photographer takes her picture with the principal and one by herself. We laugh as we see her rush off the stage.

After the ceremony, we waited for her outside. People were taking pictures and hugging each other as if they'd never see each other again. Emi finds us and takes her cap off. She jogs towards me and throws herself into my arms. I hug her and kiss her on the lips, some of her lipstick coming off. Thena and Bell got her ready this morning. Her hair is natural and down.

"Congratulations Em," I whisper. She smiles at me like she's been waiting for this whole thing.

"Thank you."

I smile and look over her shoulder. She follows my line of sight and freezes before jumping into action, running towards the two girls both in caps and gowns, the blonde one wearing heels and a fitted dress and the other in blue jeans and Converse. *"Liv!"* she screams, drawing attention. She runs into them, hugging both of them.

Clara and Liv both embrace Emi; Liv is obviously more excited and warmer than Clara. Liv and Emi talk and hug and Thena walks by them and takes pictures of the three of them before leaving and going to talk to her mom. Bell has been the main communication line between Emi and their mom, but Thena is the one who plans and handles everything.

Emi hugs Liv one last time before walking over, her smile the widest it's been all day.

"Come on, we need to take pictures," Thena tells her, brushing past both of us.

Emi takes pictures with her whole family, even one with Bell and Tristan, which is awkward to look at. Bell stands in between them, and Emi can barely force a smile. Emi and her Mom's picture is uncomfortable for everyone, and Rick squeezes between them to dissipate the tension. When it's time for Emi and me to take pictures, I wrap an arm around her shoulder and hug her. After the first few pictures, I pull my tie off and put it on her. A year ago, we took this same picture, only I was wearing my gown, and she had on my cap.

For every milestone, we've been there for each other, and that'll never change. Nothing could make it.

Chapter 94

Emille Kate Van der Berg

I'm waiting in the backyard for Jay. He's coming to pick me up and take me to Thena's house for the night. My duffel bag sits on the ground, my knees pulled to my chest. The house is quiet and lonely. Rick went on an overnight trip with Eric and Mr. Yates, so it's just Mom and me here. I couldn't sit inside any longer, so I came out to the backyard.

The back door opens, and I turn around, expecting to see Jay. Mom stands still, her arms crossed and her eyes locked on me.

I don't say anything, even when she sits down. There are less than two feet of space between us.

"Are you staying the night with Thena?" I nod, and she nods back.

"Can we talk?" I don't want us to keep living and moving around each other. I don't want this to be permanent. *"I'm sorry-"*

546

She shakes her head, her eyes filling with tears. *"No, no, you have nothing to be sorry for."* Her voice is firm as she tries to hide its tremble. *"This is my fault. I wasn't there for you when your dad died, and I think deep down I knew you were like him in more ways than one."* She wipes her cheeks with her fingertips and looks at me. *"I met your dad when I was a teenager, and I liked him. I liked how easy-going he was and how, no matter how bad I was feeling, he could make me laugh. But the more I got to know and love him, I knew there was more. Emi, your dad was sick. He'd sometimes be so happy and all over the place, and other times I had to bring you and your sisters to him, just so he'd get out of bed."*

I think I buried those memories of him lying in bed, his back to us, me lying with him and talking enough for both of us, Mom crying and calling Rick because he wouldn't get up.

"Is that why you guys divorced?"

"He divorced me. He said he couldn't keep me from my true love anymore. He said he loved me and thanked me for giving you guys to him. Your dad was so sick, and when he died, I knew you needed me, but I could barely look at you with out seeing him. Oh Emi, your big love, your easy vulnerability, your creativity…you were so much of him." Her lip trembles, and for the first time in a long time, I see her, and she sees me.

"I didn't need you to be him. I just needed someone. Maybe you couldn't have prevented any of this. But you could have kept Allison from terrorizing me." I wipe my face and clear my throat. *"I just needed you to be there for me. I need m-my mom."* A cry escapes me, and I can feel my shoulders shaking. She moves closer and holds me while I cry.

The years of closeness we've missed, the pain we've caused each other, and everything in between. We'll never have the relationship I had with my dad, but I know there will never be another relationship like that. I just want her to be there for me the best way she knows how.

"I'm here, Emi. From now on, I'm here, and I see you. I promise I see you, my crotee."

I laugh with tears streaming down my face. She's here now, and I believe her.

Everyone is already inside the house. I could hear laughter from outside the front door. Bell is in the kitchen making her twice-baked potatoes, and Nick is outside grilling while Thena chops up vegetables and whatever other side she's making.

I hug both of them, kissing Bell's cheek and wrapping an arm around Thena. She moves away after a few moments, overwhelmed by my raw emotion, but leaves one hand on my back, rubbing in comforting circles. I lean against the kitchen counter, eating some of the chips Thena put out. I can't remember the last time we were all together, and the air felt this light - my brain unmarred by fog - my heart unburdened from secrets.

The front door opens and Clay walks in with a plate of desserts and a small smile. Bell quickly walks to him wiping her hands on her apron; they talk quietly, and their eyes never stray from each other. Bell grabs his plate and walks into the kitchen with him following at her heels.

The plate is filled with brownies, different types of cookies, and a few mini pies. Bell and I both groan and eye it. Clay laughs and slides it away from us.

"What are you making?" Clay asks Bell. He lifts one of her apron strings and lets it slip back through his fingers with amusement. I reach across the island and take one of the cookies.

"Twice-baked potatoes; they're Emi's favorite."

Clay looks at me. *"They are?"*

I nod and take another bite of the cookie. It's crispy and warm, with a hint of sweetness from the chocolate chips. My eyes close involuntarily to savor the perfect combination of sensations.

"Congratulations on winning the art competition," Clay says, pulling me back from my cookie revelry.

"Oh, Thank you!" I point to the cookies and then give him the okay sign. *"These are fire."*

"I'd say I baked them, but I'd be lying." He points to Bell. *"I didn't know the model could cook."* Belle whips around and gives him a look I can't decipher.

"You cook a lot?" he asks Bell.

She narrows her eyes. *"Why? Is that something you like?"* My eyes widen, but I wait for Clay's answer. *Where did that come from?*

He smirks. *"I like everything you do."*

"Oh really? Like what?" Bell presses, loading the potatoes up. Thena is distracted by whatever she's stirring on the stove.

Clay looks at her, and Bell's cheeks tint. I take another bite of the cookie.

"The way you talk. The way you laugh. They way you always show up for your family. How serious you are about your work. The way that apron looks on you right now." Clay answers in a smooth and casual voice. He leans against the counter, his tattoo sleeve on full display.

"Are you covered in tattoos?" I blurt. I shrink in embarrassment, but Clay only laughs.

"No, not fully." He doesn't take his eyes off of Bell. *"Most of my chest and neck are empty. My right hand is empty, and most of my legs."* I nod. I like Clay's tattoos; they're all neat and smooth, the writing clear, and the drawings vivid and sharp, like they could animate if you looked at them long enough. I start to ask him another question and realize that he's now peering intently over Belle's shoulder to see what she is doing with the potatoes. If she turned her face even a little, they would share an unavoidable kiss. But she doesn't. The guys come in from the backyard carrying one plate of meat. They grab Clay immediately and drag him outside to grill and talk trash with them. I see him toss a look back over his shoulder toward Bell as he goes out the door, but she doesn't look up.

Nick comes back inside, grabbing an empty glass container Thena had cleaned out for him. Before he goes back outside, I stop him, and he waits for me to speak.

"Does Clay have a girlfriend?"

Nick shakes his head. *"Not that I know of."* He's back out the door before I can ask anything else.

I don't want to break up Bell and Tristan, but I wouldn't be sad if Bell broke up with Tristan for Clay.

We all eat in the living room. After my third potato, I'm stuffed and lying across Jay. He and the other guys were outside smoking earlier, and I can smell it on his shirt. I snuggle further into him. I can't believe that I am really done with high school.

Clay sits on the floor by Bell, and Thena and Nick sit on the same couch, closer than I've seen them since Nick returned.

"I'm going to hang out with Liv tomorrow. Clara invited me to her graduation party," I tell Jay

"Are you excited?" Jay asks me. I look up at him. *"Yeah,"* I say with a yawn. I think I might be the first person to fall asleep again. I turn my head, and before I close my eyes, I see Clay and Bell whispering to each other, a shy smile on Bell's face.

Chapter 95

Emille Kate Van der Berg

I wake up around ten and find everyone downstairs eating breakfast. Clay must've slept over because he sits at the kitchen table eating bacon and eggs with Bell, Nick, and Thena. I walk over and sit beside Bell, who slides her plate over to make room for me. I grab a slice of bacon off it and take a bite.

"Where's Jay?"

"At his apartment. He wanted to shower and change," Thena answers, getting up to get me a cup of coffee. I thank her and take a generous sip of it. *"What are you doing today, Emi?"*

I yawn behind my hand before answering. *"I have to go to my school to get something I forgot, and I'm attending a graduation party tonight. I was going to go at ten and leave before midnight. Do any of you want to go?"*

"To a high school graduation party? I think I'll pass," Clay answers with a smile. Bell tries to hide her laugh while Nick lets his smile show. I narrow my eyes at the three of them.

Thena's the only one who thinks about it. *"You should go and spend time with your friend Liv, and I'll pick you up."* She nods like that's the final plan, and I nod in agreement.

After breakfast, Nick gets up and tells us he has to go to work for a little while. Clay offers to give Bell a ride back to her apartment. She agrees, and I go upstairs to change. When I come downstairs, Thena is fixing her hair with a cotton T-shirt, scrunching it, then dropping it. When she finishes, she grabs the pieces and twirls them until she can easily clip her hair. Thena the perfect embracing her curls is still a shock for me to see.

I slide on my Birkenstocks and grab my backpack and follow her outside. She drops me off at home so I can get my car and then drives back to the city. It was completely out of her way, but that's the kind of person Thena is. Driving myself is easily one of the most exciting benefits of having really stuck with therapy this time.

I drive to the school and head toward the front office. I grab my packet and walk toward Ms. Han's room; it's her free period. I knock on the door, and her head snaps up from her paper. She smiles and waves me in.

"Emi! How are you?"

"I'm good." I walk over and lay the painting down on the table. She looks at it and just stares for a little bit.

She traces over some of the lines and runs her fingers over some of the shaded parts.

"Your range of shades is amazing, and the lines are clean and smooth. I think you could have a career in this if you wanted." She looks at me with a soft look on her face. *"Do you want to have a career in this?"*

I think about it for a second before I shake my head.

"I love painting and drawing, but I don't want it to become a task. I want to keep them for myself."

"That's understandable. Some of the best artists in the world could be stay-at-home moms, art teachers, or even just regular people working 9-5. Sometimes a passion just stays a passion. You'll know when it should become something different."

I thank her for her class. She smiles, and we hug. I'll miss her.

I head back outside but stop myself. I want to know what Mr. Fields thinks about the journal. I can't stop the curiosity from bubbling up. I head to his classroom before I can stop myself. He sits at his desk reading newspapers. I guess he's mostly free since he only taught seniors.

I knock on his door, and he looks up from his newspaper, smiles, and sets the newspaper down.

"Hey, I just wanted to see what you thought about the journal."

At the mention of my journal, he drops his feet from his desk and springs into action. He grabs my journal from his desk and a notepad, the page filled with his handwriting.

"I read it. I read it rather fast, to be honest, and I think you have potential—a lot of potential. You're a talented writer whose characters reflect your passion, but you need guidance like most people. I can help you. If you want, I could meet you for coffee in the city, or we could communicate over email. It's up to you. Whatever you're comfortable with."

I'm stunned! His smile is wide, and his energy is infectious.

"Okay… You want to mentor me?"

"Yes, if you're comfortable, of course. I'd love to. You don't have to answer now. Here." He writes down his email on a notecard and gives it to me.

"Okay! Thank you!" He nods, and I turn around and leave. Driving back to the city I turn over the thought of being a mentee and having Mr. Fields help me become a better writer.

It doesn't sound like a bad idea.

Chapter 96

Emille Kate Van der Berg

Clara lives in a house that resembles a castle. It literally has turrets. The front gates are open, and cars line the driveway and the side of the street. I get out of the Uber and walk up the walkway half expecting to see a moat or at least a drawbridge. Music blasts from speakers, and I push my way inside. People stare at me, and I hear Bell's name as small snatches of conversation about breakdown and crazy. I sigh. This is what my mother was always afraid of, but at this moment I'm strangely unaffected.

I find Liv and Clara sitting outside by the pool. They share a patio loveseat with no one else around them.

"God, can we leave?" I hear Clara ask. Liv laughs and shakes her head. I can't imagine Liv being around all this alcohol and constantly fighting the urge to drink or fall into her old habits.

"It's your party, remember?" Liv reminds her. Liv looks up, and when she sees me, she stands up and walks over. We hugged. *"You came!"*

"Of course! I promised." She drags me over, and I sit between her and Clara. Clara tenses but doesn't shift away.

"Your house is beautiful," I tell Clara. She smiles and tips her chin up.

"It's my dad's. He's selling it in a few weeks. He and my little sister are moving." Clara looks happy about this. *"Then I'll be off to Brown."* She wistfully sighs and leans back, more relaxed.

"Where are you going?" I ask Liv. I haven't had time to ask her about her future plans.

"Brown. I got in early admission before I had my little incident. My dad has been helping me pack up." Clara excuses herself and walks away to talk to two guys, both with looks of concern on their faces.

My eyes widened. *"You're going to Brown? I thought you didn't want to go to college."*

She shrugs her shoulders. *"For her, I'll try it out, plus I'll get a degree and be able to figure shit out. I accepted while I was at in-patient, and my sponsor assured me we'd be able to talk still."* I laugh, and Liv rolls her eyes. I think she secretly likes her sponsor, but since the guy is really positive, she acts like she doesn't.

"I'm happy for you." I lean over and hug her; she hugs me back. "You know, I consider you one of my best friends."

"You're my best friend, Emi. You're one of the best people I've ever met."

My eyes water. I wipe them with the back of my hand and smile. She rolls her eyes and playfully pushes me away. I talk to Liv for a little bit longer. I ask her if she's okay being here, and she thinks about it.

"I look around and see all these people drunk and high out of their minds doing and saying stupid shit, and I'm happy I'm not one of them. I like being here with you and with Clara. I don't want to be in a haze because when I wake up, iI can't even remember what happened. I like being awake and in love. It's nice."

"It is nice," I agreed in a whisper.

Liv and I talk for a little while longer, sipping lemonade and eating bags of chips that Liv snuck from the kitchen. She checks her phone and pokes me in my side. I look at her, and she's already standing. *"Come on."*

I follow her through Clara's backyard. It's kind of on a slope until you hit a flat land. We stand there, and I wait for something to happen. Just as I was about to ask Liv what was happening, a loud bang went off. I look up and see fireworks lighting up the sky. People yell and cheer.

The fireworks heat up the air. As more fireworks go off, we feel a breeze. We hear the sound of bodies hitting the water and music getting louder, and it all amplifies this moment. Makes it seem more real and permanent.

"We made it, Emi." Liv says almost in awe. *"We graduated high school. And we got better."*

July

Chapter 97

Emille Kate Van der Berg

I sprawl out on Thena's bed and roll over; she's getting ready for our country club brunch. I've decided I'm wearing jean shorts and one of Jay's T-shirts, and that's it. I've stayed mostly at her place since graduating. Occasionally, I go back to Mom and Rick's, but it's really just to grab clothes.

Today, I will announce what I'm doing with my future. I've talked it over with Liv and Thena, and I'm confident in my decision.

Thena comes from her bathroom in a blue sundress, her hair slicked into a high bun. Bell came back from L.A. last night. She went straight to her apartment when she landed. Nick stayed late last night. For a second, I thought he would spend the night, but Thena walked him out. The way he touched Thena's arm on the way out spoke volumes about where they were now.

Nick and Jay are downstairs. Thena is planning something, but I don't know what. She's been on the phone more, writing in her black leather journal, and has reminders going off randomly. She likes being busy.

"Come on. Bell is probably waiting for us." I roll off her bed and follow her downstairs.

"Spain?" I hear Jay ask. When I come into sight, they both get quiet, and I walk over to him and narrow my eyes suspiciously at him. He just smirks at me and plants a kiss on my lips. *"Ready?"* I nod, and we all climb into Nick's car.

"Plans for this summer?" I ask Jay, holding onto his hand. Jay shrugs. *"Whatever you want."*

"Ice cream and movies. Can we go to the beach?"

"I like the beach."

###

Bell is waiting for us as we walk towards the table, and I notice an empty chair beside her.

Rick walks in with Clay. *Clay.* I think we all freeze when we see him. He shakes hands with Mom and Mr. and Mrs. Yates before he moves over and sits down by Bell. Jay gives him a slow clap while a smile spreads across both faces.

"I told you! Rick Van der Berg likes you, and now you're screwed. You're stuck," Jay tells him, and Clay shrugs like he doesn't mind at all.

"Where's the boyfriend?" he quietly asks Bell. I can hear them, but I don't think anyone else can. No one else is trying to.

"*Oh well, uh, he's not really ever invited.*" She clears her throat, her cheeks tinting. "*Rick doesn't think he should come, so he doesn't.*"

Clay nods, reaching for his water. He takes a sip. "*Mmh.*"

Bell makes the same sound, mimicking him, and Clay rolls his eyes before smiling at her. Bell looks away and then redirects her attention to me. She just caught me staring.

"*So tell us, what are your future plans?*" She's good at random subject changes.

I take a deep breath and clear my throat.

"*I've decided to do small work with my drawings for books or whatever and work with my teacher, Mr. Fields on my writing.*"

"*And your living arrangement?*" Mom asks, her voice soft and curious. I smile at her.

"*I'm going to move in with Thena. It's more realistic, and I can grow and do what I need to do there. So yeah, I'll be moved out by the seventh.*"

The table is silent. I look around. Clay nods like he's impressed, Nick smiles at me, and my sisters both have looks of encouragement on their faces. I look at Mom and Rick, who both look happy for me, but I see the sadness lingering in their eyes. I'm the last one out of the house, and Alexander and Thena will never return. Bell and I visit, but I don't think either of us will move back full-time.

"*Have you decided what you want to do for your twenty-first birthday?*" Bell asks Thena, redirecting the attention.

Thena smiles and perks up. "*I've decided to go to Saint Tropez, and I want you guys to come.*" She realizes our parents might be listening, so she lists off our names. "*Emi, Bell, Clay, James, and…*" she grumbles out the last name "*Nicolas.*"

Nick beams and nods. *"Send me the dates, and I'll be there."*

"Will you?" Thena snaps back sarcastically.

"Promise," Nick calmly replies. Thena smiles against her will.

"When are we leaving?" I perk up. I want to go. *"I'm over America and the paparazzi that comes with it."* They posted a picture of me and Jay kissing in his car. A little embarrassing to see out of nowhere.

"Same. I can't hide out in my car anymore," Bell admits. Clay bumps shoulders with her, and she grins. I didn't know she had to hide out in her car.

"We leave in a week, and we'll come back close to the beginning of August," Thena announces. *"Can you come?"* Thena asks Clay.

"I can. I'll probably be working on new music, but I'd love to come," Clay answers. I wonder why he'd *love* to come.

I look at Jay. *"Saint Tropez!"* I gush. I can tell by the easy smile that he's not surprised. *"You knew?"*

He shrugs. *"She wanted to spitball some places. I know she loves France, and you love the beach, so it was an easy win."*

I wrap my arms around him and hug him.

"Did you all see Bell's new cover?" Mrs. Yates asks. I pull away from Jay and look at the magazine. Bell is on the cover in a green suit jacket and a button-up shirt with the first three unbuttoned, her hair slicked back and a soft twinkle in her eye.

She's on the cover of *Harper's Bazaar*, one of the biggest magazines in the world, and her Instagram followers have grown by the day. More people will follow her, and she'll be in more demand. This isn't the end; everything will keep growing, and so will Thena. From what I heard her and

Nick say, her business has hit a quarter high, and companies are requesting exclusive partnerships on certain designs.

More people will know the Van der Berg name, and in turn, they'll learn mine. I won't be invisible anymore. But maybe that's okay. It'll be okay with Jay, my sisters, and even Clay and Nick. This is the beginning of something. Whatever it is, I know I can handle it. No escaping it this time.

Jay wraps an arm around my shoulder, drawing me to him.

"You know I love you, right?"

"Yeah," I say with a smile, "you know I love you too, right?"

THE END

If you or someone you
know is struggling or in crisis,
help is available.

Call or text
988
or
Chat
988lifeline.org